TUNE UP

ALSO BY JOE KLINGLER
Missing Mona
Mash Up
RATS

UPCOMING IN
THE SECRETS OF MYLIN SERIES
Burn Up (Fall 2017)
Lock Up (Spring 2018)

Joe Klingler

TUNE UP

The Secrets of Mylin - Book I

A Qigiq and Dreeson
Thriller

CartoSi LLC

CARTOSI LLC
P.O. Box 3520
Los Altos, CA 94024

This book is a work of fiction. Names, characters, places, and events are either a product of the author's imagination or are used fictitiously. Any resemblance to actual incidents or locales or persons, living or dead, is entirely coincidental and not intended by the author.

Cover design by Ansel Niner
Photograph of model by Iconogenic
Viola image by 3drenderings
Artwork used under license from Shutterstock.com

ISBN-13: 978-1-941156-06-3
ISBN-10: 1-941156-06-1

To my siblings:
Joanne, Mary, William, Helen, Robert, Dolores, Catherine, Charles, Lawrence
who each in his or her own way helped make me crazy enough to want to be a writer.

Acknowledgements

First and foremost, thank you dear reader. It is your interest in and support of my novels that allows me to continue to work. Thanks also to the many readers who have taken the time to write reviews of my books. Each one is greatly appreciated and helps to reach new readers in the vastness of the book industry.

Thanks to Michele Bighouse for plowing through an early manuscript and providing thoughtful insight and detailed analysis. A special thanks to Amie Chang for her helpful comments and crosschecks on culture and storyline. Thanks to my long-term colleague, Jim Elliott, who has read my work from the first paragraph and whose precision copyediting skills keep me out of loads of trouble.

I would like to thank Randall Gates, the maker of the real-world *Dream Cycle* and the man who donned a tuxedo in the wilderness, for inspiration. And also Lindsay Maxwell for introducing me to the incredible art of Cai Guo-Qiang.

Once again I had the privilege of working with my longtime editor, Robyn Russell, who finds problems within problems, and helps sort them out with gentle humor and keen intuition.

Lastly a warm thank you to R, who continues as first reader and tireless supporter of my literary pursuits.

TUNE UP

"A bird does not sing because he has an answer.
He sings because he has a song."
—Joan Walsh Anglund

PROLOGUE

MRS. CHONG TOUCHED HER GRAY CURLS to ensure they were in place. The same dark blue dress she always wore on Monday hung from her thin shoulders—feng shui indicated blue was auspicious for the start of her week. She had made the dress herself on the sewing machine she operated all day long to make a living. The owner hadn't even charged her for thread, though she had to provide her own fabric. But she didn't mind. She loved America, and never felt so free as she did in her little apartment in Chinatown so close to the enormous bridge of gold.

Sometimes she wished for a larger apartment away from the alley. But she wished more that Mr. Chong hadn't smoked himself to death at fifty-two. She picked up the picture of him standing on the pier beside the gray steel ship that had brought them to America thirty years ago and gazed into his dark, ambitious eyes. She kissed two fingers of her right hand and placed them on the picture, adding another smudge to the glass. She said softly:

"Good day, Mr. Chong. I am off to work. I hope you are having a beautiful life with our ancestors." Dr. Fan at the Chinese hospital had warned her about talking to herself too much as she grew older. But she wasn't talking to herself, she was speaking to her husband's ghost so he would leave her in peace.

She replaced the black lacquer frame on a pearl-colored doily. Glancing right, she sighed, and lifted a photograph of two preteen girls in yellow dresses down to their shins wearing white orchids in black hair.

"I miss you and your wonderful music. Please call.

Remember I cared for you when your mother..." She sniffled and blinked back tears. "In that bad bad year when your father smuggled us into Shanghai. And now..." She waited for a deep breath to lift and lower her chest. She replaced the picture. As she positioned it carefully, her gaze touched a third picture.

"You left our homeland to escape the one-child policy of our fine government. And look what has happened to us." She shook her head, then turned away.

She touched her hair again. The oversized numbers of the bamboo clock on her lovely cherry wood nightstand glowed 6:40. She had made sure the clock was made in China before paying the man at the pawn shop for it. Helping the people of Asia with money she made working in America made her happy. The Buddha taught the connectedness of all things, and surrounding herself with the words *Made in China* helped her feel connected to a homeland she hadn't seen in decades. And with Mr. Chong gone...

She pushed the word *never* from her mind before forcing her face into a smile. Americans didn't want to see the sadness of an old Chinese woman, so she was careful not to show it to them.

She walked down to street level, being careful of her posture, and squeezing the rail with her stiff fingers. Only two flights, but she knew that every bit of exercise was a wellness prescription for her aging body.

She tried to be glad the old building had no elevator.

The heavy main door stuck. She pushed hard with her shoulder, caught her balance as it swung, and stepped outside to the sidewalk. A misty fog glowed orange in the sky. She pulled her sweater to her chin and turned right toward the factory: the spare room where she and three other women manufactured anything the boss could get an order for. She liked the baseball caps with their emblems and bright colors best. Doing a beautiful embroidered logo, or someone's name, made her happy—though the boss said she was too slow. She told him,

"Haste makes waste." He would grumble, but leave her alone to work. Not so with the younger sewers. He was always talking to them, and rubbing against their bodies. Some quit, but most couldn't afford to.

She walked two blocks and stopped at an intersection with a group of pedestrians. She needed to turn left, but the little walking man she thought of as a friendly Chinese man helping her navigate the chaos of San Francisco wasn't there. A red hand glowed. She waited. A tall white man bumped her with his brown shoulder bag. She knew it contained a computer. Her boss had one and gloated that it let him keep track of every stitch they sewed. She turned around; a dozen people had gathered behind her.

She smiled. She liked people close by. They gave her comfort, as if she were a small part of a larger whole like the Buddha taught. But the autos zooming through the streets scared her. Always so fast. Pushing bicycles and people out of the way as if cars were special. Bullies. She didn't have a car—and didn't want one. They were a kind of opium that made people crazy and rude, disconnected from the Earth: the root of all life. No, the Buddha would have walked. So she walked. Not that she could afford a car, even a small one.

Her walking man friend replaced the hand.

The human mass around her moved into the street. She tried to stop at the curb to look both ways, but her small body was carried forward. A white van was stopped to her left. A light green car sat next to it—one of those curved ones that look like hungry fish. Her boss said they were the future because of the wind.

She stumbled as her toe found the street, but with so many people pressed together she wasn't in danger of falling. She squeezed her cream-colored purse closer to her chest and took small steps to get past the front of a towering black truck with a grill of immense shiny teeth.

She told her feet to move faster in the Oxfords she struggled to tie each morning.

The woman near her left elbow screamed.

A lion roared. She looked toward the sound, worried the truck was coming to crush her. A shoulder bag slammed against her chest. The screaming woman jumped away. A blur of moving colors washed over Mrs. Chong's eyes.

"Too fast," she whispered.

The crowd was gone. She was alone partway across the street with light all around her. The roar became the buzzing of a giant insect caught in a trap. Her head filled with:

Run, you must run.

She shuffled backwards. Within her spinning world a black hand reached out from the truck. She tried with all her might to leap. Up over the curb. Reach safety—but she wasn't sure she was even moving.

The black hand slapped her right shoulder, then the hip the doctors said she should be careful of because older women often broke hips because of weakness in their bones. Oh, how she hoped her hip wasn't broken.

She spun like a whirling Sufi and the orange-gray fog of the morning spun and the insect flew past like the train whistles of her youth when she would stand on a platform and watch enormous train engines fly by, hoping one day to ride one all the way to America.

She hit the pavement. The sound of a tree branch losing a battle with the wind reached her ears. Rough stones pressed hard against her cheek, then...

———

The driver of a black delivery truck paid careful attention as a motorcycle blasted across the intersection against a red light. Pedestrians scattered, car horns blared, asphalt-tortured tires squealed. The bike swerved behind a Mustang that was braking hard to avoid an SUV arching into its lane. A Toyota sedan ran up the curb and cracked a plexiglass bus stop that was empty, the departing bus only a few yards down the street.

Voices cursed at the rider's back, now a quarter of a mile away. A crowd formed around an elderly woman in a shabby blue dress and a torn sweater lying in the crosswalk.

She wasn't moving.

Cell phones lifted to ears.

The driver ignored the green light and the horns blaring behind him, dialed the 911 operator on his cell phone, and crawled down from his cab. When the dispatcher answered, he read the street names from a black and white sign.

"No, she isn't moving," he said. "Okay, we'll leave her be. I have the lane blocked. Thanks." He hung up.

The woman was breathing, but her shoulder was bleeding, and she was lying very still. He leaned against his chrome grill and fished a Camel cigarette pack out of his jacket.

Traffic backed up behind his truck for blocks. The cigarette was half gone when a cop weaved a bulbous motorcycle through traffic. He parked to the far side of the prone figure, protecting her from cross traffic. As he dismounted the crowd thinned fast: people figuring the cop had things under control, or maybe reluctant to get involved.

Half-a-minute later two paramedics with a stretcher jumped out of a red vehicle parked half on the sidewalk. The truck driver drew on his cigarette and watched them work: smooth and coordinated, like a good hockey team. Traffic inched to the right of his truck and moved within a couple of yards of the woman's head.

The cop took notes from a woman who said she had been walking beside the victim. But she managed to run across the space between the lanes where the motorcycle had shot through. He then talked to a guy carrying a shoulder bag who had also been near the woman. As he finished with the bag man he noticed the trucker sitting on the front bumper staring at him.

"It's okay to move that now," the cop said, gesturing with his writing hand. "We've got to get traffic flowing."

"Sure, officer. In a minute."

The cop looked up and was about to speak when the trucker said: "I'm a witness. I was right up there." He pointed to his cab with what remained of the cigarette.

The cop flipped a sheet on his pad.

"Bill Perkins. Perkins Delivery Service. I've been waiting for you."

The officer stopped writing.

"Waiting? Why would you wait? We appreciate it, but there are dozens of witnesses."

"Did they all tell you what happened?" Bill asked.

The cop nodded. "A motorcycle split lanes, which is legal in California. He was going fast, ran the red light." He flipped his pad closed before adding, "Which isn't legal in any state in the Union."

Bill took a long drag, pressed the butt out on the front bumper, and slipped it into the front pocket of his overalls.

"I was elevated," Bill pointed with his thumb. "Unique perspective."

The cop pursed his lips, nodded, said nothing.

"Bird's-eye view if you know what I mean."

"You have a point Mr. Perkins, but your truck is blocking morning rush-hour traffic. Where is this going?"

Perkins tapped another cigarette out of a squished soft pack. He lit it while the cop tapped the handle of his holstered pistol with this thumb.

"Officer," he leaned forward to read the badge, "Marsail...did I say that right?"

The cop nodded, softening a little.

"Officer, the guy riding the motorbike hit her on purpose."

Officer Marsail stood straighter and frowned.

"I saw him coming in the rearview. He waited. Waited for

her, the woman in blue. And timed it almost right. But as his bike entered the crosswalk she was moving slower than he had planned, so she was still in front of my left front fender."

Perkins inhaled through his Camel. Marsail reopened his notebook.

"The guy had clear road. The noise of that bike had parted the crowd like he was Moses. But he didn't go straight through. He swerved. A nice accurate swerve with his body to the inside like a racer boy. Had his butt hanging off the machine when he hit her with his shoulder and knee. Easier for him to maintain control than if his handlebar had clipped her. That might have sent him flying."

The cop met Perkins' eyes.

"You're sure?"

"Officer Marsail, I'm sure enough that I missed my seven o'clock delivery this morning to wait for you. And I left my truck right where it was so you can see the view I had."

The cop pointed up.

Bill nodded.

The officer climbed up and sat behind the wheel of the Mercedes box truck. Bill stepped up on the running board.

"He took her out on purpose, Officer. I hope you can find out why."

The officer slid down from the cab, walked to his motorcycle, and picked up the radio handset.

CHAPTER 1

I OWN ROBERTS PHOTOGRAPHY, which is really just me and a Chevy Suburban with framed pictures, cameras, and a kiteboard in the back. Shooting was what I was doing that first time—back in July at the Ann Arbor Art Fair in Michigan. I was crouched behind a low hedge of nannyberry, the moon two days shy of full. I always check the moon phase for night shooting—there are few things better than the ghost-flavor of moonlight to make a good picture mysteriously great. She had stepped from the shadows between the 38-foot-tall stone columns of Hill Auditorium where the highbrow concerts were held. I remember her skin most of all—golden silver as her cigarette lighter illuminated the smooth curves of cheeks. Asian. I guessed Chinese, but I don't have much experience with beautiful women from the Far East.

She had smoked half of her cigarette, drawn from a black-and-white box I didn't recognize, when blinking lights beckoned concert goers to return to their seats. In the few minutes between the lighter and the blinking I filled a memory chip with RAW digital images. Normally, I would review my work. Instead, I ran across the street with my Canon banging against my hip to buy a seat in the thirteenth row. My luck was good; she was sitting in row eight. The orchestra consisted of thirty-three women from Asia according to the program I hid behind while examining the smoker girl. They were about to play Mozart.

Of the 342 pictures on that memory chip I committed six to the archival ink of my Epson professional printer on 46-by-30-inch canvas using a giclée process that helps a photo look like a painting. One of those six prints hung six feet in front of me at an art show in the chain of shows I've done for three summers in a row trying to scratch out a living as a creative photographer. This weeks' show had my display tent pitched in the warming mountain air at Kings Beach beside the incomparable blue of Lake Tahoe, California. To pass the time I was reading a novel about a portrait painter from Shanghai who had been sold into prostitution. Her incredible resilience was inspiring me to continue my modest effort to become an artist whose work spoke to people. The shuffle of shoe leather against pavement drew my attention. I closed my book and prepared to play *meet the artist*. With luck I might sell a print—or at least get an email address, and strive to sell something, someday via my newsletter.

My eyes stopped mid-rise.

A slender woman in boots was staring at the print entitled *Smoking Girl #6, my* favorite from the series. The girl in the photo stood in partial profile, beginning to lower a lighter, its flame almost extinguished—just enough remaining to form an auric glow around the slender fingers of her closed left hand. Her hair was shorter on the right side of her head, parted above the right eye and swooped to the left—seemingly making it impossible for her to see from her left eye. Her slim body appeared miniaturized by the massive column of stone beside her. Yet the composure of her face made them both appear strong—maybe she even more than it.

This girl was standing the same way now.

This girl had identical hair.

It seemed improbable in the extreme. I was two thousands miles from Michigan. Yet here she was, standing inside my tent.

The professional in me wanted to grab the camera beneath the seat of my stool and capture the magic of the subject examining the subject. I would title it *Smoking Girl #7*. I made a living taking photographs on a planet where anyone could hold up a box of electronics and ("say cheesy") get a picture. My real job was to find ways of seeing the world that people would never discover on the screen of a cell phone.

For this, I needed rarity. I roamed the world hunting for it— like at the top of those stairs that night at Hill Auditorium.

This was such a moment.

Yet I couldn't move. Short breaths dried my mouth. Blood pulsing in both ears joined the slow rhythm of waves washing the beach behind me. She stood quietly, like that stone column, color swirling behind her from art show attendees strolling by.

I tried to say hello, but my lips wouldn't part. Seconds passed. A muscle in my left biceps twitched. I grabbed the camera below me, found the on switch, and fired three quiet clicks before realizing what I was doing.

She didn't turn.

But she did say, "Did you take this picture?"

The thought of lawyers stampeding in my direction un-hypnotized me. Naturally, shooting in a public place, I hadn't asked her to sign a model release. And here I was, selling her image. At best I was in a gray area of the law. At worst, I owed her money I had already spent.

But lying wouldn't help.

"Yes. A few weeks ago. During an art fair in Ann Arbor."

She turned toward me. My legs went slack—beautiful was too small a word to capture her up close in the flesh 3D presence. I was glad I hadn't stood up.

"You were in Michigan?"

I nodded, not sure my speech would hold up to the intensity of her dark right eye; her hair still completely covered the left. Hair that was touched with silver sparkles, and streaked with a strand of purple.

I wanted to lift my camera again.

"She looks a lot like me," she said, turning her eye back to *Smoking Girl #6*.

I cleared my throat and managed, "Do you think so?" I

would have sworn on a couple of Gideons she was smoking girl, but my response was automatic when anyone said a picture looked like someone they knew. It had slipped out before I realized how stupid I sounded.

The girl stared at the picture while I stared at the girl, all five feet, maybe three or four inches of her. Midsummer, yet she wore high-heeled black boots that hugged her calf to just below her knee. Then nothing but golden silky thigh to the lower edge of purple shorts. Short purple shorts that matched the streak in her hair. My eyes were lifting to study the fog-gray silk clinging to her chest when her head spun towards me.

"I was in Ann Arbor once."

It didn't sound like an accusation—more a proclamation of worldliness. I found part of my brain and said:

"Did you like it?"

Her red lips, maybe with a hint of purple, parted to show gleaming white teeth that had needed an orthodontist when she was in middle school. No matter, even slightly crooked her smile had the intensity of the Luxor beam in Vegas. She said:

"I went to my first ever concert in America to learn about new music." Her eye grew distant. "Computers and wires and hands waving in the air with dozens of speakers all around me." Then she whispered. "The energy was so intense. I didn't know humans could make such sounds."

I tilted my head toward #6. "Is that the building where you attended the concert?"

She shook her head. "No, that was the GO Orchestra. I didn't play that night, it was my turn to listen." She grinned. "I snuck outside to smoke. My father doesn't allow me to smoke."

Confusion seeped into my head alongside the taser-stun effect of her presence. I threw myself back in time trying hard to remember other concerts during the art festival. Blank. There had been dozens; I only remembered one.

"I heard your orchestra. They're fantastic."

"We work very hard."

"It shows. Really." I was being overly enthusiastic. Obvious. A klutz. I tried to calm down. "I only saw the second half, it was..." I needed a non-obvious word, but I was a photographer not a writer, "great."

Her eye bored a hole in my forehead for an instant. She turned back to #6.

"You took this during intermission, didn't you? Then you wanted to see more of me, so you bought a ticket for the second half."

I tried to read in her voice if this was good thing. But her tone was flat, like she was reading from a teleprompter.

I cleared my throat.

She turned to face me. All of her this time, including the toes of her black boots.

"That's okay. I'm told men like me."

My knees did their Jell-O imitation. I made an effort to sit taller on my stool.

"I was, um...curious about the concert. And hoped to show you the pictures."

Her smile came back and a giggle joined it. She leaned forward toward my display case where I kept anything smaller than 11 x 14. The summer air carried the scent of lilacs to my nostrils.

"You," she read from my business card, "Mr. Roberts, professional photographer with the big...lens, are a terrible liar."

She had caught me, and my brain was still running slower than...my grandfather came to mind saying *Molasses in January,* something I had never even seen. While I sat mute, trying to balance a better lie and the truth, she picked a card from the stack and stared at it the way she had been staring at #6.

"You're right," I managed. "I wanted to see you up close."

Her eye danced between the card and my face, and settled on the card.

I said, "Do you live in Tahoe?"

She shook her head slowly, eyes still on the card. "I had to work last night." She looked up. "Do you know this place CalNeva? It sits on the state line. A wide stripe runs right across the floor, dividing the two sides into different worlds: one dusty and boring, the other filled with light and sound and energy."

I had read about that casino in the local paper while trying to find my name in the listing of artists for the show. Frank Sinatra and the Rat Pack had performed there decades ago.

"Never been there."

She shrugged. "I saw a poster for this art show. I love art and music." She took a deep breath. "And the amazing sunshine in the mountains. I'm waiting here for my s—" She looked back down at the card, said, "Um, my ride." Then she glanced over her shoulder at *Smoking Girl*.

I guessed her thoughts. "Would you like to have that picture?"

She stepped back as if I had shoved her. "Oh no." She shook her head so emphatically I got a glimpse of her left eye, then added softly, "I don't have a place to hang it."

Now *she* was lying. There was a reason she was refusing the picture; a reason that frightened her. Thankfully, I was finally together and only said:

"If you ever want one, just contact me." I nodded toward the card she was holding with both hands. "I'll be happy to deliver it to you. Or perhaps to your family. Maybe they have a place to hang it."

She took another step backward, shaking her head again.

Couldn't I do anything right? I figured her family would love my picture of their lovely daughter.

"If you ever change your mind. Call me, okay?"

She stopped moving backward and turned to face #6 again. She said:

"Are there more?"

"There are five others. That's the last one of the series." I chose not to mention the dozens of reprints I had sold thus far, my most successful series yet.

"Your picture is...beguiling," she said in a breathless whisper most people saved for places like the Grand Canyon.

"Thank you. So is the subject." I should have stayed shut up, but it was true.

"May I see the others?"

"They're in my truck; booths don't hold much. I put one of the series out at each show. Would you like to go with me to get them?" I spoke before realizing that might sound like a proposition.

Her face turned slowly toward me and the brow over that one eye lifted slightly.

"Who will watch your booth while you're gone?"

My mind flashed to her lips pressed against mine on the floor of my Chevy while the most valuable items I owned were carted away in broad daylight—better than a fair trade.

"Good point." I waved my camera hand toward the other tents. "We usually watch out for each other, but today is Monday. Still lots of tourist traffic from the weekend. People stop by early, then head home at lunchtime."

Her eye dropped to my hand, perhaps because it was holding the camera. You shoot enough pictures, your hand just feels normal with a camera in it.

"You want to take my picture?"

Now what was I going to say? All of my work was clandestine. As soon as someone knew their picture was being taken, the mystery drained from their bodies and the results were empty shadows of life. I desperately wanted to take her picture, her phone number, her virginity in the unlikely event she still had it. But a posed portrait?

"Well, usually I—"

"Take sneaky pictures of people who don't know you are

there," she said, not asking a question.

"It's not like I sneak. It's just—"

"You hide where we cannot see you." She smiled. "It's okay. If you don't want to..."

"No. I mean, yes. I'd love to take your picture. Just turn back toward the *Smoking Girl* picture."

I lifted my camera. A woman wearing a pink top, pushing a dark blue stroller, and towing a kid in a yellow dress passed the booth; putting far too much color in the background. I shot anyway. I wanted to record every inch of smoking girl's turn, and the stillness she had shown when studying the picture, which is exactly what she did—as if she knew what I wanted and was making an effort to give it to me.

When I had burned through enough megabytes, I said: "Turn this way and let's see that smile when you told me how good a liar I am."

I shot her smile, and instantly wished I owned a house to hang it in. Then managed twenty more shots, and decided I would put one on the lock screen of my smartphone until I had that house.

"I'll go look for the other pictures if you mind the store. Deal?"

She glanced at her wristwatch, a slender silver thing nearly too small to read. She looked up, her face passive.

My heart sank at the thought she was about to run away.

"Deal," she said.

I'm not the most organized of people, but I found *Smoking Girl #2* and *#5* in less than five minutes in a breathless search. The others were in the truck somewhere. Except for *#1*. I sold that in Ann Arbor to a young cop who claimed to like the way her body had been backlit when the door to the auditorium was opened by a woman wearing a sapphire-blue gown. I'd bet he just liked her shape in silhouette. Since then I'd been on art-show highway—too busy to set up my printer.

I stepped under the Roberts Photography sign just as smoking girl was selling a small version of *Girl #6* with no frame. The customer, a slender woman in her forties in tight red slacks waving a brown 100mm cigarette with her left hand, was jabbering about how thrilled she was to buy a picture from the very model who had posed for it. And it depicted what she called the "lost art" of smoking a cigarette so that men would notice, the orally fixated bastards that they were.

Considering that she might put me in that group of bastards, I hung back from the conversation, not wanting to jeopardize a sale. People often lost their enthusiasm when they found out the "great photographer" was a somewhat disheveled surfer dude only a few years out of art school. I combed my raggedy blond hair with my free hand. As the woman turned to leave I stared at a picture of a Utah rock like it was a living specimen.

"You made a sale?"

"That was my third." She shrugged. "The cash is under this napkin."

"Amazing. Would you like a sales job?" I smiled.

"I have a job."

Right. Musician. What had she called it, the GO Orchestra?

"You can play in the booth—anything you want."

She looked up fast, startled.

"Your fiddle...uh...you never told me which instrument you play." I knew there were other instruments in an orchestra besides the violin, but couldn't name them.

"You didn't ask."

I hesitated. Should I ask now?

She smiled. "Viola. See?" She pointed to a spot on her neck that looked like a love bite from a sailor who had been on a slow boat. She must have read my eyes.

"It comes from holding the *fiddle* with my chin." She tilted her head to demonstrate with an air instrument. "The viola is larger than the violin, with a sweeter tone, but is held the same way."

"I never knew there were hazards in fiddle playing."

"Many." She stepped from behind my makeshift sales stand. "You found more pictures of me?" She brought both hands together under her chin like a kid awaiting ice cream.

"Two. But there are others. I didn't want to keep you waiting."

"It was fun. People recognize me right away. They wanted to know how I take pictures of myself."

Of course they would assume she was the Roberts of Roberts Photography. An obvious mistake; still, I felt like an intruder in my own booth.

"What did you tell them?"

She lowered her eyes and grinned with closed lips. She took a step toward me and whispered, "These modern cameras are wonderful," into my right ear.

Neither confirm nor deny. Smart girl. No wonder she was making sales.

"Very clever," I said, smiling. I was smiling a lot since she walked into my booth.

I took down #6 and put up #3 with her staring over my shoulder. The nearness of her body caused me to almost drop the picture. Twice. When I stepped back, she was locked in her staring stance again.

In #3 she again stood beside the column, but I had cranked the zoom to a longer focal length—so large that blown up on the print, her face was triple life size. It was just barely possible in this photo to verify that she did indeed have a dark and glistening left eye behind that swoosh of hair.

But that wasn't what most people noticed.

They noticed she was looking up—chin lifted, eyes upturned so far the whites showed below the irises. She had been gazing at the moon, whose light created the whitewash softness on her cheeks. But there was no way for the observer to know about the moon. Only her upturned face covering the entire canvas, lips pulling on a cigarette, its embers glowing crimson from the effort was visible.

"Do you have trouble?" she asked.

I had loads of trouble, most of it related to scratching out a living with a camera as I wandered in my search. And most recently keeping my knees solidified in her presence. Even in my lust-induced stupor I doubted that's what she meant.

"What kind of trouble?"

She waved her hand at #3 with two fingers extended like she was holding a cigarette, though she wasn't.

"Selling these."

Ah. "I sell a few."

She shook her head vigorously.

"I mean the smoking. Americans do not like. I try to stop. My father hates for me to smoke unless..." her voice drifted off. "But sometimes I am tense."

She had a point. More than once a woman, almost always a woman, often dragging a kid by the hand, would stop to chastise me for my photographs and blab about how I was promoting a disgusting habit, ruining the young, etc. If I was in a good mood I would respond that artistic license gave me free rein to have a perspective that showing smoking promoted beauty and eroticism—not smoking. And if I wanted to start a discussion I'd add: maybe the world needed more of both. Then the little one would usually interrupt to ask, "Mommy, what's rot-siz-him?"

If I wasn't in a good mood—say at a craft show I should have skipped on artistic grounds where people let me know they were insulted by my prices for a mere *photograph*—I would suggest she buy the picture to take it off the market before it could harm impressionable young minds. Once I offered a loud, obese woman wearing ballet slippers and leading a child on a red leash to help burn the picture after she paid for it. In cash. She was not amused.

The smoking girl was staring at me.

"Sometimes people complain." I shrugged, then smiled. "I just take the pictures. Can I help it if you smoke?"

"Sell better without smoke, you think?"

I repeated my shrug.

She stepped up to *Smoking Girl #3* and held her hand up to make the cigarette disappear. She observed for a moment, tilting her head left, then right. She said:

"Better with smoke."

She was right. I could have timed that shot differently, but something about the geometry of the straight cigarette and the curve of her cheekbone had made me wait.

"Right you are." I chewed my lower lip, decided to take a chance. "Are you performing in the area?"

Her head jerked to face me.

"The viola," I said, pointing to my neck. "Are you playing anywhere I can come see you?"

"To take pictures?"

Maybe that would have been a better move, most women like to have their picture taken. But I was trying to get personal.

"If you like. If you don't, I won't. Either way I would enjoy hearing you play," which was true. It wasn't all I would enjoy, but it was a start.

"Not here," she swooped a long curve with her right hand in a sort of Tai Chi move. "We travel."

"I travel too," I said with a grin, hoping to swoop along her path in my old truck.

She shook her head. Too emphatically for the current state of my ego. I said:

"Are you staying here in Tahoe?"

Her eyes widened. "No."

That no clearly meant no.

"Not staying," she added. "I am here to visit Pé." She paused. "If possible."

I breathed a little sigh, hope rising slowly upward from my toes.

"This art show is over in a few days, then I'm on to Reno for the Hot August Nights street fair."

Something like surprise slipped out before she got her left hand up to cover her mouth.

"You come to Reno?" she said, her voice barely a whisper.

"For over a week." I searched for a way to grab this moment. "Will you be there?" It hit me. "I'll dig out the other pictures of *Smoking Girl* to show you."

Her hand didn't move, but the corner of her eye was smiling even as she shook her head no.

Time to persist. "How can I reach you in Reno? Phone? E-mail?" I paused. What a fool. "I'm sorry, I just realized I've never introduced myself." I held out my hand. "Hello, by name is Joe Roberts. I'm a photographer."

Without lowering her left hand from where it covered her charming, slightly-tilted teeth, she lifted her right arm, took my hand and did a little curtsy.

"Pleased to meet you," she said through her hand.

No name. I half-smiled with my right cheek. My rational forebrain was insisting that she hadn't given her name because she had no interest in Mr. Roberts, and I was trying to ignore it.

"Shall I just call you Smoking Girl?"

Her hand came down. She bowed as she said:

"I am Mylin. I choose name after famous architect who designed your war memorial. I dream of the magical art she creates. She is so free. And powerful." She hesitated. "My father does not approve, but he allows this little rebellion so long as I do my work."

"A pleasure to meet you, Mylin," I said, with a butterfly whacking its wings against my chest. I figured she meant Maya Lin, the famous architect from Yale. I experienced her incredible Vietnam Veterans Memorial during a DC art show, designed while she was still a student.

"Does anyone work here?" a deep voice said from behind her.

I glanced over her shoulder. A husky guy made of about 250 pounds of muscle was holding the *#3* I had just hung on the booth's wall. His salt-and-pepper growth hadn't been shaved for a few days. Before I was able to put my mouth in motion, Mylin said, "I'll be right with you, sir." To me she said, "Please write your address here. I'll be sure your picture is sent today."

She moved with a sideways hopping motion over to the husky guy.

"How may I help you?"

For the first time since I had met her she reached up and brushed the multi-colored strands of hair back from her left eye. Something dark flashed beneath it near her temple. The hair fell back into place before I figured out what it was.

The guy glanced down at the print of *#3* he was holding in two huge paws hardened from physical labor. He looked up at Mylin, back to the print, up to Mylin.

"Is that you?"

She used her dim-the-sun smile and said:

"Oh yes. That was taken by moonlight in Michigan. I was staring at Orion wondering about our small space in the giant universe, and enjoying the little lift tobacco gives the soul."

"I'll be damned," he said. "A hot chick who understands why I smoke. How much is it?"

"Well, that depends," she said.

The man's jaw hardened.

"We want to be sure that our art goes to the man who appreciates it. You know there are wealthy people here at Lake Tahoe who buy only to match their carpet. They don't feel the heart of the picture. Like those rich boys in Hollywood who buy a chopper, but can't change oil."

Biker was a good guess. And by the look on his face,

correct. But how did she know this stuff?

"I know the type," he said. "I do my own custom work. Every bit of chrome I put on myself."

She nodded, still smiling. "Would you like to make an offer for my picture?"

My ego felt a speed bump rumble under its spinning wheels. Her picture?

"Well, I guess I—"

"Shhh," she said with a finger to her lips. "Don't say it aloud, bring bad luck." She reached down her blouse and came up with the small pad of paper I usually have on the counter. Somehow a miniature ballpoint appeared.

"Write down what you think would be fair. I will check with accountant."

The guy carefully lowered the print like it was a small child, putting the frame on the toe of his boot so it wouldn't be scratched by the asphalt.

"Will you sign it?" he asked.

She nodded. "On the back. Write that down too, just the way you want it."

His hand dwarfed hers as he gently took the pad.

"Take your time. I'll be right here." She walked backwards and stopped next to me.

"How much?" she whispered from the side of painted lips.

A little arrow speared my wallet; she might have made those three sales in five minutes by low-balling the price. I should have counted the money under the napkin.

"I'm flexible."

The guy waved her over and slipped the paper into her palm like they were doing a cocaine drop. She held up a finger for him to wait. Back in our corner she unfolded it. Out front the guy held the pictures in two hands and shifted weight from one foot to another—like he was waiting for a date who was late, worried she might not show.

I glanced at the paper. His price was fifty bucks over the asking I would have put on it—she was doing a bang up sales job. I shook my head; the guy frowned. I held out my hand for the magic appearing pen, crossed off the number, subtracted a hundred, and wrote a new one. Her eyes studied me with disapproval. She half-brushed her hair again. I read the inscription he wanted.

I gaze upon you longing to feel the vibrations of your life fill me.

I swallowed hard. This guy did custom chrome work?

I whispered to Mylin, "You okay with that?"

She shrugged with her right shoulder, took the slip of paper, and held it up for him to read, since both of his hands were holding the painting.

His unshaven face didn't look happy. "Why?"

"Because we have sale price for the right buyer. I want you have this picture...with your poetic description."

He swallowed hard. I'd bet his mouth was as dry as mine.

"Deal," he said, and shook her hand while carefully balancing the painting.

After she signed it, and we carefully wrapped the picture for travel, the biker gave her a big hug, and strutted away smiling. She tugged at my sleeve.

"Why did you do that?"

"Do what?" I hesitated. "You did all the work. I just watched."

She shook her head. "His offer. You didn't take it." Her visible eye carefully studied my face.

"He offered more than I normally ask."

"So?"

We gazed at each other. I tried really hard to keep my mind on our conversation. Finally I said, "I wanted to be fair."

She stared at me, not moving. "What is this *fair?*"

Since I didn't respond she continued.

"You could have gotten more," she said, like I had missed the winning touchdown in the homecoming game.

"Sure. But now he feels great about his purchase, and I feel great having sold it to him."

Her right eye scanned my face. She brushed her hair again.

"And this feeling great? Is more important than money?"

Since I work alone, I hadn't ever needed to explain this to anyone. But I tried.

"This feeling is why I do art. Art to make people happy. Art to make me happy."

Her eye didn't move.

For lack of a better idea, I stared back. Finally, her lips curved upward. She said:

"Me too."

She got me. Maybe this was the moment.

"Would you have dinner with me after the show? It closes at seven."

Her smile faded; her lips stiffened; she stepped away.

"I'm sorry, Joe. I can't do that."

My mouth formed *Why?* but my brain got there in time to strangle it. "Another time then." My heart was sinking, but I remembered something she said. "Maybe in Reno. I'll be there all week."

Her head wagged. "Not a good idea." She froze. "You don't know me."

That was a twist. Girls usually said: *I don't know you.*

"At least let me buy you a drink." I was grasping. "For helping with the booth. And these pictures are of you. It's the least I can do."

Hesitation clouded her gaze. It struck me she might be married; of course she couldn't take a picture home. Or maybe she didn't even like men.

Very softly she said, "I have to work."

"I'd really love to hear you play." That was true. Her lithe body and slender fingers coaxing sound from an instrument would make me like any kind of music.

Her head shook.

My hands felt cold, my feet stiff, like standing in wet sand.

Without warning her head stopped moving and the visible half of her brow furled. "I must go," she said as she spun in a single motion like a ballet dancer exiting the stage.

She was out of earshot before I recovered enough to say, "Wait."

She didn't look back.

The growing crowd enveloped her.

I took three steps in her direction and stopped. She wasn't just playing hard to get; she didn't want me to follow her. I returned to the tent and slumped on my stool. Potential customers strolled past. What had I learned? Her name. Her instrument. And she was employed by the GO Orchestra. She was working less than an hour drive away, but I didn't know when, or where.

The blank space where *Girl #3* had been hanging gaped at me. Without enthusiasm I dragged myself over and hung #6 back where it had started. I stared at the girl by the pillar and felt California's summer sun heat up my black cargo shorts. Then a smile found its way onto my face. An hour ago I had nothing. Now I had a name (maybe false), a musical instrument (probably real), and an encounter with a beautiful woman I had thought I would never see again in my life.

The day was going quite well, and the sun was barely up.

CHAPTER 2

QIGIQ WAS NAKED WHEN THE PHONE on the teak nightstand emitted the rumble of an Italian V-twin. He took two steps, grabbed the wireless handset and pressed it to his ear as he continued to the bamboo dresser that stored half of the clothes he owned. Only his partner would call before breakfast.

"Hello, Kandy."

"Someday it's not going to be me, Qi."

"Who else would call a hardworking stiff like me before coffee on a Monday?"

No hesitation. "Anyone who knew of a possible homicide on Richardson because her buddy Marsail was on that beat this morning. Vic is on the way to the hospital. Perp's a motorcycle hit and run—right up your two-wheeled alley. A witness claims premeditated action. Let's go get a head start."

Qigiq pondered the idea that he was having a dream of rising early and receiving a baffling phone call from Kandy. Or maybe...

"You're making this up, right? I've done something to annoy you and this is payback."

"You should be so lucky. ETA in three minutes. Did I catch you at a bad time?"

"Just looking for underwear to match my boots. I'll roll in five."

"Fifteen thirty-four Richardson. Take Charlotte, turn north. One way."

He hung up and grabbed synthetic shorts, well suited to sitting on the narrow seat of the rented Aprilia 850. Its automatic transmission had let him keep riding while his ankle healed from a conversation with a Mercedes. Two minutes and fifty seconds later he thumbed the starter, missing the low rumble of his Moto Guzzi.

Twelve minutes of focused riding ended at Charlotte and a row of creeping commuters. He unzipped the leather bag strapped to the gas tank, pulled out a round block the size of a hockey puck, flicked a switch with his thumb, and powerful blue and red LEDs began strobing. He stuck the box to the top of his white helmet and eased the bike to the left between two lanes of cars. He motored four blocks before seeing the black Mini at the curb. No Kandy. He continued crawling past stopped cars for three more blocks and found her talking with a motor cop on the corner of Richardson.

"Nice hat, Ronald MacDonald would be impressed," Kandy said as he pulled to a stop along the curb. He removed the lights and switched the bike off.

"Tom Marsail, my partner Qigiq from Alaska," Kandy said. "Would you mind telling a short version again?"

Marsail moved his gaze away from the black shirt adorning Kandy's nearly six feet of gazelle-muscle. She preferred athletic clothes that didn't hinder movement in an altercation. Since she didn't know when there might be one, she wore them all the time, violating a number of department regulations that Captain Jasik let slide because she was good at her job and babysat the sabbatical guy from Alaska without complaining about it.

"Got the call at 7:39 this morning. Elderly lady down, unconscious. She's in transit to the UCSF Medical Center." He glanced at his watch. "Maybe there by now. She was crossing Charlotte," he pointed, "with at least a dozen other people. Charlotte light was red, her walk light was go. A motorcyclist split lanes between cars, fast enough to knock her down on impact. Rider crossed the intersection against the red, swerved through traffic, and rode away."

"Drugged-up kid using the city as a video game?" Qigiq asked.

Kandy shook her head. "Even the lowest of the low don't party on Monday morning. And—" she nodded at Marsail.

"And," Marsail continued, "we have a witness over there driving a box truck. Says he was the first vehicle in line, saw the guy coming in his rearview. Claims the rider *aimed* for the old lady."

Qigiq frowned. "Do we know the ethnicity of the victim or the perp?"

"Woman was Asian." He shrugged. "Probably Chinese given we're in Chinatown. No info on the perp. Full-coverage racing helmet. Dark shield."

Qigiq looked at the lanes the bike had split. "Dark shield at seven-thirty on a foggy morning? Not safety first."

Marsail's eyes moved between Kandy and Qigiq.

"Weird," Kandy added.

Marsail said, "Black. A witness said the bike was a late model black Triumph. But he also said there were no markings so I don't know how—"

Qigig held up a hand. "Did the witness say something like, 'Vertical twin, black engine, one tail pipe on each side?'"

Marsail nodded and tapped his notebook with a pen. "And—"

Qigiq added, "It *sounded* like a Triumph."

Marsail smiled. "Exactly."

Kandy scanned up and down the street, tracing the path of the motorcycle with her eyes. "What do we know about that witness?"

Marsail flipped a page of his notebook. "Mechanic at a place called Munroe Motors, here in San Francisco."

Qigiq pushed both hands into his pants pockets. "Triumph for sure. A mechanic who works on European bikes wouldn't be mistaken about an exhaust note."

A boy of about eleven wearing a green windbreaker appeared next to Qigiq. He held a silver camera in his raised hand, but didn't speak.

Qigiq dropped to one knee. "Would you like me to take your picture?"

The boy's head moved slowly from side to side.

Qigiq pointed. "Would you like to sit on officer Tom's motorbike?"

Marsail's face showed surprise, but he didn't comment.

The boy smiled, and continued moving his head.

"Do you want to show us something?" Kandy asked.

The boy nodded.

"Anthony!"

A woman raced toward them with powerful strides, her low brown heels stomping the sidewalk. She continued loudly:

"I told you to leave the police alone, they have important work to do."

She grabbed his free hand and pulled him along Charlotte in the direction of the traffic jam, her shoulders rocking with each step.

Kandy and Qigiq's eyes met. She said: "Our conversation won't end well."

Qigiq trotted after the woman.

"Excuse me, Ma'am. I'm detective Qigiq. May I talk with you?"

She stopped and spun on her heel. "I'm in a hurry. Are you arresting us?"

He drew up with her body between him and her son—a mama bear protecting her cub.

"No, Ma'am. An elderly woman was seriously injured on this corner a few minutes ago. If you or your fine son could help us understand what happened, it would greatly assist us in our work."

She said: "What happened?" Then shrieked: "What

happened!?"

Qigiq resisted the temptation to cover his ears. He frowned to appear serious.

"I'll tell you what happened. I was over there in that dry cleaners." Her free hand pointed diagonally across the intersection. "Waiting waiting waiting. They didn't want to open until 7:30, but I pounded on the glass. These Orientals are so lazy. There I was, the customer, ready to pick up my dress and they wouldn't let me in. When they finally opened there was a wrinkle in it, so they can just do it over before I pay."

"Yes Ma'am, I understand." Qigiq said, giving no indication of what he was beginning to understand.

"As I was leaving that...that...*madman* on a devil machine roared into a bunch of pedestrians crossing the street. I don't know why we allow them in this country; they're dangerous. Only hoodlums ride them. And they pollute more than a car. Can you imagine that? Only one person, and it pollutes more than a car!"

"Not all—"

"And he *raced* through that crowd of nice folks trying to get to work to make a decent living, which is getting harder and harder to do with so many illegal aliens sneaking in and taking our jobs."

Kandy had been prescient.

"That rider—" She stopped. The little boy was tugging at her printed skirt.

"Leave me alone, Anthony. Can't you see I'm talking to this nice policeman?"

She turned back to Qigiq.

"That rider never even slowed down. He drove that evil thing into those people like they weren't even there, and knocked that poor lady—" Another tug.

"Anthony! When we get home!"

"What does he want?" Qigiq asked gently.

"He wants to show you pictures, but he's too shy to ask. All the time he's taking pictures and pictures and more pictures and wants to show them to people. Let me tell you, it can try the patience of the Almighty."

Qigiq dropped to one knee and spoke directly to the boy.

"May I see what you have?"

Without looking to his mother for approval he rushed to Qigiq and held the camera up with both hands. The screen showed the intersection; the boy had also been inside the corner dry cleaners. The box truck faced him. A crowd stood on the corner to the left. It verified the positions described by the witnesses, but wasn't otherwise helpful.

Qigiq started to rise, but the crowd began crossing the street. He leaned closer.

A tiny movie showed a motorcycle moving toward the camera.

It toppled a woman in a blue dress. Zigzagged through the intersection.

A car careened onto the sidewalk.

The motorcycle disappeared.

The woman in the blue dress didn't move.

Definitely a Triumph.

———

Qigiq leaned forward and placed both elbows onto a light blue desktop blotter that would never see ink because he used a pencil and a laptop. He said:

"Tell me again why Captain Jasik gave us this corner office?"

Kandy smiled across the double-wide desks they had positioned back-to-back in the middle of the room so they could converse without turning around.

"You already know why. We pulled him out of the media fire on that serial explosion thing."

"But that's our job."

Kandy leaned back and dropped the heel of a leather boot on top of her desk. "He just wanted a reason to be nice to you."

"The visiting gumshoe whose Alaskan name no one can pronounce? That usually means the basement."

"Unless..." She lifted an eyebrow.

"You mean we get this palatial office on the third floor with an actual view because the captain wants me to stay?"

"Feel the love, Detective Key-jeek," she said, tapping her laptop with one hand. "But..."

He waited. Kandy usually had a punch line.

"Now we have another case."

"And the captain has a short memory," Qigiq said.

"It's not that. It's just..."

"You're only as good as your last case," they said in unison.

When they stopped laughing, Qigiq tapped the arrow key on his laptop. The movie on the screen jumped forward one frame. His formal computer training had been a couple of classes in college, so he was unsure how much to trust a recording from a kid's pocket camera. That was why he had applied for a sabbatical in San Francisco, the land of geeks, where he learned something new every day.

"How do you read Anthony's movie?"

She blew a stream of air at their big window that provided a view of fifty feet at the top of the Golden Gate's south tower. It was barely identifiable, but just knowing it was the famous bridge reminded him of the special place he was living—and the special crimes it harbored.

"Given that I've only watched it," she glanced at the corner of her screen, "forty-eight times so far this morning. I don't yet have a final analysis."

"First impression?"

"The guy might swerve for a million reasons, especially if he were drunk or high. So many bodies and colors moving in his visual field, being trapped beside the box truck. Had nowhere to go. He could have panicked."

"He could have stopped," Qigiq offered.

"Sure, stopping is the primary maneuver to avoid an imminent crash. But it's not the only one."

"You sound like a courtroom lawyer," Qigiq said, letting the movie play in slow motion. "He never reached for the brake."

"True." She stepped her movie ahead. "He definitely committed to swerving instead of stopping."

"See his right wrist drop in frame five forty-one?"

She leaned close to her screen and bumped the movie ahead. "Yeah."

"He accelerated."

She shrugged. "So? He saw an opening in the crowd and wicked it up to blast through the daylight before it closed off, like a running back trying to score."

Qigiq lifted his eyes and smiled. "Wicked?"

"Racer talk."

"Good thought. Maybe he has track experience. Does it look like intent to you?"

"Maybe." She dropped her feet and stood; took five long paces to the window; stared down at the street. "Maybe just a kid splitting lanes too fast. With that tall truck in his way he didn't see the red light until it was too late to stop. Or..." she turned to face him. "He saw the light go yellow and was trying to make it through. He just arrived late and overconfident."

Qigiq stopped his movie. "And as he reached the crosswalk, he was surprised by the crowd because he had been fixated on the light."

Kandy leaned against the glass. "That might explain what could be construed as a survival reaction when he swerved."

Qigiq remained still.

"You don't believe it?" she asked.

He leaned back, rubbed his chin and sighed. "Not sure. Did you see how he rode through the intersection?"

"Fast," she said.

"Expert rider. Not everyone can make a bike weave through moving cross traffic at forty miles per hour."

"Ferd'll calculate the speed for us. I'll get the movie up to him."

Qigiq slid his lips across each other, thinking.

Kandy said, "You think expert rider means something?"

He shrugged without looking up.

She said, "Lots of riders in the city. They survive on the ability to react to rapidly changing conditions."

"I've seen them ride."

"Meaning?" She lowered her rear end to the fresh pale green paint on the windowsill.

"Most...what's that term you use to describe the way Americans drive?"

"Suck," she said. "More interested in cell phone chit-chat and text messages than the tons of lethal metal in their hands."

"Exactly."

"So what about this guy?"

Qigiq met her eyes. "Seeing how he moved his body, I think he's spent time on a track. Maybe a young racer, maybe just an enthusiast."

"And you conclude?" she pressed. "Please hurry, I need more coffee."

"Let me put it to you as a question, Detective Dreeson. Why was this rider able to avoid," he glanced down at the movie, "three vehicles moving perpendicular to his path, one of them an SUV?"

"And not the fast moving Chinese woman shuffling along the crosswalk?"

"Curious," he said.

"You want a coffee?"

"You buying? Molly likes the office kitty overflowing with love."

"Nope, but I deliver," she said as she stood from the windowsill.

He dug into his pocket for dollar bills and handed them over. "Decaf please."

She took the bills. "You smoking again?"

"No, why do you ask?"

Kandy shrugged. "I figured you were trying to compensate. How can you drink coffee without caffeine? It's a crime against nature."

"Trying to sleep better."

She laughed as she turned toward the door. "You're a detective. You only get to sleep when you're dead or on vacation." She stopped at the door and looked back. "And we're too busy for vacation."

The hydraulic cylinder let the door swing slowly closed behind her.

Qigiq stared at the fog lifting off San Francisco streets on the other side of a hundred square feet of glass, then at the screen of his laptop. The man knew his bike. Coincidence, or handpicked for this job? An odd job. A Chinese woman (ethnicity not yet verified, he reminded himself) injured in morning daylight at great risk to the rider. Made no sense. Failed homicide? Why an elderly woman?

For the umpteenth time, he stepped the movie a single frame at a time. Was the dark shield a conscious choice to prevent recognition, or a kid with good eyes who wore it as an anti-glare strategy? Like teenagers who wore sunglasses at night and were shocked that everyone else didn't.

"How do I find you?" he said to the rider in the video. "Might you be a woman?" There was no definitive evidence for anything except skill, and thousands of women rode motorcycles. Some even raced the boys, and beat them.

The door flung open as Kandy backed into the room with two oversized steaming mugs. She lowered one to Qigiq's desk while raising the other to her lips.

"Careful, it's really hot."

He nodded thanks. "Was the rider a woman?"

She sipped. Frowned. Sipped again. "Nothing says no. Not many girls ride like that though."

"Might be a good reason to use a female. Figure we wouldn't expect a girl." He sighed. "I need something to grab hold of."

"How about a sandwich?" she said.

"It's only ten-thirty."

"Mid-morning snack?"

He rolled back from the desk and patted his stomach, which was flat, but not rippled like he knew Kandy's was. "Some of us don't work out as much as you do."

"And whose fault might that be?" She grinned, or maybe snickered; he wasn't sure.

He got up and walked to the window, resting his eyes on their little piece of bridge in the distance. "We have a great view."

"Yeah, you can watch the world go by while we get nothing done." She kicked her chair over to the front of her desk and dropped into it without spilling a drop. "I stopped and saw Ferd. Said he'll take a quick look at Anthony's movie this morning."

Qigiq stared at the traffic two stories below drifting along at no more than a brisk walk. Fast movement caught his eye. A motorcycle half a mile west sliced toward him between the rows of cars.

"Maybe we can follow the bike," he said.

"Sure. Black bike. Black leathers. Black helmet with a shiny silver design that could be a bird or a monster or maybe my fairy godmother, depending on which witness you think had the best eyes."

"Sounded like a Triumph though."

He felt her staring at his back.

"Terrific," she said. "The Brits have only been shipping bikes to the U.S. for what, half a century?"

The bike snaked along. "They closed down for a spell in the seventies."

"That'll help a lot."

That time she snickered, he was sure. He turned around. "Do you have binoculars in your desk?"

"Do I look like Army surplus?" With coffee in one hand, she pulled out the lowest drawer with toe of a boot, removed a stack of Black Belt magazines, and dropped them on the floor. "You should hire a Sherpa to follow you around." She huffed a soft laugh; her head disappeared. She came up with a pair of green glasses nearly a foot long and tossed them in one smooth motion to Qigiq.

They arched high directly at his chest. He managed to get two hands on them. "You live dangerously. The captain wouldn't appreciate your breaking our new window."

Kandy leaned back with her coffee. "Breaking glass doesn't even register on my danger meter, Qi."

He searched for the bike. "It's black."

"One."

"Dropped clip on bars like our movie bike."

"Two. It's *our* bike, huh? Thanks for sharing."

"Vertical twin. I'd guess Triumph, though I can't see well from this angle. No markings on the tank. Rider in black leather."

She bolted upright. "Is it our man?"

"Relax," he said. "Way too tall. This guy makes ours look like a gnome."

"How's he ride?"

"No finesse, but he's comfortable muscling the bike around with raw strength."

She sat back down. "Helmet?"

"Black with a silver insignia. I'd say dragon, or some kind of otherworldly monster, maybe from a movie."

"I thought you read books."

"Saw a bus wrapped with a giant furry creature a couple of weeks ago. I've only seen monsters in movies."

"Never been married, huh?" she asked, huffing.

"Torment the over-thirty guy on his love life at a time like this."

"I can see how stressed you are, peeping out the window, probably ogling a mini-skirt at a hundred paces."

The glasses shook as he chuckled. "It's leather. Union Jack on the back. Looks good on her."

She launched herself to the window. "What in hell are you talking about?" she said, peering in the direction the glasses pointed.

"Three blocks up, heading this way. Our boy has stopped and is chatting with an Asian girl on the sidewalk. They keep looking this way, like they're watching us watching them."

Kandy put her hand above her eyes to block the brightening sky and squinted. "An Asian wearing a Union Jack? What is going on here?"

"Chicks dig bikers."

She punched him in the arm and he handed over the glasses. She studied the scene for thirty-seconds before saying: "They're focused on this street corner. And know each other well."

"You can read a relationship at five hundred yards?"

"Woman's intuition."

He waited. The couple was partially obscured by a vintage light pole. Finally he said, "I didn't know intuition had such range."

She lowered the glasses. "The kiss she gave him was a hint."

"Chicks dig—"

"Oh shut up."

She crossed back to her desk, dropped the glasses in the low drawer and tossed the magazines in after them. "Let's go chat."

"Official?" He reached for his riding jacket. The fog was lifting, but the dampness of San Francisco chilled his bones in a way Fairbanks never had.

Kandy was halfway out the door when she replied, "Nope."

CHAPTER 3

KANDY AND QIGIQ DOUBLE-TIMED DOWN two flights of stairs and out the McKinney side of the building to remain invisible to their quarry. They passed the biker and Union Jack girl on the opposite side of the street, crossed at a corner lacking a street sign, and strolled back toward them. The bike sat parallel to the curb, its rider straddling the seat, one hand on the handlebars, the other on the girl. The two alternated between jabbering, kissing, and staring down the street toward the SFPD offices.

As they approached, Qigiq said: "Nice bike."

The guy released the girl's waist and rotated. His eyes sized up Qigiq in one sweep and landed on Kandy. They took longer to size her up.

"Yeah," he agreed, his eyes on Kandy's chest.

"Triumph?" Qigiq asked.

The girl punched his upper arm.

He grinned. "New one. Built in Hensley."

"Looks vintage," Qigiq said.

"Like your jacket," the guy offered.

Qigiq had been wearing his Brooks black leather jacket since college. Maybe it was time to update.

Kandy said, "Doesn't riding in the city suck?"

Eyes turned. The girl scowled.

The rider's grin widened. He seemed happy to be talking to Kandy's shirt.

"Nah, it's great. Cars are wallowing whales. I slice around them like a jet fighter." His right hand demonstrated.

Qigiq put him in his mid-twenties, Caucasian with a hint of something, perhaps Hispanic. Or maybe Native American, like himself.

Kandy said, "Isn't it dangerous?" stepping closer to the bike. She reached out her left hand and stopped an inch short of the gleaming black fender. "OK to touch it?"

There wasn't a mark on the bike. Not even dust. But the guy said, "Sure. Be careful, it's hot."

Qigiq knew he meant the exhaust, but it made him want to know how the guy had come by the shiny machine.

Kandy stroked the fender with her fingertips near a license plate mounted on a hinge low on the left, and flipped in so it couldn't be read from behind.

"It's smooth."

The Asian girl crossed her arms over her bosom.

The guy said, "I rub it with clay. Makes it shine."

"Is it fast?" Kandy asked, straightening and meeting his eyes.

"Fast is a relative thing," he said, lifting a thigh across the saddle to face Kandy. "It's faster than most cars. And it's fast for a Triumph. But there are extreme motorcycles that are outright faster."

The honesty of the answer surprised Qigiq; he had been expecting: *Yeah, Babe, like me.*

The rider watched Kandy, as if Qigiq and the Asian girl had gone off together for lunch.

"Nothing is faster through the city though." He gestured forward, "Narrow bars squeeze between cages," and down, "loads of torque." He paused before adding, "I never get caught in the city."

That sounded like the voice of experience to Qigiq.

The girl wearing the Union Jack skirt interrupted. "Michael."

He shot her a glance that contained a few daggers.

"Where did you get it?" Qigiq interjected. The girl visibly relaxed.

Kandy walked slowly around the rear of the bike so Michael and Qigiq faced each other, and the two women were on opposite sides of the machine. And its rider. One of Michael's eyes tried to follow her.

"Got it new from Munroe Motors. Had it worked on by a guy."

"I've always wanted a Triumph," Qigiq said, which was true. He wanted a '69, if he ever found one in decent shape.

"Watch Craigslist," Michael said. "Good ones show up out of the blue."

The mention of Craigslist reminded Qigiq of his first case in San Francisco where an ad had been rigged to trigger an explosion. Quite an unnerving experience with Internet technology.

Kandy squatted to admire the bike; Michael tried hard not to stare.

"What kind of modifications?" Qigiq asked.

"Michael," the girl said with more insistence.

Michael didn't bother to look at her. "Rebuilt from the ground up. Suspension and everything. Only way to get it right."

"Maybe your guy will help me?"

Michael shook his head. "He only works by referral. Sorry, I don't know you," he turned towards Kandy, "and your lady, well enough."

Kandy popped up from a full squat. "Yet," she said with a wide smile.

He hesitated, clearly torn between two paths, maybe considering the one less traveled.

Qigiq suppressed a grin and let the moment play out.

Michael made his decision, turned towards the girl, pulled the clutch and fired the bike. "Gotta go," he said to Union Jack. "I'll call you tonight."

"You'd better," she said, adding a quick kiss before he slipped into his helmet.

"Hey," Kandy said. She pointed to his head, "Great graphics."

"Custom."

She leaned in close, her body between his bike and traffic— blocking his only means of escape. "Don't tell me, custom guy only works by referral."

His cheeks puffed up with a smile inside the full-coverage helmet. "Bye."

Qigiq put the departing exhaust note at 100 decibels—above the legal limit, but it was just a guess.

Michael slipped his machine into traffic where there appeared to be no space, crossed deftly between moving cars, and accelerated into the narrow lane between them.

"Why is lane splitting legal in California?" Qigiq asked rhetorically.

"Because it's cool," the Union girl said as she turned away.

Kandy took long strides. The first over the spot on the pavement where parked cars dripped oil. The second up the curb. The third put her beside the girl.

"Hey," Kandy said.

Qigiq stared in the direction of his office trying to figure out what the two had been looking at, kept quiet, and listened.

"Hey, what? Stay away from my man."

"How about helping me?" Kandy said.

The girl stopped. "Why?"

"We only stopped to admire his bike."

"Yeah, I saw you admiring."

"I want one," Kandy said.

The girl began correcting her smeared lipstick with a finger. "You want a bike?"

Kandy shook her head. "No. A man with a bike."

The girl started to turn away.

"Not your man. Someone, uh, shorter."

"Like that guy?" the girl asked, flipping her hair toward Qigiq.

"We just work together. You know..."

The girl laughed. "Something with better performance?"

Kandy shrugged. "I thought you might know some bikers."

"Bikers are everywhere. You just have to know where to look."

Kandy held out her hand. "Kandy."

The girl hesitated, "Trina." She shook lightly once.

They watched each other in silence. Trina finally said:

"They love to talk bikes in the cafés: Drive Chain, Zeitgeist, Ton Up, Lucky 13, even Old Princeton Landing down in Half Moon Bay." She walked away, her heels clicking softly below the swaying Union Jack flag of the United Kingdom emblazoned on her skirt.

Qigiq was studying the pavement where the bike had been when Kandy returned. New Triumphs didn't leak like the old ones.

"Find anything?" she asked.

"Recent chain lube. Doesn't seem useful."

"He's careful about maintenance, and likes lube," she said with a laugh.

"Make a new friend?"

She dug into the front pocket of her black jeans and came up with a half-empty yellow pack of gum. "Friend would be an exaggeration, but she gave me a tip: biker bars." She proffered the pack.

He held up a hand. "I heard the list. Ton Up will be café racers, maybe some Brit bikes."

"Let yourself go, it's only sugar."

He drew a stick, palmed the wrapper into his pocket. "It'll have vintage race bikes on display. Place will be frequented by kids trying to capture the mysterious essence of the 60s when making a motorbike go 100 mph took more than a credit card and riding it away from the dealer."

"Your kind of place."

He shrugged as they started back towards the office. "My kind of decor. What do we find at the Ton Up?"

"Boys and bikes," she said as she chewed. "Maybe a connection to our hit-and-run machine. And more black Triumphs."

Qigiq rolled his lips together. "We don't know if the rider was male." He glanced down at his orange-faced wristwatch. "They're wearing full-coverage helmets—safe, but not retro. Hides their faces." He paused, considering. "Think the Ton Up is open for lunch?"

Kandy pulled out her cell phone and asked for the number. Before she placed the call, it vibrated in her hand. She tapped speakerphone and said, "Dreeson."

"Hello, Detective. A rush order this morning, I see."

"Sorry we can't arrange attempted homicides for your schedule, Ferd. The bad guys won't cooperate."

"But the time stamp on this movie data is 7:28 am. It didn't arrive on my desk until 9:04."

"Sorry, Qigiq and I wasted time studying it. I should have just taken it to your lab, but we didn't want to bother you if there was nothing there."

"And how did you ascertain that without bringing it to me for analysis?"

"You win, Ferd. At least we were smart enough to realize you needed to see it."

"As I understand the situation, a child was astute enough to realize that. And please Detective, my name is Ferdinand."

"Sorry, Ferd." She laughed. He laughed with her. So?"

"I've done a first order analysis that has produced results you will wish to see. Thus, my personal phone call."

"Thanks, two minutes. Really. We're only a couple blocks

away." Her phone disappeared into a pocket.

Qigiq read her expression. "What's wrong?"

"Ferd has results he wants us to see right away. But..." She pointed to her left.

Four black Triumphs glided between lanes of traffic and parked near the oil spot where Michael's bike had been. The machines ceased roaring together.

The crawling traffic was library quiet by comparison.

He said: "Must be ride your Triumph to work day."

While one man dismounted, Qigiq studied bikes that could be part of a top-secret government cloning machine. From a distance they matched the one in little Anthony's movie. And Michael's bike, though not nearly so clean.

A short man strode the half-block between them wearing his helmet. He stopped facing Qigiq. The entrance to the Footwear Etc. store to the left reflected in the dark shield.

"You the one asking questions?"

The voice was male, young, slight accent.

"About what?" Qigiq said.

The man pushed him on his left shoulder, moving him back a step.

Kandy inched closer.

The helmet turned. "So you're the chick that has Trina upset?"

Qigiq glanced at Kandy. She nodded.

"I was talking to Michael about his bike," Qigiq said. He leaned slightly to look past the guy's shoulder. The other three riders sat astride their machines, barely paying attention. "It looked a lot like yours."

From Qigiq's left Kandy said, "His helmet looked like yours too."

"Not your business." He turned to Qigiq and lifted his hand into the gun imitation kids use. "You stay away from Trina."

"I never looked at Trina," Qigiq replied truthfully.

The guy pushed him again.

"That's not the way she tells it."

Kandy moved in another inch. "What did Trina have to say about Michael?"

The finger moved toward her. "You came on to him. Tried to find out about," he waved his other hand toward his buddies, "us."

"Us?" Qigiq laughed. "I see four guys who dress pretty and ride motorbikes. You could be Shriners, though they prefer red."

"Don't push me old man."

"What's your problem?" Kandy said. "We only chatted about British bikes and how underpowered they are by today's standards."

The helmet's shield flicked back and forth between them.

"Too many questions. Consider this a warning to stay away. You only get one."

"Oooo," Kandy cooed under her breath.

Qigiq took a guess. "So we're not welcome at the Ton Up club?"

The guy's titanium enhanced racing glove came up fast. Qigiq dodged left. The punch grazed his right ear. Kandy's elbow doubled the guy in half with a thud.

His knees smacked the pavement.

His friends materialized on the sidewalk, but stopped ten yards away when he raised a hand as he wheezed inside his helmet.

Qigiq prepared for him to leap up.

But he gestured and his buddies returned to their bikes, fired them up, and left. He stood slowly and surprised Qigiq by flipping up his face shield and glaring directly at him. He was Asian, with black, angry eyes and a narrow straight nose. The helmet limited his peripheral vision; maybe he wasn't aware that Kandy was the one who had hit him.

"Would you tell me who mods your bikes?" Qigiq asked.

"Not a chance."

"I'm glad we're still on speaking terms. What's with the design on the helmet?"

A gloved hand reached up and perfectly traced the image. "Our mascot," he said, turned and headed for his bike.

"You going to let him leave?" Kandy whispered.

"You want to do paperwork on this?"

She flexed her hand and rubbed her elbow.

"Was he wearing armor?" he asked.

"Not where I hit him. Did you notice the plates?"

"Flip mounts so the plate can be folded flat to the bike, can't be read from behind. Harley ships some bikes with that feature."

"Does it have any legal use?" she said.

"Looks cool. Keeps people from tripping over it in a parking lot." He smiled.

"I got Michael's, by the way: 20J2254. Easy to read while stroking his fender."

"I'll bet his fender enjoyed it too." He tilted his head in the direction of the office. "Shall we?"

Halfway back Kandy said: "Four guys. They must have figured you'd be tough."

"Or you."

She slipped her thumbs into the front pockets of her jeans. "Guys rarely figure that right."

They stopped to wait for a cable car to trundle through the intersection on steel rails, then hustled across with a small group of pedestrians.

"Even after they've met you?" he asked.

"Even after they've met me."

They walked a block in silence. He thought about bikes. Gangs. Criminal organizations built around riding. He eventually asked:

"Who are they?"

She shrugged. "Local club. Drugs, babes. Hot bikes. All

black, no markings, trick license plates. Don't want anyone to see what's going on."

"Related to the injured Mrs. Chong?"

She chewed her gum for a second. "Or just an accident. They're aggressive riders."

He stopped and faced her. "What was our rider doing out of bed at seven-thirty on a Monday morning?"

Her head bobbed slightly. "A point worthy of consideration over a fine lunch."

"I bet the Ton Up has British food."

She turned toward the office and picked up the pace.

"Let's go see what Ferd has for us first. I promised we'd stop by right away."

CHAPTER 4

KANDY AND QIGIQ STOOD BEFORE A DOOR half-filled with frosted glass emblazoned with the words Electronic Evidence Recovery in black letters. Kandy tapped the glass with two fingers, each tap slightly louder than the previous one. Ferdinand hated being disturbed, and had instructed her on his preferred method of being knocked at.

"Enter," came from within.

"You first," Qigiq said. "He likes you best."

Kandy turned the knob and whispered, "Chicken."

They entered an open room with rows of long tables that reminded Qigiq of his high school cafeteria, only these tables held computers in various stages of disassembly rather than students in stages of development. A lone figure draped in a knee-length white lab coat sat in the center of the room leaning over a binocular microscope.

"Hello, Ferdinand," Kandy called across the room.

Without looking up he said, "Trying to sweet talk me now, Detective? You must have another stalled case that requires my skill to save your—" He paused for a moment, "Reputation."

"Cute, Ferd," Kandy replied. "But you can save my pert little ass by waving your digital voodoo wand anytime you want."

The white shape rolled his armless chair away from the scope.

"Please, Detective, must we be so suggestive?"

"Only if it helps you think," Kandy replied with a one-huff laugh.

Ferdinand removed thick glasses in gold aviator frames and rubbed them with his lab coat. His eyes lifted toward Kandy.

"Vulgarity is hardly necessary to power my thinking apparatus."

Kandy stopped beside Ferdinand. "Did you like our movie?"

"Anthony did a fine job for one so young. Of course, today's digital cameras are remarkable."

"Which means you have something for us," Kandy said, smiling in Qigiq's direction.

"When, Detective, in the years I've been saving your—" Ferdinand paused.

"Did you just smile, Ferd?" Kandy asked.

"When have I *not* had something for you?"

Kandy said, "Well, there was the time I brought you that Blackberry."

Ferdinand returned his glasses to his face and stared over them. "The one the Boeing aircraft had run over?"

She shrugged. "It wasn't in the best shape..."

Ferdinand nodded a hello to Qigiq that contained a grinning hint of *how do you put up with her?* He walked briskly to a far corner of the lab, waving for them to follow, and reached into a deep pocket of his coat. The room lights faded to candlelight.

"Overspend your electric budget again?" Kandy said.

"Give your eyes a moment to adjust. You will see much more with less ambient light."

Three large monitors arranged in a curve lit up. They held a frozen frame from Anthony's movie, greatly enlarged. A single motorcycle sat far back in traffic.

"We begin," Ferdinand said. A blue line emanating from the bike's headlight shot across the screen between the cars. "This," he pointed to the screen, "represents the bike's speed and direction of travel. Its velocity, if you will."

The movie began playing in slow motion; the bike inched along the blue line.

"Now," Ferdinand said.

A green line glowed from the forehead of a woman in a blue dress and extended out into the crosswalk.

The movie stopped. "Using these two lines, we obtain the following."

A rectangle the size of the bike, and an ellipse the size of the woman moved across the still frame.

"He should have missed her," Kandy said.

"Correct," Ferdinand said. "If he had simply maintained his speed and direction—"

"Velocity if you will," Kandy interjected.

"Correct. No collision would have occurred."

"Damn, you're good," Kandy said. A tiny grin flickered at the corners of Ferdinand's lips. "But we knew that. Witnesses saw the bike swerve."

Ferdinand shook his head. "Witnesses are much less reliable than science."

A red line lit beside the blue one. This time the box moved along the line, veered to the rider's right as it reached the front wheel of the truck, and made contact with the ellipse.

"How much time?" Qigiq asked.

"From here," Ferdinand pointed to where the red line veered away from the blue one, "to here at the collision. Six-tenths of a second."

"An old woman can't move that fast. She had no chance," Kandy said.

"How fast?" Qigiq asked.

Ferdinand pointed to the bike far back in traffic. "Here. Zero. He's stopped between lanes."

"Zero?" Kandy said a bit too loud. Her voice echoed in the long room.

The frames of the movie flashed past until the motorcyclist made contact with the woman. Ferdinand tapped a keyboard. Numbers popped up beside the image of the biker.

"Forty-three miles per hour." She whistled.

"Zero to forty-three in?" Qigiq asked.

Ferdinand pointed.

Qigiq read. "Two point eight seconds."

"Was he trying to beat the pedestrians?" Kandy asked.

"Ah, yes. The human's motivation," Ferdinand said. "Science does not help so much with that question."

Qigiq leaned closer to the screen. "So he hit her on purpose."

Ferdinand shook his head. "This we don't know."

"I love your voodoo wand, Ferd," Kandy said. "But I gotta tell you. I'm not learning anything new here."

Ferdinand's eyebrows shot up. "You knew he was going forty-three miles per hour?"

"Uh..."

"From a standing start?"

"Well, no, but..."

"So you have learned something, Detective." Ferdinand met Kandy's eyes. With a perfectly straight face he said, "Shall I wave my wand again?"

Kandy burst out laughing.

Ferdinand fought a grin.

Qigiq said, "Do you have any coffee? I left mine in the office when we ran out to meet the Union Jack girl."

"Fresh." Ferdinand pointed to the far left corner.

"Want one?" Qigiq said.

Ferdinand declined.

In the corner Qigiq found a pair of personal computers whose internals had been replaced by Krups drip coffee makers: one regular, one decaf. A third computer frame held a bean grinder. The fourth concealed a bright red espresso machine. From most angles they looked like a computing array that only the anointed should approach. It was Monday, still before noon, but an ugly case was already on his desk. Caffeine would sure be welcome. To postpone the decision he drew a cup for Kandy. As it filled, a compromise suggested itself.

He filled a ceramic mug half full of decaf and finished filling it with full-on Colombian blend, and a dash of cream. He would ease into caffeine reduction.

"You mean Ferd has decaf?" Kandy said. "You didn't give me any did you?" She stared suspiciously into the dark liquid.

Qigiq shook his head. "Never."

"You're drinking decaf?" Ferdinand asked. "I thought only the VW driving, flower-on-the-dash yoginis who work for me drank black water?"

"Trying to cut back," Qigiq said. "Helps me relax."

"I know you have more, Ferd," Kandy said, after a sip. "You have that look in your eyes."

Ferdinand held up one finger. "Perhaps just a little."

Ferdinand typed and talked. "There wasn't a great deal more movie to analyze. We can, of course, tell you the curvature of each swerve, the acceleration forces involved, and the one place where the rider touched his brakes."

"Conclusion?" Qigiq asked, blowing across the top of his cup.

"First class rider. Most street riders would be unable to make such rapid changes of direction." He turned. "Based on accident analysis, riders often crash when the bike could have saved them." He paused. Sighed. "Sadly, the same can be said of automobile drivers."

Movie frames flicked by on a large monitor until the bike was directly beside the truck, not yet in the crosswalk.

"We were very lucky," Ferdinand said.

Kandy looked up. "You science guys believe in luck?"

Ferdinand gestured at the screen. "We were fortunate that our famous fog was present to diffuse the morning light. It allowed me to perform this analysis."

The image zoomed in until the helmet filled the screen. The graphics the guy who tried to punch him had traced with his finger grew into a dancing dragon. Or lizard.

"Note the dark shield to protect against sunlight. We see only a deep green."

Kandy caught Qigiq's eye and shrugged.

"But there is more data here than meets the naked eye," Ferdinand continued. He stroked a flat pad with his thumb and middle finger. The remainder of the frame became very bright, but an image emerged from the face shield.

Qigiq stepped closer and stooped until he was on the same level as the dark eyes now staring out from behind the shield. He said:

"That was there the whole time?"

"Oh yes," Ferdinand replied. "But not where your eyes could perceive it. By expanding and shifting to the range of the monitor, we see this."

His hand stopped and the image quality improved as the computer filled in higher resolution data.

"Eyes," Kandy said.

A portion of a face was visible above the cheek pads of the helmet. Qigiq compared it to the guy who had swung at him on the street.

"Yes," Ferdinand said. "And asymmetrical eyebrows. The left is slightly longer."

Kandy nodded. "Not enough for an ID."

"True," Ferdinand agreed. "But enough for something important."

The movie zoomed out until the rider was back beside the truck. The blue line of his direction of travel appeared, then the red of his veer to the right. Ferdinand brushed his pad and a new yellow line was added parallel to the blue one.

"Watch this yellow line," Ferdinand instructed.

The frames played in slow motion. The woman appeared from the left side of the screen. The bike moved forward. In an eye-blink the yellow line flashed to the rider's right, connecting his face shield with the face of the woman in the blue dress.

Ferdinand stopped the movie.

"You didn't?" Kandy said.

"I most certainly did. And with great accuracy."

Qigiq sipped his half-decaf and listened. He had moved to San Francisco to learn computer tricks, after all, and Ferdinand was delivering a master class.

"You tracked his eyes?" Kandy said, incredulous. "From that tinted fog you showed us behind the face shield?"

"Some effort was required," Ferdinand admitted. "But the computer and I are both highly confident in our findings." The movie moved forward. The timer readout told Qigiq that the eye movement towards the woman occurred a half second before the veer began.

"He saw her," Qigiq said.

"Most definitely."

"And swerved to hit her?" Kandy asked.

"Assuredly."

"On purpose?" Qigiq asked. "Or target fixation?"

"For that we need further analysis."

"It takes practice to break the instinct to stare at a threat in the road," Qigiq said. "And staring almost guarantees you'll hit it."

"Speaking from experience?" Kandy asked.

He grinned. "I've hit a few things. Falling rocks as they roll into the road. Wild animals in the dark. Eventually learned to focus on the escape route at an off-road riding school."

"So we still can't know if he meant to hit her?" Kandy said, as she drained her coffee and began pacing the length of the three monitors.

"Detective, have you no faith in our skills?"

The movie played. The bike straightened, the yellow arrow went left into the gap behind an SUV; the bike went left. The arrow straightened, pointing across the intersection; the bike straightened. Arrow right, two car lengths in front of a Toyota. Bike right. Left, right, left as cars swerved and slowed, the Toyota and a Ford colliding, the bike weaving through them like a halfback on amphetamines.

"And this tells us?" Ferdinand asked.

Kandy stopped pacing. "The bike goes where that yellow line goes first."

"It follows his eyes," Qigiq added, "for all subsequent turns."

"So he swerved right at her, intending to hit her," Kandy said.

"Maybe kill her," Qigiq added. "He was going fast enough."

"Forty-three miles per hour," Ferdinand said. "Sixty-three feet per second."

Kandy shook her head. "Crazy stunt...running a red light straight into a busy intersection."

"The time of day was key," Ferdinand said. "Early morning traffic creeps through there. Gave him opportunity for evasive action."

"Something else," Qigiq said.

The room quieted.

"He knew?" Kandy said.

Qigiq nodded. "Yes. He knew she would be there. Probably knew the time within a minute or two."

"I agree," Ferdinand said. "Most certainly premeditated." He spun his chair. "I'll have that coffee now, please."

CHAPTER 5

I SAT IN THE BACK OF MY ROBERTS photography display tent ruminating. It was Monday; the Kings Beach Art Show ran through Wednesday. But Mylin had sold in one day what usually took me a week. The organizers would be upset if I left empty pavement where a booth should be, and Roberts Photography might not be allowed in next year. I wouldn't be the only one though; two spots had been barren all weekend from artists who hadn't shown up at all.

On the other hand, if I finished the show, I couldn't break down until Thursday morning because the end-of-show auction shindig lasted until after midnight Wednesday. That would put me in Reno Thursday afternoon. Would I still be able to find her?

Find her? What was I thinking?

Yes, she was mesmerizing. And showed interest in my pictures. But not me. What would she want with a traveling artist anyway?

A twenty-something couple with six tattoos between them passed by without glancing in. I sighed. My body energized every time I recalled her voice, conjured her face, or glanced at *Smoking Girl #6*. Fate had made our paths cross a second time. I needed to *carpe diem*.

And when I found her?

I stood and inhaled hot summer air; a Greek food tent upwind was roasting lamb. I stuffed two twenties from Mylin's stack on the counter into my cargo shorts, and rolled the rest into a canvas whose surface I was preparing for archival inks. The school of hard knocks had taught me that cash was safer hidden than where pickpockets could easily reach it.

On my way out of the booth I stopped to admire *Girl #6*. I turned to leave. A hand wrapped around my left biceps and dragged me backwards. A second hand gripped my opposite wrist and yanked it behind my back. Someone had seen me stash the cash. I twisted and caught a glimpse of straight black hair and a gray sport coat.

He didn't speak.

My instincts yelled *run*. I forced my panic down. What did I know about being robbed? *Remain calm. Don't resist. Give him no reason to hurt you.* I inhaled like dragging on a cigarette, a habit I had dropped after the peer pressure of high school went away. His grip held firm. Didn't relax, didn't tighten, just pressed like surgical tubing squeezing blood from my arms.

Surely a thief would tell me what he wanted.

I counted silently to ten, then blabbered: "If there's something I'm supposed to do, I'm happy to oblige."

Breath hotter than the California sun hit my neck as a voice whispered: "Be quiet."

A couple, perhaps in their fifties, strolled by. The man glanced at #6, the woman at me.

I smiled.

She frowned.

They didn't enter my booth.

The hand remained fixed—like I was trapped in a machine that had lost power. I waited, afraid to ask another question.

An Asian gentleman strolled into the booth and stopped in front of #6. His hair was nearly white against sun-darkened skin, and long enough to cover his ears. August in California, but he wore a dark blue suit with a subtle light blue stripe; maybe the stripe was his concession to the heat. His leather loafers had the aerodynamic look of something designed in Italy.

"She is quite a beauty in her way," he said.

Did he mean my picture? The girl? Was it okay to talk?

"This was taken in Michigan," he said.

It didn't sound like a question.

The hand shook my arm.

"Uh, yes it—" I choked, cleared my throat. "Ann Arbor. About a month ago."

The old man stared into her eyes. "Yes, quite a beauty."

He stepped closer to the picture, clasping his hands behind him as if he were being careful not to touch it. He said:

"Do you know this woman?"

"Not exactly. It's a long story."

A shake. Maybe the old man liked long stories and the guy holding me knew it. As I prepared to tell the story, I also sought an explanation. This old man wasn't here to rob me. I began:

"When I took that picture, I had never seen her before."

A second shake.

"Truly. I was taking pictures of the crowd attending a concert."

"The GO Orchestra?" he asked.

I hesitated. "At the time, I didn't know who was performing." A tighter squeeze on both arms. "Please let me finish," I said rapidly to avoid being treated like a salt shaker. "I took that picture and several others. Then started selling reprints from my booth at art shows."

"You have her permission for this?" the old man asked.

"No," I answered quickly. "Not then. I've been selling them for a few weeks, and today that girl, the one in the picture, walked into this very booth."

"And the girl with her?" the old man said.

I rewound my mental reel. Had there been a girl with her? Was I so distracted I had missed her friend? I sure hoped not. I said: "She came into the booth alone," preparing to be shaken. But nothing happened.

The old man turned to me, oblivious to the crowd behind

him and the guy behind me.

"And?" he said.

"She was here for a few minutes." I ran the scenario through my mind, trying to push away the images I had of her legs in those purple shorts, her boots, her smile, her one-eyed look. "She liked the picture. I offered to give her one but she declined. I told her there were others."

I was not being shaken so I continued.

"I went to my truck, found two more. When I got back I learned she had been selling pictures for me. She's quite a good sales person."

The old man smiled just a fraction.

"We hung *Smoking Girl #3* right there where *#6* is now, and a guy came by and bought it while she was still here; in fact, she sold it to him and—" I coughed. I was going to say she signed it, but something stopped me.

The old man cocked his left eyebrow. It was almost as white as his hair.

"She did a really good job. So I put," I gestured with my head, "Number six back up."

The old man was silent, though his mouth moved like he was sucking candy.

"One more thing," I added.

The man lifted his eyes and gazed through me, as if remembering something important.

"She talked about a GO Orchestra. Is that the one you asked about?" I didn't want to give him new information that could put Mylin in danger, but did want to appear cooperative.

Thumbs dug into both arms. Questions were not okay. And I was going to have bruises.

The old guy's face remained blank as he said: "You saw no other girl. About the same height, slightly heavier, round face?"

I shook my head slowly and emphatically.

He said, "I'll take your number six, Mr. Roberts. My

colleague will remain to settle the account."

He turned 180 degrees in place, the way soldiers do, and was gone.

The hands released me. My left arm was numb, the right had goosebumps. I started to turn around but froze when it occurred to me that being able to identify the man's face was a bad idea.

I was wrong about that too.

He stepped around me and lifted the picture from the wall of my display tent, then turned to face me. He was only five foot seven or so, and as thin as the old man. He wore industrially faded blue jeans and Jordans below his gray sport coat. His hair was the same length as the old man's, but pure black—though reflections from the lake were tinting it midnight blue. He held the painting in front of his chest and smiled, his teeth straight and even.

"How much?" he asked.

I swallowed. I had assumed they were going to just *take* it. I pointed and said, "There's a sticker on the back," so he would know I wasn't making something up. "But I can discount it if you wish." Ever the power salesman.

"No need."

He held the picture under an arm and peeled off hundreds with his thumb like a one-handed card dealer. I counted eight, but he was awfully fast. He held out the money and said:

"Tell her to call grandmother."

I reached for my stash to make change. "Would you like me to package that for travel?" When I looked up he and the picture were gone and hundreds fluttered to the pavement.

I retrieved the cash, then sat on my stool to compose myself.

The August sun heated my tent. The aroma of lamb hung in the air.

I began shivering.

CHAPTER 6

"YOU REALLY WANT TO GO WITH US?" Kandy said, staring across the monitors at Ferdinand. "A lab rat venturing onto the mean streets with lowly detectives."

Ferdinand sipped a double espresso with precisely two centimeters of foam. He had constructed it after showing the video of his eye-tracking experiment four times.

"Lab rats must eat, Detective."

A scientist in a biker bar? Qigiq recalled being at a crime scene with Ferdinand when they had been fired upon. Ferd was a quick-thinking, observant guy, but he wasn't fast on his feet. He said:

"We have no idea of the quality of the food at this place. It might be dangerous."

Ferdinand nodded emphatically. "Ah, this risk I will accept."

"You're both crazy," Kandy said as she stood. "You want me to drive?"

Ferdinand caught Qigiq's eye and lifted an eyebrow.

Qigiq said, "We should arrive on bikes."

"Won't be able to procure them on short notice," Kandy said. "Do you ride, Ferd?"

"A motorcycle? Long ago, yes." He shook his head. "Never in the city."

"Park around the corner." Qigiq said. "Walk in"

"No element of surprise," she said.

"This isn't a raid. We're going over to have lunch," Qigiq offered.

"A limousine," Ferdinand suggested. "We shall arrive at the

entrance in a chauffeur driven automobile, and have the driver wait for us."

Qigiq stood. "Expensive lunch."

"A limo?" Kandy shook her head. "Why the heck would we want to dance in with that? Not low profile."

"My friends, you wish to gather information, do you not? We must be noticed."

———

Thirty minutes later Qigiq sat with Ferdinand in the back of a pewter-gray town car. Kandy rode shotgun beside a driver named Mark who Ferdinand had borrowed, along with the car, from a local tech CEO he had helped with an analysis he wouldn't talk about.

Kandy sat rigid.

Qigiq knew she hated being in a vehicle she wasn't piloting. He was impressed with her restraint though; she had only corrected Mark three times.

The front entrance to the club was a windowless door midway down the block on 6th Street with "Ton Up" stenciled across it in black paint. They were only blocks from the beautiful glass and stonework of the enormous Moscone Convention Center, yet here were surrounded by beige industrial buildings, littered streets, and rusting chain-link fence.

The once-white front door was closed. Rusted hinges and dark streaks from repeated rains suggested it had last been opened during the Bush administration. No one milled about on the sidewalk. They drove around the block and rolled slowly along a gravel alley toward the rear of the building, the limo's doors passing within inches of parked motorcycles.

Kandy rolled down her window. "Think it's here?"

"This is difficult," Ferdinand said. "Even to my trained eye they all look the same."

Qigiq compared the bikes through darkened rear side windows to the five he had seen on the street. Something wasn't quite right.

From the front seat Kandy said, "Guys form clubs around a marque all the time. Look at you and your broken Moto Guzzi. Doesn't male bonding require the same toys?"

"Almost the same," Qigiq answered. "Riders usually personalize their ride: paint, custom seat, flashy wheels. There's an odd red or green one here, but the rest look like they came from Henry Ford's assembly line."

"Any color you want so long as it's black," Kandy said, and laughed.

Ferdinand leaned forward, speaking quietly. "You're saying there's a reason these bikes show so little variation? Perhaps they race and wish to allow no advantage?"

"Can't race the paint," Kandy said.

Qigiq shifted in the car's supple leather. "If you were seeking maximum performance, you would at least choose different bars for your height and riding style."

"Maybe these guys are all the same size," Kandy said, still laughing.

"Highly improbable," Ferdinand offered.

Kandy twisted around to face the back. "Not as improbable as you, Ferd."

Ferdinand relaxed against the seat. "I'll take that as a compliment, Detective."

Gravel crunched. More bikes scrolled past the window. Even the tread pattern on the tires appeared common. Maybe they purchased in bulk.

Ferdinand rolled his window down and lifted a camera smaller than his palm.

The driver stopped ten yards from a screen door held open by a piston doorstop with the connecting rod still attached. A young white male stood beside an Asian girl, both in black leather pants and tight synthetic shirts: hers puce, his white. They stared at the car but made no move except to lift cigarettes to their lips.

"His tattoo mean anything?" Qigiq asked.

"Haven't seen uneven bars like that before," Kandy said. "I'll run a database search using Ferd's pictures."

A tilted wooden sign over the open door read "Ton Up" in letters that had been burned in by a blowtorch.

Kandy got out first. The boy's cigarette stopped in front of his chest. The girl looked at Kandy, then flicked her eyes to the boy.

Neither moved.

Ferdinand rolled his girth out and stood beside Kandy. Qigiq exited on the driver's side and waited for the car to back away before joining the others.

Two cigarettes were ground out under thick-soled boots and the leather-clad pair disappeared into the cave darkness of the club.

Qigiq closed his right eye, as he suspected Kandy was doing. "How about me first?" he said, and stepped through the open doorway. He opened his eye. Accustomed to darkness from being closed, it gave him the layout of the club's important features: two men standing in shadows to his left, and two to his right. He turned and said:

"How's this place for lunch?'

"Depends," the man closest to him said. His face hadn't been shaven for a few days. His straight black hair was short enough to be brushed straight up.

"On?"

"What you ride."

"Who wants to know?" He hoped for at least a first name.

"I would," came a voice from behind him, belonging to the man furthest away to his right. "This is a private club."

"Your statement is in disagreement with your website and online reviews of the Ton Up," Ferdinand said. "They distinctly state: 'Everyone welcome, bring your friends.'"

The man turned to Ferdinand, who was wearing a light tan jacket in place of his ever-present lab coat.

"Who are you?"

"A hungry patron," Kandy said from behind Ferdinand. "When did the club go private?"

"When I said it did," the man replied.

Qigiq kept the two to his left in his peripheral vision and studied the speaker: Asian and lean, probably fast with his fists. Qigiq said:

"How do we join?"

Ferdinand moved forward past Qigiq until he was opposite the man speaking. "There is no need to join." The man stood straighter, but he was still small next to Ferdinand's bulk. "We're here for a bite of good British food."

Qigiq knew that was hard to come by, even in England.

"And to hire a rider," Ferd added.

Qigiq didn't want to show his surprise, so he smiled.

"What kind of rider?" a man out of sight to the left said. He was the first one who sounded made in America. So who was in charge? Probably someone they hadn't met yet.

Without hesitation Ferdinand said, "One who can handle a vintage British machine in a challenging situation. My colleagues suggested this might be the place to find such a man."

The girl who had been outside shuffled across the back of the room past a glowing jukebox and sat down at a table with two other girls—one was Trina.

"Or woman," Ferd added.

Qigiq couldn't even guess what Ferdinand was up to.

"I'm getting hungry standing here." Kandy touched Ferdinand's arm. "Can't we get some food?"

The three girls eyes flashed from Kandy's hand, to Ferdinand, then to each other.

The man who had declared the club private said, "Pete, get the man a table, we need to talk."

Qigiq caught Kandy's eye as they moved slowly between tables scattered in the room. Her left shoulder twitched in a tiny shrug.

A thin waitress in fishnet stockings and boots with heels thick enough to protect her from floodwaters led them to a round table for four. It sat between a skylight with wire hexagons in the glass and the table of three girls. Qigiq wondered if Pete had sent her, or if maybe she was Pete.

One of the guys by the door came over alone. "You want to talk then eat, or eat then talk?"

Qigiq was more sure now: square jaw, thick arms, blond wavy hair. American. Probably a California native.

Ferdinand said, "Please, join us. We would welcome the company, wouldn't we my friends?"

Qigiq nodded. Kandy looked the guy up and down twice, then smiled like a *Vogue* model.

He swung his leg over the back of a chair that had more nicks than a carving board and dropped to its seat. He said: "You're looking for a rider?"

Ferdinand nodded. "And a recommendation for lunch. This is Kandy, and my friend Qigiq. My name is Ferdinand."

"I'm Stolz." He shook hands all around. "Get the fish-n-chips, everything else sucks. What'd ya need a rider for?"

"A reenactment," Ferdinand said.

"You mean like Remember the Alamo?" a man said, stepping up behind Kandy with his eyes on Qigiq.

Qigiq watched his hands carefully. He sensed that this was the guy who had swung at him on the sidewalk. But he didn't have the asymmetrical eyebrows of the rider in the video.

"Nothing so extravagant," Ferdinand said. "But an expert rider is required. And a period accurate motorbike."

Stolz said, "We're experts on accuracy, aren't we Prime?"

Still standing behind Kandy, Prime said, "We're experts on lots of things. What's this rider have to do?"

"Jump a fence," Ferdinand said without hesitation.

Kandy's eyes asked a question. Qigiq shrugged.

"A fence?" Stolz said. "Like a stunt?"

Ferdinand said, "I prefer to think of it as an accurate reenactment of an artful moment."

"What moment?" Prime asked.

Ferdinand rotated his hulk forty-five degrees to the left and pointed at the far wall where movie posters including *On Any Sunday* and *Girl With a Motorcycle* had been pasted up in a wallpaper patchwork of motorbikes and young ladies who couldn't afford much clothing.

Stolz frowned.

Prime stared at the wall.

Qigiq found it; wondered when his colleague had first seen it.

Ferdinand motioned the fishnet girl to the table. She bent forward far enough to reveal a pink bra while he whispered in her ear. Then he slipped a folded bill into the top of her garter-supported stocking beside two other tips. The cash poked upward like little warning flags below a swath of leather impersonating a skirt.

She swayed on her heels to the back corner of the club and reached up high, pointing with her left index finger and flashing a slender bottom. She tapped the finger against a black and white poster partially covered on three corners by pictures of race bikes from the seventies.

Her finger landed on a fence. Actually, two fences: one of barbed wire, the other of wood.

Stolz looked from the girl's finger, to her bottom, to Ferdinand, back to the finger, the bottom, and finally stopped at Ferdinand. He said:

"*That* jump?"

"Precisely," Ferdinand replied.

The fishnet girl returned. "Ready to order?"

She departed with a request for four orders of fish-n-chips—
two tartar, two vinegar—and five 2-Strokes: a local beer named
for its distinctive aftertaste.

Prime wasn't having lunch.

Stolz said, "That's an easy jump."

Ferdinand raised his right eyebrow. "Really?"

"Sure. Robbie Maddison jumped 119 feet to the top of the
Arc de Triomphe in Paris. And back down again. A fence is
nothing."

"Paris?" Kandy said, genuinely surprised.

Qigiq said, "The one in Nevada."

Stolz nodded vigorously. "Yeah, in Vegas. A lot higher
jump than that." He pointed to the poster on the back wall.

"This Paris jump," Ferdinand said. "Was it accomplished on
a 1962 Triumph motorbike...over a barbed wire fence?"

"Nah," Stolz shook his head. "Robbie used a Japanese
motocrosser. Honda I think."

Prime, who had been quiet and motionless, said: "Two-
stroke Yamaha."

Stolz shrugged, "They're all the same."

Qigiq shifted in his seat. "You think this jump reenactment
would be easy on a dirt bike?"

Prime looked at him directly. "Easy by today's standards.
Robbie's records are over 100 feet high and 350 feet long.
Unassisted except by ramps. No weird rockets or anything."

"Impressive," Kandy said, cooing a bit like the waitress.

"It was," Prime said, meeting her eyes for the first time.
"The hang time felt like minutes. At night on New Year's Eve. I
thought for sure he'd overshoot the landing ramp on the way
down."

"A tense moment indeed," Ferdinand said. "But we're not
talking about jumping by modern standards. We, or shall I say
one of you, will be jumping by the standards of 1962, simulated
to look like the World War II era. The bike, suit, helmet.

Everything period accurate for an iconic moment."

Stolz looked at Prime and leaned back against his chair, locking his fingers behind his surfer hair. "That's harder."

Qigiq noticed Stolz's wrist: two bars like the guy outside.

"Precisely my point," Ferdinand said, looking up to smile at the fishnet waitress who had returned with two orders of fish and chips and was placing the first in front of Kandy and the second in front of him. She didn't look as young as Trina and the other girls, or quite as naive.

"Don't wait to eat," she said, "it's better hot."

"Why bother?" Prime asked. He stood erect, balanced, his thin face calm and unsmiling like a statue of Bruce Lee. Not threatening or yielding—just *there.*

Ferdinand already had fish in his mouth, its crumb coating sticking to his beard. He held up a finger. When he had washed it down with a swallow of 2-Stroke he said: "Quite a smooth flavor. You gentlemen are correct about the after-bite, heats the mouth like an exhaust chamber. But I digress. To your question. Why do anything?" He cleared his throat.

They all waited.

Ferdinand continued, "For satisfaction. Not only for oneself, but for others."

"You mean money," Prime said.

"A crude measure of satisfaction," Ferdinand replied. "But adequate in many cases. I believe people will pay to see this jump."

Stolz crossed his arms and nodded. Qigiq figured the prospect of money appealed to him.

"How much does the rider get?" Prime asked.

Ferdinand spoke between bites. "Whatever is necessary."

"So we're talking big bucks," Stolz offered.

"Big is relative. If we use a stadium, or perhaps a race track, sell television privileges, obtain rights to the original clip of Steve McQueen from the movie for comparison, then many things are possible."

"But McQueen didn't make that jump," Prime said.

Ferdinand put a finger to his lips like he was asking everyone to be quiet.

"Mr. McQueen made a practice jump—but crashed. We know that someone else did the jump for the movie, and we will admit to it in the fine print if necessary." He glanced around the room, now filling with black leather for the lunch hour. "How many people in this room, a club based around European motorcycles..." He bit into the fish and chewed before continuing. "And not just *any* European brand. No, the Triumph brand used by Mr. Cool himself to make the immortal jump. How many of these people know who jumped in the film?"

Prime took the time to scan the room like he was hunting illusive prey. "Ten, maybe twenty percent."

"And the other 80 percent?" Ferdinand said. "Are they *aware* of the jump?"

"Oh yeah. All bikers know about that jump," Prime said. "And most movie people."

"And who do they think made it?"

"McQueen," Stolz said. "I run into blokes all the time who swear it was McQueen."

A video of a black bike colliding with a blue dress replayed in Qigiq's head. A few months ago he wouldn't have understood the statement he was about to make.

"But with social networks, won't the truth become instantly apparent?"

"And who'll care?" Prime said. "So some guy makes a jump that a hundred kids could do with a Honda 250?"

"Retro is always in vogue somewhere my friends. Reproducing this jump will draw thousands."

"He's right about the Web," Prime said.

Ferdinand smiled so wide his teeth showed behind his dark beard. He said:

"If we are lucky, blogs and tweets will light up the Internet like a little boy's eyes seeing a motorbike for the first time. Each mention will bring more customers. There will be so much attention on our jump, regardless of who made the first, that we will be guaranteed an audience." He wiped his hands on a green napkin with a tiny Union Jack in the corner. "That is where the money comes from. We will, of course, secure sponsors. The funds to begin construction have already been secured."

Prime and Stolz were silent. Qigiq figured they were contemplating the size of the paycheck, and who would be making the jump to get it.

Ferdinand finished his beer and sighed. "There is, however, a problem."

The eyes of the bikers snapped to his face. He didn't wait for them to ask.

"The bike. Using a 1962 Triumph isn't really fair."

"Why not?" Stolz said. "That's what Steve used." Eyes flicked toward him. He shrugged his broad shoulders. "OK, whoever jumped."

"Yes," Ferdinand said, "this is true. But at the time, the bike was brand new. A vintage 60s Triumph today is half a century old."

Qigiq sat back and sipped a beer that was forthright in its flavor. He admired Ferdinand's mastery of logic, and the way he used it in the field. But watching Kandy eat was making him hungry.

Stolz grinned but didn't say more.

Prime met Ferdinand's gaze, then flicked his eyes toward Kandy and back. "If you can get the specs, we'll help you build a brand new bike that even Triumph would swear was made in Hinckley."

―――――

Back in the town car Kandy asked, "Ton always seemed like a strange term to me."

"There are several theories," Ferdinand said.

"And I bet you're going to share them."

"Just one. A hundred pounds sterling is referred to as a ton in British slang, much as a yard is one hundred U.S. dollars. So a hundred of anything in Britain is often known as a ton."

"Ah. The magic triple digits," she said. "Ton Up—a hundred miles per hour and above."

"Exactly. Not fast by today's standards."

Qigiq said, "Fast for vintage bikes. Fast for the street."

Kandy twisted in the front seat to glance back at Qigiq and Ferdinand. She burst out laughing.

"Okay," Qigiq said. "Fast for the street for average, law-abiding citizens."

"These black motorcycles. How much over a hundred might they achieve?" Ferdinand asked.

"Depends on modifications," Qigiq said. "The British Vincent Black Lightning from the 1950s managed 150 mph with a guy in a bathing suit lying on the seat. They could finesse these machines into that territory with today's engine technology."

Ferdinand nodded. "I once did a computer simulation. Do you realize that driving on the highway at 150 mph, dodging traffic, is the same relative velocity as if the traffic were parked and a driver weaved through them at 80 mph?"

"A hundred and fifty is worse," Kandy said. "Other drivers throw curve balls at you. They can't do that parked."

"Speaking from experience, Detective?"

Her left cheek twitched before she said: "Thought experiment, Ferd, just a thought experiment."

"The tattoos mean anything?" Qigiq asked. "Stolz had those two vertical bars."

Ferdinand added: "Depends on how widespread use of that particular pattern is in the city. Or perhaps the country. Many tattoo artists work from a common set of drawings. Have you seen the art on the Internet?"

"Not lately," Qigiq said.

Kandy scoffed. "I thought all bikers were into tattoos."

"Hardly," Ferdinand said. "While I understand the practice to be popular, there are over nine million registered motorcycles in the United States. I doubt those riders all have body ink."

"Body ink?" Kandy said. "Ferd, you hipster, I hardly recognize you."

"Research, Detective. As soon as I saw that a motorbike was involved in today's incident, I did some reading."

"I'll follow-up on the wrist art," Kandy said. "On one condition."

Qigiq listened up. Kandy's last condition had cost him dinner for two.

"And that is?" Ferdinand asked.

"You tell me what this Steve McQueen jump is all about."

Ferdinand smiled, but remained silent.

"I didn't realize you had an interest in bikes," Qigiq said.

"I simply read the history of Triumph, thinking it might be useful to speak their language."

"And the *we need a rider* story?" Kandy asked.

"Improvisation. It's always better to be buying when seeking information. As a detective, I'm sure you're well aware of the methodology."

Kandy slid lower in the front seat. "You're full of surprises, Ferd."

"Why McQueen?" Qigiq asked. "That was a long time ago."

"The Triumph history mentions this jump; I thought it odd that a 1962 machine was used in a movie set in the forties. Second, Hollywood. Many people are familiar with the jump because of their interest in the iconic image of Steve McQueen and action movies. They often know nothing about motorcycles."

The car stopped in a left turn lane waiting for an arrow. The blinker pulsed softly. He shifted his head to peek at the driver's rearview mirror.

Kandy said, "You saw the movie?"

"Several times. An amazing story of an incredible tunneling operation. But there was one other thing."

Qigiq studied the mirror.

Ferdinand said, "I saw the poster. It occurred to me that a reenactment would give three strangers a bit of credibility in their world and act as a natural conversation starter."

A dot in the mirror moved sideways. He turned in his seat, but the view out the rear window was blocked by a green van with reverse lettering on the front for a French laundry named Peninou. He leaned forward and swung his eyes back to the side mirror.

Kandy said, "You saw that poster on the back wall from our table? Good eyes."

"No. I saw it while standing in the doorway. Once we were seated, it was no longer in my line of sight."

"You were really studying that place," Kandy said. "There were a hun...a *ton* of posters back there."

"Scientists are trained to be observant."

"Hah," Kandy said. "Okay, Mister Observant. When Miss Fishnet reached up to point at the poster, what color panties was she wearing under that tiny skirt?"

The limo turned into the left hand lane of a one-way street.

"She wasn't...um. Sorry, I don't recall," Ferdinand replied.

"We're being followed," Qigiq said. "They're tagging. Bikes look the same, only the size of the rider changes. Makes no sense."

Kandy said, "They figure us for cops?"

"Prime saw us twice in one day. He probably suspects something," Qigiq replied.

Kandy turned toward the window. "Five cars back. You think Prime told the others about our encounter?"

"Encounter?" Ferdinand said.

"Kandy had a conversation with Prime earlier today," Qigiq said. "We saw a black bike near the office and walked over to investigate."

"And this bike belonged to Prime?" Ferdinand asked.

"No, it was Michael and Trina," Kandy said. "She was one of the girls at the table next to us."

Qigiq checked the side mirror; the bike disappeared behind traffic. "Prime showed up later, tried to scare us away. He and Kandy had a chat."

"That explains the enthusiastic welcome," Ferdinand said.

"Why tail us?" Kandy asked, staring out the back.

"Simple. They believe we are lying, have a hidden agenda that includes exploiting them, and are following us in an attempt to obtain information." The town car moved through lunch-hour traffic. "Driver, would you please turn right at the next opportunity, and take us to Noonon's headquarters?"

"The financial district?" Kandy said.

"Misdirection," Ferdinand replied.

CHAPTER 7

I WASHED THE GYRO GREASE off my hands in the steel sink
of the restroom at Kings Beach park. A dented steel plate bolted
to the wall acted as a lousy mirror, made worse by guys who had
attempted to scratch their initials into it. I couldn't stop
worrying. Mylin drifting into the Roberts Photography booth
might have been happenstance—a synchronicity of events larger
than me. *That* I could accept. But the two guys who followed
weren't a coincidence; they wanted something specific. Those
calm, slow-moving eyes of the old guy were the eyes of a hunter
accustomed to getting his prey.

The shivering returned, even though I had sat in the sun
through lunch. The gray-haired guy had asked about the girl with
Mylin. I placed my hands inside a metal box that roared like a
wind tunnel. Was the other girl the target, or was Mylin in
trouble?

Maybe both.

What could I do? Not much. But I had to do something.

White light hammered me as I exited the concrete block
restroom. I squinted, but still got an instant headache. Fat chance
she would get help from a struggling photographer who couldn't
stop thinking about her. Again. It had taken weeks to stop
imagining her every minute after printing the pictures from the
Ann Arbor shoot. Now I had talked to her. And seen her at close
range without a lens between us. I had even touched her when...

Her card.

I pulled it from my pocket as I walked. The shiny black
surface held my thumbprint. I was so paranoid I figured that was

intentional. Red ink in an elaborate script spelled *The GO Orchestra* above a ten-digit phone number. I flipped the card over, comparing the writing to what she had written on the back of #3 for the guy who did his own chrome. The "n" dropped below the line, the "e" had a little tail. Yes, Mylin had written:

Do not use your real name.

Sweat soaked into the band of the wide-brimmed hat I used at summer shows. My heart felt lighter—she was warning me of danger. Danger in the form of the two guys I had just met. But that meant she thought I might follow her.

Maybe she *would* have dinner with me in Reno.

I stopped walking. Maybe she was only interested in the other pictures. But why the warning?

The image of the young Asian guy holding #6 and saying *Tell her to call grandmother* came back to me. I felt fingers tighten around my right arm and spun fast trying to break the hold.

I was alone on the asphalt, my heart racing.

A little girl on a push bike had seen me spin and chanted: "Dance, dance, dance."

I rubbed my arm, smiled kindly at her, and felt stupid for the false alarm. I walked away fast, my spine vibrating like a cable under tension.

The show crowd was thinning as the heat of the afternoon sun reflecting from a mile-high lake drove tourists to beach umbrellas and detective novels. I reached my booth and stood in the shade rolling her card across my fingers: a magician practicing a trick.

What to do?

Find her. I pulled out my cell phone, had three bars, and tapped out five of the ten numbers before her voice in my head said *do not use your real name*. Cell phone metadata could be analyzed; everyone who had heard of Edward Snowden knew that. The phone would even reveal its location if the right people asked.

I deleted the numbers and paced the length of my booth like a prisoner in solitary.

"What's wrong?"

The guy across the aisle had called out to me. He stood under a sign that read Bear Naked Leather. The booth was filled to bursting with belts, vests and hair clasps for bikers.

"Need to make a call." I pointed at the phone in my hand. "Cell phone's dead," I called back.

All 250-plus pounds of him meandered over wearing a deep blue grease-spotted T-shirt under a black leather vest, despite the heat. He held out a small green phone in a big paw of a hand, the arm covered with dark hair reminding me of a California grizzly before they went extinct.

My call would be traced to his phone. I didn't know what was going on between Mylin and those men. No way I could involve a generous stranger.

"Uh, that's okay, I'll use a pay phone after I close up. It can wait, but thanks for the offer."

His face didn't change expression. "Not many pay phones around anymore." He held the green box toward me.

"Really, it's okay," I mumbled, thinking too slowly to offer an explanation.

"Make any call you want. This baby is prepaid in cash. No name to trace back, no records. I use it to make special calls to Reno. It ain't Vegas, but it's close and handy." Surprisingly soft brown eyes studied me. "And if you ask me, the Reno girls are friendlier. Like that Asian babe hanging around earlier. She a model or something?"

I wanted to say *or something*, but my mind was busy trying to figure out what a *special* call was, and if that's what I was about to make.

"If you really don't mind," I said. "It'll be short, and I'll pay you for the minutes."

He held up his other paw and shook his head. "We artists have to stick together. Life is tough enough with tourists." He placed the phone on my makeshift counter. "If you feel the need to pay me, drop off one of these little pictures you make. I'll put it up in my shop. He headed back toward his leather goods.

"Thank you," I said, maybe not loud enough for him to hear. The cover of the flip phone had been painted metallic green. It appeared to be smiling at me, as if it knew more about what I was moving toward than I did.

"It's just a phone," I said aloud, and picked it up.

A woman with an accent a bit like Mylin's answered, "Girls of the Orient, Reno, how may I help you?"

Thoughts skittered through my head: Mylin played viola, in an orchestra called GO, in Nevada, the state of legalized sin.

"I, uh..." I managed before it struck me that *GO* meant *Girls...Orient*.

"Hello. Take your time, we know this decision can be challenging. But be assured, whatever your needs, we can help."

"I'm looking for a particular girl...."

"Yes." A pause. "What would you like? Piano, violin? A singer perhaps? What event would this be for?"

I managed to eek out, "Just dinner."

"I see. Well, a string quartet would work nicely."

Mylin's card said not to use my name, but didn't mention hers. It was probably fake.

"Mylin."

"Your what, sir?"

"Mylin. Do you have a girl named Mylin?" An obvious approach finally found its way into my head. "I need a girl who plays viola."

"Viola isn't our most popular instrument, sir. Let me check our records."

Could there possibly be more than one woman in Reno named Mylin who played the viola? How many violas did an orchestra have, anyway?

"Sir? Yes, I found her. But I'm sorry, she's on vacation. Would a guitarist do?"

Vacation?

"No, thank you. Do you know when she'll be back?"

"She's not accepting appointments until seven tomorrow. That would be Tuesday evening, sir."

"Dinner at seven, please?" Now that I had met her, the stress of waiting 24 hours would probably give me heart palpitations.

"Surely. Which restaurant? Or is this a private affair?"

"I don't know the area well," I replied truthfully. "Could she meet me at the Reno airport?"

"Yes. Your name?"

Her card stared at me like the warning on a pack of cigarettes.

"Phillips, with two L's. Karl with a K."

"Thank you, Mr. Phillips. We accept Visa, MasterCard, and American Express to guarantee your reservation. Your card number please?"

While sitting in my booth in Ann Arbor, I had read an article in the paper about a madam in Washington D.C. She had threatened to expose the credit card records of politicians who used her service. Her life ended hanging by the neck in Florida from an apparent suicide. I said:

"Sorry, I don't use credit cards."

Long silence. "You, uh...I'm sorry, you don't have a credit card?"

"That's correct. I believe the way banks track spending behavior violates my constitutional right to privacy." I didn't bother to mention my somewhat challenged credit rating, or the fact that I wasn't Mr. Phillips.

"We accept cash, Mr. Phillips. However, we will require a two hundred and fifty dollar deposit to cover the two-hour minimum. There is also a one hundred dollar surcharge for the airport location. If you can have three hundred and fifty in cash ready when Mylin meets you, I will go ahead and book your meeting."

"Thank you, I will." I gave thanks that the old guy and the biker had both paid cash for their *Smoking Girl* pictures.

"Mylin will meet you near the main entrance of the Reno International Airport terminal. You will see a row of chauffeurs holding signs. Just look for your name, Mr. Phillips."

"Seven o'clock tomorrow then."

"That's correct, Mr. Phillips. Thank you for calling Girls of the Orient."

I pressed end. A prepaid cell phone and assumed name were even stranger than clandestine photography. Then I smiled. Mylin and I would be together in twenty-nine hours.

CHAPTER 8

KANDY LOWERED THE BLACK HANDSET to the cradle on her desk. She said:

"Mrs. Chong is mumbling in Chinese. The doctor says it's a good sign."

Qigiq's eyes shot up. Reviewing Ferdinand's findings and reading witness statements in an attempt to identify the mystery rider hadn't left him with much hope.

"No, we can't see her yet," Kandy said to his unasked question.

"Maybe she'll mumble something important."

"The guard will call us if Doctor Fan agrees to let us question her."

Qigiq turned to the wide corner windows. The skyscrapers of the financial district weren't visible from this angle. He saw retail storefronts, shoulder-to-shoulder houses in pastels, a lonely grassy hill, a handful of sailboat masts rising from the bay, and their little piece of the Golden Gate. Except for the bridge, he could be a hundred places. He said:

"Do you think she knows?"

"Why someone ran her down?" Kandy sipped black coffee. "I think she might guess, but she won't give the law anything. Not with someone in Chinatown trying to kill her."

"We haven't confirmed that," he said toward the window.

"Hurt her then." Kandy pushed her chair back and lifted her booted feet to the desk. "Or at least scare her."

Qigiq turned away from tracking traffic. "Ferdinand's analysis convinced you it was intentional?"

She nodded. "Seems right to me. The guy...okay, rider, could have missed her. Just didn't want to."

"So we find the bike, then the rider."

"Cookie-cutter bikes, faceless rider. Should be easy."

"If it were easy—"

The ringing phone cut him off. Kandy glanced at the incoming number, then picked up the handset.

"Hey Ferd, enjoy lunch?"

Her eyes danced with interest.

"You do?" She reached for a pad of paper and scribbled with the nub of pencil from her center drawer. "Uh-huh. Yeah, got it. Let me talk to Qu." She listened. "No fancy stuff, promise. Protect the source? Won't be hard since you won't tell me who it is. You sure this is reliable?" She tapped the flat eraser of the tiny pencil against the pad. "If it's good enough for you. Later, Ferd." She lowered the phone. "Ferd got us the builder's name."

"Should I ask how?"

"He usually brags about his scientific powers of logical deduction. This time, tight-lipped. Claims it's good though, ninety-seven percent confident."

Qigiq stood. "So he's not sure."

"He doesn't use the word *sure*. Everything has a probability in the Land of Ferd. Even sunrise."

Qigiq sat back down. "We need an approach plan. We barge in with questions, it might alert the people we're trying to find."

Kandy smiled, "Now you're thinking, Detective." She turned the pad toward him, "That's the guy."

Qigiq read *Murphy*. Then an address. "Mission District?"

"Deep in. Fair number of people moving drugs, prostitutes, stolen goods. Some of it feeds the yuppie engineers from tech companies seeking recreation."

"So what's a welder with one name doing there?"

Kandy laughed. "Uh...welding?"

Qigiq stood; strolled to the window; leaned against the

vertical metal bar between two huge sheets of glass.

"What is our mystery man welding?"

"Considering our source, he probably repairs bent motorcycles. Maybe does some sculpture. Artists love the Mission."

Qigiq's eyes drifted over the traffic below. "Kandy, you're a genius. Maybe we should present Mr. Murphy with a challenge."

"You don't mean your Moto Guzzi paperweight? Grojini said it can't be fixed."

"Maybe Murphy has unique expertise. Or can fabricate a new one. I'd sure like to have my bike back."

She remained silent.

"Don't get me wrong. I truly appreciate the loaner you arranged. It's kept me sane," he held his left leg up at a 45 degree angle and rotated his foot, "while this ankle healed. But a motorcycle that shifts itself..." He shrugged. "Besides, who knows if Murphy can repair my frame; the crash didn't leave much to work with."

"The attempt on your life you mean?" She smiled. "OK, let's get your relic back on the road, so long as you appreciate the effort I went through to get approval for that Italian rocket— and you not even a motor cop." She picked up the handset. "I'll warn Munroe Motors we're coming."

"What about Mrs. Chong's residence?" Qigiq asked. "Should I get a search warrant?"

Holding the phone to her ear with her left hand, she pulled a document from her back pocket and waved it.

————

The rubber sole of Kandy's right boot pressed the raised black knobs of an alloy brake pedal and the Mini came to a stop like it had run into a giant sponge. Qigiq released his hold on the passenger's grab bar and flexed his hand.

"Record time," Kandy said. "Mrs. Chong's apartment."

"Who are we racing?" Qigiq asked.

She laughed through her nose. "Father Time."

He popped his door, glanced down. "Six inches."

"Was there any doubt?" Kandy said, exiting the vehicle like water from a pipe. The next moment she stood beside his open door, her eyes moving up the sidewalk to the cross street and back.

Still seated, he said, "Quiet neighborhood."

"Chinatown residential neighborhood on a weekday. Everyone's at work, including the illegals." A Chrysler mini-van passed, its formerly red paint faded to a chalky pink. "He should wax that."

"What do you make of the building?"

Kandy's eyes stopped following the van and turned to the pastel green three-story townhouse tucked shoulder to shoulder between identical three-story townhouses of different pastel colors.

"Old. Well kept. Rent control: ours or theirs."

"Theirs?" Qigiq asked.

"We're in Chinatown. Whole blocks are sometimes owned by a single family who rent only to Chinese people they trust. Translation: relatives."

"And the rent is controlled by these families?"

"Let's just say, if you want to live here, it pays to have the right genes."

Qigiq unfolded an 8 1/2 x 11 sheet of paper from one-eighth its original size and read, "425 Mason. Apartment five."

Kandy's eyes danced to the corner, back to the front door. "Yep." She tapped a flat outline in the left pocket of her jeans. "GPS is dead on."

Qigiq stepped over the curb to the sidewalk, favoring his left leg. "You and your gadgets."

"Better living through technology," she said to the breeze as she stepped toward the door under pressed metal digits reading 425.

By the time Qigiq strolled up the two steps leading to the door, Kandy was knocking because no one had answered the buzzer in any of the six apartments.

"We have a warrant," he said.

She turned to face him, her mouth grinning like a wrecked Edsel.

"Okay." She pulled the wrinkled warrant from her back pocket and slipped it into his hand. "Cover me."

Qigiq moved close behind her, blocking the view of her hands from the street.

Kandy put her right hand against the door and reached her left underneath, working a scratched American Express card into the jamb. The door swung open.

"Old," she said, stepping through the doorway.

Qigiq clicked the door shut behind them, making sure it locked.

Kandy moved softly up stairs covered with blue all-weather carpeting that was new or recently cleaned. Qigiq followed her to the third floor. They stopped by a white door, its four panels painted a bright red that brought the hallway alive.

"Good feng shui," Kandy said.

"Did he make doors?"

She lowered her brows. He grinned. She said, "Shall we?"

Qigiq tapped the door with the index knuckle of his hand holding the warrant.

Silence, save for the wind-rush of oversized tires rolling by on the street below.

He tapped again. Met Kandy's eyes. She shrugged. He lowered himself to one knee, then examined the door knob and the keyhole above it. He said:

"Yale deadbolt."

"Not a great neighborhood to live alone," Kandy said. "Elderly people are attacked far too often. Thugs think—" She held her breath.

A creaking moan filtered through the door.

Kandy whispered, "Window." Then she spun on her heel and bounded down stairs three at a time with one gliding hand using the railing as a rappelling rope.

Without rising, he turned to the door and reached into his boot for a white-handled knife and a pouch containing tools a dentist might use. Except these were black.

He knocked again. "Delivery for Mrs. Chong. I need a signature, ma'am."

Holding the knife with two fingers of his left hand, he used the remaining fingers and his right hand to nudge a tool into the keyhole below the "L" in the old YALE lock. He tried to recall how many U.S. Presidents had attended Yale versus Harvard so his mind wouldn't interfere with the sensations his fingertips were receiving.

A screech erupted from beyond the door. His fingers slipped. He closed his eyes and wished for a tumbler gun that would open the door in an instant. Shooting the lock off was an option, as was kicking the door in. But if he opened it to Mrs. Chong's hard-of-hearing sister struggling to open a window because the room was too warm, locksmithing was a whole lot easier to explain.

He refocused and counted down from ten. The lock snicked. He rocked the door fore and aft to ease the bolt along its path, then shifted his body to the side, and pushed the door inward. It squealed for the first half of its journey, went silent, tapped a doorstop, shuddered for a moment, and stopped full open.

He rolled the knife handle in his left hand. Living area to the right, a short refrigerator humming along the back, kitchen window to the left. No movement. He drifted silently over a floor runner woven from bamboo towards the only other door in evidence. As he reached the fridge, it hit the end of its cycle and became stone quiet. He stopped. A wall clock with calligraphic numbers ticked; passing car tires sizzled; a giant tuning fork hummed low.

Iron fire escape.

"Stop. Police," rang up from the alley. Kandy was giving chase.

He took quick steps to the bedroom door, ducked, pushed it open, swept his eyes over the room three times, and rushed to where pale curtains covered an open window. Two stories below and far to his right a black spec disappeared around the corner of a pale yellow building.

A handful of minutes later Qigiq leaned against the side of the Mini and stared up at Mrs. Chong's kitchen window. Kandy sat on the hood cross-legged, like a Buddha drafted for ninja duty. She unwrapped a green and white candy.

"Mint?" she asked.

"I thought you chewed gum?" he replied, without turning away from the apartment. "How long was he in there?"

"Dentist wants me to cut down on the Juicy Fruit. I don't want to pollute my body with aspartame. Might have been hours."

"Mints are better? What was he looking for?"

"Doc didn't mention mints. Could be anything."

The August wind whirled an orange matchbook cover past his feet, reminding him why he had smoked for years: the hours of inactivity spent contemplating clues. He held up two fingers and rubbed them together where the cigarette would be.

"Gut feeling?" she asked, her voice muffled by the mint she held between her lips.

"Black clad figure, agile, not tall, probably male based on gait. Can't conclude much. Someone looting an empty apartment?"

"Coincidence? Don't buy it," she slurped out.

"Me either. Nothing was disturbed. No tossed clothes, slit mattress. None of the Hollywood stuff when the perp is trying to find the heroin being trafficked by grandmother's sewing club."

"No quest for the Golden Fleece. Maybe he left something."

Qigiq nodded. "That means he expects someone to come looking for it. Who might that be?"

"Us?"

"Planting evidence? Possible. But we didn't find anything."

"Maybe we aren't looking right."

Qigiq stood. "Or maybe he did take something. No muss and fuss because he knew exactly what he was after and where to find it." He took three steps toward the apartment, stopped on the sidewalk, and gazed up at the building where an elderly Chinese woman lived alone.

How was he going to find something that wasn't there?

––––––

Twenty minutes later a rap on the door of the apartment interrupted their musings.

"Hi Ferd," Kandy said as she opened the door to the hallway.

"I imagine you've contaminated the site by now," he said with a smile.

"Wouldn't want to make your job too easy."

He shook his head as he stepped passed her.

"Hello, Qigiq. What are we looking for?"

Qigiq was sitting across from the fridge on a futon whose back depicted a long boat in still waters. "Something that's not here, but should be. It was here when we arrived, and is small enough for a single man to carry and still run fast."

Ferdinand's smile faded. He stood in the middle of the room and turned slowly, his eyes scanning every surface.

"Or," Kandy said. "Something that's here that shouldn't be."

Ferdinand frowned. "So we are looking for something that is out of place, either by its presence or absence?"

"That's our best guess," Qigiq said. "Unless you have a better explanation for why a guy would be in here, then run like hell when we came to the door."

Ferdinand's expression didn't change. "He was looking for information. Found it, memorized or photographed it, and has moved on, having what he needs."

"That's even worse," Kandy said.

"Shall we look for fingerprints?" Ferdinand asked.

Kandy said: "He was wearing gloves when he came off the fire escape."

"We know he opened the bedroom window," Qigiq said. "I heard it screech."

"I will check," Ferdinand said. He sat down beside Qigiq. "This room is spotless. Did he touch anything else?"

Kandy closed the outer door to the apartment. "Nothing we've noticed on a visual scan. We haven't touched anything."

Ferdinand nodded for several seconds, then said: "Hypotheses?"

Kandy said, "The old woman had something the guy wanted. He put her in the hospital so he'd have free access to take it." She paused. "Doesn't make sense though. Mrs. Chong worked everyday, easy enough to sneak in without the road drama."

Ferdinand nodded. "So he wasn't taking something. He was planting something."

"Looks that way," Kandy said.

"Why this timing?" Qigiq asked. "She goes to the hospital. Someone hits her apartment."

"These events are related, of course," Ferdinand said. He steepled his fingers and touched them to the tip of his nose. "I will determine how."

CHAPTER 9

QIGIQ AND KANDY STOOD TO THE LEFT of a badly distorted Moto Guzzi motorcycle frame. Mr. Grojini faced them from the opposite side. They were surrounded by partially assembled motorcycles and spare parts, far in the back of Munroe Motors shop.

"Cannot," Mr. Grojini said, shaking his head. "The damage, it is too much."

"Can part of it be salvaged?" Qigiq asked.

"Salvaged?" Grojini frowned. "A little." He pointed. "This rail, this hub. Much work. Better to find old bike, steal its frame."

"Not impossible?" Kandy asked, sucking on a mint.

"Nothing impossible. But make no sense. Take many hours and difficult to make right. Maybe not ride so good."

"Okay if we take it?" Qigiq asked.

"Sure. Maybe find man who work magic. My shop too busy to fool with bent metal."

"Will you search for a new frame?" Qigiq said.

Grojini smiled widely. "Of course. I find frame. You put this," he waved at the twisted steel structure between them, "in living room. Make beautiful art. Have nice memory of surviving big crash."

Qigiq didn't need a reminder of the Mercedes pushing him off the highway; the ache in his ankle when fog rolled over his houseboat was sufficient. They folded down the rear seat of Kandy's new turbocharged Mini, inserted the frame diagonally, and closed the barn-door style rear doors. Qigiq slipped into the passenger seat, his knees in his chest. "Do you think Murphy has heard about our visit to the Ton Up?"

Kandy eased into traffic, heading west. "At least about the jump."

Qigiq considered how to approach Murphy for information, and if the man was really good, maybe get his frame repaired. Oddly, he wasn't being tossed from side to side.

"You okay, Kandy?"

"Sure, why?"

"We're going the speed limit."

"Just so happens I have precious cargo in the back."

Qigiq grinned. "The cargo rates, but your passenger doesn't?"

"My passenger understands the nature of risk." She swung south.

"What do we think about Mr. Murphy?"

"We think he's owns a welding shop. Does repairs. A little sculpture. Ferd didn't have much else."

"Why do the Ton Up boys use him?"

"Good question. How many bikes can one club wreck in a month?"

Qigiq mentally counted the riders in the club at lunch. "How big do you think?"

Kandy swerved. "Maybe three, four times what we saw, call it forty riders. Fifty tops."

Qigiq reached a hand back to steady the cargo. "Were all those frames custom?"

Kandy glanced at him and back at the six lane road. "You're asking me about motorcycles? What does Mister Bike Fanatic think?"

"None looked stock. Custom clones, if that's not an oxymoron."

"Weird." She turned right down a concrete street whose uneven flat sections tested the suspension on the Mini. Shoulder-to-shoulder houses drifted by.

Qigiq said, "I've only been to the Mission District a couple of times. Does this become industrial?"

"Loads of immigrants in the Mission. They do whatever they need to."

"Welding shop in a living room?"

Kandy braked at a stop sign. Checked traffic. Turned left and slowed.

Qigiq was surprised by how quickly shoulder-to-shoulder houses became low metal buildings. He followed the rising street numbers. Kandy pulled up in front of a building that had once been a small gas station. The pumps were gone, but their cracked islands remained in front of a pair of panel garage doors with blacked-out windows. An empty shop that had likely sold cigarettes and soda pop was attached on the left. A hand-painted sign above the garage doors declared *Murphy's Customs* in careful red script. Four motorcycles sat along the right side of the lot; none of them matched the bikes from the Ton Up.

"Shall we?" Qigiq said, as he popped open the passenger door.

Kandy locked the car before following Qigiq to the entrance door, whose glass was also blacked out. And barred.

Qigiq turned a shiny brass doorknob and stepped inside. Strains of a string quartet seeped through the wall to the garage to his right. Kandy followed him into a room that still contained a three-door cooler. The leftmost section was stocked with red and white Coke cans from top to bottom. The other two contained glass beer bottles. Qigiq recognized Sapporo, Rolling Rock, and Coors before he stopped looking. Past the cooler a restroom door stood half open, the blue-man insignia still screwed on at shoulder height. To the right a closed white door with no windows blocked the way to the work area.

Invoices were scattered across a low wooden table to the right of the door. A red plastic chair had been shoved underneath. At the far corner a silver school bell sat below a sticky note on the wall with *RING FOR SERVICE* hand printed in block letters. As Qigiq reached for the bell, the white door flung toward them and banged against the table. The string quartet grew louder.

Kandy stepped backward, creating space between herself and the man who had just entered.

"Sorry, didn't know I had customers," the man said.

He was six feet tall with the rail thin body of a distance runner. His tanned face was partially hidden by safety goggles beneath straight sandy hair. He wore white gloves and a long white coat much like Ferdinand's, the two front pockets weighted down with hand tools.

Qigiq blinked hard as the overpowering smell of paint from the work area reached him.

"Just arrived," Kandy said. "We were about to ring."

He glanced at the silver bell, then back at Kandy. "What can I do for you?"

"We have a problem with a motorcycle frame," Qigiq said.

The man peeled off his gloves and stuffed them into the front pocket with his tools. His eyes narrowed. "A frame?"

Qigiq caught Kandy's glance: *what's special about frames?*

"An older wrecked one. Maybe beyond repair. We were hoping for an expert opinion."

The man looked them over, taking his time, like he didn't much care what they thought. Finally he said, "And you think I'm an expert?"

"If you're Murphy," Kandy said.

He nodded, "I'm Murphy." But he didn't offer his hand.

"Would you have time to look? It's in the car," Qigiq said.

Murphy stood in the doorway where he had stopped. "Maybe." He moved into the room, turned, and closed the white door to the work area. "Depends."

"Sentimental value," Qigiq said. "I've been riding this bike for nine years. But we had an accident a few weeks back."

"We?"

"The bike and I."

"And you came to me?"

"Heard you were the best," Kandy said. "Word at the club."

"The best?" Murphy's blank expression curved into a twisted smile, as if he were accustomed to praise, but didn't believe it. "At some things. Let's go look at your frame; unique problems intrigue me."

Kandy led the way out the front door, unlocked the Mini with electronic emphasis, and swung the barn doors out to their stops.

Without a word Murphy slid the frame halfway out of the car. He motioned to Qigiq to hold it while he ran slender fingers over the tubes. He paused to stroke one tube repeatedly with his fingertips, the way some people touch money, then moved on. He wrapped his entire hand around a tube at the front and moved up and down like he was polishing it.

"What did you hit?" Murphy asked.

"A car pushed me down an escarpment."

Murphy nodded. "You were thrown off, but the bike found the bottom."

"And concrete."

Murphy shook his head, saying no to something. He pulled the frame the rest of the way out of the car and with Qigiq's help lowered it to the pavement. Murphy straightened, then circled the frame, examining it like a horse he was about to bet on. On his third lap he said, "Moto Guzzi loop frame. Ambassador. Bent bad. See these cracks in the surface? Twists. Difficult to take out and have any strength left. You sure you want to fix it?"

Crinkling cellophane told him Kandy was unwrapping a mint.

"I'd like to get my bike back on the road. It's an Italian police bike. We haven't been able to find a replacement frame."

"Hard," Murphy said. "The ones left are mostly rust."

They stood in silence while Murphy lapped the frame again. He stopped at the front and squatted; closed one eye; stared.

"What do you think?" Qigiq asked.

With his eye still closed Murphy said, "I think you should buy a new bike, step into state-of-the-art technology. You'll be amazed how well they ride."

Qigiq had a rented Aprilia. It rode well, but it wasn't a Moto Guzzi.

"Not like the classics, though."

Murphy nodded. "Nothing rides exactly like the classics. Sort of like music: once Mozart is born and composes, everything else is just...different."

Kandy suppressed a grin.

"Can you do anything with it?" Qigiq asked.

Murphy stood. "I can always do something. Not sure what. I'll need to study that steel, see if I can salvage bits of it. Too much new material and it won't handle right. You in a hurry?"

"I'm looking for another nine years," Qigiq said.

Murphy's head bobbed. "OK, let's drag it inside."

Kandy held the door to the office open. After they passed, she nudged around behind the frame, slid past Murphy, and reached for the white door. "You want it back here?"

His eyes made a quick decision before he nodded. She swung the door open and Murphy backed in, pulling the frame and Qigiq along with him.

A first glance reminded Qigiq of Ferdinand's lab. Overhead light panels were mounted on movable fixtures. The far side of the two-car garage was covered with bright red workbenches and wall-mounted tools so clean they could have been in a catalog. The back wall held a row of power tools. The floor was cleaner than the counter in the station's cafeteria. If possible, Murphy was even neater than Ferdinand.

The string quartet changed to solo piano.

They stopped inside the door while Murphy's head twisted back and forth. A motorcycle frame hung in the center of the room with a vertical twin engine in it.

"Back here," Murphy said.

Murphy led the way to the far corner and a space between a bench and a door with a shiny silver padlock. They lowered the frame and slid it carefully across the floor under a four-foot poster of a crash-test rocket sled. The caption read: *Then someone will do it!*

Qigiq looked from the poster to Kandy. She shrugged. He said, "A rocket sled?"

Murphy glanced up at the poster. "You've heard of Murphy's Law. I get ribbed about it all the time. So I did some research. Turns out it all started with sensors being incorrectly placed on a test suit for an Air Force sled. What Edward A. Murphy really said was: 'If there are two or more ways to do something, and one of those ways can result in a catastrophe, then someone will do it.' So I had a friend paint that picture of the MX981 sled. Reminds me to build things people can't get wrong."

"Your friend's a fine painter," Kandy said.

"He does custom gas tanks. Been thinking about putting that sled on one of my own bikes. Haven't gotten around to it."

The muffled sound of a Formula One car screaming through a hairpin interrupted.

Kandy said, "That's me," and reached inside her jacket. Before she got the phone to her ear, the bell on the front desk binged twice.

Murphy looked down at the frame, then at the door to the front office and up to a round white-faced clock hanging over the red bench. It was just past four o'clock. His slim face revealed nothing.

Kandy cupped her free hand over her mouth and spoke quietly.

Murphy said, "Give me a minute." He pointed to the frame hanging in the center of the room. "The paint's wet." He pulled the white door closed behind him.

Qigiq was impressed Murphy could paint and kept the place so clean. A circle of lightweight parachute-like cloth billowed from the ceiling. Maybe it descended to create a paint booth.

Kandy was still on the phone.

The machines along the back wall included a saw with a diamond blade and a drill press. Standard fare to work with steel. The tools over the red workbench were countless and included a few he had never seen that could be pipe-fitting devices. A poster of an exotic motorcycle in shades of black made by Bimota hung above the tools. The name Oronero was inscribed below the picture. He stepped closer. The poster informed him the name meant *Black Gold* and was the first production motorcycle to use a fully carbon-fiber frame.

Kandy touched his arm; shook her phone. "Jasik. We have a new problem."

"It's only Monday afternoon. Already another problem?"

"Think of the job security," she said. "Missing persons."

"Has homicide fired me?"

"You should be so lucky. A woman is in his office screaming a weird story about her husband—"

The white door swung open; Murphy stepped through. He turned to a panel beside the door, unlocked it and hung a key with a half-dozen others. He relocked the box before turning around.

"More work and it's still Monday," Murphy said.

Kandy smiled.

"Will it slow down my frame?" Qigiq asked.

Murphy shook his head. "No, I was expecting it." He crossed the concrete floor until he too was standing in front of Oronero. "Nice bike isn't it?"

"Carbon fiber seems exotic for a street bike," Qigiq said.

"The black looks good," Kandy said. "Real black, not like the watery gray some people call black."

Murphy nodded. "Italians are particular. As for the carbon, light and stiff. And unique, which is the market for that bike. They don't make many."

"Faster than my Guzzi," Qigiq said.

Murphy laughed. "By a wide margin. But not nearly as comfortable. Let's talk about your frame. I'll X-ray the tubes to know how much I can use and how much has to be scrapped. Might have to replace everything. You okay with that?"

Qigiq hesitated, aware that custom fabrication came with a price tag.

"Yeah, he's okay with it," Kandy said with a grin.

"What the lady says," Qigiq said.

"I can't give you an estimate until I get a better look. But I will before starting."

"Sounds good," Qigiq said. "Do you need anything else from the bike?"

"Not now. If there's info I can't get from the vehicle data, I'll call you. It's pretty old, I might have to guess here and there."

Qigiq said, "I appreciate your taking this on."

Murphy held out his hand. They shook.

"It's what I do. If you find a replacement frame though, let me know right away, so I don't waste my time...and your money." For the first time, Murphy smiled. His teeth were remarkably white, with one slightly twisted incisor.

————

Kandy's Mini played stop-and-go on Van Ness Avenue, a boulevard with three lanes in each direction, all bumper-to-bumper. Craggy trees spaced along the median marked their limited progress. Six-story block stone buildings on each side blocked the sun. Qigiq empathized with lab mice in a maze.

Kandy said, "So this woman thinks her husband is being

blackmailed. Claims to have found electronic letters—not emails, but scans of actual paper letters—along with incriminating pictures with a girl she believes is a prostitute."

"So we're back to being the Missing Persons Department?" Qigiq said, staring at a Ford pickup whose frame had been elevated a foot, its rear bumper hanging dangerously close to their windshield.

"Jasik is repaying another favor; they're overloaded. And we don't have the homicide of the day—yet. Maybe he's going easy on you, hoping you'll want to stay in this crazy city. Plus," she paused and inched the car forward, "statistics show missing persons often end up dead. Think of it as us getting a head start. This lady thinks her husband ran away with the babe in the pictures."

"And she misses him?"

Kandy made a right turn. "She wants him back so she can sue for divorce before he spends all their money on the hottie."

"So he's not really missing?"

"Missing in the sense she can't find him. Hasn't heard from him since Saturday night, and thinks something terrible has happened based on threats in the letters."

"Maybe we do have a homicide." He paused, but she didn't laugh. "Does the money match the demands?" The truck bumper pulled away.

"Nope. Way more is missing. She won't say how much, just that it would buy a house, though she didn't say where. The letter asked for only ten thousand in cash."

They made good progress on Marina Drive heading away from the Golden Gate Bridge. Late afternoon traffic in the opposite direction was nearly gridlocked. Beyond, two girls in shorts played Frisbee with a dog, and a guy sat alone, staring out at the shimmering waters of the bay, strumming an acoustic guitar.

"You got all this from a phone call?"

"The Captain, bless his soul, put her on. She screamed at me. The rest I got from the documents."

"We have documents?"

Kandy downshifted. "On your phone. Jasik had them emailed so we'd be prepared by the time she confronts us. I barely had time to glance at them, but they sure are interesting."

Qigiq dug for his phone. "She *confronts* us? Already we're on the defensive?"

"You've been warned."

Qigiq stared at the screen waiting for his email to update. Ever-present electronic communication sure was fast—barely gave him time to think.

The first message arrived: portrait of a male, 40 to 45 years old, graying slightly, puffy face. Charcoal suit with a dark blue tie.

"This the guy she's been tormenting?"

Without taking her eyes from the road she said, "Let's not take sides until we've met the woman."

"Confronted, you mean?"

Kandy laughed.

The second email was a spreadsheet that described a series of payments over a 24-month period under the title Exhibit A. The total was six-figure substantial.

"What's this guy do for a living?"

"Probably says somewhere," she said.

Qigiq scrolled the documents. "Lawyer. Age 44. No income information." He opened the third email. "This is a blackmail letter? It looks like a contract."

"A contract?"

"Yeah. A Mr. Spooner agrees to make a series of payments to Brintworks LLC for..." He read for half a minute. "Can't find what the payments are for. The closest to a detail says: 'the continued efforts of Brintworks LLC on behalf of the client.' Doesn't say what kind of efforts."

"So the wife is overreacting?"

"Nothing to react to," Qigiq said. "Unless she doesn't like the budget."

Two more emails arrived. The first had ten attachments. Qigiq tapped it open and whistled.

"Something good?" Kandy said, slowing the car slightly and glancing at Qigiq's phone.

"Mr. Spooner has been a busy man. She's about twenty-five, Asian, and lightly clothed. Good clear shots of Mr. Spooner, but none of the girl's face."

"No wonder the wife is screaming. How did she find them?"

"Get this. The pictures are titled Exhibit B. But there's no reference to an Exhibit B anywhere in the contract."

Kandy stopped at a light and flicked her turn signal on. She stretched her arms overhead and rolled her shoulders. "A hint to sign the contract, which is then enforceable by law, or Exhibit B will be used to make you wish you had."

Qigiq studied the wife's statement. "She says her husband didn't come home Saturday night, which is rare. Then not on Sunday either, which is unheard of. She called their friends and learned nothing. She checked the appointment book on the computer in his den, and guess what?"

"Trysts with the Asian girl were logged under a code name. Trixie...or no Trish, maybe Vicky. I vote for Trish."

"Cute. No entries in the entire book. None. Wiped clean. Everything on the computer had been erased."

"So Mr. Spooner knew he wasn't coming back." Kandy made a left, gunned the engine in first and shifted smoothly to third, settling into traffic. "And he had time to delete evidence from his computer."

"But not the automatic backup system, apparently. Or he didn't understand it well enough to know the files had been copied."

"He received this in email?" Kandy said. "We might be able to trace it."

"Doesn't say. Just that when she saw everything missing from his computer she went right to the backup system and looked for the latest files. That was Sunday morning, according to her statement. She found files containing the contract and pictures. There's no mention of email."

Kandy stared straight ahead. "And what did she conclude from the files? He's a lawyer; he must deal in contracts all the time."

"Only says that she wants to find him. He's missing and she wants us to find him, to be more accurate," Qigiq said.

Kandy pulled around to the rear parking area and stopped the Mini. She turned in her seat.

"Before Mrs. Spooner starts yelling at us, what did you think of Murphy?"

"Clean. Organized. Specialized equipment like that diamond-bladed saw. Knows his bikes."

"Get any vibes?"

"Awfully well organized for a guy who works on bikes."

"I got the same vibe. Wondered if he's just a perfectionist—"

"Maybe was military. Picked up the habit of precision."

She nodded slowly. "Or there's something more important than motorcycles going on?"

He looked at her, eyes wide. "More important than motorcycles?"

She shook her head and punched his left biceps. "Let's go interview the delightful Mrs. Spooner."

"Confront, you mean?"

He laughed and popped the passenger door open with one finger.

CHAPTER 10

THE INSTANT QIGIQ WALKED through the entrance to their new office a woman in the corner leapt from her chair and started toward him. Two steps behind her trailed Molly, Captain Jasik's administrative assistant, who must have been handy when the captain wanted to be rid of the woman.

"Finally! Are you the Detective that will find my Rudy? That mean black guy has been making me wait for hours."

The first lie.

He said, "Let's determine if he's missing."

She stopped in her tracks. The woman wasn't over five-five, even in the heels she was wearing. Qigiq generally tried to ignore such things, but visible cleavage beneath a snug powder-blue blouse suggested augmentation. He put her at about 35, including gym membership, personal trainer, and tanning bed.

"What do you mean? Of course he's missing. I told you he didn't come home Saturday night and I haven't seen him since. Rudy never does things like that. Didn't you read the form that mean guy made me fill out?"

Qigiq smiled. "That's our captain, Mrs. Spooner. He's quite thorough."

"I don't give a dirty rat's ass about your captain. I want you to find my husband. That *captain* told me you were the best."

"He exaggerates," Kandy said from behind Qigiq. "It's his most endearing trait."

Mrs. Spooner frowned deep enough to crease her makeup.

"Please, won't you have a seat," Qigiq said. He turned, "Thanks Molly, we'll help Mrs. Spooner."

Relief washed over Molly's slightly plump face, followed by a wide smile. "Thank you." She walked around Mrs. Spooner like the woman was radioactive. Before exiting she turned and met Qigiq's eyes. "I'll be down the hall if you need me." She glanced at Mrs. Spooner, and raced from the room.

Mrs. Spooner's eyes followed Qigiq as he walked around his desk and sat down, her frown cast in plaster.

"You're just going to sit there? Go do something!"

From across the room Kandy met Qigiq's eyes, her lips pressed together, her shoulders shaking with suppressed laughter.

Qigiq looked to Mrs. Spooner. He pointed to the chair beside his desk. Spooner's eyes danced between his face and the chair.

"Oh, all right," she said. "But I've been waiting and waiting and waiting since coming down here."

"Would you prefer to stop?" Qigiq asked. "We can work from your statement."

"I'd prefer someone found my husband," she snapped, lowering herself to the hard wood of the guest chair and crossing her legs. Her skirt rode up nude hose. "And found him quick, that little prick."

Kandy lowered her head and coughed twice.

Qigiq pulled his phone from inside his jacket.

Mrs. Spooner sat up taller and straightened her skirt. "You're not going to make me sit here while you make a phone call are you?"

He placed the phone on his desk. "No, Mrs. Spooner. I just wanted to have the documents relevant to your case available."

"You handle important cases with a crummy cell phone?" she said, pointing.

He nodded. "The Captain wanted us to start immediately, so he had them sent electronically. I read them in the car."

Her faced relaxed. "I see." She swallowed. "What do you think?'

Kandy walked across the room and slipped quietly into her desk chair facing both Qigiq and Mrs. Spooner.

"We have questions and would greatly appreciate your help in answering them," Qigiq said. "For example, why did Mr. Spooner erase his home computer?"

"So I wouldn't find the pictures of that...that...trollop he's involved with."

Qigiq nodded slowly as he mentally sorted puzzle pieces. He said:

"But why have incriminating pictures on his computer in the first place?"

Mrs. Spooner leaned back against the hard wood of the chair. "You know very well why."

Qigiq wished he knew. The reason behind the pictures could help determine if her husband had simply bailed out on a woman who was driving him crazy. Made Qigiq wonder about their relationship: to each other, and to money. And the source of the money. Was this just a guy in midlife crisis who ran away with a girl like thousands of other men? Or something more sinister that also involves Mrs. Spooner: blackmail, extortion, and money flowing through this Brintworks corporation.

She looked back and forth from Kandy to Qigiq.

"Oh come on. You know he had them so he could hide in his den pretending to be working and pull on his little pecker like all men do."

Kandy coughed again.

Qigiq cleared his throat. "Would you like something to drink, Mrs. Spooner? Coffee? Or water perhaps?"

"Water."

Kandy pressed an intercom button on the phone.

"Hi, Molly. A water, a decaf and a coffee, please? Thanks."

"So you believe he had them for personal reasons?" Qigiq asked.

"Why else have pictures of a young girl? They're surely not

art."

"That's what we'd like to find out," Kandy said.

Qigiq said, "Perhaps, Mrs. Spooner, if you told us what you think is going on, we can determine our best next step."

"Your next step is to find the prick so I can sue his ass for divorce and take every dime he's ever going to earn. My attorney is drawing up papers."

Qigiq nodded, holding his face neutral.

Kandy said, "You believe your husband is romantically involved with this woman, and they ran away together?"

"Of course."

"Have you checked your personal bank accounts, Mrs. Spooner?" Qigiq asked.

"He wouldn't!"

"He'll need money if he's going to run very far," Kandy said.

"He can't run very far. He has to go to work. He should be there right now. He'll never make full partner if he screws around like this."

"What can you tell us about this contract with," Qigiq glanced at his phone, "Brintworks LLC?"

"Never heard of them," Mrs. Spooner said.

"Why did you bring it?" Kandy asked.

"Because it was in the same place as the pictures. I just put everything on a memory stick."

Qigiq rubbed his chin. "Does your husband know much about computers, Mrs. Spooner?"

"Rudy? Are you kidding? He can barely turn one on." She paused and blinked. "A computer I mean."

"Does he know about your automatic backup system?" Kandy asked.

"He did know." She uncrossed her legs. "But his office installed it a long time ago, and I don't think he ever used it. He might have forgotten."

"If he didn't forget," Kandy asked, "would he know how to remove files from it?"

"You can't," Mrs. Spooner said.

"Can't?" Kandy asked.

"Well, if you can, it's really hard. It's supposed to be some kind of secure thing for his legal documents so you can track changes and all that stuff, but never lose anything."

"So he knew the pictures were on the backup system?" Kandy asked.

Mrs. Spooner squinted. "It only makes copies every so often. He might have thought he deleted everything before it was duplicated."

"Why are you familiar with this system, Mrs. Spooner?" Qigiq asked.

Her shiny blue eyes sized him up like she was about to have him thrown out of her dinner party. "Because I like to know that our financial records are secure, so I made the guy who installed it explain it to me."

"Mrs. Spooner—" Kandy began.

"Please, call me Rachel."

"Rachel, that contract doesn't make sense with those files. And if your husband had been...um, using those files for a long time, they should be in many backups, maybe over a period of weeks. Were they?"

Rachel shook her head. "No. I went back one day at a time. They were in only one place, about a week ago."

"So he took them off his computer. Do you know how they got there?" Kandy asked.

"I only know they weren't in the email backups where I usually find things."

"Did you find emails to the girl?" Qigiq said.

Rachel was shaking her head again. "Nothing. I looked everywhere for his little love notes. There's nothing."

"Yet you think he knows this young woman well enough to

run away with her?" Kandy asked.

Rachel Spooner crossed her arms under her ample breasts. "How well does a horny middle-aged man have to know a young woman?"

Qigiq slipped his phone back into his pocket. "Did you find any reference to Brintworks?"

"Just that contract. I suspected it was a secret code name for his whore so I searched all the backups. Nothing." Rachel appeared disappointed, as if she wanted more material to bury her husband under.

He said, "Have you read the Brintworks contract?"

Rachel nodded. "He usually works on much bigger deals. Tens of millions of dollars. This is tiny by Rudy's standards."

Nearly a half-million dollars, and no end in sight once the blackmailers got that piece. Qigiq figured maybe that wasn't so tiny against Rudy's personal net worth.

Kandy leaned towards Rachel. "We have to ask. Has your husband done anything like this before? Another woman, someone at the office, even a prostitute?"

Rachel sat stock-still and gazed straight ahead. Her eyes defocused as she spoke the softest she had all day. "I sometimes thought he wasn't really working late. You know, when he claimed he was. But I never caught him at anything before. Until this."

"What's he driving?" Qigiq asked.

Rachel blinked. "Driving? I don't know."

"What does he normally drive?" Kandy said.

"His BMW. But it's in the garage."

"He left without his car?"

Rachel suddenly stood and straightened her skirt. "Yes. He didn't take many clothes either. And the Tumi luggage I bought him for our anniversary is still in the bedroom."

"No car, no suitcase. But you're convinced he ran away," Kandy said. "He's not just taking a long weekend in the mountains to relax?"

Rachel replied, "If he is, he won't be relaxed when he gets back." Her shoulders shuddered under her sweater. "He doesn't answer his cell phone, his office doesn't know where he is, and he didn't even take his car." Tears suddenly escaped her eyes. "He loves that car. He wouldn't run away. But that's all I can think of. He found another woman and he's gone." She smoothed her skirt again. "What am I going to do?"

"Rachel," Qigiq said quietly. "Would you please check with your bank to see if funds have been recently removed from any accounts: yours, his, joint? First we will find Rudy. Then we figure out what's going on, and take it from there."

Molly arrived with a tray and three drinks. "Sorry it took so long, I had to brew the decaf."

Rachel lifted a water glass from the tray and drank slowly, as if the clear liquid was a comfort to her. She returned the empty glass and said, "I'll be leaving now."

Molly followed her out the door.

They sat in silence, sipping coffee.

"The usual?" Kandy said. "Follow credit card transactions. Maybe score a car rental."

"Can we pass that back to Missing Persons? They have people who specialize in following data trails. Probably check for Spooner's name on flight manifests too." He paused. What he really wanted was a reason for—

"That contract bothers you, doesn't it?" she said.

He nodded. "Can't make sense of it. If Rudy Spooner fell for the girl and is running away, what's the contract for? If the contract is blackmail leveraged by the compromising pictures, why run away with a girl who is blackmailing you?"

"Who says he ran away with the girl?" Kandy said.

"He left his car."

She grinned. "Just because you wouldn't leave your bike doesn't mean he wouldn't abandon his car. It'd be a bullseye on

his back. Plus, it's probably not paid for, so he lets Rachel deal
with it."

"We'll know more if Missing Persons finds something.
Maybe they'll even want the case back so we can focus on this
hit-and-run the truck driver thinks was intentional."

The phone jangled. Kandy's hand shot out.

"Dreeson. Hello, Rachel...I see...Please calm down, we're on
it. We'll call you right away. Yes, I have your cell phone
number. Thanks for letting us know...bye."

"Fast," Qigiq said.

"She called 800 numbers to check on her accounts while
waiting for a taxi. There's one that's over two hundred thousand
lower than she expected."

"Too much for the first payment. He's running."

"Drawn on Saturday morning," she said. "I bet he notified
the bank in advance to be sure they had it ready. I'll also bet it
was a commercial account he set up to be exempt from Treasury
reporting requirements. He's a lawyer, probably knows all about
that stuff."

"Last minute decision? He's had the contract for almost a
week."

Kandy tapped the phone. "You know, it's not illegal for
Spooner to take money from his own account and go on
vacation."

"Some vacation. But I'd like to find the girl...or these
Brintworks people."

"Think they called him? There had to be an if-you-don't-pay
ultimatum delivered somehow," Kandy said.

"I'd guess the girl slipped it to Rudy after an encounter.
Deliver the documents by hand, nothing goes through the
Internet or phone system. Nothing for us to trace."

"You're getting the hang of this electronic stuff," she said
with a smile.

"Intense teacher." He propped both feet up on his desk,

crossed at the ankles. "How did he meet her? How did they communicate if not by phone or email? How long has this been going on? They must have put hooks into him pretty deep before delivering that contract."

"You leaning blackmail?"

He sipped his cooling decaf. It wasn't the same without the caffeine kick, but it tasted fine.

"Only explanation for the contract. Unless you think it's simply the document he happened to be working on when he loaded the pictures, so the files accidentally ended up in the same place on his computer."

"Funny that the pictures are titled Exhibit B then, huh?" she said.

"Yeah. And he deleted the files, including the contract."

"We had better find Mr. Spooner before Brintworks does." Kandy stood and reached around her back to touch her weapon. "And where's the girl?" She started for the door.

Qigiq leaned back. "You have a plan?"

Kandy stopped, her hand on the doorknob. "Yeah, I was going to the restroom while you figure out what we do next."

A loud knock erupted from the door.

Kandy whispered, "Don't tell me she's back." Qigiq grinned. She pulled the door open.

"Detective Dreeson, so nice to see you," Ferdinand said, stepping through the door carrying an envelope. He stopped at Kandy's desk. "May I?"

Kandy waved her hand. "Be my guest. Did you bring us a gift?"

He opened the metal clasp and withdrew a stack of pictures. "These are from my printer, so they are less than ideal." He spread a series of four prints left to right. "I am awaiting budget approval for a new one. We must stay one technological step ahead of the criminal element if we are to be successful."

Qigiq moved around the desks to stand beside Ferdinand.

The first two pictures showed the dresser in the bedroom at Mrs. Chong's apartment. Then the framed picture of two girls. And one of a man in his 50s or 60s. Perhaps Mr. Chong. The second two looked like a blurry Rorschach test.

Ferdinand pointed to the first picture. "This is the location in which I found the pictures when I arrived. I assume you hadn't touched them?" His eyes moved between Kandy and Qigiq. "Good. Now, based on microscopic analysis of the surface, I believe Mrs. Chong kept the pictures here." He pointed to the second print.

"There was a third picture?" Qigiq said.

Ferdinand nodded. "Precisely. If you look at this print, you will see striations on the surface where the third picture had been located. For comparison, the fourth print shows the striations from the leftmost picture in the second photograph. Careful analysis of the location of the pictures as you found them would indicate they had spent very little time in that location."

"Maybe she moved them recently," Kandy said.

"Possibly," Ferdinand answered. "But there was no dust buildup to indicate they had been sitting long. A much more likely explanation is that your burglar wished to remove a picture, and didn't want you to know it had been there. So he simply rearranged the remaining two."

"Now you're going to tell us what was in the missing picture, right?" Kandy said.

Ferdinand smiled. "I am not a magician, Detective Kandy. But I have another gift." He removed a smartphone from his pocket and placed it on the desk. "Listen carefully."

A male voice spoke what Qigiq judged to be Chinese. He didn't understand a word.

Kandy stared at Ferdinand, arms across her chest, an index finger tapping her left biceps like it was sending Morse code.

"I will translate." Ferdinand read from a slip of paper. "'In your absence grandmother has taken ill. She is in the Chinese

Hospital. You should come home and go to her to pay your respects. While she is alive.' My friend Dr. Liu translated the Mandarin for me. He is quite reliable."

"Where was it?" Kandy said.

"The answering machine," Qigiq said.

"Excellent guess." Ferdinand returned the phone to his pocket. "This is the outgoing message I found on the machine."

"Outgoing?" Kandy scooted one butt cheek up onto her desk to half-sit, studying the pictures still lying there.

"How long do you think it's been there?" Qigiq said.

Ferdinand slipped another set of pictures from his envelope. "Not long." He placed onto Kandy's desk a photo of a plastic answering machine sitting on a black table with curved legs and a glass surface beside a lamp of intricate white porcelain. In a semicircle around it he laid down five more pages, each showing fingerprints. "These two prints are from the number buttons, and I suspect will match the owner of the apartment, Mrs. Chong. However, look at the prints from the menu buttons required to record a new outgoing message."

"Gloves," Kandy said.

"Yes, Detective. One might surmise that our friend who stole the picture also left this message, though we cannot prove it."

"Who is he expecting to call?" Qigiq said, staring at the smudges Ferdinand had lifted from the menu buttons. "And why?"

"Somebody he can't reach directly," Kandy said. "Everyone has a cell phone. Who wouldn't be reachable?"

Qigiq said, "Someone who doesn't want to be reached."

"Exactly," Ferdinand agreed.

Qigiq considered the slip of paper containing the translation. "He uses the imperative: 'You should come home.'"

Kandy added, "And given what we now know about Mrs. Chong's accident, a not-so-veiled threat: 'While she is alive.'"

"I'm not certain this is meant for an individual," Ferdinand added. "'You should return,' might mean a couple, a family, maybe a group of people who are together only temporarily."

"What does your Mandarin expert say?" Kandy asked.

"The message is for one or more individuals who are somehow absent. He wouldn't commit beyond that."

"Would he guess?" Kandy asked.

"Yes, based on inflections. He feels this man is communicating with someone he considers subordinate to himself. Very likely a woman."

"Another missing person," Kandy said. "I hope she's as much fun as Mrs. Spooner."

Qigiq choked on his decaf.

"But he insists that she visit," Ferdinand said.

"So she's away without his approval," Qigiq said.

"Precisely."

"Is this a setup?" Kandy asked. "He knows this missing woman will go to her grandmother, so he creates an accident."

Qigiq said, "There are easier ways to find someone."

Ferdinand stroked his long, well-groomed black beard. "Yes and no. If the woman is on the run, perhaps his best option is to force her come to him."

"Old school funeral strategy you mean?" Kandy said. "Mrs. Chong was supposed to be killed, this woman shows up at the funeral. They nab her."

"Extreme," Qigiq said.

"Men are weird," Kandy said, but she was smiling.

"That is a long deductive chain with very little evidence," Ferdinand said. "But possible."

"Can we get the log of calls to Mrs. Chong's phone?" Qigiq said. "Maybe starting Monday morning. It hasn't been long, shouldn't be many."

Ferdinand nodded.

"I'll get it," Kandy said. "And put a watchdog on her line in case there are more." She stood and walked to the window, lifting a cell phone to her ear.

Ferdinand stared at the photos on the desk. He repeated, "Very little evidence."

"What was in the picture?" Qigiq said.

"The man's face, of course," Ferdinand said. "The remaining pictures are of familial relations. The missing picture was also, with a high probability."

"Which man?"

Ferdinand's head bobbed. "Ah yes, who? This question has been haunting my thoughts. Perhaps the rider. But why bother, we have no way to see the rider's face. Then who else might concern us? He would naturally assume we would search Mrs. Chong's apartment. Someone did not want us to see this picture...a picture this someone was aware of."

"It would lead us to him. Without it? No visible link."

Kandy returned from the window. "We'll have a call log shortly. Did you solve all our problems, Ferd?"

"Not all, Detective. I would like to remain and help find a breakthrough, but I must be leaving."

"Hot date with a computer, Ferd? A fast new model?" Kandy laughed.

Ferdinand tilted his head and examined Kandy over the top of his glasses for a moment. Then shook his head and turned for the door.

As the door clicked behind him Qigiq sighed. "Not much to go on."

Kandy unwrapped a mint from her pocket. "You mean the missing picture, or finding the enchanting Mrs. Spooner's husband?"

"You pick," Qigiq said, scanning the photos strewn across Kandy's desk.

Kandy stepped up beside him. "A missing photo and a message on an answering machine. You really think they're trying to trap someone?"

Qigiq tapped the note with his index finger. "You should come home."

"Maybe he misses her."

Her cell phone blared its revving Ferrari. She grabbed it. "Dreeson."

Qigiq waited. There were two people in each of the other pictures. How many in the missing one?

"Thanks," Kandy said, and hung up. "One call."

"Hmm."

"An hour ago. Phone booth here in San Francisco. A bar on Fisherman's Wharf called Lou's Blues."

"Public place. Lots of people. Not much hope of tracking who made the call."

"We might get lucky."

"Long shot," Qigiq said. "But maybe. We have a man on Mrs. Chong's room, don't we?"

Kandy nodded. "I'll stop at Lou's on my way, ask a few questions. Maybe find that luck."

"Want me to tag along?"

"No need," she said. "I'd rather you find Rudy Spooner so I don't have to talk to his wife again."

CHAPTER 11

I PUSHED ANOTHER PICTURE into the back of my truck, hating that I'd need to trek to the booth in the sweltering sun a dozen times to empty it. Show sponsors frowned upon a vendor leaving early, but after meeting Mylin—and the guy with strong hands—my heart was no longer into selling art to tourists. I'd make an excuse. And donate a large format print for the show auction. Just maybe they'd invite me back next year.

What I really wanted was to shoot more pictures. Of Mylin. I leaned against the open truck door, closed my eyes, and imagined her in a black bikini on the beach at Emerald Bay. I would hide behind a corner of that ancient Viking house made of huge round stones and capture her enjoying the crystal blue waters of Lake Tahoe. My cell phone rang.

I didn't recognize the number.

I debated letting voice mail handle it, but my cell phone number was on my business card. Might be an easy sale.

"Roberts Photography."

"Yo Bobby. It's Bear. You just got a call on my little green monster."

"Sorry, Bear. A call for me?"

"Yeah, nice lady. Sweet. Wouldn't meet me for dinner. But she gave me a message for you. Well, actually for Mr. Phillips. But I figured you borrowed my special phone for a reason, and that reason might make you Mr. Phillips. Capeesh?"

I capeeshed. They had grabbed Bear's phone number; and I had no idea what I was dealing with. "She left a message?"

"Your chickadee has come home to roost early."

"How early is she roosting, Bear?"

"Nice lady said she can move you up to 5:30 tonight. Dinner only."

I glanced at the dash of the truck. 4:18.

"And get this, Mr. Phillips. Your chick has another performance in the same area so they are waiving what she called the 'airport pickup fee.' This is your lucky day, my friend."

Save a hundred dollars and meet Mylin in less than an hour? My knees wobbled.

"That's great Bear. Thanks for the call."

"You gonna go see her?"

Darn right I was. "Do I need to call back to confirm?"

"Already did," Bear said. "Figured you wouldn't want to wait."

"You figured right. How can I thank you?"

"No need. Have fun with your girl. Anything else comes up, call Bear. I'll be sittin' here in the shade for a couple more days."

I shoved my phone in the pocket of my shorts. With the cash from today's sales, I was set for weeks. What was I going to wear to meet Mylin for dinner? And the pictures? I still had to load. I stood tall and craned my neck. Two women in pastel summer dresses were visible walking the show in the late afternoon heat. Left, right—no cops.

I closed the white barn doors of my aging Chevy Suburban. It was long enough inside for my artwork, the kiteboard, and two inflatable kites that let me experience the freedom of the wind. So far the Tahoe breeze had been too light for real fun, and I had been too busy. The V8 rolled over and started, I checked over my shoulder and made a U-turn across four lanes of traffic, drove at 5 mph, then turned right into the parking area next to the show. I scanned again for cops, then twisted the wheel to guide the SUV down the wide walkway toward my booth.

The two women stepped aside to let me ease past. An obese woman in black slacks walking a small poodle with a blue ribbon around its neck stopped, turned, and stared through the windshield directly at me. She stood in the middle of the path between rows of tented booths, blocking my way.

I waited.

She didn't move.

I eased the pressure on my brake pedal to let her know the truck was indeed coming in her direction.

She wagged a finger at me. "You're not supposed to bring that thing in here."

I rolled down my window, feeling the heat from the afternoon sun roll in against the Chevy's air conditioning. "Yes, ma'am. I'm sorry to inconvenience you. I have an emergency in Reno and have to clear my booth."

"I've been coming to this show for ten years. You're supposed to carry your stuff to your vehicle."

I nodded, wishing her dog would chase a squirrel to stop her reciting the rules to me. I knew the rules, and was quite aware I was violating them. "I'm sorry, ma'am. But I have to be at the airport by five-thirty and this is the fastest way. If I'm not there, I don't know what she'll do." Which was true, I dreaded the thought that Mylin would show up without me there to meet her.

"You get that truck out of here. I'm not moving. I know the rules. They make me carry all my stuff back and forth during the show; you can too."

Ah, an injured artist. I was doing something she wished she could do.

A tall man with a gray beard and large straw hat walked up to the driver's window.

"If you're going to bring that in here, at least keep moving will you? You're blocking everybody."

I met his eyes from the high seat of the SUV. "Sorry. But the lady," I tilted my head in the direction of the artist, "has the walk blocked."

His eyebrows lifted as his head turned. He took three long strides and put his hand under her arm. "C'mon ma'am, let's keep things moving. These struggling artists need to sell stuff, and the only way they can do that is to let people get through."

She stared up at him, but started walking. The little dog trotted behind and sniffed the heels of his running shoes.

I eased the brake and crept forward. Thankfully, the man turned at the first aisle; she and the dog tagged along beside him. When I reached my booth, Bear was moving in the shadows inside. By the time I hopped out to open the back doors, he was standing there holding six giclée prints stacked like pancakes.

"Heard some lady was bitching about a guy trying to squeeze a huge truck down the sidewalk. The nerve of some artists, bringing a vehicle in during sales hours. What's this world coming to?"

"Thanks, Bear." I unstrapped the kiteboard and stacked the prints against it. There were three more large pictures in the booth, my stool, the counter, and the roof with its folding infrastructure of aluminum poles. I glanced at my watch; it was already 4:31.

"You coming back?" Bear asked.

"Not tonight." Would Mylin be busy on Tuesday? "Not sure about tomorrow either."

"Just take the pictures. I'll tell them you got called away and are coming back on Wednesday. They won't be happy, but it's better than an empty space."

I nodded. "I've got a picture I can leave up."

"Leave business cards, too." He smiled. "The picture might get stolen."

"I'll risk it." I tossed the three pictures in and dragged out one I had coated to make it waterproof for those days I tried to sell art in the rain.

He nodded like a giant bobble-head guy, approving my plan.

"Safe travels," he said, holding out the pre-paid phone. "Toss it in the trash when you're done."

I hesitated, thanked him, and took the shiny green phone. Then I dug around in my truck and gave Bear a matted and framed 11-by-14 print of *Smoking Girl #6*. He held it out in two hands, examined it, tried to give it back, but finally he smiled, wished me luck, and we shook hands.

Within minutes I was climbing north on Rt. 267 out of Kings Beach toward the 7208 feet elevation of Brockway summit, crossing my fingers traffic wouldn't slow me down before I reached I-80 to press east.

Forty-five minutes, no speeding tickets, and a clean blue shirt (that I struggled into while driving) later I reached the Reno airport. I located the short-term parking garage and reached out to insert a credit card into the reader. *Do not use your real name.* I pulled my arm back and stared at the slot in the metal box, imagining connections to faraway computers. I pushed the green button to eject a paper card, pulled it, and in my haste almost crashed the slowly rising gate. I shut off the truck. The dash clock read 5:37. I took three deep breaths, jumped onto the pavement, and dropped my shorts to my ankles while stepping out of my sneakers. Two gray-haired ladies dragging wheeled bags slowed, stared for a long moment, and swung away. I slipped into black slacks and Puma shoes that didn't look like sneakers but sorta were. I didn't own anything better.

5:39.

The truck locked with a bleep and a flash and I tried to slow my heart rate by telling myself I was fashionably on time as I jogged through the parking structure. I crossed eight lanes of traffic that dutifully stopped for me, and slowed as I entered the terminal. I stopped near a twenty foot tall sculpture of a downhill ski racer cast in bronze, including the slope and the gate his body was bending as he made a turn.

Travelers towed bags in all directions. Dozens of slot

machines with TV show themes jangled while taking tourists'
money. A row of limo drivers stood across the aisle holding
white signs: Smithern, Hampton, Donner.

I spun around to face a bookstore window.

The reflection in the plate glass showed Mylin standing at
the end of the row wearing a fitted green dress to her knees. She
held a sign that read *Phillips* in beautiful indigo calligraphy. A
small black case that suggested a submachine gun in a mafia
movie sat at her feet.

My own eyes stared back at me from the glass.

In my rush to be on time, I had forgotten she wasn't
expecting Joe Roberts; she was waiting to play the fiddle over
dinner. A book cover caught my eye: a teenage girl with a
mountain of curly hair who looked like a doll with a cigarette
and nail polish. *Soiled Doves—Prostitution in the Early West.*
The book beside it depicted silver mining in the 1800s in a black
and white photo.

Mylin's reflection hovered beside the silver mine: elegant,
composed, yet with the strength to pull Jupiter out of its orbit. I
lowered my head and backtracked toward the entrance, crossed
behind a stairway, slipped through a golf shop, and came up
behind her.

"Excuse me, are you waiting for Mr. Phillips?" I asked
softly.

She turned her head slowly, smiled without showing teeth,
and turned the placard towards me. "Yes I am."

"You've found him. May I carry that for you?" I pointed to
her case.

She nodded.

I leaned over, picked up the case and offered my arm. "Shall
we?"

"We shall."

As we walked toward the entrance she dropped the Phillips
card into a recycling bin without slowing. "Does Mr. Phillips

have something for me?"

I dug into my pants for the envelope, considered the wisdom of making a payment in the airport, registered that this was Nevada—the land of outlaws and casinos—and handed it to her.

She smiled as the cash disappeared into a shiny black purse clutched in her hand.

We walked in silence across the wide one-way street back to the parking garage. When we reached my truck she asked: "Where would you like me to play tonight?'

I shrugged. "I wanted to see you. You don't have to play unless you want to."

She frowned. "Not play?" Her eyes searched my face, but the frown didn't go away.

"Would you like to have dinner?"

She nodded slowly, the frown in place. "Then I play?"

"If you like. I'll be happy to listen."

A smile emerged. "Only two hours. I must be at the museum before eight."

"I'll drop you off after dinner." I opened the door and gave her elbow a boost as she stepped up into the SUV. Her skin was soft and her arm tiny inside my hand. My body began heating from the inside.

We drove around a semicircle to exit the airport.

"Where are you taking me?"

I didn't know Reno well, didn't have much to spend, and had no idea what she liked. She crossed her legs and the green dress slipped upward. Concentrating on driving became more difficult. My mouth was dry when I answered, "Someplace close, I don't want to spend our time together driving."

"When you could be hearing me play," she said, then laughed.

I rolled up the on-ramp to Interstate-395 because I hadn't been paying attention to the road.

"See that sign?" she said.

To the right of the highway an electronic billboard three stories high encouraged me to play a game called *Sex and the City*, then switched to invite me to a country music concert. I nodded.

"Let's go there." She pointed. I waited for the exit and eased onto the ramp. "They have many restaurants. Anything you like."

Anything? I smiled. I would like to touch her. Kiss her. But I tried to keep my mind on food.

"It's close, too. More time for playing."

I coughed.

She laughed again: a soft, gentle sound I hadn't heard before.

We passed through a wall of glass doors into a jungle of jangling slot machines and the aroma of burning cigarettes competing with a perfume factory. She carried her tiny purse with my money, and I carried her fiddle because she didn't trust leaving it in the truck. The soft touch of her hand on my arm guided me. We strolled through a long open bar to a seafood restaurant named The Fin.

"Hello, do you have reservations?" a slender girl in a shiny black dress asked.

I shook my head, but Mylin held up a V with the fingers of her left hand. "Two for Phillips."

The slender girl ran a long two-toned fingernail down a computer screen. She looked up, studied Mylin's face, turned back to the screen.

"Oh yes, right this way please."

We were led through a wood and stone bar area, down four steps into a dining room surrounded by flowers, and past water streaming over a rock sculpture that filled the room with the burble of a brook. She dropped us in a booth in the back corner where the sound of a cello playing smooth jazz riffs all but made the casino disappear.

Mylin's visible dark eye dashed over the menu. Her hair covered the other one.

She suggested fare from the appetizer menu because she didn't like performing on a full stomach. So we ordered a salad and coconut encrusted shrimp to share.

She looked at me, half-smiled, and didn't look away.

"If it's not too personal, why do you dye your hair purple?"

She still didn't look away. "Because I don't want to look like any one else."

"You're beautiful either way."

"Thank you. My father insists that I have absorbed too much of your American idea of the importance of the individual. He preaches about duty and honor to family and country. But he lets me keep it because it helps the audience remember me after I perform." She paused. "Maybe it even makes more money for the orchestra."

"Marketing people call that branding." Her smile faded, but didn't go completely away. "It helps differentiate you from all the other players. So you stand out." I coughed. "Of course, it's your playing that really matters, but most people, especially consumer-obsessed Americans, can use a little visual helper to prop up their memory."

The salad arrived on separate plates. It had at least eight different vegetables that I could name, and little seeds that I couldn't.

When the waiter had gone, she said: "Do you need a visual helper to remember me?" Then she laughed.

"No. But I have one."

She stroked the hair over her left eye with her left hand. "You mean the purple?"

"That too. But I meant the way you smoke. The first time I ever saw you, you were smoking, I have dozens of pictures of you smoking, and I looked at pictures of you smoking for weeks while printing them. The light was so low the night I took your picture that I barely noticed the purple. Your hair really jumps out in sunlight."

"Smoking," she said. And ate her salad. "Father says it will ruin my assets, age me before my time." She hesitated. "Like it has done to him."

"Do you like it?"

She nodded. "Sometimes. I know it's a drug, and it is the drug I crave, not the smoke. But sometimes when life becomes...difficult, it helps me to relax and be strong."

A circle of golden crustaceans with dark dipping sauce in the center arrived on a blue plate.

"I can see where performing would make you nervous. So many notes. All those people staring at you."

She smiled and showed her crooked tooth as she bit into a fried shrimp the size of my middle finger. I said:

"I just take pictures."

"And no one even knows you're doing it." She laughed again.

"True. The pressure comes when hundreds of people walk into my booth and walk out empty handed. Day after day. Makes me wonder if I'm any good at all."

She watched my eyes. "That would feel horrible. Like playing a concert and everyone walking out during the climactic movement." She shook her head. "I'm so sorry."

"Don't be. I sell my fair share of work. It's just that a lot of people have to see it for a few to buy. The rejection gets to me sometimes. But hey, you did a great job selling today." I gave her my best thank-you smile.

"It was easy," she said softly. "Your work is filled with the joy and wonder of the beauty in the world. The right people will want to own it."

I swallowed, super pleased she liked my work. "I had an amazing subject."

She lowered her eyes. But she was smiling.

I was about to flag down the waiter for the check, but she asked for a dessert with layers of peanut butter and chocolate made fluffy, insisting that sugar was instant energy. My attention roamed between the tip of her tongue licking her lips, and the intoxicating depth of her right eye that carried me back to the *Smoking Girl* pictures. They reminded me that I hadn't told her about the men who visited. As she once more licked creamy peanut butter from her upper lip, I said:

"Someone came to see you." I cleared my throat. "At the art show. Before I called the GO number."

A forkful of choco-peanut moved in slow motion toward her mouth.

"Who look for me?"

"They weren't looking for you exactly. They somehow knew you had visited my booth, but thought you should be with another girl."

Her brow not covered by swooping hair grew a deeper crease. "They?"

"Two guys. A slender elderly gentleman with gray hair, and a young guy who never took off his shades. They were both wearing sport jackets, and asked if another girl had come in with you."

Her bright red lips squirmed as her tongue worked its way through the peanut butter. "What did you tell them?"

"That I had never met you before today, except for the secret pictures in Ann Arbor."

She looked straight into my eyes, maybe concerned I lied. "And?"

"And that I hadn't seen anyone with you. And you hadn't mentioned anyone. We also talked about the *Smoking Girl* series. The old guy bought #6."

Her mouth slowed.

"I didn't tell them I had your card."

She nodded, shifting the purple streak in her dark hair back and forth over her left eye as her gaze drifted to a spot on the wall somewhere over my right shoulder. She sat up straighter. "They followed me."

"Don't know how else they would have found my booth, unless you told them you were going to the art show."

She acted as if she hadn't heard. "They thought I would go to her."

Her. The second girl the old guy asked about. I waited.

Mylin whispered, "They haven't found her yet." Her eyes flashed around the room, stopping on faces until she returned to mine. The relaxed peanut-butter smile was gone.

"Before he left with the picture, the young guy told me if I saw you again to give you a message."

"Why would he think you would see me again?"

"He acted very serious when he said, 'Tell her to call grandmother.' That was the entire message, 'Tell her to call grandmother.'"

She lifted her left hand to cover her mouth. Her eye grew shiny. "Those bastards." She leapt to her feet. "I must call."

"I have a cell phone."

"It can be traced," she said, turning from the table.

"Wait. This is a throwaway my friend gave me. You might be seen wandering the casino."

She sat down, took the phone, dialed, listened. Closed the phone. Whispered, "Bastards," again. Then turned to a large clock beside the faux babbling brook.

"Will you go with me to the museum?"

"I, uh, thought we only had two hours." I immediately kicked myself for making the glass half empty.

She nodded. "Our time is almost up. I must perform, but you come along." She hesitated, stared down at the chocolate, found her fork and dug into it. "When I finish playing, we will take a drive." She licked the creamy dessert from the fork. "And not be followed."

I wanted to ask about her grandmother, the guys tailing her, the girl she hadn't met. But I didn't. Instead, I followed her to the truck and let the map on her cell phone navigate us to the Nevada Museum of Art on West Liberty Street.

It was 7:46 pm on the dash when we pulled past a giant metal ring with a pyramid on top into a nearly full parking lot beside an alley. Golden light spilled outward through the tall narrow windows of the museum, splashed over a giant iron flower resting on the sidewalk, and across cracked asphalt. I said:

"Sign says the museum closed at five."

"I am playing for a charity. Raising money to buy new art."

I stepped out, walked around, and opened her door. The sight of her body in profile beneath the green fabric made my skin vibrate. "You said private." My eyes drifted down her calves to leather straps around each ankle and an ankle bracelet with a green stone held by finely woven strands of delicate gold wire. "I don't have an invitation."

She handed out her viola case with a smile. "I invited you."

She slipped off the seat until her heels touched the pavement, and clicked briskly toward the building. We walked through the tall doors of the main entrance, turned left, climbed a flight of stairs beneath an inverted copper tower pointing down at us like an artillery shell, and made a U-turn toward an exhibition hall crowded with people talking and drinking wine from long-stem glasses.

I stopped. "Mylin, I'm not dressed for this kind of party."

She smiled. "Take pictures as my photographer. They won't mind. Everyone knows we artists are nonconformists." She crossed the threshold into the noisy room.

I followed on her heels like the blue-ribboned dog at the art show.

Immediately a tall slender woman with gray hair and an elegant gown the color of midnight on the ocean noticed us.

Light twinkled from her dress as she approached.

"Mylin, sweetheart, I'm so glad you came to play for my little soirée. The natives grow restless. I'm afraid food and alcohol can hold them off for only so long. And you know..." she leaned in to whisper, "we need them in the right mood for the auction."

"Hello, Ms. Carson, it's good to see you again. This is my driver, Mr. Phillips."

The woman switched her wine glass to her left hand and offered her right. Her eyes were alive like a teenage girl's telling a secret, but wrinkles in her cheeks spoke of a long life.

"Nice to meet you, Mr. Phillips. I trust you are taking care of our jewel."

Her hand felt like it had come from a freezer. I shook gently and bowed slightly.

"Doing my best."

"Ah, you are so warm. My hands turn to ice in air conditioning; you'd think this museum was filled with mummies instead of paintings. Come my dear, let us get you to your audience."

She led us to a corner where a single microphone on a stand and two overhead spots formed a makeshift stage set among glass domes on the floor, some clear, some milky white, each less than a foot high. There were no chairs or other musicians in evidence. Half of the men were in tuxedos. I glanced down at my charcoal Pumas and felt like I was letting Mylin down—even if I was just a driver.

She touched my hand to take her case from me, sending tingling energy up my arm, and went into the corner to tune up her instrument. I drifted to the wall to be out of the way and found a plaque describing the domes. Each one represented the clarity of Lake Tahoe at some point in the past and were part of an exhibit called Tahoe: A Visual History. The name and signature of the artist popped off the metal plaque:

Maya Lin.

My mouth felt dry.

Below her name: *NO PHOTOGRAPHY ALLOWED!*

At that moment, Ms. Carson found me. "Isn't she a lovely girl?"

I wanted to tell Ms. Carson how images of Mylin's eyes and lips had been haunting me since shooting a hundred photos in Ann Arbor. But I said, "She's always so pleasant."

"Pleasant? You haven't heard her play, have you?"

While trying to guess what she meant I scanned the room for a spot where an underdressed guy could hide.

"Will you be staying for the performance?" she asked.

"I don't want to intrude; I'll wait in the truck." I added, "This is quite a formal affair."

"Oh pish-posh. Just a bunch of people with too much money. I do like some of them, though. Come."

She was three strides ahead of me and sipping her wine before my feet moved. I glanced back over my shoulder. Mylin was facing the wall and bowing furiously, though quietly. Ms. Carson led me from the noisy room and toward the back of the building. She said:

"Have you worked with Mylin long?"

"No. This is my first time as her driver."

"It's nice that your company sends someone to look after her at these affairs. Men sometimes like her too much."

That I could understand.

She stopped walking and examined me from my shoes to my forehead. "You don't look the lifelong-driver type. You must do something else too."

Fabricating an entire career was beyond my skill set, so I said, "I'm a photographer."

Her teen-girl eyes studied me.

"Fine art," I added.

She said, "Really," like it was three separate words.

"I'm exhibiting over at Kings Beach. I'm in the Tahoe area this summer for art shows."

"And driving too. Do you specialize?"

"Impromptu street photography. I call it un-modeled, sort of a musique concrète of the camera. At least that's what one critic at the Ann Arbor art show called it."

She turned right. "I often have guests," she gave me a once-over, "especially artists, who aren't dressed for a fundraiser."

We stepped into a room that could have been costuming for a small stage play. One rack held jackets, ties and slacks, with a row of men's shoes beneath, and another dresses of so many colors it suggested a giant peacock.

Ms. Carson faced me and placed one palm atop each shoulder. "Forty-four," she announced and pulled a gray sport coat from the rack. She fingered through several dozen ties, stopping at one with splashes of yellow, "And this." She handed me the tie and said, "Tell me about these un-modeled pictures of yours."

I slipped the tie around my neck, but she took the ends away and began tying it herself.

"I collect specialized camera equipment that helps me take pictures without being noticed. Then I wait for an unusual image to present itself."

"You must be a patient man."

I had never felt patient. Maybe a tad lazy. "It's fun watching images go by that could be grabbed forever. Waiting for that sense of something important."

She pulled the tie against my neck. "There, now the jacket." I slipped it on; she nodded approval. "You'll do fine. Let us go find Mylin and get this party started."

We found her still facing the wall, gliding her bow gracefully back and forth. Above her head hundreds of four-inch steel nails protruded from a pure white wall. At a distance they formed the image of a giant amoeba emitting jagged lines of static electricity. I wanted to shoot, but using a camera would get me thrown out. I said:

"What are those nails?"

Ms. Carson replied, "They are Maya Lin's representation of the Tahoe water shed. The blob in the middle is the poor lake that is suffering from our modern ways." She turned to Mylin. "Are you ready my dear girl?"

Mylin turned with the instrument, her face calm like the girl staring upwards in *Smoking #6*. Her nod was barely perceptible.

Ms. Carson tapped the microphone. "Your attention please. Before we show you the wonderful items we have for auction tonight, please turn your attention to a young lady from the GO Orchestra. Her father's company graciously donated this performance to our fine museum this evening. If you are ever in need of musicians, please remember GO. Now, ladies and gentlemen, may I present Mylin and her viola."

Ms. Carson stepped aside with a sweep of her hand. The lights in the room, save for the two over Mylin, dimmed. Conversation faded like a wave crashing on a sand beach, leaving the room hovering in shadowy silence.

Mylin glided to the microphone and closed her eye.

I wondered if she had a last name. Or if Mylin was her brand, like pop singers who only used one name.

I inhaled, and held my breath.

She began with a sighing tone that threatened to go on forever, then unleashed a torrent of bow strokes. I was mesmerized by the sound, the speed, the rawness, her skin, and green flashes of dress as she moved like Steve Vai playing the devil himself in *Crossroads*, one of my favorite classic movies. I had no idea what energy inside Mylin drove her instrument, but it had the force of a tsunami smashing an erupting volcano.

She played and played and played.

And stopped abruptly on an upstroke.

The room burst into applause.

Mylin bowed from the waist three times, then retired to the corner to return her viola to its case. Her face glistened with perspiration. The outline of her body inside the green dress from the overhead lights made lustful suggestions. She carried the case over and held it in outstretched arms.

"Please care for my instrument."

I wanted to say something profound about how her playing impressed me, but only managed, "You were amazing."

Her lips danced toward a smile, then turned serious. "Thank you. Now I must mingle." She flicked the hair off her eye, spun on a sharp heel, and stepped between the glass blobs on the floor to melt into the crowd.

I was still standing there like a schoolboy, staring at Mylin's case, her performance echoing in my ears, when a hand touched my arm.

"Are you going to play that, or would you like a drink?"

Ms. Carson had returned. "Definitely the drink. You sure don't want to hear me play."

She handed me a very full glass of red wine.

"So tell me about un-modeling, Mr. Phillips."

"Not much to tell. It's all about being in the right place at the right time with the right equipment." I sipped the wine; it didn't taste like my budget.

"Like some other activities I can imagine." She suppressed a smile. "What subjects do you favor?"

"People. Specifically, people who are out of context."

"Un-modeled and out of context. How do you plan for that?"

"It's not planning. It's seeking a perspective and waiting for the right creatures to arrive."

"Oh my, creatures we are then?"

I smiled. "Sure. Consider your party here. If I took a shot of the crowd from eye level, it would be just another group of rich folks at an art gathering and the viewer would glance at it, register it as familiar, and dismiss it." I moved closer to her.

"But what if I had a camera mounted in the front of a viola case, and we strolled along, focusing on that painting on the far wall of a woman in armor. Already a bit unusual. But now, my camera is low and if we position ourselves just so..."

We slipped through the crowd with Ms. Carson holding onto my right elbow.

"Then I kneel," I lowered myself, she held my shoulder, "and shoot between the woman in the red dress and the man with his back to her, low to show bodies, but not faces—only the face of the woman in the painting to set context. Their relative position, his back to her, would register as tension. Is he angry? Is she about to approach him? Are they enemies? What's the metaphor of the female warrior in the background? Suddenly we have a question."

"An un-modeled question," she said.

I stood. "Exactly. A question the viewer is now asking herself: *what is going on in this picture?* And her attention engages. If she likes the answer she invents, she might even buy a copy, or tell her friends about it."

"Do you find many such pictures, Mr. Phillips?" she asked, upending her glass.

I had shot thousands of pictures, but most were only close.

"Failures. I take a lot of failures."

Ms. Carson laughed, an alto rumble that shook her slender frame.

"It takes good luck for everything to balance: lighting, body position, facial expression, shadows. Sometimes I'm running with the camera to reposition myself with only seconds to get a shot."

"Patience," she said. "You must wait."

I nodded. "Wait yes, but quietly and hyper-alert. Like hunting for an animal you've never seen before."

"Oh, that sounds so exciting. When might I meet these animals?"

Mylin stood across the room talking to a tall Caucasian guy in a banker-gray three-piece suit. His gut bulged under the expensive tailoring, and he used something shiny in his hair. His face had a square-cut jaw that made him look like a politician, and was tanned from the top down as if he spent a lot of time on yachts. She was chatting away. A little empty spot ached inside because I wasn't part of it.

Ms. Carson was staring at me; I hadn't answered her question.

"I carry samples in my truck. You can see them whenever you like."

"Is it nearby?"

I broke my eyes away from Mylin. "In the lot."

"That's wonderful. Let's go look at your animals; I'm freezing in this air conditioning. My guests can take care of themselves for a few minutes."

I hesitated, unsure of taking my eyes off Mylin now that we were finally together. But I had her viola; she wouldn't go far without it. I relaxed and said, "After you."

Ms. Carson dragged me to the bar for more wine. We traversed the perimeter of the crowd, snuck down the stairs beneath the inverted copper sculpture—that from this new angle suggested an inverted Eiffel Tower—and out through the main entrance, Mylin's case still in my hand. I pointed:

"Over by the alley."

At the truck I unlocked the rear doors. "What would you like to see first?"

"Animals." She giggled like a schoolgirl, her face a soft rose color.

I placed Mylin's instrument inside the truck and removed a wide canvas of a picture I had taken in Yosemite National Park. While hiking and gazing at cloud formations, a person in the distance on a boulder drew my eye. No big deal, just someone in the backcountry taking a break. I set up a tripod, zoomed in for a better look, and thought I was hallucinating from the altitude: a young, muscular guy was squatting on a rock wearing a tuxedo—the full deal, down to shiny black dress shoes. I took dozens of pictures. The one in my hand was my favorite: he was facing the sun, eyes shut, smiling with closed lips, as if dreaming of his lover.

I placed it across the rear bumper.

Ms. Carson stepped back to take in the panoramic print.

"Before you ask," I said. "No, I did not insert him with computer software. He was really there."

"It's wonderful. That un-modeled surprise you told me about. Whatever was he doing in a tuxedo way out there in the wilderness?"

I shrugged. "I never talked to him. He was miles away across a valley."

She sipped her wine, which was already half gone. "So it's a true mystery. How exciting. Does the park really look like that?"

"Yes, the rocks glow orange in the late afternoon sunshine."

"So much beauty hidden away from the eyes of the civilized. It's such a shame I can't walk very far anymore. My hip seems to have gotten older than the rest of me."

The sadness of age in her eyes squeezed my heart. Then I smiled. "That's why I take pictures."

Her eyes flicked to mine. She nodded, her wine-moistened lips curving slightly. "Yes, you are quite right. Art sustains us. I should be happy I'm even here to see your pictures."

I slid the Yosemite picture carefully back into the rack and considered *Smoking Girl*. Yes, Ms. Carson would appreciate it. I pulled out *#3;* placed it on the rear bumper. "This was taken during a concert intermission in Michigan." I stepped out of the way.

A sharp intake of breath preceded a whispered, "Oh my."

I held the picture with my left hand while her eyes roamed the canvas—close up, then from further back, then close again, like a sniper absorbing every detail of an enemy encampment. She was quiet for a long moment before reaching out to stroke the hair over Mylin's left eye.

"You have captured a moment of perfection, Mr. Phillips. I congratulate you."

Motion to the left drew my attention.

"I would love to have this for the museum," she said.

Mylin was crossing the parking lot on the opposite side of the museum on the arm of the guy with the yachting tan. They seemed to be walking...a bit too close.

"How much?" Ms. Carson asked.

"On the back. But I'll discount it for the museum. I'm not hanging in any museums yet." I smiled, but my focus was on Mylin as she passed the rear fender of an aquamarine car. A car I now realized from the logo on the trunk was a Bentley: convertible, subtle yet extraordinary. Her companion opened the door for her. The green dress slipped upward as she flowed into a black bucket seat.

"Oh no, we don't want to starve our starving artists. Let's take this inside and add it to the auction. And Mr. Tuxedo too."

Ms. Carson followed my gaze.

"Our musical girl has a new friend."

"Do you know him?"

"All of Reno and most of Nevada knows of Thomas Bartholomew; his family has been here since cowboys shot each other in front of the brothels of Virginia City. Started out with his father's mining operations. Moved into contracting for the casinos. He owns so many companies I bet he can't even name them all."

The Bentley's license plate read AGANDAU. I spun toward my truck wishing I had an eyeball in the back of my head to keep on Mylin. It registered that Ms. Carson wanted two large prints.

"Are you sure you want the tuxedo too?"

"Oh yes. These folks will love their tuxedo world translated to the wilderness. It'll make them feel like hardy mountain men as they battle lawyers and accountants. Does it have a name?"

"Tuxedo Junction."

She grinned. "That's wonderful. Let's take them inside before the bidding begins."

I carried *Smoking Girl #3* under my left arm, Mylin's case dangling from my fingers, and one end of *Tuxedo Junction* in my right, while Ms. Carson led the way carrying the other end. When we reached the party on the second floor, two women wearing bright blue gowns with handwritten name tags declaring them auctioneers took the paintings away.

"Is there a minimum bid?" I asked.

"Maximilian will come up with something. But don't worry, he'll drive the price way up before he lets them go."

Her head swiveled around like a hockey player looking for the puck and landed on the nearest bar. I followed. She handed me another glass of red wine. I hated to when such quality was at hand, but it was time to sip; I needed to be ready to drive. I said:

"Should I stay for the auction?"

She shook her head. "None of the other artists are here. It's easier for us to lie about them that way." Her smile didn't tell me if she was serious. "It would be helpful if you came back to sign them for the buyer."

"I'd be honored. When should I be here?"

She sipped wine and gazed at me over the glass, brown eyes twinkling in the light from the overhead spots. "When we get back from tailing our musician."

Follow Mylin? That seemed extremely —

"Mr. Phillips, it's obvious you would like to know where Mylin has gone."

I tried to remain professional. "I have her instrument. As her driver, I feel responsible for her safe return."

She ignored me. "You tell me you are a skilled hunter of

pictures."

I nodded. "Yes, I—"

"Then let me hand this boring old party to my good friend Maximilian, and you can take me hunting."

She dashed off in the direction of a table stretched across the back of the room where auction items sat on display, leaving me holding the viola. I followed quietly. A pair of ten-year-old posters lying flat on the table advertised a long past *Burning Man* festival with images of humongous bonfires. My pictures had been hung on the wall behind the table: *Tuxedo Junction* on the right with three bright spots spilling orange onto the viewer, and Mylin smoking on the left under a single bulb nicely simulating moonlight. These people knew their stuff.

I stared at Mylin's upturned right eye.

The woman in the picture remained a stranger to me.

CHAPTER 12

QIGIQ SWIVELED HIS OFFICE CHAIR toward the window. Flares of deep orange behind swirls of gray filled what sky was visible between the buildings. The sun had begun its trip into the Pacific. His coffee was cold. He was hungry for a nice relaxing dinner without questions strafing his brain. Kandy was on her way to Lou's. He could go visit Mrs. Chong, but would need a translator if she was able speak. Rudy Spooner and a pile of cash were both missing.

He'd bet Spooner wanted to be missing.

He walked to the door, lifted a leather jacket from a hat tree that had started its life as black, and grabbed the white and black helmet the moto-cops had given him as an honorary member of their special fraternity. The gift included goggles with high-impact lenses: clear for night and the city's ever-present fog, but that grew dark when exposed to sunlight.

He flicked off the overhead fluorescent light. Orange from the window washed the wood floor to a fireplace glow. The captain had provided a quality office—the SFPD was treating a nobody detective from Alaska better than said detective was currently performing.

He passed no one on the way to the rear exit. He sat on his rented Aprilia 850 and flexed his ankle: it was ready to shift again. He tried to imagine the glistening frame hanging in Murphy's garage inside one of the Triumphs at the Ton Up club. He thumbed the starter, activated the Bluetooth system Kandy had suggested, and pulled black gloves with padded knuckles and long cuffs over his jacket sleeves. It was late summer, warm everywhere in California except San Francisco. He nestled the goggles into place and rolled slowly into the alley.

He chose the long way home.

Marina Boulevard. The Golden Gate's twin towers silhouetted against the sunset. The smell of salt air growing stronger. A rider makes a premeditated swerve. The Ton Up visit—nothing he hadn't seen in a hundred bars that catered to fans of vintage motorcycles. Except the Asians. That was new for him, but not for California. Asians had been in the Golden State since before the first railroad. So a few had adopted the iconic bikes of the 60s. That's what he had seen at the Ton Up: vintage as retro, not vintage as nostalgia. Those kids hadn't been around when British bikes leaked oil and shorted out headlamps. But then, neither had he. He just knew about old bikes because he liked bikes.

Maybe he wasn't so different from the teenage guys.

He climbed the curved two-lane road towards the bridge and cruised straight through a row of toll booths that operated only for southbound traffic. He kept his eyes moving, maintaining a buffer in front and behind. He let them drift west for an instant to take in the expanse of the Pacific Ocean reflecting remnants of sunshine. The water 245 feet below his spinning tires reminded him that this bridge was the number one place in the entire world to commit suicide.

Maybe Spooner wasn't missing—he was dead.

But what would a dead man want with a quarter of a million dollars?

The breeze on his cheeks grew cooler. He checked his buffer in front, glanced in the mirror. Glanced again.

Two black bikes cruised side by side five cars back.

He moved into the exit lane for the vista point on the north side of the bridge. The two bikes changed lanes behind him; together, as if they were one vehicle. The off-ramp made a U-turn back towards the bay into a curved parking lot with slots facing blue water. He slipped the bike into a spot beside an Econoline utility van, left the motor running, and watched his mirror. If necessary, up the curb and down the sidewalk provided an escape route.

A green Volkswagen slowed, spotted his bike at the last second, and moved on. He tapped the top of his boot with his fingers to be sure his knife was in place, and considered extracting Kandy's titanium loaner from his jacket pocket. She had been right, it was so light he hardly noticed it after the first week.

A mini-van cruised behind him, followed by a red sedan, maybe a Chevy.

The low rumble of idling British twins approached.

The owner of the white van parked to his right arrived and swung the driver's door open.

The two bikes went by, helmets scanning left and right like search beacons. Both passed without slowing.

He listened to their engines fade. The driver started the van. The man backed out. A stream of cars crawled into the lot, people hurrying to see the sunset. No more bikes. He rotated to check the exit.

No sign of the two riders.

He frowned. Maybe the population density of California was making him paranoid after the comfort of Alaskan ice fields with no inhabitants. Straddling the bike, he stood tall. A woman with a side-by-side stroller carrying two tiny girls passed.

She glared at him, the idling bike, back at him.

He rolled the bike backward, preparing to leave. The speakers inside his helmet chirped. He spoke to an in-helmet microphone: "Who is calling?"

A synthetic voice that flashed him back years to a student in an orange miniskirt at U of A Fairbanks said, "Kandy *Dree*son." He let the bike roll forward into the parking space. "Accept call." A click, then silence. "Hi, Kandy."

"At Lou's. Bartender remembers the caller. Maybe. His shift started at noon."

"I'm at the vista point on the north end of the Golden Gate. A pair of black bikes followed me in."

"He remembers an Asian girl about five-foot-three. Says she stood on tiptoe to dial the old pay phone they have here."

"I parked. They passed behind me. No sign of them now."

"Bartender remembers her because she looked hot in tight slacks. A tall white guy paced back and forth while she was on the phone. He remembered being irritated by the guy's sneakers squeaking on their wood floor. Pisses him off that white guys get the sexy Asian chicks, and he's a white guy himself, but can't seem to find one."

"I'm guessing they're from the Ton Up."

"Might be because he's a bartender, doesn't shave, and carries a bowling ball above his belt."

"I'll contact you when I get to my place. Shouldn't be more than ten minutes."

"Tried to get the bartender to ID our missing person. He couldn't say one way or the other if the guy pacing was Spooner. Admitted he spent most of his time looking at the girl's pants."

"You think she's one of the girls on Mrs. Chong's vanity?"

"Depends on when that picture was taken. Bartender claims she was twenty-something and cute: curls, tight top, bracelet that jangled like she was going to a party. But then, he was mostly looking at her rear end...not so dependable."

Qigiq watched his mirrors. "Anything from the hospital?"

"Mrs. Chong is stable but not talking. We got a hit on her apartment phone. Prepay that hung up. Call came in from Reno."

"Talk tonight."

No movement in his mirrors. No black bikes. He reran it: young girl maybe calling a relative, man with her, a quarter million in cash, Reno.

He pushed his bike backwards again, then idled through the

lot behind a green and white taxi driving close to the rear bumper of the car in front of it. He checked his mirrors for a helmet or handlebar, then rolled onto the entrance ramp for CA-1 North.

Two bikes were sitting on the shoulder.

The exhaust pipes were puffing, riders straddling, just as he had done.

They hadn't talked to him in the parking lot. *Too many witnesses?* He didn't want to lead them to his houseboat. He slowed to allow maneuvering room between the taxi and his front tire. Both riders' heads were twisted over their left shoulder. Helmets covered faces. No weapons were visible.

The on-ramp was one-way and made of smooth concrete with a gravel shoulder on either side—plenty of room to escape. He approached their position and prepared to accelerate—or brake.

The green and white taxi passed the two bikes.

Their heads rotated to follow it. With a deafening roar both machines accelerated from the shoulder, rear tires flinging gravel.

In front of him.

The nearest rider spun his left hand in a circle, then pointed straight ahead.

Qigiq followed them onto the highway, carefully checking his mirrors for a vehicle that might box him in. He and the mystery riders traveled in staggered formation like bikers on a road trip. They were wearing black leather and helmets with the silver swirl pattern he had seen that morning. The front rider could be Prime from the Ton Up club; he was the right size. But it was barely a guess.

Turn indicators blinked.

The lead bike peeled onto the exit ramp toward Sausalito. Qigiq debated staying on the highway, but if he wanted information—risk was the price to get it. The three machines cruised single file downhill on winding two-lane blacktop toward town.

No one exited behind him.

They rode along Bridgeway Drive within a stone's throw of the bay and stopped in front of a restaurant called Taste of Rome. The pair rolled the bikes backward to the curb in a red no-parking zone, switched off, and dismounted.

Almost choreography.

Qigiq braked twenty yards short of their position and backed his bike in, concerned they knew his houseboat was less than a mile away. He killed his engine, hopped off, stepped up the curb—and stopped short. They were motionless, arms crossed, wearing helmets, leaning against their bike seats.

His machine ticked erratically as it cooled. A woman seated at a sidewalk table behind him complained about bikers who ignored no-parking zones. A minute passed. He leaned against his bike seat with his helmet still on and studied the riders. One medium. One short and slender. They hadn't removed their gloves. He pointed to himself and into the café. The smaller guy shook his head no. Held up two fingers.

Two minutes. And they wanted him on the street.

Qigiq checked south. A Prius went past in hybrid-electric silence followed by a gold Lexus sedan. He faced north. The lane was empty. Gallerie Electra, one of half a dozen small art galleries in town, was directly across the street. A poster in the window advertised *The Art of Burning Man* with a picture of fire consuming a matchstick man.

More minutes passed.

The guy closest to Qigiq stood, looked up and down the street, pointed to the right, then walked into the café. His partner followed.

Qigiq gazed north at a single car moving toward him: a dark BMW sedan, black, maybe midnight blue. Thirty yards before reaching him it turned right into the parking lot for the Gallerie.

Alone in the lot, it swung an arc and stopped facing the side door. There was no license plate on the front. The driver door opened to reveal a lean Asian man wearing a gray sport coat and running shoes. He was about five-seven. The trunk lid popped open, followed immediately by the passenger door. A slender white-haired man slightly taller than the driver rose from the far side of the auto. He was wearing a dark business suit.

Qigiq didn't recognize either man, nor did he understand what the bikers wanted him to witness. His instincts told him to stay invisible, not affect whatever was going down, and make sure neither man could identify him in the future.

He shifted around to the left side of his bike and squatted low, feigning opening a fuel valve the bike didn't have—since it was injected, unlike his Guzzi. He peeked over the gas tank. With two hands, the driver lifted a flat rectangle from the trunk and followed the white-haired man into the gallery. The trunk lid closed slowly, as if the hand of a ghost were guiding it.

Qigiq scanned the retail section of the building through the front display windows. It was unoccupied. He waited. The bikers came out of the café and rode north without a glance in his direction. As the sound of their engines faded a voice behind him said, "You can't park that thing here." A uniformed man on a Segway waved an arm at him. To avoid a discussion that would surely attract attention, he nodded, hopped on, and pulled out slowly, glancing back at the BMW once.

There was no plate on the back either.

Qigiq pulled into the marina north of Sausalito, gravel crunching under his tires, the smell of the sea in his nostrils. It finally occurred to him to wonder about the subject of that painting in the trunk. Kandy was right, he shouldn't stop drinking caffeine.

Kandy.

He pulled out his cell phone. She answered on the second ring.

"You all right?" she asked.

"Yeah. Weird experience."

"That was a long ten minutes."

"Sorry. Making a call earlier would have destroyed the mood."

"Now you're scaring me."

"Those guys following me. They switched ends and led me from the vista point into downtown Sausalito."

"Did they buy dinner?"

"No. They parked on the street and waited. Never even spoke to me. Then pointed out a car and disappeared into Taste of Rome. Two guys got out of the car and carried a painting into an art gallery."

"What was the painting of?" she asked.

He definitely needed caffeine.

"Don't know, only saw the back. Looked like canvas stretched over a wood frame."

"They all look like that from the back. Then what?"

"Cop threw me out of my illegal parking place. I didn't want to cause a scene that would be remembered so I headed home."

"Anyone look familiar?" she asked.

"Not at a distance. Two Asian men. An elderly gentleman with silver hair, and a guy about Prime's size. But it wasn't him."

"Don't tell me they all look alike to an Alaskan native."

"Funny. I'm only part Inuit. Maybe a touch of Aleut from way back. You never know about seal hunters."

"So our friends from the Ton Up are trying to tell us something?"

"They never took off their helmets. But the bikes fit. One guy was Prime's size, but he didn't get close enough to say hello."

Neither spoke for a moment.

"What's for dinner?" she asked.

"Leftovers. I'm eating in. Been a weird Monday."

"Yeah. Weird even by my standards," Kandy said. "Since I'm here, think I'll grab a bite at a biker bar. See if they have opinions on our friends at the Ton Up. By the way, Rachel called three times. Wants to know why I haven't found her husband."

"Anything new?"

"Not only did he not take his BMW like Rachel told us, he also didn't take his Ferrari or his Jaguar SUV. The Ferrari is at the shop getting new brakes, and the SUV is parked in the office garage. If he's driving, it's something he doesn't own."

"Rental show up?"

"No action on his credit cards or cell phone. If he's running, he's being careful."

"Like he knows someone is chasing him. Besides his wife."

"That's a good bet."

"I wonder if he's the kind of guy who would know how to run. The background check come through?"

"Dribs and drabs. Rudy studied at Dartmouth, then Princeton. Finance. Law. National Guard. Served in Iraq. Twice."

"Not a fun place."

"He's been in California for four years, working his way up in a law firm called Becket and Becket. His current assignment is for a company called Clinical Recovery Systems. Has something to do with toxic spills."

"Becket know anything?"

"Left the office Friday for an offsite meeting. Haven't heard from him since."

"The BMW sedan at the gallery didn't have plates."

"Paperwork should be taped to the inside of the windshield."

"I wasn't that close."

They said goodbye. Qigiq left the bike on the gravel and walked the long dock to his rented houseboat, his boots clumping heavily on the wooden planks. He let himself in, placed the bike key and boots by the door, and gazed west through the window over the kitchen sink at the pink sky above the Marin Hills.

If Mrs. Chong regained consciousness, would she know the why of what had happened to her?

He went back to his boots and reached into the left one to remove a slender knife with a white handle. He examined the blade, then walked outside to the open rear deck of the houseboat. He stood about ten feet from the door, held the knife by its blade, reached back over his shoulder, and tossed. The knife stuck parallel to the ground just to the left of the door. He stepped forward to remove it from a board with a thousand dents, then walked backward. He threw with the opposite hand, letting his mind wander through a world of black motorcycles, a slate-gray BMW, and a quarter of a million dollar withdrawal.

CHAPTER 13

I STOOD MESMERIZED BY MY PICTURE of Mylin on the wall while making a mental checklist of the things I didn't know about her: city where she was born, where she went to school, did she graduate, how had she ever learned to play the viola so well, how did she get a job with an orchestra, did she have a boyfriend? I shook my head to erase that last one. I was happy the GO Orchestra had turned out to be music for hire. When I dialed I thought it might be a front for the girls of Reno that Bear talked about. But why had Mylin told me not to use my real name?

The wine glass in my hand was still full.

I ignored it and turned my attention to the *Burning Man* poster on the table. If it hadn't been faked digitally, a structure the size of a casino was being destroyed. How much heat would a fire five-stories high give off?

A tap on my arm almost spilled the wine.

A waiter in a white shirt with a tray of crackers covered in green mush balanced on his arm handed me a four-inch envelope with *Mr. Phillips* written on the front. I took the envelope and reached into my trouser pocket to tip him, but his shoulders sliced into the crowd, and he was gone.

The envelope was sealed.

Inside a folded note read: *Meet me at your truck.—R.*

I picked hors d'oeuvres off trays on the way out, found a bag designed for wine bottles, and grabbed two glasses of wine in plastic cups with lids.

A stakeout needed supplies.

When I reached my truck a slender woman in a black scarf, blue jeans, black sneakers with lavender laces, and a hooded sweatshirt was leaning against it. She looked at me through round sunglasses. I felt overdressed, so I handed her the supplies, and removed my jacket and tie.

"Ms. Carson?"

"Call me Ruth," she said. "I thought the dress far too conspicuous. And don't all spies wear sunglasses at night?" She laughed. "How long will we be gone? I should make an appearance before the auction finishes."

I had no idea where Mylin had gone, what she was doing, or if we could find her. "Let's say an hour to get a few pictures, or we give up."

"Good. They'll hardly miss me."

She walked around to the passenger side; I blipped the truck open. As we pulled onto the street she asked, "How do we find these un-modeled pictures you take Mr. Phillips?"

"Call me Karl," I said.

She stared at me from behind dark lenses and smiled.

"Okay, Karl. How do we start?"

"First we find a model who doesn't know what we're doing."

"Well, that would be Mylin and Mr. Bartholomew wouldn't it?"

I nodded. "Good choice. But we don't know where they are."

"Turn right at the next light."

I glanced at Ruth. She was staring straight ahead, her lips pressed in concentration.

She said, "I bet Mr. B will take her to the best casino in town."

"There's a best one?"

"No, they're mostly all the same. But Mr. B. likes sports, so maybe the Silver Legacy. But if he wants privacy, the Grand

Sierra."

I turned onto a one-way street.

"I lean Grand Sierra," she said. "It has luxurious suites. Stay on this until you reach Plum Drive."

It took only minutes to reach the hotel: the very same thirty-story dark glass tower constructed in the shape of an "X" where Mylin and I had dined. Two minutes later we walked into the lobby with my smallest pocket camera equipped with a long optical zoom, and the flash turned off. Ruth was still in her sweatshirt. I wore my black leather jacket with a special eyelet in the pocket for the lens.

"Where would he take her?" Ruth asked rhetorically.

I figured there were only a few options: the gaming tables to impress her with money, a high-end restaurant on the ground floor for wine and food, or a hotel room. I hoped for the first two.

"Let's stroll," Ruth said, slipping her hand around my arm.

We walked the perimeter of the expansive room, examining gaming machines, marveling at the sheer brightness and noise of the place, and watching dozens of people toss money at the gods of chance on a Monday night.

Ruth pulled on my arm, dragging my ear towards her.

"Don't turn around. Behind me. At the craps table."

I faced away from the crowd and found a mirror. Mylin was leaning forward to blow on ruby-colored dice in Mr. Thomas Bartholomew's fingers. He tossed them and the people around the table either smiled or frowned.

"Now what?" she whispered, not that anyone could hear us over the rattle of betting machines and babble from televisions showing sports. Except for one, it had news. A male talking head gestured, and was replaced by a picture of a Caucasian girl of perhaps fourteen with the word "Missing" in bold white letters beneath it.

"Now?" I said. "Now we take pictures."

I traded glasses with her so I peered out through dark lenses like a rock star hiding his cocaine eyes, and she wore the pair with a built-in heads-up display that was receiving the visual feed from the camera in my pocket. I said:

"Just touch your chin when you want me to shoot. Remember composition. Think background. Angle. Something you've never seen before."

She stepped up to a slot machine that provided a good view of the craps table. I wandered away, right hand in my pocket—one eye on Ruth, the other on Mylin—trying to frame a decent picture using geometry instead of a viewfinder.

Mylin leaned forward to blow again and Ruth tapped her chin with one finger. I clicked the shutter release manually. Ruth smiled. It must have been a good roll because Mylin hopped up and down. Ruth touched again, I clicked.

We managed five more shots, including one of Mr. B. in mid-roll, then he ran out of luck and the dice passed to a pudgy guy in a shiny suit that shone silver beneath the casino lights. His red cheeks almost matched the dice. I made my way back to Ruth whose first words were, "This is fun."

"Casinos frown upon it."

She shrugged. "They're getting away."

I resisted the urge to spin around. Instead, I scanned the mirrors, but didn't see Mylin. "Let me know when the coast is clear."

Ruth pushed a button on her slot machine and it spit out a slip of paper with her credits. "I'm winning," she said, taking my arm and dragging me across the casino's main floor. "I bet they're headed for the elevators. What do we do now?"

"Getting caught following them might lead to a difficult conversation. How about we go back to your museum and taste wine?"

Smiling, she shook her head. "Silly boy, it's not my museum. I just help them raise money."

"I like your wine."

"But aren't you curious?" She squeezed my arm.

I was so curious my insides were hot and vibrating. But I didn't want Mylin angry with me for tailing her. And only part of me wanted to know; suspicion was more easily ignored than fact. I took a breath. "Stroll by the elevators?"

"Now you're talking," Ruth said.

So we did. Past rows of slot machines, an unlit stage with dark cloth draped over towers of speakers, an empty dance floor, and into seating area near a bar. From there we watched Mylin and Mr. B. pass into a wide alcove between two rows of elevators. I stopped to wait. Mr. B. didn't look nervous. Neither did Mylin, standing close by his side.

"Do they know each other?"

"No," Ruth said. "I just introduced them tonight."

"Hmm."

"They are quite friendly," she said.

They stepped into the middle elevator on the right side. I said, "Let's go."

We crossed an aisle wide enough for a pair of Peterbilt trucks to pass each other, and ducked into the elevator alcove. I pushed the up button.

Ruth faced their car. It served floors 15 through 26. A ding announced the arrival of another car. Doors spread open behind us. We stepped in backwards.

"Which floor?" I asked.

"Mr. B. will go for the best."

I pressed 26. "There isn't much we can do now. They'll see us in the hallway. And once they're in a room..." I shrugged.

"Are you always so optimistic, Karl?"

I opened my mouth to tell her my name was Joe before being yanked back to the web of lies I started with Bear's green phone. I mentally repeated, Karl, Karl, Karl, as if summoning a ghost with a Ouija board. But she was right. My pictures depended on luck. I knew that; why had I forgotten?

The parting doors at the 26th floor revealed an empty foyer. We stepped out and found ourselves at the middle of the building's X. Room-number arrows pointed in four directions.

"Feeling lucky?" she said.

"One in four. Not bad odds."

The elevator chimed behind us. I tensed, afraid that we had beat Mylin's car, they were just arriving, and I was about to have to explain why I was standing there. But a guy with a head of gray hair like a cheap rug and wearing thick black-framed glasses struggled under the load of two shopping bags in each hand as he passed to my left. His wife must have been on quite the spree, but he was alone. Halfway down the hallway he lost his grip. A shiny black bag hit the floor and spilled boxes across the carpet. He sighed loud enough for us to hear and lowered himself to one knee.

I turned to Ruth. "What would you like to do next? I don't want to make you late for your auction."

She pushed up the sleeve of her black sweatshirt to expose a diamond-framed watch face. It was 10:00 pm. I'd been awake only 13 hours. Sleeping in the truck let me get up and be in my booth in 5 minutes.

"Let's stroll a little," she said, grabbing my arm and dragging me in the direction the shopper had gone.

The room doors were all the same until midway down the hall where one side had oversized double doors covered with brown leather.

"I'll bet this is the best suite," Ruth said.

I agreed. It was also where the guy had dropped his bag and fumbled picking up boxes. My gaze traveled across gray sculpted carpeting to the base of double doors covered in smooth leather, up to a brass inlay, down the other side to—a tiny shape I instantly recognized. I glanced up and down the hallway; the man was gone. I lowered myself to one knee and retied my

Puma not-quite-athletic shoe while studying the object. Then I stood and whispered:

"Let's go."

"Can't we stroll more?" she said, titling her head toward the far end of the hall.

I brought a finger to my lips, trying to keep her quiet as I pulled her back toward the elevators. When we were safely inside a car by ourselves she said, "Whatever is going on?"

"Your optimism. We have to get back to the truck fast." I smiled. "Make sure that viola is safe."

She shot me a quizzical look.

I was sure of what I had seen. Almost.

As we passed out of the air conditioning into the warmth of the evening she said, "Are you going to tell me?"

"I might be wrong. It's a long shot."

"We're at a casino. Of course it's a long shot," she said, laughing.

"Remember the man carrying those bags?"

"Oh yes. I wish a man would do that for me when I go shopping."

"He left something."

"Left? As in dropped? I didn't notice anything on the floor."

"Left. As in the packages and the cheap toupee were a cover for him to plant a surveillance device."

We crawled into the back of the truck. I shifted paintings out of the way to access my bag of electronic goodies for un-modeled pictures—what most people called eavesdropping.

Ruth said, "This would be more exciting if you told tell me what we're doing."

I let out a slow sigh. "The bag man installed a camera under the door to that suite. At least that's my hypothesis." I held up a slender rod with a tiny glass tip the size of a pinhead. "Fiber optic camera. The narrow body is the antenna. Takes a special battery."

Ruth's eyes widened like a child eyeing a great deal of candy. "He put that under the door?"

"It won't stay in place if the door is opened; it'll become a smashed bit of metal and plastic for someone to vacuum up. He arrived moments after we did. If your instincts picked the right room...coincidence?"

"Do you think that's Mr. B.'s room?"

I smiled. "How optimistic are you?"

"Oh very," she said. "Life's more fun that way."

"If you're rolling sevens, Mr. B. took Mylin to Suite 2611. Our friend with the bags slipped a camera just like this one under the door and positioned it in the carpet so it can see into the room."

She held out her hand; I placed the tiny camera in her palm. She stared as if it were a gemstone freshly dug from the earth.

I said, "These are so small, they rarely contain encryption software."

She looked in my eyes.

"The pictures are broadcast on one of several channels, usually in a simple raw digital format. They're generally used for surveillance, so secure transmission isn't the issue. Seeing is."

"Oh, don't tell me, Karl. Do you have?"

"I do. I use them for shots I could never get with my hands. They're easy to hide in a bush or a tree. Have you ever tried to photograph a hummingbird? They're quick." I reached into the bag, came up with a box smaller than a pack of cigarettes, and extended two antennae from its top.

"That's small, too," she said.

"It's just the receiver." I dug into my pants for my smartphone. "This is the display." I pressed a cable into the box, and the other end into the bottom of the phone. "I hope your luck is running hot. That camera has to be broadcasting on one of the channels this can handle." I lowered the window on the casino side of my truck, set the box to scan, placed it on the roof...and hoped.

CHAPTER 14

THE LARGE FLAT PALM of the tall American named Thomas Bartholomew (who insisted: "Call me Barth, I don't care for Tom.") moved slowly down Mylin's back and beyond the curve of her waist. She turned her head and pressed the right side of her face against his chest. Her left eye gazed through hanging strands of purple hair and found the hotel's digital alarm clock. They had been together in the room for eight full minutes—all should be ready.

She pushed him gently away and smiled. Running her hands down the sides of her green dress she said: "You like?"

Barth's breathing was elevated, but he managed, "I like Mylin very much."

Exaggerating the errors in her English because she had been taught American men found it alluring, she said: "You like see more?"

He stepped forward and pulled her against his chest, mauling her backside again with his big clumsy hands. It was good that he had a financial mind, because he surely did not have the gentle touch of an artist. His fingers roamed upward and fumbled for the zipper on the back of her gown.

She rotated on a bare heel; her shoes had been the first to go. "Please be careful not tear gown. I use to perform."

"Don't worry, Mylin," he said, his breath hot on the nape of her neck, and his deep voice full of the authority of men who give orders for a living. "I'll buy you a hundred gowns."

She wished for a brief moment it were true: that he would buy her a closetful of beautiful dresses she would wear to perform in famous concert halls all around the world before thousands of music lovers. But it never happened that way. It was never about music. It was never even about her. The zipper reached her waist. His fingers pushed the gown forward over her shoulders. She caught it by crossing her arms over her breasts, then turned to face him.

He stepped back, his eyes roving over her body like there were words printed on it he didn't quite understand. He sat down slowly on the edge of the bed—and stared.

She was thankful his hands were away for the moment; the wrong hands made her tremble inside. She moved backward in small half-steps until she was lined up with the door to the room, then she inched her dress down to her knees, and stepped out of it. His eyes never wavered. She pulled down the left side of her black thong panties with one finger, revealing a swirl of tattoo.

"Is that the number thirteen?"

"No." She caught his eyes with hers. "These too?"

Barth cleared his throat. "We need to talk business first."

Mylin shook her head. "No business. You want, you can have. Mylin ready."

She gauged his reaction carefully. He was still wearing the jacket he had worn to the art auction, and hadn't even removed his shoes. He reached for the glass on the nightstand. His eyes hung on her body as he swallowed a gulp of the single malt on the rocks he had carried up from the bar. He said:

"Don't tell me you like me."

She smiled broadly. His hands were harsh, but he was acceptable: overweight like most Americans over 40, but no rolls of blubber. His face was boyish, but good-looking. And he was tall. She felt safe with tall men, as if they could protect her—though none ever had. And big men were sometimes big where it counted. Yet few knew the secrets of the jade stem. She preferred the elegant imagery of the Chinese and its implication of beauty and strength on which she could build pleasure. She hated the sound of the hard, ugly words Americans used—as if they despised their very bodies.

Now she needed a convincing lie, so she hid inside jumbled language, which almost always worked wonders on overheated men. With a playful tone she said:

"Of course I like you, Mr. Barth. Why you think I here?"

They had reached the critical moment when male ego battled lust. She had known which would win ever since Ms. Carson introduced them.

He drank again. "I think you're here because you're a starving classical musician, and I'm a rich businessman who can help you if you're nice to me."

Mylin feigned surprise, though she would be elated to trade places with a starving musician. "Many artists struggle. But I have a good orchestra job." She paused and tilted her head. "Did Ms. Carson say I was starving?"

Barth smiled with only half his face. "She didn't have to; it's in your eyes. You don't look like a girl in confident financial control of her life."

Her smiled faded to a pout as she tried to hide the way his words cut into her; Father never let her forget who controlled her life. Except for one thing. "I like to play my instrument. Takes much time."

"And you play it very well indeed. But most people don't care to hear a viola. Even one played by such an attractive young woman."

"I do OK," she said, without moving.

He put his glass down with a thud. "OK is no way to live, Mylin. I don't want to insult you, but I like to negotiate my contracts up front."

She crossed her legs at the ankle and lowered her arms slightly.

"We are negotiating?"

He shook his head. "We've been negotiating since you got in

my car little lady. So. What is it you want?"

Mylin raised herself to the balls of her feet, put her arms over her head like a ballet dancer, and spun in a circle. "What I want is to not negotiate, my Mr. Barth. If you like to give me gift, Mylin would be most grateful. But such generosity is not necessary."

Barth tilted his head, hesitated, then sighed.

"OK, you win." He reached inside his jacket and pulled out a silver wallet made of something like spun titanium. "I would like to buy you a gown for your next concert. If you will humor me, I prefer dark blue. Something extravagant, but not overly long." He retrieved her green dress from the floor, crossed to a chair beside the entrance to the bathroom, bent at the waist to block her view, and gently placed her dress on the chair.

She would count it later.

She walked backward until she felt the wall behind her with her left hand. She raised her right hand and pointed at his jade stem with her index finger, then curled it toward her. He crossed the room in two strides and placed both palms against the wall above her head, leaned down, and kissed her.

CHAPTER 15

"OH MY," RUTH GASPED. She lowered the hand that had been covering her mouth while staring at Mylin's image on my phone. She turned away. "Oh my," she said more softly, fanning herself with her bare hand. "And I introduced them."

"It's not your fault. They're adults."

"Yes, I know. But so, um, quickly. And...did he offer her money?"

I said, "Rich guys move fast," trying to unknot the tension in my stomach.

"I feel so guilty."

"Oh, Ruth." I grinned. "How many wealthy men have you known with trophy wives, and mistresses, and a string of romantic encounters on top of that?"

She blushed. "All right. Yes, I'm a bit jealous. She is quite beautiful."

"And she plays with such intensity."

"A female Pied Piper of sorts," she murmured.

I let the phone record the pictures that came in every few seconds, but turned off the display. Ruth didn't care to watch. I couldn't; Mylin was messing with my heartstrings. And despite the fact that I took clandestine pictures for a living, this pushed my limit. Mylin had a right to her privacy; though a part of me hoped the camera would capture something as good as *Smoking Girl.* I said:

"Does your Pied Piper lure men away from this town?"

"At least *a* man," she said. "A very rich man."

I faced her. "So Mylin is just after his money?"

She shrugged. "A young foreign girl. She could be after many things. Money. A job. Marriage and a green card. Or..."

Ruth's eyes met mine. The corners of her mouth twitched slightly. She was going to make me ask, so I gave her a melodramatic: "Or?"

"Or a good time," she said, and burst out laughing. "He is rather handsome."

I shook my head, slipped out the back of the truck, and helped Ruth step to the ground.

"We had better not be here when they come out."

"Oh no, that would be difficult to explain," she agreed.

"To the auction?"

"To the auction," she said, and pecked my cheek with a light kiss.

―――――

I stood in the second floor ballroom with Ruth, sipping my wine. She had her left hand on my forearm, and would squeeze and whisper in my ear who was going to bid next. She had been right three times in a row. A sculpture of a snow-ski racer that appeared to be a miniature of the one at the Reno airport was being placed on the auction table when the sound of the glass door at the top of the stairs snuck through the bidding. It wasn't loud, and wouldn't be noticed by someone not listening. But I had been listening for over thirty minutes.

I turned my head slowly and found the entrance. Mylin had come in alone and was strolling toward the nearest bartender. She wore the green gown I had seen drop to the floor via the hidden camera.

"She's back," I whispered to Ruth.

As Ruth turned to look, Bartholomew pushed open the glass entrance door.

"Oh good, Bartholomew is back too. I was worried he might go home for a nap. Better he comes here happy and spends money." She grinned up at me and turned back to the auction.

The bidding for the skier statue opened at twenty-five hundred dollars.

He passed behind Mylin without speaking to her and crossed to the far bar. Maybe they had fought after we left the parking lot. Wishful thinking. More likely they had agreed not to be seen together in public any more than necessary.

I whispered, "Is he married?"

Ruth studied my eyes before answering. "Was. Twice. Not now. Probably isn't looking, after what Olivia cost him in the divorce."

He took a chair and an assistant handed him a paddle with number 73 on it. Mylin remained by the bar holding red wine and chatting with the gray-bearded bartender.

The bid went to $2600. Then $2750 when an elderly woman in a wheelchair raised paddle number 14. I wondered how long it had been since she had skied on snow.

I nursed my wine. Mylin had mentioned a drive after the museum; I didn't want to fall asleep on the highway. Another paddle went up. I wanted to go to her, but debated: when she left, she told me to wait—shouldn't I hang out until she came to me? For all I knew, she was still doing whatever it was she did.

"Five thousand," Ruth whispered. "You watch."

"Seems high, but I believe you. You've done this before."

She smiled.

The bid went to $3000.

"Bartholomew won't start bidding until everyone else slows down," she said.

"You think he wants the sculpture?"

She nodded. "He's an avid skier. But there's something he wants more."

My eyes landed on Mylin and my teeth clenched. Ruth followed the direction of my gaze.

"Oh yes, the girl. But now that they've had their way with each other, he has a new desire."

She read the confusion on my face.

"A trophy," she said. "He wants a trophy to commemorate tonight. I introduced them after Mylin's performance; they've only known each other for a few hours. From what I saw on your spy screen, he's smitten. He'll buy something expensive and put it in his den to remind him of this night."

"Men do that?"

"Some. Others send a gift to the woman in the hope it will help *her* remember how great it was." She glanced at me from the corner of her eye. "Or try to convince her." She finished her wine. "But not our Bartholomew. He'll want the trophy for himself."

I wouldn't need a brain crutch to remind me of Mylin, especially if I'd been in the room when her gown floated to the floor.

The bid reached $3500. Paddle 73 took it to $4000. Ruth was batting a thousand.

I was startled by a voice saying, "Can we talk?"

Mylin stood within inches of my side. "Yeah, sure." I looked around a room full of people caught in the frenzy of bidding for expensive artwork to add to houses already overflowing with expensive artwork. "Here?"

Mylin bent forward to smile at Ruth and pulled me toward the side of the room.

"Will you drive me to San Francisco?"

I glanced at the wall behind the bar: not quite 11:00 pm. "When?"

She tossed her head to move her hair aside and chastised me with both eyes. "Now, silly."

"It's at least a four-hour drive. It'll be the middle of the night when we get there."

"That doesn't matter. I have to see my grandmother."

"At three in the morning? Does she stay up late watching reruns?"

She slapped my biceps with her palm. "No. She's in the hospital. I must go to her."

I wanted to ask why, but this wasn't the place for an emotional discussion. I kept it practical:

"They won't let us in until morning visiting hours."

She frowned.

I added, "You can talk to security. But late at night, I doubt you can get in."

"We must try."

Ruth was following the bidding. The skier had gone to $4850. No one was paying attention to us. "Do you want to stay for the auction?"

Mylin shook her head.

"Leave now?" I asked.

She nodded.

We walked over. I tapped Ruth on the shoulder. "We're leaving. Thanks for the company."

She smiled. "The pleasure was all mine. Perhaps we can take more photographs one day." Her eyes roamed my face. "I look forward to seeing the results of our efforts." She turned to Mylin. They hugged. "Thank you for your wonderful performance tonight. We'll have you back soon." She held Mylin at arms length and met her eyes. Whatever passed between them I couldn't decode.

"Yes, please do," Mylin said. "I love your museum."

Mylin said nothing all the way to my truck. Once inside she bolted upright.

"Where's my viola?"

"Hidden in back under my board."

Her body melted into the bucket seat. "I'm so worried about Laolao. She's old now. And alone. I must go help her."

It was obvious her body craved sleep, but her brain wouldn't cooperate. She had played at the museum, spent time with Bartholomew, and learned about her grandmother. Plus, she had just met me today and was now riding down the highway with a stranger.

"It'll be four hours or so; there's nothing you can do until we get there." She tilted her face to look at me, but kept her head against the glass. I peeled off my jacket and held it out to her. "How about you fold this into a pillow, lean against the window, and try to sleep? I promise to wake you up as soon as we get to San Francisco."

She took the jacket, but unfolded it and used it as a blanket, lifting and folding one arm for a pillow.

"Thank you," she said. "But I am so worried."

"Worrying won't help your grandmother as much as sleeping, then you'll have energy when we get there." I remembered her profession. "Can you hum a lullaby?"

She grinned half-heartedly. But then she closed her eyes and quietly hummed a gentle tune that mixed with the singing of the tires to create a kind a moving ambient music. In not many minutes her humming faded to silence. The slow movement of her chest beneath the jacket suggested she was asleep.

We hadn't yet made it to Truckee.

I held my eyes on the concrete rolling under the hood of my Chevy because they wanted to drift sideways to gaze at her face, and take in the slow rise and fall of breasts beneath her dress— the dress that had floated to a layer of folded green around her ankles. I had stared at those ankles at that moment, feeling uncomfortable watching like a secret agent as she disrobed.

I had seen it then, a green block I now recognized as a cut stone the size of a sugar cube. Strapped to her ankle with shiny silver cable. Or maybe titanium. When she stepped out of my truck on our way into the museum that same cable had shimmered gold.

The green stone lay in shadows against her golden skin.

Why an ankle bracelet? Maybe playing the viola with such intensity a bracelet on her wrist would be a distraction—to both her and the audience.

I drove for two hours. She woke on the west side of Sacramento when an eighteen wheeler blew an air horn at a tiny cinnamon-colored Ford that cut him off.

She blinked repeatedly, then turned her body to face me without uncurling it. "How much longer?"

"Hour and a half, give or take."

She stretched her back straight. Sighed.

"You hungry?" I asked.

"I don't want to stop, it will take too long."

I motioned with my head. "I borrowed food from Ms. Carson. It's behind my seat."

She lowered the jacket and reached down behind me. The dress strap fell from her left shoulder. I returned my eyes to the road and said, "You know we aren't going to be able to get in."

She popped a cracker and a square of dark cheese into her mouth. "I want to be there now."

I had been away at art shows in Florida last year when my own mother was hospitalized after falling down icy stairs. I knew how powerless it felt to be far away. But how arriving at three in the morning was going to help wasn't clear to me.

"I'm driving as fast as I can without going to jail."

Her mouth was still working on the cracker. She met my eyes and smiled with closed lips.

Two more crackers, another few minutes, and she was fast asleep against the window as my truck bounced along the Interstate. She hadn't moved except to shake her head no in a dream when the smartphone I had been afraid to use for the phone call to Reno led me to Jackson Street. I cruised slowly past the entrance to the Chinese Hospital. Bright light spilled out through double glass doors. No one was visible—not even a guard half-dozing behind a security desk.

I rolled slowly along Jackson in the only legal direction and made a right at the first opportunity. Driving around the block didn't reveal a parking place that gave me a view of the front door. I made another loop and this time went two blocks north. Halfway down the first block on the way back I found a spot on the left behind a red Toyota sedan—facing the hospital.

It took me a couple of tries to parallel park on the left side, but the line of sight over the roof of the smaller car gave a clear view of the front doors of the hospital. I pushed the shift up into park, and turned off the engine.

A blanket of quiet descended. Half the streetlights were off, including the one above us, leaving the street covered with shadows. Minutes passed. Mylin opened her eyes.

I gestured toward the hospital entrance.

"Have you talked to them?" she asked.

I shook my head. "Just now parked. Don't see anyone inside."

"They must be open. It's a hospital."

"Not for visitors. The emergency room is probably open, though."

She turned and brushed her hair back with two fingers. In the gray night, the wide ink-dark eyes of a young girl gazed at me as if I could solve the world's problems. "I want to see Laolao." She pulled the handle and swung the passenger door into the street.

I reached up and flicked the switch to extinguish the inside light, then took my cell phone off the dash, pulled the power cord out, and held it toward her. "Call."

She closed the door, took the phone.

I said, "I put the number in the address book."

She poked at the phone with one finger and lifted it to her left ear, hair falling over her left eye. She looked down, listening. In a moment she used her right hand to cover her mouth.

Her right eye danced toward me, then away.

I relaxed back into the driver's seat and rested my fatigued eyes on the door to the hospital. No one came or went. Mylin spoke in a language with the lilting inflections and pitch variation of a far-off land, reminding me of the barriers between us.

She pulled the phone from her ear, fell back against the seat, and straightened her left arm in one motion.

I took the phone. "No luck?"

"Intensive care. They won't let me see her before seven A.M." She stared through the windshield. "Only immediate family are allowed."

"She's your grandmother."

She was silent for nearly a minute before whispering, "But how they know?"

"Your name. Show them your ID. Do you have a driver's license?"

She shook her head slowly, her eyes gazing into the night.

"Do you know how to drive?"

She turned to me. "A little."

A little skill seemed like a dangerous concept. "Credit card? Birth certificate? Passport?"

She shook her head.

"Anything with your name on it that would connect you to her?"

"No."

I carried a driver's license because the law required me to. I had never thought about traveling around without ID. I smiled. "Maybe they won't ask."

She returned a weak smile and slouched into the seat.

The dash clock showed 3:14. "Where would you like me to take you?"

She closed her eyes. "I stay here."

"For five hours? Shouldn't we find a ho—" My mind flashed to a green dress slipping from a shoulder. "Shouldn't we find a place to sleep?" The obvious hit me. "Do you have family here in San Francisco? I—"

She shot upright. "No. Not there. I am supposed to be in Reno tonight."

We took a walk, found a 24-hour coffee shop, and used its restrooms. They sold us day-old baked goods at a discount, two large coffees, orange juice, and a bottle of water. When we got back to the truck, Mylin insisted on remaining up front to watch the door to the hospital.

I assured her it wasn't going to move. She ignored me.

I stretched out in back on a packing blanket and closed my eyes. The image of Mylin seeing herself that had started the day drifted through my tired brain...

Who was she?

A first-rate musician, yes.

But not only that. An intellect was hidden inside her like a second soul that danced with rich men, spoke foreign tongues, and maybe thought Joe the photographer was just a naive little boy.

CHAPTER 16

QIGIQ STUDIED THE SMOOTH CURVES of a shiny black motorcycle frame. This one wasn't hanging in Murphy's garage, it was sitting in the front window of the art gallery the unknown bikers had led him to. The night on the other side of the window was nearly as black as the frame, whose gleaming finish glinted gold and silver from clusters of LED lights surrounding it. The acrid epoxies that constituted modern paints and glues reached his nose. A dozen art lovers circulated behind him. A lone jazzman with the requisite soul patch and a blood-red beret sat in the corner playing a slender electronic keyboard that sounded remarkably like a piano.

From behind his left shoulder a male voice said, "Do you think it's art?"

Qigiq turned towards a heavyset man wearing black riding leathers that had likely fit in the past, but were now filled to bursting. His jacket was unzipped from his gray beard to his waist, easing the pressure on his belly.

"It's hanging in a gallery," Qigiq said.

The man smiled. "Critics think that since motorcycles move, they can't be art."

"Automotive art then," Qigiq said. The musician stopped. The gallery filled with subdued chatter.

"Still art. Like a bowl of fruit," the man said, lifting a glass of white wine to his lips. "To my mind a motorcycle is to be appreciated as much for its emotional power as an object as for its transportation utility."

In a distant corner a telephone rang.

The musician started into a piece that was part Satié and part swing.

Qigiq said, "I ride for the flow of skill that a motorcycle draws from its rider. That unique interaction of the focused mind and coordinated body with the laws of physics as embodied in metal, rubber, and gravity." He paused. "And combustion."

"You talk like a Zen head meditating on those little poems. As if riding were a religion."

The ringing persisted.

"Riding is a solid system not ruled by opinion or consensus," Qigiq said. He glanced over his shoulder. Tourists gazed at paintings filled with brilliant color. One checked a price tag. Was anyone going to answer that phone? He added, "Mistakes cause real physical damage to blood and bone."

"Still sounds like religion," the man said with a small laugh. "I just like to look. Bikes embody beauty beyond sculpture. Function, form. All that design school stuff."

The ringing grew suddenly loud, as if the phone were plugged into a rock guitarist's amplifier. Qigiq turned to see if the noise was bothering the keyboard player.

The gallery collapsed into shards of white-hot melting metal until all was a flat expanse of pale white...

A voice from a cavern low in his mind shouted: "Bedroom."

He squeezed his eyes shut, trying to bring the dream gallery back, wanting to know what the portly biker would say next.

Another jangle snapped his eyes open. He groaned and stretched his neck from side to side. On the third trip he moved it far enough to glance at the clock: 04:31 AM TUE. He peeked at the curtains. Darkness. He willed the sound to stop. It rang. He willed. It rang. He rolled onto his left shoulder and reached with his right hand. Six inches short. He stretched harder to reach the wireless handset and dragged it to his ear, hoping for a drunk trying to call his ex-wife.

"Hello."

"Qu, we have a situation."

Kandy's voice was clear and awake. He shook off the fog of sleep. "Where?"

"The hospital. George just called. He's on surveillance. Asian nurse in Mrs. Chong's room."

"It's a Chinese hospital."

"To quote John Lennon: 'Yeah, yeah, yeah.' After fifteen minutes he became suspicious; a nurse rarely stays so long. Then chanting started inside the room, so he checked with the floor nurse. Whoever is with Mrs. Chong isn't an employee."

"Is she in danger?"

"Our guy doesn't think so. So far this woman sits on the bed and speaks what he figures is Chinese. Unfortunately, we'd didn't plan on needing a multilingual officer in the middle of the night."

Qigiq sat up. "So we have no idea what's being said?"

"The room is under surveillance. We've got video and audio gear recording all visitors."

"That means you woke Ferdinand up and he's having the recording translated."

"Nope. You get to do that because he likes you best. I'm on my way to the hospital. I want to talk to this mystery woman."

He shuffled to the bathroom and splashed cold water on his face. It wasn't sufficient, so he turned the cold on, stepped into the shower, and was awake in less than a minute. Toweling off on his way to the bedroom he found his phone and dialed. Ferdinand answered on the second ring.

"Hello, Ferdinand. Sorry to trouble you in the middle of the night, but we have a situation down at the Chinese hospital."

"No problem, my friend. What is it that cannot wait until morning?"

The phone filled with soft static for a moment. "An unknown woman is visiting right now with Mrs. Chong. We're recording the conversation. Need a translation from Chinese.

Unknown dialect."

"At...four in the morning?" Ferdinand said. An unintelligible voice whispered in the background. Ferd said, "They have unusual visiting hours."

"The woman is dressed as a nurse. No ID yet. Kandy is on her way."

"And you would like me to translate the recording while you two pick the woman up for questioning. You need the translation by the time you interrogate her so you will know if she's telling the truth about what was said."

"She's chanting as we speak."

"Chanting? Well, we shall see what songs are sung in these wee hours." Static filled his ear again. Ferdinand continued, "Ask Kandy to email the access information for the recordings. I'll begin an analysis from home after contacting Dr. Liu. He'll be interested to see how our case is progressing."

Qigiq dropped the handset on the rumpled bed and tried to guess who would visit Mrs. Chong at this hour. Not someone who wanted to speak to the police. He put on a base layer, green pullover, and leather jacket. In ten minutes he was riding south across the Golden Gate Bridge with a bitter crosswind buffeting the bike. Three other vehicles were on the bridge; none were black motorcycles. Questions hammered his waking brain: How did Mrs. Chong fit? Why was Ferd awake? Where was Rachel Spooner's husband? And Kandy was right; that contract bothered him.

He stopped at a red light on Marina Boulevard and lowered his feet. To his left, a million star-like dots flickered on the open black water of San Francisco Bay. Whitecaps reflecting moonlight—lifting, rolling, dying.

The light turned green. He rolled toward Chinatown—a culture within a culture.

The pictures Mrs. Spooner discovered included a faceless Asian girl. Grasping at straws. There were thousands of such girls in San Francisco.

The city buildings blocked the ocean wind, yet the air was colder here.

CHAPTER 17

"JOE, JOE, JOE," Mylin's voice called in a harsh whisper.

I rolled over and banged my elbow into the side of the truck, sending a lightning bolt tingle up my forearm into my fingertips.

"Joe, wake up!"

I sat up fast, my head swimming. "What time is it?"

"Something is happening."

My mouth tasted like I had been siphoning gas with a rubber hose, something I hadn't done since borrowing a few gallons from Mom's Buick back in high school. I twisted toward the dash. A blurry blue spot refused to show me the time. A bit of sleep was just enough to make my body demand more.

"Hurry!" she screamed softly.

I dragged myself between the seat backs and crammed into the driver's seat.

"What's going on?"

She pointed toward the hospital. "Look."

A silver Mercedes sedan sat double-parked in the middle of the one-way street with the passenger door open. The door to the main lobby swung outward. A black-haired girl in a white dress scuttled across the sidewalk, leapt from the curb to the street, and ran toward the car.

"That's Pé. I must talk to her," Mylin said.

The door to the Mercedes slammed shut.

I reached behind my seat and grabbed the camera with a zoom I kept handy for shooting one-handed while driving. I flicked it on and handed it to Mylin.

"Point this and press the silver button on top."

Mylin looked at it like I had handed her a bomb. Then she held it out toward the front of the hospital and started clicking.

A motorcycle without a headlight approached in my street-side mirror. I waited with my lights off, found a mint lifted from a restaurant in the center console, and popped it in my mouth to counteract the gasoline.

The Mercedes pulled away and made a right at the first corner. The body lean said it was in a hurry. The moment it was gone the bike engine came alive, flashed past on our right, and dove through the same corner. Black helmet.

I started the truck.

"Hurry," Mylin said.

"You want to follow them?"

She looked at me. "I must talk to Pé. She is in danger."

Whoever Pé might be, she was riding in that Mercedes, so I pulled out and stepped on it. As I swung into the same right-hander my rearview mirror showed car headlights approaching from where the motorcycle had been. Jackson street had become a very busy place in the past five minutes.

The silver car was blocks ahead with the motorcycle between us. I drove only a single block before being stopped by a red light. I counted the seconds. Mylin's jaw tensed and released, tensed and released. A motorcycle buzzed through the intersection from left to right. It sounded different from the first one, more smooth hum than rumble. This rider wore a white helmet.

The light changed and I accelerated to chase the silver car, worried how this girl I had known for less than twenty-four hours would react if I lost them. I said:

"Where are they going?"

"Away."

Both the car and the motorcycle were visible ahead. Did the driver know the bike was tailing him?

"How far away?"

"Far."

I stepped on the gas and drew closer to the bike while scanning my memory for details of how detectives tailed bad guys in movies—something about multiple chase vehicles.

We grew closer. Mylin lifted the camera and clicked.

"Do you know if this 'far' is north or south?" I asked.

"Pé hates cold."

"I'd guess they're headed for the freeway. They could drive south down the peninsula through Palo Alto, Carmel, Big Sur. Maybe all the way to Los Angeles, even Mexico. Or they can turn east and head towards Yosemite, or Reno, or Las Vegas. Does any of that sound right?"

She lowered my camera to her lap and frowned.

I continued, "There are at least three routes south that I know about: 101, 280, and CA-1 along the Pacific Ocean. They'll have to double back to get to 101. East, hmm, I don't know much about going east. But there are a couple of bridges that go across the bay, maybe one of those."

Mylin lifted the camera and clicked. "The coast," she said, without a trace of uncertainty.

I slowed slightly. "You're sure?"

"Yes. They will escape to water. Pé has loved the sea since we were little girls."

That narrowed it down to about a thousand miles of shoreline, but I didn't have a better idea. If I followed the vehicles in front, one of them would notice a white Chevy truck on the empty streets.

I slowed more.

Five blocks later the Mercedes far ahead turned left; I took the next corner. We were the only vehicle on the street, tracing a parallel path to the Mercedes. I relaxed now that we were out of sight. A few minutes later we reached Market Street, which took us to Dolores and an on-ramp for I-280 south. I had no idea what the Mercedes had done. Was it ahead, behind, or somewhere else entirely?

The driver had pulled away from the hospital in a hurry. Figuring he had reached the expressway ahead of me, I pushed my truck toward 80 mph hoping the cops were eating donuts. As I approached a green sign indicating the exit to CA-1 and the town of Pacifica, the Mercedes zipped past in the far left lane. I slowed to the speed limit. The motorcycle came by thirty-seconds later, still with no headlight.

"You guessed right, Mylin."

She aimed the camera at a black-clad rider on a black machine. Something shiny on his helmet flashed each time he passed a streetlight.

I remained in my lane. They pulled slowly away.

A half mile later the Mercedes turn indicator blinked three times and the car drifted right across the empty lanes. The biker followed, no signal. We were soon on two-lane blacktop with a double-yellow centerline. Following here wouldn't draw much attention because there was nowhere else to go. I inched closer to the bike.

Mylin cracked her window open. "I smell the ocean."

The road curved into hills covered in the brown grass of a California no-rain summer, then wound its way upward toward the steeper Devil's Slide region of the coast road—directly into thick, wet-the-windshield fog that tossed a gray blanket over our eyes. I rolled my window down two inches and listened for the bike.

"I can't take pictures," she said.

"Maybe we'll drive above it. If not, we can switch to infrared and hope."

She turned the camera over in her hands, examining it. Then she faced me like she wanted to say something. She didn't; instead, she sunk low in her seat and gazed into the fog.

I drove using the volume of the bike as a distance gauge. After a tense quarter hour the fog lightened, and the shape of a rider emerged on the road in front of us. A few minutes later we were almost to the Slide, the fog had thinned, and Mylin started taking pictures like a metronome.

"It'll shoot video," I offered.

She held the camera out to me; I rotated a knob. She held it up, pressed, checked the small screen, pressed again, taking video each time either vehicle came into view.

I counted seconds to estimate distance; the Mercedes was a half-mile ahead. The silver car entered a left hand sweeper with an unpaved parking area on the outside of the turn between the road and the ocean. An SUV barreling around the corner from the opposite direction drifted across the double-yellow lines.

Angular fenders suggested a Cadillac.

A Cadillac on a collision course with the Mercedes.

Two words leapt to mind: *drunk driver*.

The Mercedes driver reacted with an ungainly swerve to his right. The left front fender of the Cadillac connected with the left side of the Mercedes and smacked it toward the dirt area where tourists parked to photograph the open sea.

I mashed the brake pedal and heaved the wheel left, bouncing onto a dirt fire road that twisted east up the side of the Slide. The Chevy stopped a hundred feet off the highway with the crash visible over door-high swaying grass turned to seed. Mylin pointed the camera and whispered under her breath. I flicked off the lights, leaned behind her to stare through the side window, and hoped the people down there had been too busy to notice my truck.

The Mercedes had skidded across the dirt and come to rest with its trunk pointing at the Pacific, headlights cutting parallel white swaths through the dust and fog swirling over the highway. Shadows moved behind the windshield: two heads, a gesturing arm. The Cadillac SUV that had sideswiped them pulled onto the right shoulder of CA-1 across the two-lane road from the Mercedes. I saw the driver, but the curve of the rising cliff obscured the passenger's side of the vehicle. I said:

"Shoot the SUV."

Mylin shifted her camera. The shutter click told me she was back in photo mode.

I lowered the passenger window halfway. The rumble of the bike engine reached us as the machine climbed. It pulled onto the shoulder and stopped two car lengths from the driver's door of the Mercedes.

Mylin clicked.

The rider stepped off and strode from the idling bike directly toward the car. I squinted and wished it wasn't a foggy night on the coast. The driver's window of the Mercedes powered down like the guy was going to place an order for a burger. I said:

"Let's shoot video so we don't miss anything."

She let me twist the mode nob; resumed shooting.

A scream arrived on the night air. Mylin jerked like she had been struck by lightning.

The passenger door of the Mercedes swung open; light whitewashed the interior.

The driver's arm lifted. Flames flared behind the steering wheel, followed by the thump of a boulder landing in wet sand.

The rider rag-dolled to the ground.

A second flash lit the dirt surrounding the downed rider. A second thump. The Cadillac backed up the shoulder fast, the roar of its V8 reaching them. The third flash lit the SUV as it turned sharply and slammed its rear bumper into the scooped nose of the Mercedes. The car rolled backwards to the sound of screeching metal as the driver slammed into the airbag inflating from the center of his steering wheel. The SUV pushed, its thick-treaded tires clawing dirt, until the Mercedes hung over the edge of the cliff in a moment of teeter-totter balance.

Then vanished.

The girl in white stood alone in the mist.

Mylin whispered, "Pé."

Two men leapt out of the SUV.

Her head swiveled in every direction. She bounded toward the cliff. When she reached the edge where the Mercedes had gone over she splayed her arms wide—and jumped into black air.

I pressed my lips together as the rush of a parachute jump raced up my insides.

Mylin screamed, "Pé!" far too loud for our safety.

The two men stopped, turned, and jogged to the biker. They carried him to a side door of the SUV and maneuvered him inside. One man examined the rear of the SUV, then hopped behind the wheel and drove north.

Directly toward us.

I swallowed hard. There was no traffic on the highway. We were alone on the fire road. I raised the window, switched off the truck to hide its exhaust, and reached for Mylin. Her eyes opened wide as I pulled her flat across the console between us and lay over her. I whispered:

"We must be quiet."

Her back pressed against my cheek. I estimated the odds that the driver would glance up a dirt side road; the odds he would notice a white Suburban in the darkness; the odds he would conclude it was an empty forest-service truck; the odds he would keep going. I was still calculating when the Cadillac's V8 roared past a hundred feet below us.

I began to sit up; remembered the other man. And the motorcycle.

Holding Mylin gently down with one hand I lifted my eye to the edge of the door. Dry grass blocked my view. I lowered my head, pressed my ear against the door, held my breath. Listened. No thumping bike engine.

I gestured to Mylin for the camera, then moved in slow motion: a technique I had practiced for years in order to capture my pictures. The human eye noticed movement.

With my left hand covering the back I turned the display on, dimmed it to low so it wouldn't light the inside of the truck, set the camera to record, and wrapped my right hand around the lens. With my arm behind the roof pillar I slowly inched the camera upward. When I had it about halfway to the roof Mylin nodded.

I whispered, "Is the bike there?"

Lying over the console twisted almost onto her back she nodded.

"Is there a rider?"

She nodded again.

We waited. The blood drained from my hand as I worried Murphy's Law would make the camera battery suddenly die.

My eyes met Mylin's.

She whispered, "He is walking everywhere." She wiggled two fingers like legs. "He picks up plastic parts and tosses them over the cliff."

He was destroying evidence by dropping it into the Pacific. If I backed onto the highway, he would wonder where we had come from. If I started the truck up the hill, he might follow and trap us. I was considering whether to climb the ridge on foot to get a better angle when Mylin held a finger to her lips. My hand was numb and my shoulder ached, but I waited in silence.

She gestured with two hands. The bike was continuing south; it wouldn't pass us. The tension in my chest eased.

"Is the coast clear?" I asked softly, realizing I sounded like a pulp novel; or a spy.

She nodded, and sat up.

I lowered my arm and gazed out the side window while massaging feeling back into my hand. A light, dusty fog hovered above the rocks like they were exhaling. No sound. The scene of so much activity was back to its naturally tranquil state, yet foreboding in the dark silence.

I handed her the camera. "Let's get out of here."

She shook her head hard, sending her hair flying. "We must find Pé."

The parachute-jump feeling returned. I had driven this road while traveling the art show circuit; the only thing beyond that edge was a steep drop to the ocean. I started the truck, twisted my head around to see out the rear window, and backed toward the highway.

She glared directly at my face, but didn't speak.

"Mylin, we've got to get out of here. Maybe you know what's going on, but I sure don't. The police need to be here. They'll have a much better chance of finding Pé—" I paused, stopped the truck, and looked directly into those dark eyes that made me crazy, "and keeping her alive, than the two of us wandering around in the dark."

She looked away and stared out the windshield.

I backed to the edge of the main road. "You decide."

"We must help Pé."

"Do you want to talk to the police?"

Her head shook slowly back and forth.

"Is it okay if I do?"

She remained silent; I took that for yes. We were sitting at the side of the road a few hundred feet from I had no idea what. One, possibly two, maybe even three people were dead. Every instinct in me was yelling to get the hell out of there. Especially because Mylin was clearly afraid of those men. But just leave her friend to the ocean? That would be...I didn't know what it would be. But we couldn't do it.

I pointed the Chevy north toward San Francisco. It would be easy to get lost in a place with a half-million people.

Mylin twisted in her seat and stared back at Devil's Slide, seeming to struggle to not run back and jump off the cliff to be with her friend. Then she spun forward and stared out the windshield, her jaw set tight. She started whispering again, but not in English.

I drove fast for several minutes, then swerved into a parking lot in the little surf town of Pacifica.

"Promise me you'll wait."

Her eyes squinted like she wasn't sure, but she nodded and said:

"Do you have a cigarette?"

"No, sorry."

I ran three blocks before finding a pay phone, grabbed the handset and pressed 911. When the emergency operator answered I said: "There's been an automobile accident near Devil's Slide on Route 1, a car went over the edge at the overlook near the south end of the tunnel." I dictated the GPS coordinates my camera had stored and hung up before she asked any questions. It was 5:55 AM. The sky to the east held a hint of blue. The stars were gone.

I jogged back to the truck.

Mylin wasn't sitting in the front seat. I ran faster, peered through the side windows — swore under my breath. No way to find her, and a camera full of incriminating pictures in my possession. I leaned against the truck, chewed on the tip of my left thumb, and stared east at the horizon. I stood motionless for the better part of ten minutes, trying to make sense of the past eighteen hours — what was I doing with Mylin; and most important, what was she doing with me?

I pulled out Bear's phone and stared at its shiny green surface.

Obfuscated device. Fake name. Gunshots. Car crash. And now, smoking girl was just a memory. Again.

CHAPTER **18**

KANDY WAS SITTING ON THE MINI'S HOOD, leaning against the windshield like a sunbather in a lounge chair when Qigiq pulled up to the front of the hospital. He rolled his bike backward down the crown of the road until the rear tire bumped the curb.

"George called," she said. "We missed her."

He kicked down the stand and swung his leg over the seat. "How?"

"She went to the ladies' room. He tried to watch Mrs. Chong, in case the girl was a diversion, and the restroom at the same time. She snuck out, probably used the stairs."

He walked over and put both hands against the roof rail of the Mini, looked down and studied the cracked pavement between the car and the curb. "Recordings?"

"More luck. We got audio. But our friend knew about the cameras, or figured it out. Never showed her face. The video doesn't tell us much."

"George see her?"

"Caught a glimpse when she dashed by racing to the restroom. Didn't pay much attention on the way in; nurses go in all the time."

"What did they talk about?"

"Don't know yet. George uploaded what we have." She turned from gazing at the dark sky. "You talked to Ferd, right?"

"Yeah, he was up. Wants you to send him the data link so he can start from home."

Kandy spoke while constructing an email. "Ferd was up at

four in the morning?"

"There was a voice in the background. TV maybe. Or Internet video."

She grinned. "Probably an online course: Computer Forensics—The Next 50 Years."

Qigiq leaned against the car to face the doors to the Chinese Hospital. Ferdinand had boundless curiosity; he could be into most anything. He said:

"So we wait for the translation?"

"Unless you want to listen to chanting you don't understand."

Only half the streetlights were lit, casting small pools of light onto the street in evenly spaced intervals like they were losing a fight with the darkness.

"Maybe in the morning. Coffee?"

"So long as it's not decaf," she said, jumping off the hood. "And it's already morning."

They walked to a 24-hour shop three blocks south that was baking pastries. A Chinese woman shook a finger at them to wait then returned with coffee she said was "Americana" and puffy apple pastries still warm from the oven.

Kandy had taken the first bite when her cell phone ground like a car trying to start. "Auto-confirm message from Ferd. His system has the data."

Qigiq nodded and sipped; the coffee was super hot; their case was super cold.

"Ideas?" she asked.

"Late night visit from family."

Kandy chewed, blew on her coffee. "Four in the morning? Sneak past security with a nurse's uniform?"

"Maybe she's shy." He smiled, but it didn't have much strength in it.

Kandy leaned back, kicked a second chair into position, and put her boots on it to stretch her legs.

The baker woman tapped the top of the glass counter and glared at Kandy.

Kandy grinned sheepishly. "See Qu, I've been in the office too long, losing my well-developed social skills." She moved her boots to the low rail between the chair legs. "One thing we know: she didn't want to be seen."

"Right. But who does she think is watching?"

"Us?"

He shook his head. "George was sitting there in plain sight. Why would our secret visitor care if the police were watching Mrs. Chong? Wouldn't she want us to find out whether or not this was an accident?"

"Unless she already knows," Kandy said.

He ran a finger along the green dragon tail encircling his ceramic mug. Figured it for hand painted. "If she already knows it wasn't, then she probably knows who did it." The rich aroma was starting to wake him up.

"In which case, they're hunting her. Or." Her green eyes studied the ceiling. "She's hiding from us. Maybe she has a criminal record."

"Strange way to hide," he said. "Why take the chance of being seen? Mrs. Chong is still unconscious. The hospital would have told her that." He paused. "She never spoke with hospital staff, did she? She just snuck in."

Kandy's phone buzzed again. She glanced down. "Not Ferd."

"You have friends awake at five in the morning?"

Kandy flicked the screen; her jaw moved in small circles. "Accident at Devil's Slide."

He leaned toward her phone. "An auto accident?"

"Yeah. I'm getting pictures from Dispatch."

"We've been promoted from Missing Persons to Traffic?"

"Whoa," Kandy held up her phone. "Picture of the front of the Chinese Hospital. A woman in white leaving through the main entrance, heading for a silver Mercedes."

———

Qigiq left his bike parked at the hospital and rode south with Kandy: the direction the Mercedes was pointing in the picture. As they traveled, her phone continued downloading media.

"Ferdinand needs to see these," Qigiq said.

"Wake him up again," Kandy said. "I'm sure he'd love to hear from you twice in one night."

Qigiq sighed and dialed Ferdinand's home number for the second time in an hour. Kandy downshifted to accelerate. She grinned in his direction.

The phone rang five times before a sleepy Ferdinand answered.

"Sorry to bother you again," Qigiq said, "but we have a new situation." He tapped the speaker button and held the phone between the front seats.

"Hello, Detective. You are having a busy night."

"More action on the Chong case," Kandy said. "That visitor whose audio you're analyzing, we have a picture of her exiting the hospital. Less than an hour ago."

"Your audio is with my colleague; we will have something later this morning. You say you have a picture?" Ferdinand asked, sounding more awake.

"Came through dispatch to my cell phone," Kandy said.

"Source?"

"Unidentified," she said.

"Do you know if it's real?" Ferdinand asked.

Kandy swerved to clear a pothole the City of San Francisco had missed.

"Don't know anything yet."

Qigiq added, "We're getting a new picture every few minutes."

"New pictures? Please explain."

Qigiq said, "Based on these photos, someone is following

the Mercedes and sending pictures to the police."

"In real time?" Ferdinand said.

"Real time?"

"When were the pictures taken relative to when you receive them?"

Qigiq looked at Kandy. She shrugged.

"How can we tell?" Qigiq said.

Ferdinand sighed. "Are you able to send them to me without modifying the data?"

"Sure," Kandy said. "I'll forward them."

"As soon as possible, please."

Kandy braked hard and swung the Mini to the curb beside a fire hydrant. She jumped out, ran around the back and yanked open the passenger door. "You drive."

"It'll slow us down," Qigiq said, climbing out of the car.

"Necessary concession," Kandy said. "Gotta get these to Ferd. Find out what's going on. Besides, we're not even sure where we're going."

He assumed the Mercedes had been pointed in the direction it wanted to go—a weak assumption on a one-way street. But they headed south anyway until reaching the first freeway, then headed south on that. While he drove, Kandy worked her phone.

"Head for I-280," she said. "Just got a shot of the exit to Devil's Slide. The Mercedes is on it."

"One good guess for us."

"Downloading video now. It'll take awhile...unless." Kandy studied the residential area through the side window. "Let's get off here for a minute."

Qigiq exited the freeway and took the first street toward the ocean.

"Just drive slow," Kandy said.

He left the car in second and inched along. "What are you doing?"

"Poaching." They traveled two and half blocks before she

said, "Stop here."

He pulled over.

"Won't be long."

They waited, engine idling. "Watch this," Kandy said, holding up the phone.

Together they viewed a jerky recording of a Mercedes coupe moving along the road in front of the camera. Behind it a lone motorcycle knifed through the night.

"One of theirs?" Kandy asked.

"Have to be closer for a positive ID. But another black bike is too much coincidence for me."

The vehicles climbed a hill and swept into a long left turn with a drop-off to the ocean to the right, and a rising wall of rock on the left. Partway through the curve an approaching SUV sideswiped the silver car, forcing it onto the shoulder.

"That's the blind left-hander up at Devil's Slide. I'll drive," Kandy said, as she jumped out of the car.

Qigiq played the video twice more while being tossed around in the passenger seat. He waited for more, but loading had slowed when Kandy pulled away, and essentially stopped as they neared the coast. They rode in silence for a few miles. The corner in the video came into view. Kandy downshifted.

There was nothing there.

She pulled the car far off to the left shoulder facing traffic and let it idle.

"Is this the right turn?" Qigiq asked, comparing the image on the phone to the sharp curve.

"GPS doesn't lie, although it has its moments. But check out the fallen rocks on the inside of the turn: big, little, little, big, bigger. Looks like a match to me."

"So the pictures are delayed."

"Can't be by much. We know she ducked out of the hospital just before George called." She turned to face him. "Who the hell is sending this stuff to us?"

"And why?" He leaned against the seat and scanned the far side of the road in the wash from the Mini's headlights—dirt had been thrown onto the asphalt. On the near side where they were parked, clear tire tracks marked the shoulder. "Why not just call 911?"

"Did. From a pay phone. Hung up fast."

"The video?"

"And pictures came in later. Be interesting to see if Ferd can trace anything," Kandy said. "Shall we take a closer look?"

They retrieved flashlights from the back and walked carefully toward the far side of the curve under a half moon and daylight trying to break to the east. No one came down the road. They approached from the far right and walked on rock when possible. Qigiq said:

"I've ridden through here a couple of times. Nice ride down to Half Moon Bay, hugs the ocean. Not a lot of shoulder."

Their white lights fanned across the asphalt and onto a dirt shoulder scarred from cars sliding and fighting for traction.

"How long ago?" Kandy asked.

Qigiq pointed his light at the road. "Not long. There hasn't been enough traffic to clear the asphalt of dust." He made his way carefully to the edge of the cliff. A light breeze brushed his cheeks. The lazy whoosh of waves climbed the cliff. "Nasty drop."

Kandy stepped up beside him, followed his gaze. "Silver Mercedes. Maybe an E-Class."

He nodded, leaned forward. Each wave lifted the trunk lid, then it would settle back to closed. "We'll need gear to rappel."

"Maybe we should just call the cops," she said, and laughed.

Waves worked the beach. The car rocked slightly. The light wind moved fog directly at his face. A gull cried. He held his breath and listened. It cried again, a plaintive *yeow* sound. "You hear a bird?"

Kandy shook her head. "Just wind and surf."

He listened, staring down, concentrating. Silver plastic chunks of the car's bumpers were scattered across the slope a third of the way down. "Not much chance."

Kandy sighed, not something she did often. "Steep. Must be a hundred feet."

Qigiq crawled over the rock, laid flat, and examined the slope with his light. The small white circle moved over the moonlit ground: rock, shrub, a tiny patch of white.

"Kandy."

She crawled out on the rock next to him.

He steadied his light on the spot. "She had on a white dress. But why would that be on the slope if she was in the car?"

The material shifted left—into the wind.

———

The helicopter arrived in seven and a half minutes and hovered above the cliff. Qigiq stood back from the edge as a woman in a harness spun out of the craft like a spider from the ceiling. She descended slowly toward the body wedged between a boulder and a small tree growing in its shadow.

"Any chance?" Kandy asked.

"She's moved three times."

The dangling EMT touched a foot to the boulder. A basket unfolded, and shortly the EMT and a girl in white were being winched into the sky. The thumping blade lifted the chopper out over the ocean leaving only the sound of waves massaging the beach below.

"Why wasn't she in the car?" Kandy said.

"I was about to ask you."

"Thrown out as it tumbled down the incline?"

He frowned. "Locked doors. Airbag. Seat belt. Thrown from one of the safest vehicles ever made?"

Kandy scuffed her foot in the dirt. A moment later her phone emitted a metallic rattling. "More email." She pulled it out. "One less mystery." She held it toward Qigiq.

The screen shone brightly in the predawn light. The Mercedes was parked in the overlook, rear bumper toward the ocean, passenger door standing open.

"She got out," he said, studying the image. He held the phone in front of him and walked away from the ledge, repositioning himself for half a minute. "I think here."

Kandy looked back and forth from the rock ledge to Qigiq's position. Nodded.

He turned one-eighty and gazed along the highway. He held out his left arm about twenty degrees above horizontal and pointed with a finger into the distance. "About there."

Kandy's eyes followed the direction of his arm. She spun around to double-check the ledge and turned back. "Walk or ride?"

They rolled down the right lane of asphalt slowly in the Mini, studying the shoulder surface carefully.

"Tracks are still fresh," Qigiq said. "Wide tires. SUV or pickup truck."

They continued on another hundred feet and found a service road. He said:

"Let's walk."

They climbed the road on foot with their LED flashlights helping the emerging morning light. Forty yards up they stopped and looked over at the ledge. Kandy pulled out her phone and brought up the picture.

"About here," she said.

"With a long lens," Qigiq added. "Those pictures didn't come from a cell phone."

They stood quietly studying the ground, the surrounding area, the high grass.

Kandy said, "Guesses?"

"Someone who knows Mrs. Chong. And probably our nurse in white."

"Two vehicles rendezvous at the hospital and things get

weird," she said.

"Three."

She looked at him. Turned off her phone.

"The bike," he said. "That black bike between Spooner in the Mercedes and our photographer."

"Rudy Spooner?"

"Wild guess. Flashy car. Asian girl. Blackmail. Could be coincidence, but I'm thinking Mrs. Spooner is going to yell at us."

Kandy shrugged. "If you're right, we found her husband. That's what she asked for."

"You know what they say."

She grinned. "Be careful what you wish for."

They made their way back along the gravel two-track. Qigiq stopped at the edge of the road and played the tiny light across the dark asphalt. He turned it off. Waited. Flicked it back on.

"You got something?" Kandy asked.

"The dust turns right."

She got down on one knee and leaned her left cheek toward the ground, tossing her light beam at the road. "You mean our photographer headed to San Francisco?"

"That's my bet."

She stood. "Priority?"

They knew nothing about the photographer. Him. Or her. Or them. The sky was growing brighter. He hoped the girl on the cliff would be okay.

"Girl, pictures, photographer."

"Agreed," Kandy said, and jogged for the car.

They rolled north on Highway One towards the city. Qigiq played possible scenarios in his head, and assumed Kandy was doing the same. Neither spoke. Qigiq thumbed the radio, asked for an update on the air rescue. They waited. Glanced at each other. Continued north.

The radio crackled.

"Pilot called in. Girl is screaming hysterically in a language they don't understand. They have her restrained."

Qigiq asked, "Did they sedate her?"

"Negative until they do brain scans at General. Doc is being conservative with meds at this point."

He turned to Kandy and spoke softly, "Think she's pissed or scared?"

"Both, but pissed is winning. If you're right, the getaway failed."

"Think she knows about the driver?"

Kandy shook her head and leaned toward him speaking softly, "Happened fast, unless she saw the car from the chopper. She'll go berserk when they tell her."

"Better wait for an ID." He glanced at the disc-brake face on his watch. "The boat should be there shortly." To the radio he said, "Any idea when we can see her?"

The operator responded, "Knew you'd ask, Detective. When the in-flight doctor stopped swearing he told me to tell you not before nine A.M."

He signed off and leaned back as Kandy changed lanes and accelerated.

"Think he meant it?" he asked.

"Nah, he's just trying to keep you out of there so he can care for his patient. We'd better arrive early. Next step, Ferd?"

"Breakfast."

CHAPTER **19**

KANDY TAPPED ON THE DOOR MARKED Electronic Evidence Recovery, holding breakfast burritos and coffee. She was about to knock a second time when the door swung open. A red-eyed scowl transformed to a wide smile inside Ferdinand's beard.

"Detectives, good to see you so early. It has been quite a night, has it not?"

Kandy handed Ferdinand a tube wrapped in silver paper. She said:

"Not up to your gourmet tastes I'm afraid, but excellent by burrito standards. Marlo sends his best."

"Ah, thank you. He does fine work with limited resources. Please, come in, we have much to discuss."

Ferdinand led the way to a modest conference room at one end of his lab where a tablet computer lay flat on the table beside a projector. A screen showed the image of a Mercedes twisted sideways midway through a slide across a dirt shoulder.

"I have been reconstructing the event," Ferdinand said. "We have a series of snapshots, in some cases taken minutes apart. An occasional video adds details. Many pictures were blurred by the motion of the chase vehicle." He faced them. "But there is a surprising amount of information to be extracted." He paused and rubbed his chin through his dark beard. "This is the most extraordinary data to have in our possession."

"How did we get it?" Kandy asked.

"From the tracing I've been able to do, several dozen cafés spread throughout the United States decided to send us a picture or two at about the same time."

"Faked?" she said.

"Hmm. No, I think someone was physically present in each location. They all did nearly the same thing: logged into a free email service to create a new account, used that account to upload images, then immediately deleted the account."

"Can we get info about the deleted accounts?" she said.

Ferdinand nodded while unwrapping foil. "Possibly, with appropriate warrants, but it will take time. And I suspect tell us nothing."

Kandy and Qigiq glanced at each other.

Ferdinand took a bite of the burrito. "I believe that whoever took these pictures wants us to have them so we can understand this event. However, even if we found the photographer, the delivery method implies this person would be a reluctant witness."

"And they're just digital pictures," Kandy said. "They might help us figure out what happened, but won't be a great deal of use in court."

"Precisely," Ferdinand said. "Especially since we don't know who took them, or with what, although I can make a few guesses about the equipment."

"You know what camera was used?" Qigiq asked.

"The model, not an individual camera. These photographs were very likely taken with a professional grade Canon Digital SLR."

"You're going to tell us how, right Ferd?" Kandy said.

Ferdinand shook his head. "You want to know my secrets, Detective. But since you've brought me such interesting work today, I will tell you. These images are compressed in the JPEG format. This format is a standard, but it provides a great deal of latitude within the specification regarding the quantization tables. Each manufacturer decides on his own, leaving a kind of fingerprint on the picture. In my estimation these images are from the aforementioned Canon camera, and have not been retouched in any way."

"You'd have to repeat that slowly in English for me to understand. But this helps us how?" Kandy asked.

"Well, unlike the consumer video data you brought me yesterday morning from the child who happened upon a speeding motorbike, these were taken with professional equipment."

Qigiq said: "So a professional photographer just happened to be waiting outside the Chinese Hospital as our nurse ran to her getaway car. He or she was quick enough to shoot these pictures *and* conveniently send them to us to help make the case."

Ferdinand smiled.

"You think we're being set up?" Kandy asked.

Ferdinand mumbled, "Possibly," through the burrito. "Let us review what we have and then make the decision regarding what we should trust."

Ferdinand dimmed the lights and touched the pad computer. The projected image jumped to a woman in a white uniform exiting the hospital, looking down, and running toward the open door of a silver Mercedes.

"E-Class," Kandy said, and smiled.

"I've used the timestamp on each picture, which is stored in the JPEG file, to recreate a movie in real time. This picture will hold until the next one was taken."

In fifteen seconds a new picture of the Mercedes appeared. The doors were closed.

"Did you run the plate?" Kandy asked, while the picture sat frozen on the screen.

"Detective Dreeson, do I look like a run-of-the-mill gumshoe who should be bothered with such trivia?" Ferdinand said.

She pulled out her phone to call in the plate number.

"Please check your email," Ferdinand said.

She did. "Ferd, you amaze me." She turned to Qigiq. "Came in about a minute ago."

Qigiq reached for his coffee. He was feeling better, glad he had skipped the decaf.

"Car is registered to Michaly, Brower, McKinley & Spooner," she said.

Qigiq sipped the hot liquid. "He used a company car so his wife wouldn't get suspicious."

"Or maybe throw off the tail," she said. "Which didn't work."

"We only know who owns the car," Ferdinand said. "We don't yet know who was in it."

They nodded agreement, but Qigiq would have put ten-to-one odds on Rutherford Spooner as the driver.

The picture changed to a view of a city street with both the Mercedes and a black motorcycle on the road. The light at the nearest intersection glowed red. A second motorcycle was crossing the intersection left to right, heading north.

Kandy groaned.

Qigiq said, "That's me heading to the Chinese hospital."

"You?" Ferdinand said, leaning closer to the picture.

"Yes. I was racing to the hospital to meet Kandy. We were planning to talk to the girl dressed as a nurse."

"This is quite fortunate," Ferdinand said. "It provides independent verification that the timecode embedded in these pictures is accurate."

"Glad to help," Qigiq said. But having been so close to their target and not somehow sensing it...maybe he was losing his touch.

The picture changed, the vehicles now on the highway. They exited. The Mercedes moved further ahead. One picture showed only the motorcycle, the Mercedes having disappeared around a curve—like a Hollywood chase scene in development.

The first video played. The image bounced and twisted,

clearly taken from a moving vehicle, but the HD quality was very good, even through fog roiling in from the ocean.

"I've stabilized this digitally; it will repeat in a moment," Ferdinand said. "I wanted you to see the raw material first."

The clip started again, rock solid, as if taken from a tripod.

"Nice work, Ferd," Kandy said.

The car curved right, followed by the bike.

"How fast?" Qigiq asked.

"Seventy-one miles per hour," Ferdinand answered. "Estimated from the video using the standard spacing of dashed dividing lines."

"In a hurry," Kandy said.

"The bike doesn't seem to be catching them. Why rush?" Qigiq asked.

"Speculation," Ferdinand said, rolling his burrito wrapper into a ball and tossing it into the corner basket on the first try. "They wish to lose the bike. Don't like being followed." He brushed crumbs from his white lab coat where it bulged over his belly.

"Hard to lose anyone up there on California One," Kandy said. "Nowhere to go."

"Amateurs," Ferdinand added. "They were safer on the interstate with multiple lanes and regular exits. Now they have boxed themselves in."

More images showed the vehicles climbing, the fog growing thicker.

"Where are they headed?" Qigiq asked. "Why not stay on the interstate?"

"The coast," Kandy said.

"Somewhere north of Half Moon Bay," Ferdinand said. "Otherwise it would have been wiser to remain on I-280 and travel west at CA-92."

The image switched to stable video. The Mercedes entered a sweeping turn to the left. A dark SUV appeared from around the blind corner and sideswiped the car, spinning it into the dirt. The motorcycle rolled onto the shoulder and braked to a stop, back wheel skidding on the dirt shoulder. The combination of dust and fog obscured the vehicles.

"I finished this just before you arrived," Ferdinand said.

"Where's that SUV?" Kandy said.

"It continued north after contact," Qigiq said. "Strange sensation watching a silent movie, isn't it?"

The rider stepped off his bike; the interior of the Mercedes lit up; a flash erupted from the driver's side of the Mercedes. The rider dropped to the dirt. Kandy and Qigiq jumped to their feet.

Ferdinand lowered himself into the nearest chair. "Oh my goodness."

Another flash blossomed from the driver's seat.

The SUV entered from the lower left corner of the frame. Going backwards.

"Cadillac," Kandy said.

The SUV slammed into the Mercedes. The four-wheel drive dug into the dirt of the shoulder and pushed until the Mercedes tilted over the side, then pulled away. Two men exited the vehicle and headed toward a woman in white.

She turned toward the cliff.

And ran like a ghost floating through darkness. Reached the edge. Leapt into the air like an Olympic long jumper.

Qigiq sat down.

Kandy took long slow breaths, as if meditating.

The motorcycle rider was lifted and shoved into the back seat of the SUV. It drove away. One man remained, tossed broken bumper parts over the cliff, mounted the bike, and spun the rear wheel across the area, throwing dirt and gravel in every direction.

"It will be difficult to find a blood sample there," Ferdinand said.

The bike rode south and the movie stopped on empty road, the dust drifting away from the ocean freeze-framed in the foggy air.

Ferdinand tapped the table, gazing at the screen.

Qigiq said, "Another skilled rider."

"One, two, maybe three people dead," Kandy said. "We're back on homicide detail."

There was silence except for crinkling foil as Qigiq wrapped up the last uneaten bit of his breakfast.

"Four if Mrs. Chong doesn't make it," she added.

Qigiq glanced at his watch.

"They'll never let us in," Kandy said.

Qigiq scratched his chin. Tossed the wrapped foil at the wastebasket. Missed. Stood.

"Might as well wait there as here."

Ferdinand stood with him. "You're going to talk to the girl?"

"We'll try. She's the link between Spooner and Mrs. Chong."

Kandy hadn't moved. "*If* Spooner was driving."

Qigiq retrieved the foil from the floor, backed up three paces and tried again. He was successful this time. "The girl can tell us."

"She won't," Kandy said. "She was freaking out in the chopper. Wait until detectives start asking questions."

"I suspect you have hatched a plan," Ferdinand said.

Kandy put her boots up on the table and stretched. "What do we know about our nurse?"

Qigiq leaned against the wall close to the wastebasket. "She went to see Mrs. Chong. Ferdinand is working on a translation that might tell us why. She ducked into a Mercedes. Jumped out twenty minutes later—"

"Twenty-nine minutes and forty-one seconds," Ferdinand said.

Qigiq nodded. "Shortly after that, she jumped off a cliff to escape men from a Cadillac Escalade we probably can't locate."

"Anything else?" Kandy said.

"I'd guess Asian from her size, but we don't have a good face shot: too dark at Devil's Slide. Possibly Hispanic, or African-American, or a petite Norwegian with dyed hair."

Kandy said, "Or even an Alaskan."

A cell phone showed up in Ferdinand's hand. "I'll call the hospital. They will be documenting her injuries." He headed for the door.

"And we think Spooner was in the car with her, since the vehicle is registered to his law firm."

Kandy nodded, frowning.

"You're not happy," Qigiq said. He wasn't happy either; things were moving too fast. He'd need more sleep to keep up. And Tuesday hadn't even officially opened for business.

"Bothers me that she got out of the car," Kandy said. "If it was Spooner, and they were running away together, why not stay with him?"

"He was firing a gun."

"Scared her? Pushed her out?"

"The recording showed dome light on first, gun flash maybe two seconds later."

Kandy chewed her lower lip. "Think he told her to run?"

"The car was boxed in, men coming for them. No time to do much else."

"No place to run either."

He nodded. "Well-planned ambush."

A light knock sounded on the door before it opened and Ferdinand came through. He walked directly to the pad computer and started tapping.

Qigiq glanced at Kandy and shrugged. She pulled her boots off the table.

In a few seconds the screen filled with the face of an Asian girl, perhaps twenty-five years old. She appeared to be sleeping.

The left side of her face looked like it had been splashed with purple paint.

Qigiq walked to the far end of the table and stood beside Kandy. "We've seen her."

Kandy stared at the picture.

Ferdinand waited. Then, "I have others."

"Please," Kandy said.

The next one showed deep bruises on the girl's back and right thigh.

Qigiq closed his eyes, trying to remember the face.

"What's her name?" Kandy asked.

Ferdinand said: "Jane Doe. No ID."

"How's she doing?" Kandy asked.

"Broken arm, lung damage. Stable at present, but they will be scanning for internal injuries shortly."

Qigiq opened his eyes. "Picture in Mrs. Chong's apartment." He waved his hand. "On the left."

Kandy looked at him, then spoke to Ferdinand. "You take photos of Mrs. Chong's place?"

"Detective Dreeson, my office is very thorough." He tapped the computer and images of Mrs. Chong's apartment appeared. A few taps later they were looking at a picture of two girls, perhaps in their early teens, projected beside the image of the unknown girl from the cliff.

"Dead right, Qu," Kandy said. "The one on the left when she was much younger. Do we have a name?"

Ferdinand smiled, "We are very thorough." He touched his screen and an image of the back of the photo appeared.

"Chinese?" Kandy asked.

Qigiq said, "Definitely not Alaskan Inuit."

"The language department will have something for us momentarily," Ferdinand said.

The group fell silent. Thoughtful. Gazing at the handwritten note.

Kandy said, "Our girl went to the hospital to see Mrs. Chong."

Qigiq asked, "Why now? A family visit doesn't explain the midnight crawl."

Ferdinand stood. "They should finish with the audio from her visit soon." Before he reached the door a ringtone interrupted.

Kandy pulled a phone from her jeans. "Text message from the team retrieving the car at Devil's Slide. Driver's side airbag inflated. No occupants. Close to ten thousand dollars in fifties and hundreds scattered on the sand." She lowered the phone. "The trunk is empty."

Ferdinand nodded and departed.

Qigiq said, "Let's go get my bike."

CHAPTER 20

I PUT AWAY THE PHONE I HAD BORROWED FROM BEAR, leaned against my dusty truck, and stared toward an open expanse of gray water. Bear had gotten it done through a crime reporting website with help from his biker friends around the country. I owed him another one. What the cops did with Mylin's pictures and video was now their problem.

The streets around me were devoid of traffic. Where would Mylin go? She was clearly afraid, maybe even in shock, yet had photographed a Mercedes being pushed by an angry Cadillac. I turned to the truck. A sleep-deprived guy stared back from the dark glass side panel of the Chevy.

"OK, Roberts, photographer at large, what's your next step?"

I nearly jumped out of my Pumas when a woman behind me said: "Breakfast."

I spun. Mylin was rounding the corner of a wooden fence at the edge of the parking lot. The green dress clung to her swaying torso, and a cigarette hung from the left side of her mouth. My heart pumped hard. She carried a steaming cup in each hand, and dangled a white paper bag from her left pinky. I said:

"I thought you had gone."

The half of brow not covered by hair furled. "Gone where?"

I shrugged, feeling stupid for jumping to conclusions. She handed me a coffee and half-danced, half-skipped around the front of the truck reminding me of a lonely child pretending to be happy. She slid into the passenger seat. I got behind the wheel, wondering if she was in denial about what we had seen.

Her profile with the cigarette took me back to Michigan, and the days before life got complicated.

"Can we go to a park?" she asked. "I want to be near nature."

I turned the key, trying to read her eyes. "Sure. Do you have one in mind?"

She shook her head, sending hair flying in every direction, still holding a cup in one hand, the bag in the other, and the cigarette in her mouth.

"How about we go walk the Embarcadero along the bay?"

She drew on the cigarette, its glow conjuring my photographs, and exhaled without touching it. Then she shrugged.

I drove to the multilevel garage on Howard Street. We walked two blocks to a bay still cast in mist and glowing orange in the sunrise, and sat on a bench near the ferry dock.

"Will this do?" I asked.

She nodded, but her face and eyes were as expressionless as a rock star in a Vegas wax museum. She handed me the bag in slow motion. A whimper escaped her lips. I didn't need to ask to know she had returned to Devil's Slide.

Two bites into an egg and cheese croissant she whispered: "Why did you do this?"

My mouth opened before I realized she wasn't asking me. I slid closer. Our legs touched. She sipped from her cup using two hands, then stared straight ahead and continued:

"You knew we can never get away."

I had witnessed the jump with my own eyes, yet the past tense sent shivers through me. I blamed the cool air coming off the bay. Questions formed in my head: *Who was she? Who was in the SUV? Who fired that gun? Was the motorcycle rider dead?* I took a bite of croissant, willing myself to keep my mouth shut, and waited.

Mylin eventually turned toward me, but her eyes focused out

over the water.

I said, "Would you like to walk along the bay?"

She blinked. Almost smiled. Nodded once.

I took her hand. Carrying our coffee, we strolled past the ferry terminal, away from the ballpark where the Giants played, and toward the business district. I searched for the right thing to say. This wasn't it, but she needed to know.

"Those pictures we took."

She glanced at me, her expression blank, hair back across her left eye.

"I, uh, a friend helped me. We figured a way to send them to the police anonymously."

She squeezed my hand. Holding the coffee hadn't worked, her fingers were still icy.

We walked another fifty yards before she said: "What will they do?"

"No idea. But they know something happened up on the Slide. And it wasn't an accident."

"No," she said. "Not an accident."

A street light flickered as it came on. Traffic was still light, but we were no longer alone on the sidewalk as Tuesday business stumbled into action.

"The police will want to talk to us," I ventured.

"No police," she said without breaking stride. "Very bad."

"How else can we help her?"

She stopped and turned her head to look up the street to the left, then the other way, like a kid before crossing.

"We cannot help her; she is dead."

"We can't be su—" She pressed a finger to my lips.

"Shh. Listen."

A car honked, tires whooshed behind me, a ship's foghorn bleated.

She said, "Motorbike."

I strained my ears. The deep potato-potato sound of a Harley was loudest. A sports car revved far away. Then something else—something not a car.

She said, "It's them." Color left her lips. "They..."

She closed her eyes. Her hand released mine.

I turned toward the something sound. It grew louder. A lone biker three blocks south of us was headed in our direction.

"Are they looking for you?"

She shook her head.

"But it's bad if they see you because you're supposed to be in Reno?"

She nodded fast.

I peeled off my leather jacket and flung it over her shoulders to cover a dress that might attract attention. I searched for a place to hide, but no buildings were close, just the street behind me and a picturesque view of the bay in front. Run? Bad move to *not* draw attention.

We needed to hide in the open—I had experience with that from shooting pictures.

I slipped my right hand into the jacket's outside pocket where I carried a small camera so I would never miss a picture. With my left arm, I pulled Mylin close and gazed over her head at the street. The bike was passing through an intersection.

A woman in a beige business suit walked north, heels clicking on the sidewalk. I dragged Mylin backward two steps so the woman would block the rider's line of sight.

"Ma'am, would you please take our picture?"

She studied me carefully, but slowed. She had a brown briefcase in her left hand. I pushed the camera towards her right. Instinctively she reached up to take it. "I don't know much about photog—"

"That's okay. We just want a memory of our visit."

I spun around and pulled Mylin to my chest. Her eyes popped wide with surprise. I wrapped both arms around her, easily hiding her petite frame behind my body.

Then kissed her.

Her lips were hard together. I held mine to them.

"I don't really know much about...oh my, well let me see," said the woman's voice from behind my back.

The briefcase ticked as it touched the sidewalk.

"There, it's on now."

Mylin's lips softened.

The motorbike was closer, the pitch rising as it approached.

"Okay, ready. Ahem, yes, well smi—oh that's silly."

The shutter clicked. The motorbike sailed by.

I put my energy into a firm hug and focused my attention on Mylin.

She didn't pull away.

"Let me take another one."

The bike was barely audible now. I pulled back slightly and risked a glance over my left shoulder. The rider was two lights away and accelerating.

I turned to the woman, whose face was flushed red.

"Thank you so much."

She handed me the camera and bent over to retrieve her case. "I'm glad to help." She walked over and leaned towards Mylin's ear. I stepped away, scanning the horizon for signs of the bike. When I turned back, the woman was humming to the click of her heels as she walked along the sidewalk.

Mylin suppressed a grin.

"What?"

She shook her head and remained silent.

I checked the camera. The woman had taken three decent pictures of us kissing in front of a bay painted gold by the morning sun. I held it up for Mylin.

She giggled.

"What did she say?"

Mylin whispered in my ear. "I wish my husband would kiss me like that."

"I'm sorry, I just wanted to hide you from the—"

She pressed her finger against my lips. "It was nice kiss."

I looked into the darkness of her eyes and smiled. Then, as if reflected there, Pé in her white dress leapt over a rock ledge.

CHAPTER 21

I PURCHASED TWO SANDWICHES AND A NEWSPAPER inside the ferry building so we would be prepared to wait all day if necessary. After leaving the Howard Street garage I refueled the truck and could drive to Reno and beyond. Mylin still wanted to see her grandmother with her own eyes, so we went back and parked on a narrow side street three blocks from the hospital to hide. I rifled through the paper, not expecting to find anything. But I did.

"Headline here reads: Motorcycles Pose Threat to Pedestrians. An elderly woman was injured in a hit-and-run accident, then taken to the Chinese hospital. She was unconscious at the scene."

Mylin ignored me.

I said, "You don't know who's waiting for you up there. Look what happened to—" I stopped.

"Pé disobeyed," she said, for the umpteenth time.

"You're supposed to be in Reno. What happens if they find you here?"

We sat in the back of my truck with a lightproof curtain pulled across behind the front seats: a human duck blind I often used to take photographs. People rarely noticed a parked vehicle unless they saw motion inside. In the semidarkness from the heavily tinted windows her eyes turned up towards me.

"Really, what happens?" I said softly. "Will they fire you from the orchestra?"

She stared for a moment. "No."

"Will they deport you? Send you back to—" I stopped. She

could be from a thousand places in the Far East. None of which I had ever seen.

"That is the past." She hesitated, her voice uncertain. "They will not send me there."

"Let's go back to Reno. We can call the hospital for updates."

She was squatting low, her hand absently toying with the bracelet around her left ankle. She frowned at me like I had added two plus two and got five.

"How about if I go in? No one knows me." Which wasn't true, the two guys who visited my booth would remember me.

She shook her head. "Do you speak Chinese?"

"I could take a note in for you."

She frowned again. "I must see her."

See? Of course—seeing was my specialty.

———

I walked alone through the entrance. The lobby was empty, white floor tile gleamed, lights glared above red chairs. No one occupied the desk that sat behind a cutout in the wall dividing visitors from employees. I had a black earbud in my left ear and my phone on my belt like a cowboy buckle. It had been simple to rig a cellular connection between my smartphone and a tablet computer so Mylin could see, hear, and speak while staying out of sight in the truck. Though she had suggested I was crazy, she agreed to give it a try.

I said: "Hello." Mylin's voice came through the bud: "I see an empty counter."

A middle-aged Chinese woman in a light blue smock and dark slacks came around the corner and up to the opposite side of the door-sized cutout.

"May I help you?"

I glanced at my watch: 8:24 AM. "The operator told me visiting hours start at eight. I'm here to see Mrs. Chong."

The woman, who stood a bit over five feet, ran a fingernail

coated with red and gold polish down the page of a computer printout. "Sorry, she's in ICU. Immediate family only."

"She's my grandmother."

The woman locked her eyes on me, her body language shouting that I was lying.

"By marriage."

She nodded. "Where's your wife?"

"She's working in Reno. She asked me to find out as much as I can." I hoped making a couple of true statements would help my face appear more trustworthy. I added a smile.

"You'll have to be quick," she said. "Mrs. Chong hasn't been awake much."

"But she has been?" I said. "Awake?"

The woman flipped through papers. "Check with the floor nurse for details." She pointed to my left. "Elevators are that way. Fourth floor, take this." She handed me a visitor badge that resembled a credit card with a silver clip glued on the back.

I attached it to the pocket of my leather jacket. "Thank you very much."

"Remember. Keep it short." She studied my face.

I gave her a warm good morning smile, trying to calm her intuition that I was lying.

She disappeared into a side room. I was alone in the hall. A minute later I was alone in the elevator. "Still there?"

"Yes," Mylin said. "I hope grandma is awake."

"Me too," I said, a bit surprised that the connection worked inside the elevator car.

The double doors slid opened on the fourth floor and the clean-chemical smell peculiar to hospitals wafted over me. A central nursing station to my right was occupied by half a dozen women and two men, all dressed in blue and white. I headed for it, shifting the camera slightly left and right.

"Who's that?" Mylin asked. I waited for her to elaborate. "That man at the end sitting on the red chair."

I lowered my head down, checked my watch, and whispered, "Cop."

When I reached the circular desk, I stopped and held up my visitor card. They ignored me.

I waited.

And waited.

A tall woman with red hair finally turned her head away from the conversation she was having. Her eyes landed on me. She came over. "Yes?"

"Mrs. Chong, please." I held my visitor card higher.

"Immediate family only," she said.

"I'm married to her granddaughter. The family asked me to visit to get the latest information, since I live closest."

The redhead frowned. "And you are?"

"Karl Phillips."

"And your wife's name?"

I hesitated, not knowing what name Mylin would give. To cover the passing time I turned my head to the side and coughed. The nurse stared at me like I had smallpox.

"Allergies, sorry. Must be the air."

"Tell her, 'Chi Phang Wen,'" Mylin said in my ear. "Her daughter Phing's daughter."

I repeated the names exactly as Mylin had given them to me, pronouncing each as carefully as possible.

"I see." She flipped pages, and turned a book toward me. "Sign in please. And be sure to sign out when you leave. Fifteen minute limit." She glanced at my buckle. "No cell phone calls on this floor. None. That means zero." She studied my face; I tried to look innocent and harmless. "Really. Don't break any rules. We had a...commotion on the night shift. Everyone is still on eggshells."

"Thank you." I signed *Karl Phillips* above a faint green line. By the time I looked up she had returned to chatting with her colleague, the coffee never having left her hand. Room 458 was printed at the top of the page; below it, handwritten names and times of visits were arranged in neat columns. I didn't read them, but I did stand on the balls of my feet, and tilt the book so the camera got a look.

"Son-in-law has visited," Mylin said.

She didn't continue, so I turned around and searched. Room 458 was to my right. The numbers went up in the direction of the cop in the red chair. This could get more complicated. As I approached 458, the cop lifted his eyes from a magazine. He was wearing a medium-gray business suit that was a little baggy all over. No badge or gun in sight, but I'd bet he had both.

"Hello, is this Mrs. Chong's room?"

He nodded, and directed me in with a swing of his thumb. His eyes didn't follow me, but after I walked through, I noticed the door didn't close all the way.

Mrs. Chong's bed was to my right, the head tilted up slightly. She was alone in the room. I had expected tubes and wires and machines, but there was only an IV in her right arm, and an EKG monitoring her heart with a green line stroking across a screen. She looked asleep, had a bruise on her left cheek, and was much smaller than the hospital bed.

"Oh, Laolao," came through my earbud. "What have they done?"

I walked to the left side of the bed with my back to the doorway. I touched her hand, which was cold and wrinkled but surprisingly soft, except for callouses on the index finger and thumb. I had no idea what to say, so I said, "I don't know what to say grandmother," hoping for help from Mylin.

I listened carefully. Mylin was sobbing. I glanced over my shoulder; the cop had an eye on me, but pretended not to. I said softly, "Chi Phang Wen sends her love." Mrs. Chong squeezed my hand so gently I might have imagined it.

A stream of sound filled my ear, but it wasn't English, and it was far too fast for me to repeat. I almost said Mylin's name, but caught myself.

The stream continued between sobs.

I removed the bud from my ear and leaned over to brush Mrs. Chong's hair with my fingertips. I hoped the camera angle would show Mylin what I was doing as I placed the ear bud beside Mrs. Chong's ear and raised the volume.

"I can only stay a minute grandmother," I said. "If you have a message for M...my wife, she's anxious to know if you're all right."

Mrs. Chong didn't move, except for the slow rise and fall of the white sheet over her chest. The green line on the monitor jumped in what I hoped was a normal fashion. I waited with no way to know if Mylin was talking, or if Mrs. Chong heard. I stroked her hair and watched her face for movement. Her hand grew warm in mine. I glanced back, the cop was staring down at a picture of a fast red car in a magazine, or pretending to.

Mrs. Chong's lips moved, but no sound emerged. I lifted the bud back to my ear and made sure the camera pointed at her. For he benefit of the cop I said, "I'll be back as soon as I can to check on you." In my ear Mylin said in very clear English, "Get out of there. Now!"

I jerked upright and pushed the bud tight into my ear.

"What? Why?" I whispered to the tiny microphone.

"Go. They are coming."

Go? Where was I supposed to go? I spun around. The cop was leaned back and flipping pages. I shuffled to the door and checked the hallway.

Empty.

I nodded to the cop as I walked by, trying to keep my shoes quiet on the hard tiles. "They" would use the elevator. Red Exit signs glowed at the ends of the halls. I didn't want to be seen ducking into a stairwell; the cop might follow me. I took a deep breath and turned away from the nursing station and the elevators, moving along the row of patient rooms. In the glass window at the end of the hall my reflection walked toward me. A door to my right was narrower than the rest. I grabbed the knob and begged the universe to let it be unlocked.

It rotated.

I swung the door out to the right and hid behind it. A small closet held a bucket on wheels, mop, and stacks of toilet paper. I stepped into the room, crouched and checked the reflection in the window. The elevator doors were open and two men had almost reached the sign-in counter. The redheaded nurse sipped her coffee and ignored them. The blurred reflection told me the older man had been in my booth at the art show and now owned a print of *Smoking Girl #6*. The young guy seemed stockier than the one who had twisted my arm.

"What are you doing?" Mylin insisted in my ear. "Where are you?"

I moved deeper into the closet and whispered. "Two men. I'm hiding."

"Get out of there. They must not see you."

She was right about that. Explaining why I had been at Kings Beach and was now in the Chinese Hospital would be very tricky.

I pushed the bucket partway into the hall to block the door open. The closet held no place to hide, and walking past the nursing station would attract too much attention.

The redhead was staring at the open closet door. The two men were still waiting. She placed her coffee mug on the counter and pointed to the book where they were to sign. Then she started in my direction at a brisk walk. I eased the bucket into the hallway and held the door open against its spring with my left arm. Her soft shoes swished up the hall.

I smiled when she came around the edge of the door.

She gave me a stern look, but before she had a chance to speak I held a finger to my lips, motioned her into the tiny closet, and let the door close. We stood where the mop bucket had been. A sliver of light slipped beneath the door

I whispered: "Are there members of your family that you would rather not see?"

"What?" Thankfully, she automatically whispered back.

"Those Asian men who just came in. They're unhappy that I married into the family. It's better if they don't know I'm here." I crossed my fingers and hoped luck was on my side. "I had to come here myself because we, uh, can't really trust what they tell us."

"Oh...oh, I see."

"Where are you?" Mylin shouted into my ear. "Who are you talking to?'

The redhead studied me. I needed her mind at ease. I said:

"The police think something criminal might have happened to my grandmother. I'm glad they put an officer here to watch her room. But if those guys see me, there's a good chance there'll be a scene that shouldn't happen inside a hospital."

She chewed her lower lip for a few seconds. Then said:

"My brother-in-law is like that. Every time he sees me he makes snide remarks until there's an argument. He didn't want me to marry Mark because a nursing career isn't good enough— I'm only a lowly blue collar worker bee. He needs to get over it; we've been married nearly two years."

She took a breath, which gave me an opening.

"Can you help me sneak out?"

She smiled for the first time. "Oh, that's easy." Turning away she brushed my chest with her back. The woody aroma of forest after a rain filled my nostrils. Packages made crackling noises as she ruffled through them. She handed me a flat, stiff bundle.

"Put this on," she whispered.

I pulled at the material and it fell open into a blue lab coat. I slipped it on over my leather jacket.

"And this." A cap. "And this too." I held the flat mask up to my face and she tied it expertly behind my head.

"OK," she said. "Here's what we do. I'll open the door and check to make sure those guys are in Mrs. Chong's room. That's who they've been coming to see. Twice a day."

They were watching the old woman closely. That motorcycle behind the Mercedes hadn't been a coincidence. It had been waiting.

She continued, "When I nod, step into the hallway and walk beside me."

"Thank you," I said, the sound muffled by the mask.

"Once you're in the elevator, take that stuff off, and leave it at the front desk."

"I really appreciate your help."

"Don't mention it. My brother-in-law is a jackass too. I completely understand."

She held up a finger. I steadied my breathing. After a few seconds that felt like an hour she lowered her finger and we stepped out of the closet. She positioned herself between me and the door to Mrs. Chong's room. The cop was flipping pages. I pushed the bucket into the closet with my toe and eased the door closed.

As we started toward the elevator the redhead, whose name I still didn't know, said: "Doctor Mathews, Mrs. Chong remains unconscious. Vital signs are normal. The I.V. is working with no trouble and she makes sounds, but nothing intelligible so far. In the next room is Mrs. Fischer. She gives us all kinds of trouble, but her heart monitor hasn't detected another episode since last night..."

I nodded my head at regular intervals, trying to appear thoughtful.

The door to Mrs. Chong's room was half open. I forced myself not to look in, but caught a glimpse of a body on either side of the bed. I gritted my teeth and hoped the old guy didn't recognize me.

At the elevator my redheaded friend stopped talking in mid-sentence and held out her hand. We shook business style.

"If you need help again, call this floor, extension 4401. Ask for Malissa, with an 'A.' I'll come down and figure a way to get you up here."

"I can't thank you enough," I said through the mask.

She smiled. "That was intense. But sort of fun." She blinked twice. "I need coffee."

She walked away as the space between the elevator doors narrowed.

I slipped the cap off and struggled to untie the mask. As the car jostled to a stop I slipped out of the blue gown and folded it into a crude rectangle. From the rear of the car I waited for the doors to slide open, then surveyed the hall. Empty.

I walked to the unmanned counter and placed the blue clothing in a pile to one side. A woman's voice in a back office drifted toward me.

"Another one? Those things should be illegal."

"Less dangerous than a swimming pool according to those Freakonomics guys in Chicago," a male voice said.

"People don't shoot themselves cleaning a pool."

I frowned, wondering—

"Where are you?" Mylin insisted in my left ear.

I hurried through the double doors into the long shadows of tall buildings created by morning light.

CHAPTER 22

QIGIQ SAT IN A CONFERENCE ROOM LIT only by the projection of the frozen image of a silver Mercedes being pushed over a cliff by a full-size SUV. Kandy chewed her lower lip. Ferdinand alternated between scratching his beard and rubbing eyes circled with fatigue.

"But the airbag went off," Kandy said.

Ferdinand nodded. "Yes. This implies the driver was in the car upon impact."

"He for sure was in the car when it was pushed," Qigiq said. "Any chance he got out before it hit the water?"

Ferdinand rubbed his right cheek. "Open the door and dive from a falling car like a Hollywood stuntman? Possible, if he were very fast, and out near the top. But then, why did so many airbags deploy?"

"We could send a team up to look for blood on the rocks," Kandy said.

"And the gun," Qigiq added. "Where's the gun?" He paused. "And the money. Ten thousand blowing around the beach. Is that all of it, or is there more? Maybe a lot more?"

The room was quiet save for the humming fan cooling the projector.

Ferdinand stepped the video backwards until a face became visible through the open driver's window of the Mercedes. The image was dark, fuzzy, and taken from a distance.

"Can't swear it's Spooner," Kandy said.

"Should we show it to his wife?" Qigiq asked. He slid his chair closer to the computer and moved the video backwards one frame at a time. The SUV moved forward and the Mercedes followed as if attached by a powerful magnet. The vehicles separated. He continued until the driver's window filled with a flash. He moved the video forward and back until the flash lit the face behind the wheel. "How's that?"

Ferdinand said, "Let's ask her."

Kandy made a call. Halfway through she grinned and shook her head. Hung up.

"You won't believe this."

They waited.

"Our friend Mrs. Spooner was in Jasik's office before eight this morning, demanding to know why we haven't found her husband. He's having her escorted over."

Qigiq glanced at his watch. "Maybe we should head to the hospital and try to talk to the girl they airlifted in?"

Ferdinand shook his head. "Detectives, you really should be here for the identification. I must return to the lab."

"Nice try, Qu" Kandy said. "Thanks for the video analysis, Ferd."

The door closed behind Ferdinand.

"You think it's Rudy?" Kandy asked.

"The girl on the cliff matches the pictures in Rudy's contract, what we can see of her. The car is registered to his company."

"So where is he?" she asked.

Qigiq studied the picture. "Is the seatbelt buckled?"

They both stared. Kandy walked up to the projection and touched the screen.

"Here, I think."

"So if it's buckled at the top, hard to imagine he was able to get out fast."

She nodded. "So he went down with the car?"

"Yeah."

"But now he's gone."

"And the seatbelt?" Qigiq asked.

She frowned in thought. "You mean, is it still buckled?" She slipped her smartphone from the front pocket of her jeans and pressed it to her ear.

Female voices approached from outside the conference room. Qigiq overheard, "Why does Mr. Jasik keep sending me away?" just before three quick knocks rattled the door.

"Come in."

The door swung inward and Mrs. Spooner flew through the opening wearing a gray jacket and slacks. Molly stopped in the doorway and let the door swing halfway closed. Her hair was down to her shoulders today. She smiled quick and ducked away.

"Not you two," Mrs. Spooner said. "Have you found my husband? You're supposed to be looking for him. What are you doing in here watching..." her eyes turned to the screen. For a brief moment her mouth stopped moving as she studied the image. She took a small step forward. "Is that Rutherford? That looks like..." She blinked long, probably fake, lashes.

"Thank you for coming, Mrs. Spooner," Qigiq said.

Kandy stood with the phone to her ear and moved to the back of the conference room.

"Is that?" Mrs. Spooner began.

"Please sit down, Mrs. Spooner," Qigiq said. "We would like you to help us identify—"

"Is he with that slut?" she interrupted.

Qigiq coughed.

"He is!" She crossed her arms on her chest. "That worthless two-timing prick."

Qigiq tried again. "Please, Mrs. Spooner, have a seat."

"I don't need to sit down. That's Rutherford. So where is she?"

Mrs. Spooner's eyes flashed from the screen to Qigiq and back, as if she were daring him to speak.

"First, Mrs. Spooner. Would you please identify the man driving the silver Mercedes?"

"Identify him? Of course, you fool. That's Rudy and his company car. He drives that monstrous penis-extension whenever he wants to impress the whores."

"Thank you, Mrs. Spooner."

Kandy returned to the table. "Unbuckled," she said.

Qigiq nodded slightly.

"Where is he?" Mrs. Spooner demanded.

Qigiq said, "We know where he *was*."

"And where is she?"

"If by she," Kandy interjected, "you mean an Asian girl. We do know where she is."

"Good," Mrs. Spooner said, still standing. "Then Rudy will be there too." Mrs. Spooner moved close to the screen. "What's that bright light?"

"This is an ongoing investigation," Kandy said.

"So?" Mrs. Spooner said to the screen.

"That means all information must remain confidential," Qigiq said.

Mrs. Spooner spun on her heel. "You mean you won't tell me where he is? I'm his wife. You tell me right this instant or I'll have my lawyer in here—"

Kandy stood. "Enough lady. Sit down and listen."

"You can't talk to me like that. I'll have your job."

"You couldn't handle my job," Kandy said. "You want information? Sit down and stop talking. We would like you to identify someone."

Mrs. Spooner's eyes flashed to Qigiq, who was studying a ball point pen, and back to Kandy. "Well I never. Wait until the girls at the club hear about this." She stomped the length of the table and sat at the far end away from the screen.

"Thank you," Kandy said.

Qigiq swiped the surface of the pad computer to move the

video backwards until the girl was on the screen, then played it.

"There's that bitch," Mrs. Spooner said.

"Who is she?" Kandy asked.

"You don't know? What kind of detectives are you?"

Kandy sighed loudly. "We are the kind of detectives who want you to tell us if *you* know who this person is."

Mrs. Spooner frowned. "No, I don't know exactly who she is. I know we met her after a concert." She studied their faces. "You know, when the patrons who donate money to bring these foreign orchestras to town get to go backstage for cheap wine and crappy food and talk to the *artistes*."

Qigiq and Kandy remained silent.

Mrs. Spooner touched a pink-painted fingertip to pink-painted lips. "It was early in the summer, a concert by an all-girl band Rudy wanted to hear. He has a thing for Asians, you know, that yellow fever "preference" that runs rampant in the Bay Area." She waved her hand. "All that exotic, submissive crap. They think every Asian woman is a geisha trained to bring them pleasure."

"That's where you first met her?" Kandy asked.

Mrs. Spooner nodded. "Yes." She was quiet. "I saw her again at another concert a few weeks ago. The three of us chatted over wine." She grew quiet again. "From those pictures I gave you, apparently Rudy saw more of her." She gazed down at the floor.

"But you recognize her?" Qigiq asked.

"She moves with a grace that's evident even in your horrible video. That's her."

"Do you have a name?" Kandy asked.

"It was a one-syllable Asian name. Pi or Pee or maybe Pay. Yes, I remember teasing Rutherford that if he ever touched a foreign girl I would make him pay."

No one laughed.

"So where is she?" Mrs. Spooner asked. "You said you

knew."

Qigiq said, "She's in the hospital."

Rachel Spooner showed surprise and frowned at the same time, giving her face the overemphasized features of a stage actor. "And my Rudy?"

He ran the video forward.

Mrs. Spooner inhaled and held her breath. Softly, she said, "Is he dead?"

In a matter-of-fact monotone, Kandy said: "The car was found in two feet of water on an ocean beach. Rutherford Spooner wasn't in it." She paused. "We haven't yet located his body."

Mrs. Spooner appeared to deflate for a brief instant, then sat bolt upright. "So, you still haven't found my husband. Then what are you doing here?" She pointed to the door with a pink-painted nail. "Go look for him."

———

At least it wasn't a hassle getting rid of her," Kandy said as she flipped open the driver's door of her Mini with one finger and hopped in.

"I'm grateful, but the Captain isn't going to like us," Qigiq said.

"He'll like us fine when we figure out what's going on."

The car backed out slowly then leapt forward like a compressed spring being released. They rode in silence through the city as Kandy wound her way toward the UCSF Medical Center. She stopped at a red traffic light, the fifth car in line.

"Did he survive?" she asked.

"Let's assume no. Who would have known about the accident and been able to get down there to remove the body?"

"The perps knew. And whoever sent us the pictures." The light turned green.

"Who would have known in advance?"

Kandy upshifted. "Someone watching when they left the

Chinese Hospital."

"Say I buy that. How did they get the body off the beach? There's no way down without mountaineering equipment."

Kandy made a left turn at Van Ness. "Had to be a boat."

"How about divers?" Qigiq asked.

Her lips pressed together. "Maybe." She stopped and drummed a rhythm on the steering wheel with her index fingers.

"How about they dragged the body and money out of the car and swam a mile north or south? Walked out and drove away."

Kandy made a tick tick tick sound with her tongue. "No boat? Can't say why, but I think there was a boat. It's faster. Outdrives can get in close, even beach. Drag Spooner out, or his body, the money, then idle fifty yards offshore, and float away like a hundred sport-fishing yachts."

"Easy way to hide," Qigiq said. "Right in the open."

"Why leave ten grand in the sand?"

"Only one reason I can think of," he said. "In a hurry."

She slipped the black car into a street parking spot across from the ER entrance.

"So Rudy was alive," she said. "Not much reason to be in a ten-thousand-dollar hurry in the middle of the night with a dead body."

Qigiq stepped to the sidewalk and closed the door softly.

"Why try to kill him, then keep him alive?"

She walked around to his side and leaned against the car. "Why bother with the body at all? Why not just take the money and leave the body for us? Car goes over cliff. Driver dies. No big deal."

"Do you think they know we have that video?"

She shook her head. "Not a chance. They were too careless. I bet they don't even know it was recorded."

He sat on the front of the car, the hood still warm from engine heat. The warmth suggested its opposite. He said:

"In the winter, watch the snow."

"Has to be an Alaska saying," she said, digging deep into her pocket. "I'll bet it means something like the snow can reveal the past if you read it right. In the winter here we watch the rain, when we can see it through the fog." She extracted a green mint and unwrapped it, stuffed the paper back into her pocket.

"How much money was in the trunk?" he asked.

She rolled the mint over her tongue. "My guess, everything missing from Spooner's account. Close to a quarter million. More if he tapped accounts we don't know about yet."

"Then he's alive, takes the money from the trunk, spills ten grand from an open zipper or a high wind; no time to clean up, races to the boat."

She bit through the mint with an audible crunch. "Who's the skipper?"

CHAPTER 23

IT TOOK TWENTY MINUTES to locate the name of the doctor who had treated the young woman brought in by helicopter, and another twenty waiting for Doctor Simmons to find time between his patients. They waited in the emergency room area with a dozen others, including a woman with two children, while Kandy consumed mints as fast as she could unwrap them.

The doctor erupted through a pair of swinging doors.

"Hello detectives, yes I treated the young woman. From what I understand she is lucky to be alive after such a fall."

"Fall?" Kandy said.

"Her guardian told me they were hiking at night up near Devil's Slide. One moment she was admiring the moon and the next, she slipped. Apparently it took hours to retrieve her and get her here for treatment."

Kandy's eyes flashed to Qigiq. She said: "But the car?"

"He didn't mention a car."

"Did the emergency crew mention a car?" Qigiq asked.

Doctor Simmons frowned. "I didn't talk to the crew directly. What's this about a car?"

Kandy said, "There was an auto accident in the area. We thought it might be related."

"I see," the doctor said. "Well, Miss Zhang's injuries were nothing like those from a motor vehicle accident, and believe me, I see plenty here in San Francisco. From a medical standpoint, those self-driving cars can't get here soon enough."

"Zhang?" Qigiq said.

The doctor turned. "Yes, Pé Chu-Zhang. I remember the

name clearly on the discharge papers."

"She's been discharged *already?*" Kandy said, a bit loudly for a hospital.

"Against my recommendation. She hadn't been conscious long, and her back was badly bruised. I was concerned about internal injuries and advised keeping her here for observation. But he insisted she be transferred."

"Her guardian?" Kandy said.

"Yes. An Asian man of about 50, gray hair, quite professional, brought in her work visa and medical records. Those records showed she was up to date on vaccinations required in the U.S., so I didn't need to be concerned about imported infections. They also contained a medical power of attorney."

"What about—" Qigiq began.

"The girl said very little, and none of it in English. I tried to persuade her to stay with us, but she deferred to the gentleman."

"Do you know where they took her?" Kandy asked.

Doctor Simmons shook his head. "My nurse rolled her out of here in a wheelchair as required by protocol. That's the last I saw of her."

Qigiq said: "You mentioned her injuries were nothing like a motor vehicle accident."

The doctor hesitated. "Correct."

"She was present at a crime scene," Qigiq said. "It's important we understand what happened."

"Motor vehicle trauma is directional, typically forward against a seat belt and airbag as the vehicle rapidly decelerates in the collision."

Kandy leaned against the wall of the hallway.

"Miss Zhang's, on the other hand, were everywhere. One side of her face was hairline shattered like an eggshell, but still intact. Remarkably, her nose wasn't broken. She had rolled, because gravel was embedded in gashes on her knees, hip, shoulder. X-rays indicate one ankle was severely strained, but not broken. Something hard stopped her descent, and in doing so bruised her back in multiple locations. It's here that I am most concerned, swelling in the spinal region can have tragic consequences, including paralysis of the limbs."

"So she should be under observation?" Qigiq said.

"Most certainly," Simmons replied. "She needs to be in a good hospital and monitored carefully. But she was conscious and refused to stay. I can't hold someone against their will, no matter how important I think it is. Except—"

Kandy reached into her pocket. "Except if you suspect abuse?"

"Correct," Simmons said. "But Miss Zhang's injuries were completely consistent with an outdoor fall."

"I see," Qigiq said.

"However..." Simmons said more softly.

Kandy stopped her arm moving the mint.

The doctor swept his eyes up and down the hallway.

"This girl has been injured before."

Kandy's arm hung in midair. Qigiq didn't move.

Simmons continued. "She has scars." He pointed at his brown wingtip shoes. "Soles of the feet."

Kandy slipped the unwrapped mint back into her pocket.

"What can you tell us?" Qigiq asked.

"I can only speculate," Simmons said. "Burns. Razor cuts. These are consistent with self-inflicted injuries. Often seen in teenagers. Girls mostly. Have you read the book *Prozac Nation?*"

Qigiq shook his head.

"Individuals with certain kinds of personality disorders, borderline usually, but also depression, PTSD, schizophrenia, are prone to deliberate self-harm. DSH. Feeling the pain is therapeutic for them." He paused. "Or this may be something else."

"Like what?" Kandy asked, still holding up the wall.

"Pure speculation?" Simmons asked.

Kandy nodded. "Pure speculation. We're not taking notes."

"Pimps torture their prostitutes with similar techniques. We see them here in the ER when things go too far. Makes them work hard and remain obedient. But of course, pimps don't want to mark the body; it has far too much street value."

Kandy's breathing deepened. Qigiq tried to release the tension in his jaw. Silence stretched across seconds.

"There's something else," Simmons said. He turned and started down the tiled hallway.

Kandy pulled away from the wall, caught Qigiq's eye.

They followed Simmons past a row of curtained rooms, beyond a nursing station where he nodded to an African-American nurse wearing a maroon top, around a corner past a wheeled machine with a dozen knobs, and into a dark room lined with white panels. Two of the panels held X-rays hanging from silver clips. One of the panels was lit, backlighting a shadowy image Qigiq guessed was a lung.

Simmons flicked off the box, found a large yellow envelope, withdrew a film and slipped it onto an empty panel. He reached under the ledge. The box lit up.

"Miss Zhang's ankle," he announced. "I had this printed from our digital system. Sometimes I prefer film."

Qigiq stared at the picture, found the foot, the angle of the ankle, impressed that doctors could interpret these shadows.

"We suspected a fracture because of the extent of the swelling. But the X-ray reveals nothing. If there is a fracture, it's not visible from these angles. She is a strong woman who, according to the records, is a month shy of her 24th birthday."

Kandy slipped the postponed mint from her pocket to her mouth. "But?"

"I thought her feet were somewhat small when I examined her, but naturally I was focused on her injuries, especially the spine and the ankle."

"And this X-ray tells you something?" Qigiq said.

Simmons picked up a blue ballpoint pen missing its cap and used the writing end to point.

"Notice this curve. And the shape of the bones of the toes."

Qigiq studied the ghostly shadows. The toe bones reminded him of a claw.

"Not right?" Kandy asked.

"Unusual," Simmons said. "I've only ever seen it in a textbook."

"Rare disease?" Qigiq asked.

"Not sure I'd call it that," the doctor said. "And not as rare as one might hope."

Kandy moved closer to the film, tilted her head left, then right.

"Can't be," she said.

"The practice wasn't outlawed in China until nineteen forty-nine. After lasting a thousand years," Simmons said. "Cultural habits die hard."

Qigiq looked from one to the other in confusion.

"Are you sure, Doctor?" Kandy said.

"I need more scans. And would prefer to consult an expert, if I can locate one. But I am suspicious."

"Of what?" Qigiq said.

Simmons said, "This girl's feet were bound as a child. Perhaps for a year, maybe two. Then it must have been stopped, or the damage would be more severe."

Kandy's breath hissed out like a deflating tire.

———

They waited across the street from the hospital, sitting side by side on the hood of Kandy's Mini. Qigig absently stroked his chin. Kandy chewed gum, two sticks at a time.

Qigiq said, "There's one thing bothering me."

"Besides that mysterious guardian?"

"Spooner couldn't have known in advance his car was going to be pushed over a cliff at a particular curve on California Highway 1."

"Agreed. That had to be a surprise."

"But we think he survived?"

"Yeah," she said. "I've been thinking about that. The car was sitting in the ocean like a rowboat. Why didn't it flip over in the fall? Crush him." Her jaw worked the gum.

"You've figured it out?"

"We have to check the car. I'm thinking Spooner knew something about driving, and when he was being pushed over the edge, he slammed the transmission in reverse; and floored it."

Qigiq pulled a rumpled sheet of paper from his back pocket and scribbled on it with a tiny pencil.

"You always write things down?"

"You're going to tell me why he would do that. I'm preparing to take note of your explanation." He smiled.

"You ever watch racers go down sand dunes?"

The thousand mile race down the Baja peninsula in Mexico that tortured man and machine for days on end came to mind.

She continued. "If it's steep, don't brake. Too much chance of rolling over the nose."

"You think Spooner accelerated backwards to keep the car from going end over end?"

"That Mercedes is a rear-wheel-drive coupe. I would have. If the car is sitting in reverse, the odds go way up."

Warmth from the hood rose up through his body. He checked his watch: 9:30 A.M. He said:

"But."

"Ferd is analyzing the crash dynamics."

"Still leaves me with a question," Qigiq said. "Somehow Spooner makes it to the water alive and conscious. The girl isn't there; he figures the bad guys grabbed her."

"And?"

"We're speculating that a boat picked him up."

"Good a guess as any," she said, staring in the direction of the low-hanging sun.

"So, if Spooner didn't know where he was going to be and therefore had no plan to rendezvous in advance, how did the boat find him?"

The sound of cracking gum filled the air. "Cell phone."

"Probability of sufficient coverage on that tiny stretch of beach, sitting below a wall of rock?"

Kandy hopped off the hood. "Maybe the boat was patrolling the coast, waiting for him."

He faced her. "How much coastline was it watching? What are the odds it was close? Where, in fact, was Spooner headed before his trip was interrupted?"

"That's more than one question," she said with a grin.

"What's for breakfast?" he added.

"We had breakfast in Ferd's office."

"Brunch then."

She pulled open the driver's door. "Stress eating works for me. Let's go."

CHAPTER 24

MR. WU PACED THE SEMIPRIVATE ROOM located in a remote wing at the rear of the first floor. Right beside the alley. The shirt beneath his suit coat was beginning to stick to his back in the stuffy space, made worse by the presence of four people. His friend Fan had been most helpful in arranging admission; he would send the good doctor proper compensation for his discretion.

He turned at the locked entrance door and walked slowly back towards the covered window. The room was lit by fluorescent tubes that cast sharp shadows from the stark white furnishings. Lying in the first bed was a boy—some would say young man—with a collapsed lung and a hole in his chest. He was conscious, and breathing with the assistance of a machine whose hoses reached down his throat.

A fool.

Four more steps took him to the second bed where a badly battered girl lay connected to a heart monitor and an IV drip. Not only had she not followed orders, she had forgotten her familial duty and willfully disobeyed him.

He reached the window; stared at its pale tan shade; imagined his Cadillac parked in the alley on the other side. He felt exposed here and wished to leave. But these two must be dealt with.

He sighed and turned around.

Across from the beds sat a second young man slightly older than the others. He hadn't been involved. His mistake was that he had not anticipated correctly, instead spending his time playing with motorbikes like an excited teenager. The man doubted that either boy would ever be dependable; yet, they were his blood. They must learn. Eventually he would die, and they must be ready.

He crossed to the girl and stared into her eyes. She blinked but did not turn away. He reached for her left hand, held it in his, then slowly squeezed the fingers together.

"What did you think you were doing, Pé?" He squeezed harder. "What if you had damaged your hand?" Harder still.

She winced and twisted away from his gaze.

"How would you be able to play the violin you love so much?"

She squealed.

He held his grip. "That ridiculous Western music you have worked so hard to master would all stop," he released her, "if you injured even one finger. And where would you be? Another Chinese whore begging to marry anyone who would have her."

He placed his palms on the bed on either side of her prone body, then bent forward until his nose was within inches of the mottled black and blue of her damaged cheek. He waited until she turned to him.

"You know you must be punished. But first heal, so you can perform. The concert is soon. You must be present."

He straightened.

"What do you think, my little violinist in whom I have invested so much? Will your Mr. Spooner try again? Or will he pay as instructed?"

She pressed her eyes closed, and didn't speak.

"He knows much about you, doesn't he? What can he prove? And who will he tell?"

He was letting them hear his thoughts. The children needed to understand what mattered—and what didn't. They were no longer teenagers; he was growing weary of repeating the lesson.

He paced to the locked door before turning to the second

bed. He crossed his arms.

"And you get yourself shot."

The young man's eyes tracked to the older man's face. He said with some energy: "We didn't know he was armed," his voice understandable, despite the tube.

The man nodded. "You also did not know there are eighty-five guns for every one hundred people in America. This is a land of deadly weapons, Tuson. Assume everyone is armed. Sun Tzu tells us: know your enemy and know yourself—you will not be imperiled in a hundred battles."

The man moved around the bed.

"Spooner continues to offer resistance. But this situation is the result of Pé's disobedience. You were the one to suffer, Tuson. You suggest what should be done with her."

Tuson's eyes struggled to see the girl in the next bed, but his head couldn't turn enough with the tubes attached.

A soft knock interrupted.

This was unsettling. Only Doctor Fan knew who was in this room.

He reached into his jacket for his smartphone. No messages. He returned the phone and withdrew a silver automatic. He stepped to the side of the door and waved his hand at the young man sitting opposite the beds.

The man rose and walked to the locked door. He said: "May I help you?"

A female voice said, "I have a message for Mr. Wu. Doctor Fan sent me. It is urgent."

The young man turned to Mr. Wu, who nodded, and took a step back.

The young man unlocked the door and eased it open slightly. A hand with light green nail polish reached in holding a cell phone. He took it. The hand disappeared and shoes tapped away down the hall. The young man pushed the door closed, and locked it.

Wu put his weapon away and reached for the phone. A small plastic animal that matched the green nail polish dangled from a short silver chain.

He pressed the phone to his ear. "Yes?"

"I assume you are standing in a room with a gunshot victim."

"Who is this?"

"A guy who can guess you would choose the Chinese hospital."

"I'm sorry. You must have the wrong number. I have no idea what you are talking about," Mr. Wu said. He noticed the other three staring at him and stood slightly taller.

"It was a nine-millimeter round from a Glock."

"I'm sorry, I can't help you."

"It's difficult to hide a man who's been shot. Word gets around in hospitals. People whisper. A lawyer calls and asks the right questions, he gets answers."

"I still can't help you."

"Then tell someone who *can* help me that I know Pé is there, and I'd like to propose a trade."

Who had such information? He crossed the room to the side of Pé's bed.

"I'm sorry, I didn't hear clearly, would you please repeat that?"

He held the phone to Pé's ear. The recognition was clear in her eyes. He took it away before she could speak.

"Mr. Spooner, you wish to trade? I am sorry, but that is not possible."

The man on the other end of the line laughed in Wu's ear. Then said:

"Here's the deal for your boss. Pé comes with me of her own free will; I don't go to the police with the sordid details of your little blackmail business."

Wu was irritated this naive American would think he had a

boss. He took a slow breath through his nose to relax. *A minute of restraint will prevent a hundred hours of sadness.* Then he said:

"You prefer not to sign the generous offer in our contract?"

"I prefer to shoot holes in your contract," the man said, then the line went dead.

Wu waited. It didn't reconnect. He brought the phone away from his ear and examined the little green animal. It had four arms, but the front two were short, like certain dinosaurs.

He turned to the young man, again seated against the wall, and held the phone out.

"Find out whose phone this is. Then we will go find Mr. Spooner."

CHAPTER **25**

I WALKED OUT AS THE SLIDING GLASS DOOR of the entrance to the Chinese hospital slid open, glad to be away from the men upstairs visiting Mrs. Chong. A narrow beam of sunlight streaking between buildings blinded me. My toe rammed the base of a support pillar; I tumbled forward and landed on my right shoulder, my spine vibrating.

The street rested in deep shadows from three-story stucco and brick buildings of cream and gray. Three middle-aged Asian women stood at the bus stop to my right. I stood carefully and went left toward my truck. A black Jaguar driven by a white-haired woman shot past. She didn't look my way.

I tapped softly on the driver's glass to let Mylin know I was back.

No response.

I walked to the back, as if I had just parked and needed to retrieve a package from the rear. I knocked softly on the back door with one knuckle.

Nothing.

I whispered into the microphone of my ear bud.

"Mylin, can you hear me?"

No response.

I checked the phone, it still had a connection.

I scanned both sides of the street. A red car moved through an intersection guarded by stop signs fifty yards away. The three women at the bus stop were gone. I lifted the handle to the rear door. It opened when it should have been locked. I stuck my head in and let my eyes adjust to the darkness of the interior. The astringent odor of paint thinner irritated my nose. Mylin wasn't on the makeshift bed created from packing blankets where I had left her.

My heart hammered as I imagined her being abducted while I rode down the elevator. If they had dragged her into a vehicle, she could be miles away. I crawled inside. The paintings on the left were neatly stacked and nothing was broken. If there had been a struggle, it had been brief.

I sat on the blankets and crossed my legs.

Sleep tried to overwhelm me, so I stared at light leaking around the curtain. The tablet computer was stuffed beside the passenger seat—she had no way to contact me.

I suppressed words my mother didn't like me using. Now what?

A scraping sound sent alarm bells through me. Another. From inside the truck. I turned to the pictures. Dozens of large prints leaned against the side over my kiteboard, strapped in so they...the strap was missing.

I shifted away and looked for a weapon. Nothing. Not even a wrench. My tools were in a gray plastic box buried behind the front seat. I made my way to the back of the truck without taking my eyes off the paintings. In one motion I opened the back door and leapt to the street, slamming it behind me.

I ran for half a block, ducked between two parked cars, and faced the rear doors of my truck. What was I going to do if a man with a gun appeared? As I was about to move further away, the rear door inched open. I dropped lower to stay out of sight. A hand appeared. A small hand. With black fingernails. I wracked my brain. What color was Mylin's nail polish? Not black. I would have remembered black.

A dark eye appeared in the opening. The door opened another inch. The side-swept hair was unmistakable.

I stood and headed toward the truck. When she recognized me her lips widened into a huge smile and she ran to meet me like a child welcoming daddy home.

She squeezed her body against me. "I was so scared."

I held her. "Maybe we should get out of here."

"Reno. Please. We must get to Reno," she said into my chest.

I lifted her hand; stared at her black nails.

"That little store opened. I painted them for Laolao."

——————

Ducking the guys in the hospital somehow reminded me that phones could be tracked when the GPS was on, or when they connected to cell towers. So mine was now off as I drove one-way streets trying to find a highway east. Mylin remained quiet. Finally the Bay Bridge towers became visible and I worked the truck onto one of five mostly empty lanes leading away from the city.

As I reached for the radio Mylin said: "I saw them."

"We should go to the police."

"No," she shouted, kicking the dash for emphasis. The door to the glove box sprang open. She pushed it back into place.

I drove in silence. A car pushed over a cliff. A man shot. I was certain the police could handle this better than we could. I finally ventured a quiet:

"Why?"

She searched my face. I stared at the maroon minivan in front of us.

"Nothing good will happen," she said.

"Why did you unlock the truck?"

"I saw my father."

I flicked on my left turn signal and changed lanes. "Then what?"

"He disappeared into the alley beside the hospital."

It hit me. "You were going to run?"

Her head bobbed.

"But you decided to hide?"

"I got out to watch the people in the alley."

My truck tires hummed loudly on the rain grooves in the concrete highway. I needed a question with an easy answer.

"How many?"

She was quiet, eyes closed, pointing into space with her index finger. "Four."

I tried to remember how many had been at Devil's Slide in the darkness.

"Do you know them?"

Her eyes remained closed. I guessed she was gazing into the alley. "It was very dark back there. I was hiding. They carried someone." She whipped her face towards me, eyes wide. "I think it was Pé."

A girl jumping off a cliff—hospitals had morgues. I glanced at Mylin; she was staring out the windshield.

"Hunched over. Black suit. He was there."

I pressed. "And the other two."

"Him. Him," she said loudly, her eyes vacant, fixed somewhere near Mars. She leaned back against her seat and closed her eyes again. She was shivering.

The car wasn't cold inside, but I cranked up the heater anyway.

"And the fourth?"

Suddenly she relaxed and turned to me. "I didn't see. He was in passenger seat of the SUV, far back in alley. I crawled here and hid behind your pictures." She paused. "I forget phone. Forget to lock."

"That's okay," I said, glad no one had gone looking for the person in my truck. "You're safe."

She leaned her head back. Her expression suggested that she didn't believe me. She remained quiet. Five miles later she was asleep.

———

Mylin slept through Vacaville, and Sacramento, and the climb to Donner Pass named for the 87 pioneers devastated by a snowstorm back in the nineteenth century. I neared the summit and took the exit to the rest stop situated near the pass at 7227 feet. As the truck slowed, she opened her eyes.

"Where are we?"

"About an hour from Reno."

She squinted at the sunshine. "What time is it?"

I glanced at the dash. "Almost noon."

She hopped from the truck and headed toward the restrooms. I got out, locked the truck to protect my belongings from casual rest-stop thieves, and headed there myself. When I returned, she was sitting on the front bumper rubbing her knees, still wearing the green dress from her performance pulled up to mid-thigh.

"Are you hungry?" I asked.

She looked at me like she hadn't heard the question, then jumped up and reached for my hand. "First." She dragged me around to the back of the truck.

Having asked, I realized I was starving. What was the closest town on our way to Reno? Truckee. There must be a restaurant in Truckee.

She climbed through the rear door and turned to face me. "Come here."

I was dazed from driving and the bizarre night we had been through, so crawling in behind her in the parking lot of a rest area felt normal. I closed the rear barn door from the inside and locked it. By the time I turned around she had slipped off her dress, leaving black panties and heels. She was kneeling on the makeshift bed and pressing the roof with both hands as if holding it up.

My eyes took in her sensual curves and locked onto high round breasts. I realized I was staring, looked down, and focused on the metal braid encircling her right ankle. I said:

"That's a lovely bracelet."

She glanced down at the green stone. "I wear it always." She lifted her head, brushed back the hair on the left side of her face, and said:

"Make love with me."

My thoughts arrived as if flowing through viscous fluid. She was full of surprises, but nothing had prepared me for a proposition out of the clear blue sky.

"What?"

She extended both arms toward me and opened a palm to reveal a gold foil package.

"Come. We have joy."

"What?" I said again. "I mean, why? No wait, why now?"

"We must."

I squatted on my heels, my eyes roving her face and body of their own accord.

She lowered her arms. "You not want me?"

"Of course I want you." I had wanted *Smoking Girl* since taking her picture in Ann Arbor. I had touched her in my dreams. But this agenda was for a meeting I hadn't been invited to. I said:

"I don't understand."

She frowned. "How old are you, Joe?"

"Uh, twenty-six on my next birthday."

"You are virgin?"

I laughed. "No, I just..."

She reached her right hand closer. "Come. Touch me."

I inched closer. "Mylin. We just met. We can wait. Really, we shouldn't rush into things."

She shushed me and took my hand.

"We must now. Important."

I was flummoxed. Why would this girl—who had seen Pé jump, and "them" in the alley, and a car go over a cliff—want an American she had only met the day before?

She pulled my palm to her bare breast.

"Mylin. I like you. But I don't think we're ready for such a big—"

She touched my lips with her index finger. Her nipple pressed into my palm.

"Joe, I have been away all night. There is only one reason I am allowed to do that."

I frowned.

"They will ask questions. I need answers." She dangled the condom between two fingers. "Proof will be most convincing. They will know if I lie."

She pressed my hand more firmly to her body.

I looked into eyes so brown they were nearly black. Eyes I had studied in a hundred photographs. They were very serious. And afraid. I wanted to ask: *Who they? Prove what? How? Who allows you to be out?* But I only said:

"This is all wrong. For you, me...us. There must be some other way."

She released my hand and sat back. Her breasts met my gaze. "Beat me."

I wagged my head. "That's ridiculous. I would never hurt you."

"There must be marks," she said.

I sat back cross-legged to create distance between us and raised my eyes to her face. She was not smiling.

"Mylin, I want to help you. What's the real issue here?"

"They will demand to know why I was away all night. I wasn't with Mr. Bar—" She stopped. "I had an appointment earlier. But it ended quickly. I should be at our hotel in Reno by now." She pressed her lips tight together, then said: "And I'm not."

A memory prodded me. "The young guy in my booth. He said, 'Tell her to call grandmother.' You must have called. That's how you found out where she was."

She nodded slowly, arms now crossed over her bare breasts.

"Then how about you tell the truth? You went to see her tonight. We have proof in the recording my computer made while I was inside." I was glad for my obsession with recording everything, not wanting to ever miss the perfect shot.

"But..." she said softly.

"But what? You did go to see her. You saw enough to describe her hospital room, and her condition. Plus, you have a recording. Why wouldn't they believe you?"

She reached for her dress and pulled it to her chest.

My heart pumped harder.

"They might," she said. "Please hold me."

––––––

Twenty minutes later I was still lying on the packing pads with one arm around Mylin. She breathed gently. The combination of happy and deeply troubled I was experiencing was brand new. I wanted to ask a hundred questions about her past, the cliff, the future. But she had been through enough and neither of us had slept much. Now was not the time. I said:

"Are you hungry?"

"Yes. But I must be back soon."

I shifted slightly. "Let's find a place for burgers."

"Fish?"

"Maybe tuna."

She sat up. "My favorite." Her voice was upbeat, but her face said otherwise.

It took only a few minutes to stumble upon a place called Burger Me in Truckee. We didn't talk much. She pointed once to a rock formation and said it looked like a sad woman staring up into the cloudless sky. We ordered my cheeseburger, her grilled tuna on a salad, and a chocolate milkshake with two straws. We chatted about the joy of sunshine on bare skin, how stiff my old truck rode, and the challenge of taking pictures for a living when there were millions on the Internet. I didn't bring up the events of the past twenty-four hours, and neither did she.

Until I exited on Plum Drive for the Reno airport.

"Are you sure I can't drop you off at home?"

She shook her head.

"It doesn't seem right to just leave you here at the airport."

"You picked me up at the airport." A long pause while she brushed purple and black hair with her fingers. "I must catch a plane."

I took a deep breath and reminded myself I had met her right here, holding a sign with my name on it. 5:30 pm. Yesterday. "Do I call the same number?"

She shook her head vigorously, mussing her hair. "No. Don't call."

"How will I find you?"

"You cannot. Much is bad."

She faced the windshield with her viola on her lap as I obeyed the 15 mph speed limit in front of the terminal. When I stopped, she leaned over and pressed her lips to my right cheek for a full five seconds. Then she whispered:

"You must stay away."

CHAPTER 26

I SAT AT THE CURB UNTIL A TALL woman in a dark blue uniform tapped my front fender with a knuckle and waved at me to move on.

She was definitely not smiling.

The airport exit road made a wide U-turn and dumped me into Reno. I sipped the last of the warming milkshake until it made slurping sounds. I needed to return to Kings Beach to retrieve my one picture and tent. Then I had a show here in Reno; on to San Francisco; work my way down the coast towards Los Angeles as autumn approached.

Those shows wouldn't wait. But I didn't care. All I could think about was Mylin saying:

Stay away.

I tried repeatedly to spin her words into something positive; failed every time.

Hearing it only an hour after holding her in my arms...

A horn blared behind me. The light was green. I started to move, but needed time to think. In two blocks I swung into the parking lot of a deserted video rental store. Reno. Who could help me? I dug in the console for my cell phone.

The call was picked up on the fourth ring.

A woman's voice gently said, "Bear Naked Leather."

A motorcycle engine revved in my ear. She screamed, "Phone! Keep that thing quiet." Then more softly, "Can I help you?"

"Hi. My name is Joe Roberts. I met Bear at the Kings Beach show."

"You want to talk to him?"

"If he's not busy."

She laughed. "Not busy? Wait for that and you'll be staring at his tombstone. He's supposed to be back at the show now and he's still here playing with his malfunctioning toys. Hang on, I'll get him."

I failed at trying not to imagine holding Mylin.

A deep voice growled into my ear, "Bear here."

"Hi, Bear, Joe. I'm in Reno."

There was a pause. An engine cranked over but didn't start.

"Joe, how are ya? How's the babe with the cigarette?"

Such a simple question. "It's complicated Bear. You got some time?"

The engine cranked again, came to life, and rumbled in the background.

"Nothing but. Bike won't run and I'm two hours late getting to the show. Going to have to send the assistant over in the pickup. You wanna come by? I feel the need for lunch."

"Sure. Where are you?"

"Down the street from The Tattooed Parrot. Purple door. Can't miss it." The engine roared and the phone went dead.

Neither shop name showed up on my phone's GPS, so I drove to a busy street lined with casinos. The second person I asked, a man in his forties with ink on his forearms, directed me to Virginia Street. He suggested I might like a shop called Evolution, but Parrot was excellent quality.

Bear was right—easy to find. He hadn't said purple *garage* door, but that's what it was: a one-car-wide garage door with Bear Naked Leather painted in a gold gothic font on the inside of glass windows at chest level.

I parked the truck and walked around the corner looking for an entrance.

An engine roared and settled into a rough idle, the sound coming from inside the row of buildings. I looked for an alley, but the structures were shoulder to shoulder. Finally I walked through the front door of The Tattooed Parrot into a room wallpapered with drawings. The place was empty. The engine rumbled through the wall on my left. I walked to the back of the narrow room to a closed door and knocked.

The door swung away and a middle-aged Asian woman studied me.

"You want tattoo? I call boss."

I shook my head. "I'm looking for Bear."

"Bear, he no here." The door started to close.

"Wait. Please." She stared at me. "How do I get into his shop?"

She took a step away. I was afraid she was going to close the door.

"Naked Leather. How do I get inside?"

She frowned. "Knock." She swung the door closed.

I backtracked from the Parrot, went to the big purple garage door, and knocked on the middle glass plate that said NAKED in foot-high letters.

The door raised with a clatter and hum.

For some reason, perhaps the name, perhaps his display at Kings Beach, I expected a leather shop. But the lifting door revealed three hydraulic motorcycle lifts in a row. The nearest was empty. The other two held the mass of chrome and rubber I associated with Harley Davidson. Behind them on the wall, where one might reasonably expect to find racks of tools, were rows of leather belts, buckles, jackets, hats, and boots.

I stepped in. The door immediately clicked and hummed down like a giant clam trapping me inside.

Bear stood behind the bike on the far rack twisting the grip, though it wasn't running.

"Hello, Joe the picture man."

"Hey, Bear. I didn't know you had a bike shop."

"I don't."

"These are custom leather-cutting machines?"

Bear's laugh sounded like a cross between a black bear's growl and the engine he was working on.

"Funny, picture man. These are my babies."

I suddenly understood. This *was* the leather shop; Bear used the space to work on his personal bikes when he wasn't making leather goods. The third hydraulic lift had tools scattered across it and a black plastic chair beside it. Bear's idea of a height-adjustable workbench.

"Did I catch you at a bad time?"

"Good time, bad time, you know I've had my share. Let's get some lunch."

He disappeared behind the bike and returned with two open beer bottles. He thrust one in my direction.

"So what's up with your girlie-picture girl?"

I half-sat on the workbench lift and said, "It's kind of a long story."

"Tell me the one beer summation. I know the first part. You called from my phone. You met her. You like her. Then what happened?"

I took a long swallow followed by a deep breath.

"I met her grandmother, who's in a coma. Saw a woman leap off a cliff. A motorcycle rider get shot by a guy in a Mercedes. An SUV push the Mercedes off the same cliff." I paused. "You know that part, you saw the pictures. I think the gunshot guy was brought to the hospital grandma is in. Then girlie-picture tried to make me have sex with her in my truck. And I bought her lunch in Truckee before taking her back to the airport."

He drained half his beer. "I don't believe it."

"I know it's a little farfetched—"

"No way she would have to *make* you do her. You've been drooling at that picture since I watched you put it up."

I felt heat in my cheeks.

Bear broke into a big rumbling laugh. When he stopped, he finished his beer.

"Time for lunch," he announced again.

The garage door went up. He pulled me outside and closed the door behind us. As we walked along the street he blew across the empty bottle, making boat-whistle sounds.

Finally he said, "You said it was complicated. Which part?"

"She said no police."

"Yeah, I remember. That's why my buddies did that little trick to get your pictures and movies to the cops. Did the cops do anything?"

I shrugged. "Don't know how to find out."

"Watch the *Chronicle,* they love car-pushed-off-cliff stuff. Drama sells papers. What else?"

"She said I have to go away. Don't call." I paused. "She didn't explicitly say I was in danger, but that's the vibe I got."

"Ah, the broken heart of the problem." He dropped his bottle into a green trash can. It clanged twice. "Guns fired, not safe by definition. What did you say happened to the old lady?"

"Injured. Mylin kept watching for black motorcycles. Maybe had something to do with it."

"Gonna give us bikers a bad name." He laughed some more, before asking, "How's the Squeeze Inn?"

"Never been."

"Then let's go squeeze in." He growled his laugh again, but his eyes said his brain was working overtime. "It's close, we can walk."

A couple of blocks later he turned to cross a parking lot and led us to a door on an inside corner. We stepped into a room that looked like a mad professor's garage: old bicycles hanging from the ceiling, chrome milkshake maker, walls covered with graffiti. A waitress in a pink tank top and stretch jeans a size too small waved Bear to a table along the far wall.

I sat down in a chair hand-painted with psychedelic swirls at a table that had been used for carving practice by every teenager within a hundred miles.

"The food's great," Bear said.

When the pink-topped waitress came over and smiled Bear asked for two orders of ribs. I wasn't particularly hungry, having eaten in Truckee with Mylin, but ordered a pastrami on rye anyway.

"Let me see if I understand your problem," Bear said.

"I'm sure I don't."

"You like the girl. You want to see her again. She's mixed up in something neither of us understands, but we could maybe guess. The girl likes you, is trying to protect you by telling you to go away. She sees no way forward." Two beers arrived. He swallowed from one. "Am I close?"

I stared at the beer. "You really think she likes me?"

He put his bottle on the table and looked into me. "Of course she likes you, Joe. If she didn't, why tell you to go away? Just keep taking your money until you don't have any left, *then* tell you to go away."

I sipped my beer and tried hard to understand Bear's logic. I said:

"She's a violist."

"Is that right? Do they study how to bang in the back of a truck?"

I frowned.

"Okay. On the table." He patted the carvings with the palm of his hand. "Is she a musician who plays around? Or a hooker who took music lessons as a little girl?"

"She's incredible." His eyes questioned me. "On the viola. She must have studied seriously. Perhaps still does."

"Maybe she's one of those Chinese girls whose mother made her work work work instead of playtime. Have you read *Battle Hymn of the Tiger Mother?* Best seller. Nice lady who answers my phone read it, got me to read a few chapters so we could discuss it."

"I haven't even heard of it. I lean toward kiteboarding magazines when I'm not studying photographic equipment."

"Obsession with predefined goals and other people's opinions. Light on personal expression."

"Hmm."

"Not relevant to the present situation, except for the attitude of control. You said this entire orchestra is Asian girls?"

I nodded.

"Hmm."

"That matters?"

Bear drummed plump fingers on the table and poured beer down his throat with the other hand.

"You think?" he began, and paused.

Food arrived. Bear ate ribs with one hand, ordered another beer with the other. I picked at my pastrami sandwich, figured I'd take most of it with me in a to-go box, have it for dinner.

"I'm getting a bad feeling," Bear said, as he started the second order.

"Don't like the ribs?"

He shook his head and wiped sauce from his dark beard. "Ribs are great. I'm getting a bad feeling about your girlie."

I arranged my sandwich. "What kind of bad feeling?"

He swallowed. "The kind that says she's right. You should stay away from her."

I drank my beer. Then said: "You think she's in trouble with the police?"

Bear's shoulders rocked with a laugh stuck in his chest.

"Cops? No. That would be too easy."

"Then why does she keep telling me no police?"

Bear belched. "Because she doesn't want to be deported."

I bit into my pastrami; it was thick and warm and covered with melted cheese.

"Listen," Bear said. "Your chickadee must play a mean

fiddle." He pointed to a window. "There's a picture of poster for some benefit at the art museum."

I turned around. Sure enough, even looking at the back it was clearly Mylin. I had walked right past it.

"How did she get into the country?" Bear asked.

I swallowed. "That's a weird question."

"I'll bet it has a weirder answer."

I sighed. "She was telling me stories early this morning while we were, uh, resting at the Donner Pass rest area."

Bear chewed ribs. "Stories, huh?"

"Yeah, like where she's from and stuff." I paused. "Her mother's dead."

Bear stopped chewing. "How did that come up?"

"She was talking about loving to play music, and certain pieces she dedicates to her mother every time she performs them."

Bear emptied his beer and looked around for the waitress. She nodded at him from across the room. "So? Did she fly in and walk off the plane into customs waving her work visa?"

"No," I said. "She sailed to Canada on a cruise ship where she played in a string quartet during dinner every night. She got off the ship between Alaska and Washington and traveled by bus all the way to Toronto. Then took a fishing boat across Lake Erie. They were caught in a black-cloud northeaster; the girls got seasick. She was terrified they were going to capsize and drown. Finally docked in Toledo, Ohio."

"John Denver wrote a song about that place," Bear said.

"Makes no sense to me."

"Apparently it doesn't have enough action for John."

I laughed. "Never heard the song."

"Sure it makes sense. She was smuggled into the U.S."

I stared down at my half-eaten sandwich. "Why would anyone smuggle a violist into the United States?"

Bear picked at his teeth with the fork he hadn't been using.

"Not her," he said. "Them."

I looked up from my sandwich, but didn't speak.

"Think of it this way, picture man. They play pretty music. Travel around the country. Meet people from all walks of life. But sneaking into the U.S...." He shook his head. "That means no visas. I hate to be the one to break it to you, but they're prostitutes. Moving around gives them access to a broad market. Might be a good business."

I was quiet for a long time before saying:

"She said they wanted proof."

The girl with tight-jeans came with Bear's beer. She put another down for me even though mine was only half-gone.

"About what?" Bear said.

I stared up at the ceiling. There was a rusty children's sled hanging over my chair. I could read *Flyer* in faded red paint.

"She told me it was important that I make love to her."

"I see," Bear said. "So someone is watching her every move."

I took a big bite of my sandwich to distract myself.

Bear drank.

Eventually I said, "Mylin plays so well. Why not get a job teaching, or performing, or something? Why a prostitute?"

"Only one reason," Bear said.

I wracked my brain, came up empty.

Bear said, "Because she has to."

———

After lunch I ended up inside Bear Naked Leather on the plastic work chair while Bear tuned his gleaming red motorcycle. Thinking. Eventually he shut it down and opened the purple garage door to release the exhaust fumes before one of us passed out. I said:

"I'll support her. Why can't she just leave?"

"For starters, she just met you. A move like that would take a lot of trust. Plus, she already has a job. And she's an asset that makes money for someone. That someone is going to be mighty pissed if you mess with his income. How many people in her band?"

"Something like forty or fifty players, depending on the night."

"That's a load of income if they're all working the rich-guys-with-Mercedes circuit."

My stomach squeezed oddly on the pastrami. I got out, "The cliff."

"Yeah, saw your movie. He could afford the high-priced spread."

Bear fiddled with his engine with a wrench the size of a pencil.

"What do you think happened up on Highway One?" I asked.

Bear shrugged. "Loads of options—drugs, girls, weapons—but someone powerful was unhappy with the people in that silver car. If I were a betting man, which of course I am, I'd say that the unhappy someone is the same someone your girlie is afraid of."

My beer was still half full; I probably should have stopped drinking at lunch, I hadn't had much sleep. I tipped it up anyway. Then said:

"So she sends me away."

The bike burbled to a stop. "Her only choice if she likes you."

I examined the dark bottle in my hand like someone else was holding it.

"Leaving me with no options."

A wrench clattered as it struck concrete. Bear stared in my direction. "There are always options."

I lowered my empty bottle to the floor. "Let me see. Even though I just met her yesterday, I can't see her again because she refuses. We speculate that this is her way of protecting me from "they" of the cliff crash. Because she likes me."

Bear nodded. He was smiling as he bent over to retrieve the wrench.

I continued, "If she agrees to go away with me, we'll be hunted down and bad things will follow."

"So far so good," Bear said.

I stared down at my empty bottle and contemplated opening another. Bear read my mind and disappeared behind his bike. Seconds later he emerged with two huge blue cans of Foster's Lager.

"Serious work calls for serious drink," he said, handing me a can.

"Which leaves nothing," I said over the hissing of tabs being pulled.

"Picture man, you need to fire up that imagination you use to take photos." Bear lowered himself in one motion to a cross-legged position beside his hydraulic lift.

I marveled at his ability to sit like a yoga instructor.

He closed his eyes and drank the Foster's. Then said:

"Imagine with me. Girlie cannot agree to go with you because she would be complicit in running away, thus turning against the wishes of her tribe, and the elders who lead it. She therefore must be hunted down and punished as an example to others." Eyes still shut, he placed the can on the floor by his right hip and pressed his hands together like a guru preparing to lead a chant. "She can only agree to see you on business with the approval of her superiors. Thus, the romantic relationship you desire has no future. So she has sent you away into a forest of alternate futures—none of which include her."

I took a long swallow. "I'm with you so far."

"But."

I waited. He didn't say anything so I echoed: "But."

"*You* are not bound by tribal law."

"I'm not?"

"You are an interloper. You do not accept the limits of the formal relationship allowed to you by her tribe."

"I don't?" I swung the oversized can up.

"You want her on your own terms."

"I do? I mean. I do."

"Therefore..." He stretched the word out like a jury's verdict.

I put my can down, sat back, closed my eyes, and pressed my hands together in front of my chest. I knew what he wanted so I said, "Therefore."

"You must free her from servitude."

I opened one eye. Bear hadn't moved. I closed it. He was apparently completely serious. Not knowing what else to do, I said, "Free her?"

"Imagine with me, Joe. You do not communicate with her, so she can't be discovered in advance. If, and here is the magical challenge, if you are ever caught, she had no advance knowledge, so only you will be punished."

"Would she cooperate?" I said, picturing Mylin and me racing away in my white truck like *Romeo and Juliet* with a happy ending.

"She has no choice," Bear's baritone voice echoed off the walls of the shop.

"But she'll have to agree."

"No." Bear took a slow deep breath that sounded like rolling surf. "You must proceed against her will. She must see this. *They* must see this."

I opened both eyes. Bear sat with eyelids lowered, his head tipped forward.

"You have a plan?" I asked.

Moving only his right arm, he reached for the Foster's on the floor.

"Not a plan...a *vision*."

CHAPTER 27

QIGIQ'S OFFICE CHAIR SQUEAKED as he leaned back and aimed with his right index finger. He dropped his thumb to release the tan rubber band and struck the toe of his boot up on the desk.

"Three in a row."

Kandy didn't respond. She was leaning forward with her forehead pressed to the ink blotter calendar on her desktop, both arms in her lap.

"Not impressed, huh?" Qigiq asked.

She sighed but didn't move. "This case is giving me a headache."

"Which case?"

"We're homicide detectives," she said to the floor. "Isn't there supposed to be a homicide? We don't even have a body."

"Sure we do. It's just missing. Plus, we have one in a coma. That should count half."

She sat up, put her hands behind her head, and arched her back. "I was supposed to go camping this weekend. You know, Labor Day holiday, time off, all that suburban stuff. Instead we're looking at a hit and run; screaming wife; disappearing cliff jumper; driver of silver Mercedes and cash both missing. I hate leaving with so many balls in the air. This add up for you?"

"Oh yeah. Tells me I should have gone back to Alaska instead of extending my sabbatical leave. Things make sense up there."

"Even your politics?" she asked with a grin.

"Touché."

"I can't figure how Spooner survived the drop. Or got off that beach. The guys who rescued the car said signal strength is nonexistent. How could "her Rudy" do it alone? Unless he had an inflatable in the trunk. Hard to believe he was planning for a rendezvous with the ocean."

"I think his plan went bad." Qigiq dropped his feet to the floor and pulled a crumpled sheet of paper from the back pocket of his pants.

"For whom?" she asked.

He ran a finger down the page. "First, for whoever took the original pictures and wrote that contract. He or she expected Spooner to pay, not cut and run. And take the girl with him. That was the first step in making things complicated."

Kandy nodded. "Yeah, they were forced to take action to locate Pé."

"Which worked. They picked up her nurse masquerade at the hospital." He moved his finger a half inch. "But Spooner also had a plan. And cash. I'll bet he was planning to disappear with Pé."

"So the accident was improvised?"

"I vote yes. They saw an opportunity to, please don't shoot me, kill two birds with one stone."

She groaned.

"I warned you." He continued, "The sideswipe was only meant to stop them. Then they could grab the girl, and scare Spooner into paying."

"That's two birds?"

"At least." He smiled.

"But things went wrong," she said. "Girl jumps out of car. Spooner is armed, takes a man down."

"Nasty complication."

"They react to the threat, push the car over the edge. The girl jumps rather than be captured. More complication. They clear the area and leave a man to destroy evidence. Let the police call it a single vehicle accident. High profile lawyer out late at night with a young girl; she's thrown from the car in a freak crash. Both dead, what a shame. Would barely make the back page of the *Chronicle*. End of story. A dead blackmail victim can't cause problems. Girl isn't around to tell stories out of turn. Wife gets the insurance settlement. Everyone is happy. Life goes on however it was going on before."

He fired a rubber band straight down. Missed his boot.

Kandy said: "And we only know otherwise because an anonymous party sent movies." She lowered her elbows to her desk. "Wanna guess who?"

Qigiq shrugged. "Someone following Pé, Spooner, or the biker. Spooner's camp? Or a third party representing his own interests? I don't see how the video helped the blackmailer. Unless it's supposed to misdirect us in some twisted way." He propped his feet back on the desk and stared at his sheet of paper.

"Now Pé is missing again," she said. "And the info given to Doc Simmons leads nowhere. The visa must be fake. Maybe those medical records were fake too. She might not even be 24 years old."

"Spooner is missing again too."

"You see why I have a headache." She placed her forehead back down on the blotter and spoke at the floor. "No satellite phone in his name. No calls logged from that location. I can't figure out how Spooner contacted anyone to let them know where he was."

Qigiq slapped the paper with the back of his right hand.

"Kandy, you are *brilliant*."

She lifted her head. "I know. But how does that help?"

He pulled a pencil from a desk drawer, scribbled on his paper. "You said, 'let them know where he was.' I've been trying to figure out how he made a phone call."

"So?"

"You reframed the problem. How was Spooner able to let someone know where he was without placing a phone call? Or sending those text messages you like. They need a cellular connection too."

"My headache is getting worse."

Qigiq reached for the black laptop sitting on his desk and typed. He turned it around to face her and said: "GlobalStar satellites."

The headline of the Wikipedia reference in Qigiq's browser read, *SPOT Satellite GPS Messenger*. She scanned the entry. "This thing sends its GPS location directly to a satellite?"

"Correct. I carried one on a solo bike trip into the Chugach National Forest."

Kandy continued reading. "It's only one-way comm."

"Right. The one I had let me send messages to predefined recipients. Or contact emergency service providers."

She met his eyes. "*Predefined* recipients? So there has to be an account. And a list of contacts." Kandy grabbed the phone with her left hand. "Hello, Captain. We've got a possible lead on the Spooner case. We think he owned a," she read from Qigiq's computer, "SPOT Satellite Messenger. We need help knocking down corporate doors to gain access to his account."

Spooner's account led to an email address that had received the message *Silver Streak has arrived* at 04:39 AM. The message included the latitude and longitude of Devil's Slide. Kandy tracked that email address to an account and a name. Then she searched public records and uncovered a house with a mortgage in Half Moon Bay, and a boat registration for a Hatteras GT54 motor yacht. Qigiq placed phone calls to marinas to find where in Half Moon Bay such a boat docked, and learned that the name across the transom was *Solicitor*.

———

Qigiq sipped a caffeine-free Coke. His left hand, holding egg and cheese on a croissant, rested on his knee. Kandy drove south between bites of lox on a bagel.

"Captain Jasik was really helpful," Qigiq said.

"Probably tired of Mrs. Spooner yelling at him."

She changed to the fast lane. "So tell me how this SPOT thing works?"

"It's a GPS device about the size of a good brownie. Has a couple of buttons to send messages via a back channel on the Globalstar satellite network: that's the one cars talk to for emergency assistance. Then the SPOT computers do whatever you told them to do: usually send I'm OK, or I need help, to someone. If you have a smartphone, you can send short messages through it too."

"And this works?"

"It's saved thousands of lives because you can also push an emergency button and have it summon help. Like calling 911 from anywhere in the world."

Kandy slowed and dragged a piece of salmon off her bagel with her teeth. They rolled for almost a mile. She said:

"Seems awfully special-purpose, I wonder how many they sell?"

"It's mainly to call for help, or to let someone know you're okay. But you can set it to update via the Internet so a friend can track your position on a map."

She turned her head and met his eyes, then turned back to the road.

"You're getting better at this tech stuff. I can see it now: @QigiqTheGeek posting tech tips online. Thousands of female techies swooning over your latest pronouncement. Do you think —"

Her cell phone played the roaring Ferrari. She tapped the hands-free button on the steering wheel to put the call through the car's sound system.

"Dreeson."

"Uh, hello," a male voice said. "Are you the girl who called me about *Solicitor?*"

She mouthed *Girl?* to Qigiq and said, "Maybe. Who's calling?"

"This is Max down at Pillar Point Harbor. You seemed mighty interested in that boat when we talked."

"I *am* mighty interested in that boat, Max. What can I do for you?"

"Well, it ain't me exactly. I was just sitting here watching some preseason college ball. It's lookin' like those South Carolina Gamecocks might be darn good this year."

Qigiq whispered, "What's a Gamecock?"

Kandy's lips smiled, but her forehead frowned.

"Yeah, Max. Ya never know."

"Well, like I was sayin'. I was sitting here watching some ball and I see that big Hatteras leave the basin. You know that boat has a real pretty profile. Hard to mistake her for something else."

"When was this, Max?" Kandy said.

"Oh, a couple of downs ago."

"Which way did she go?"

"Well, she went due west, right into the ocean like she was going to China or something until just a speck was left. So I got out my binoculars and followed her. I'd bet a Gamecock championship that she motored north."

"Thanks, Max." She paused, glanced in her rearview mirror. "I've never seen *Solicitor*. Can you tell me what she looks like?"

"Sure. You go right to that Hatteras Yachts website and look up the GT54. The owner bought one just like they advertise it. We joke about that name around here, figure it has to belong to a lawyer or a prostitute." Max laughed hard.

"You're the best, Max. Will you do me a favor?"

"Sure thing, little lady."

Kandy's eyes rolled and Qigiq coughed a laugh.

"If *Solicitor* comes back, call me right away at this number."

"Will do."

"And Max...do you know who took her out?"

"Sure don't, little lady. I was watching the game."

She ended the call.

Qigiq held out his phone with a picture of a sleek motor yacht in profile. He said:

"Red hull, white deck. Should be easy to spot."

"If we knew where to look."

"The man said north," Qigiq said.

Kandy nodded. "Good. Somewhere between here and Alaska."

Qigiq read from his phone.

"Says here the GT54 will run 41 knots top-end, and 37 at cruise with 1600 horsepower Caterpillar 32A diesels. The lighter weight made possible by the resin-infused hull reduces fuel burn and increases range."

"Oh great. That narrows it down to what, Vancouver?"

CHAPTER 28

THE MAJESTIC BOW OF THE 54-FOOT HATTERAS sliced through the low swells of the Pacific Ocean at 30 knots. Although the shoreline north of Half Moon Bay was covered in fog as the air mass pushed east into the foothills, the boat was running along in bright sunlight. A man with dark curls blowing in the wind stood with one hand on the wheel and one on the dual controls for the Caterpillar engines. He said:

"You know, Spooner. You were lucky."

Rutherford Spooner was stretched across the stern seat where the ride was smoothest. His entire body ached, but nothing appeared to be broken, not even a fingernail. He said:

"The Mercedes E-Class has a five-star crash rating from the rear. The best there is."

The man twisted to face him. "Damn lucky."

Spooner eased himself to standing and limped to the cabin. He wanted a beer, but opened a coke. He needed to stay sharp.

"Dale, I really appreciate your helping me with this. I can't disappear alone."

"No problem, my friend. A GT54 for one day of work is a fine paycheck."

Rudy smiled. "I don't want that bitch Rachel to get it. She's going to be real surprised when she finds out where the assets aren't." He leaned against the seat and scanned the ocean. There were no other boats in sight.

"You sure about this?" Dale asked.

"Never been more sure, as they say. Pé is a doll, and so gentle. I enjoy lavishing life on her because she appreciates every little thing."

"Not your mid-life crisis you're going to wake up from one day?" Dale said.

"You bet it's a mid-life crisis. And am I ever glad it came before I had a heart attack from listening to that bitch whine about how her diamonds aren't big enough, or the Douglases have a new apartment in Paris, or the Petersons bought another Ferrari. Oh, and her favorite: Why haven't you made senior partner yet?"

They cruised along to the throb of diesel engines. The radar showed nothing ahead for two miles.

"And you think you can get away with it?" Dale said, steering slightly to starboard.

"It's like any other deal. The magic is in dotting the I's and crossing the T's. I've got the money stashed where Rachel can't touch it. The boat's in your name. When you're done with it, sell it. We'll split whatever you get."

"The house?" Dale asked.

"Darling Rachel gets the fat mortgage. Getting my equity out was too complicated. If she's willing to sell the place, she can get by until she finds some other sucker to kowtow to her pristine ass."

Dale studied his friend for a moment.

"And all you need me to do is drop you off?"

Rudy's eyes scanned the open water ahead. "Everything's set once you drop us in Mexico. That crash screwed up my timing, though."

Dale chewed his upper lip. "I've been worried since I got that emergency email to come get you last night. We weren't supposed to meet this far north. Suppose someone saw the boat?"

"At four-thirty in the morning? They were drunk or stoned. Besides. What did they see? You didn't even anchor, just sort of drifted by like you were fishing. And I boarded from the ocean side."

"With a suitcase full of money," Dale said.

They rode in silence for five full minutes filled with wind and sunshine.

"Why are we doing this in daylight?" Dale asked.

Rudy swigged from his warming Coke can. "I'm way behind schedule. We need to pick up Pé and hightail it down to Baja while my clean vehicle is still waiting. From there I disappear."

"But in broad daylight?" Dale said, concern shadowing his beachcomber tan.

The yacht climbed a rogue wave and settled down with a rush of spray past the gunwales.

"What's to hide? This is a straight buyout deal. Instead of renting her for the monthly payments originally proposed in their lame contract, I made a counter proposal. After last night's encounter, they're lucky I don't go to the cops and have them all locked up for stupidity."

"How can you buy out a girl?"

"Easy. Look at it from the meta-level." Rudy drank from his soda; the caffeine helped to keep his excited buzz going despite the aches in his body. "She's an asset." He looked across at Dale. "Don't make any butt jokes. She's just an employee. She brings in a certain amount of revenue a year, some is profit, some covers costs. She has a working life of no more than what, four or five good years? And there's risk associated with that. She might get caught, or sick, or the market for her special skills could collapse. So I ran a calculation estimating the present value of what she's worth to them in hard dollars of profit. I even added a little to spice up the deal. From there it's just business. They can keep her and make money the hard way, or they can sell her to me for a one-time fee up front."

"Do I want to know what that number is?" Dale asked, his eyes pointing straight ahead at the waves.

"Comparable to the price of this yacht," Rudy said.

"You're not worried the girl will bail out on you after the, uh, transaction?"

"Nope, she loves me." Rudy laughed. "And even if she doesn't, I'm a good deal less work for her than if she stays with her current employer."

"And?"

"And if she bails out on me, she knows I have the means to track her down and tell her old bosses where she is. They can pick her up and double their money."

"But you're out the investment," Dale said. The boat bounced hard to port, and slowly corrected itself.

"All investment involves risk," Rudy said. "I've risked more money on some techno-weenie's wet dream that turned out to be worthless."

Dale smiled. "Ah, the mid-life crisis speaking."

Rudy lifted his can. "To mid-life crises everywhere. May they be as much fun as mine."

CHAPTER 29

KANDY EXITED I-280 A HALF-MILE before the turnoff to San Francisco airport. She pulled up to a pump in a 76 gas station. The sky to the west was filled with wispy clouds over foothills etched like the crayon drawing of a child. She said:

"At least we know where Spooner is."

"We think we know," Qigiq said.

"I'd sure like to have a chat with that guy." She stretched her hip and dug in a pocket. Came up with a yellow Juicy Fruit pack.

"Back to gum?"

"Only when I'm tense." She unwrapped two sticks and shoved them together into her mouth. The four-cylinder engine burbled.

"What do we know?" he said. "Spooner wants the girl. He can't trust the people behind the contract. So he's in need of leverage." He paused as an idea crystalized. Then he said, "Where will they make the trade?"

"Trade for what?" she asked, her jaw moving.

"Pé."

Kandy twisted in the driver's seat to face him. "You think Spooner is making another run at the girl? After they tried to kill him?"

"Where do you think *Solicitor* is going?"

Kandy chewed slowly, her eyes quiet.

Qigiq said: "Spooner was headed south from Devil's Slide. Now he's headed back north. If he's running, wouldn't he continue south, make a big dash across the ocean—Hawaii, South America, somewhere no one can find him?"

"So he's coming back for her. How gallant."

"Or maybe..." Qigiq stared out the window, listening to the rhythm of Kandy chewing. "Maybe he's going back to get the guy who tried to kill him."

Kandy shook her head. "No way, he's a lawyer."

Qigiq's managed a slow smile. "You're right, partner. Spooner would send the judicial system after the guy."

"Which means a trade. Where?"

"I don't believe Spooner has simply gone sport fishing while his girlfriend gets sprung from a hospital by a guardian with false papers."

"Hard to follow a yacht with my Mini, even with the turbocharger." She laughed low.

"Can we send the Coast Guard to search *Solicitor?*"

"We're not certain *Solicitor* picked Spooner up last night, we just know the SPOT system notified the registered owner: a guy we know nothing about. We don't know the relationship between the owner and Spooner. And, we don't know if Spooner is on the boat."

Qigiq was quiet. Maybe the yacht really had gone fishing.

They looked at each other. "The SPOT."

"Do you think he still has it with him?" Qigiq said.

Kandy pulled out her phone. "If that SPOT is moving north at 37 knots he does." She put her phone on speaker and spoke to the air. "Hello, Captain. We need your help again."

A woman's voice came through the speakers. "Mr. Jasik, it's rude to answer the phone while I'm talking to you."

They both recognized Rachel Spooner's nasal whine.

"Which mountain do you need me to move for you this time, Dreeson?"

"Same one, Captain. That satellite company can track Spooner's device."

"Spooner? Really?" he said.

"Are you talking about my husband? Well, it's about time

you people did something. I certainly hope you've found that heartless swine."

"We have reason to believe he's heading north on a Hatteras yacht named *Solicitor*," Kandy said. "We want to be there when he makes land."

"*Solicitor*. How creative," Jasik said.

The whine became a high-pitched howl. "That's his stupid boat. Don't tell me he's been off playing with that waste of money all this time? I told him not to buy that dumb thing. We could have an apartment in Paris with that much money."

Kandy frowned at Qigiq, whispered "His boat?" Then said to the microphone, "If the company can give us tracking access to Spooner's SPOT device, it would help a lot."

"Well, is he on the boat?" the voice whined in the background.

"Tell me, Dreeson. How much time do I have to make magic happen this time?"

Kandy smiled as she spoke. "As much time as you like, Captain. But we're parked near the I-280/380 junction and a witness said *Solicitor* left Half Moon Bay twenty minutes ago."

The sigh from the phone filled the Mini.

"Why won't you people do something?"

"Okay, Dreeson. He better be on that boat."

She looked at Qigiq and crossed her fingers. "Thanks, Captain. I'll call when we confirm."

"Mr. Jasik. I am a taxpa—"

The call terminated.

"We better save him," Qigiq said.

"Only if we want to keep our jobs," Kandy said.

After she filled the tank and bought a jumbo 10-pack of Juicy Fruit, Kandy slammed the car into gear and spun gravel from the front wheels as she accelerated onto the road.

"I really need all-wheel drive."

"Maybe Jasik will let you expense it if we get Rachel out of his office."

Kandy drove for two minutes in silence.

"What did she mean by 'his boat'?" Qigiq asked.

"Doesn't jibe with the registration. What do you make of that?"

"My guess? He lied to his wife."

She nodded. "But she whined about the money. How do you spend money on a boat that isn't yours?"

Qigiq called Molly, waited on hold, chatted, ended with: "Yes, a profile would be great. Thanks." He hung up. "Molly checked the registration again. Want to guess when Mr. Dale Walstein became the owner of *Solicitor?*"

"Surprise me," Kandy said. "Helps my headache."

"Day before yesterday."

"Spooner is definitely running. I wonder how Walstein knows Spooner."

Ten minutes later they were rolling north with midday traffic. Kandy's phone pinged to indicate incoming mail. She passed it to Qigiq.

"It's from SPOT LLC," he said.

"Go ahead and open it."

"'Dear Ms. Dreeson. The tracking account you requested has been set up for you at the URL below. Please be aware that it is updated at five minute intervals only so long as the batteries in the SPOT device are charged. Then there's a long string of letters. It's signed, Renée Rensler, Technical Assistant. Spot LLC."

"Tap that URL."

Qigiq touched the screen. "I'm looking at a map with a red dot."

CHAPTER **30**

SPOONER TOSSED THE SODA CAN into the under-seat cooler as he gazed at the rolling blue water through the windshield. He had never felt such freedom in his prep-school tainted life. Not even the day he was discharged from the Army, though that was close. The anticipation felt so good he didn't even crave his daily scotch.

"How much longer?" Dale asked.

Spooner pointed at the fog in the distance and said, "Golden Gate."

Dale yanked his head sideways. "We're going into the bay? Are you crazy?"

Spooner smiled. "You don't think *Solicitor* can handle the current?"

"I'm not worried about *Solicitor*. I'm thinking about a half million residents of San Francisco watching us trade a bag of money for an illegal alien."

Spooner's smile didn't change. "Dale, no one can tell she's illegal just by looking at her."

Solicitor's engines moaned as the yacht climbed a wave and pushed up over the crest. The men were silent for a moment.

"I don't like it," Dale said. "This should happen on a deserted beach with limited access where we can be invisible."

Spooner shook his head. "We try that and a lonely surfer bobbing on his board will see the whole thing and feed it to the cops." He dug into the ice chest and found another Coke; pulled the tab. "This way, we're just one of dozens of boats that swing by and pick up a girl from the dock. Happens all the time.

And..."

Spooner swigged the soda.

"...all those witnesses will reduce the chance that someone pulls a gun and goes crazy with it."

Dale guided the boat to starboard until the bow pointed at the towers of the Golden Gate poking above the fog as if floating on it. "You worried the deal will go sour?"

Spooner shook his head while drinking.

"The deal is good. Our friend, who calls himself Mr. Wu, demanded more than my initial offer, and I gave him most of it. Money is the least of our problems here."

Solicitor hammered into the back of a wave, covering the windshield with a sheet of spray. Dale backed off the throttles slightly.

"Do I want to know what our biggest problem is?"

Spooner stood and put his Coke in a plastic holder. He stared through the windshield.

"Love."

Dale burst out laughing, but stopped when Spooner's features, set in concentration, communicated that he wasn't joking.

"Love?" he said, struggling to sound serious.

"Yeah. Love. Love of money. Power. Women. Love makes men incredibly stupid. I've been trying to compensate by being super careful, but Pé makes me crazy."

"How so?"

"Imagine me, B. R. Spooner Esq., respected attorney-at-law, grabbing a young girl and trying to run away from blackmail. I end up on the side of the road discharging a firearm at a guy trying to stop me." He turned to Dale. "What the hell was I thinking, trying to run? I should have figured there something fishy right from the beginning when she got friendly at that soirée where the symphony taps patrons for donations. When I received that contract with pictures..." Rudy shook his head. "Dale, I freaked out. I stopped thinking straight."

"And you're thinking straight now?"

"Like a spun aluminum arrow. I put on my business hat after you picked me up from near death last night and started analyzing money, assets, and what these guys really care about. With very little effort that kind of thinking got us to this deal. They want money, which is usually the point of blackmail. I want the girl all for myself. We both go away happy."

"You're telling me they actually agreed to your current value estimate of the girl?"

"They listened. Sure they argued she could work longer, do more contracts than I thought. But we negotiated the fine print." He rotated in his seat to face Dale. "You wouldn't believe how much this resembles every other deal I've ever done. People have objectives, they compromise, they move forward. It feels good doing it this way, rather than running and looking over my shoulder for the next thirty years. Once the paperwork on the divorce is final, I'll have a million or two in assets to spend in Mexico where it'll last. If I run low, I'll take on freelance legal work, their government has enough problems to keep me busy for ten lifetimes."

They approached the famous bridge that spanned the gaping mouth of San Francisco Bay. Hanging in the sky only a few hundred feet above them, more orange than gold, the raw brutal strength of steel beams as wide as a car and rivets the size of baseballs were so extraordinary they seemed like something fake on a movie set. A ship to port, overwhelmed by colorful stacked boxes, plied its way out to sea in the opposite direction. Dale guided *Solicitor* to give it a wide berth.

Spooner checked his watch, pulled his cell phone from a pant pocket, and placed it on the dash. "We're right on time." He turned upward to stare at the underside of the bridge. "I'm going to miss this city. It's been very good to me."

"Get false papers and a disguise. Come visit," Dale said,

chuckling.

"You jest," Spooner said. "But this is a big change for me. It'll take some getting used to."

"I thought you were tired of Rachel?"

"I've been tired of Rachel since paying the bill for the honeymoon suite. But San Francisco? I love this place."

Dale slowed to 25 knots. "Don't let that love thing make you stupid."

Spooner nodded. "Good point. Let's get on with this. Soon as I take a piss." He disappeared into the forward cabin. He returned with the strap of a black backpack in one hand, and a second cell phone in the other.

"Head for Sausalito, the Cruising Club," Spooner said.

"Cruising? Those sailing guys hate us."

"I like the way their docks are laid out. We can get in and out fast."

Spooner bent over to open a curved zipper on the pack.

Dale said, "Fast?"

"No reason to dally. Just allows more time for things to go wrong. Would you bring it down to maybe fifteen?"

Dale slowed the boat; the wind softened to a breeze.

Spooner held the pack open with his toe and scooted around for a better angle on the content. He took a picture with the smartphone, then waited for it to encrypt the file. He wrote an email to the agreed upon address that said: *Pick a number between 1 and 7.*

He attached the encrypted picture, and pressed Send.

CHAPTER 31

MR. WU STOOD ALONE AT THE VISTA point on the north side of the Golden Gate bridge gazing across mud-blue water at office towers and high-rise apartments that reminded him of a medieval castle trying to protect a mountaintop. Americans never ceased to astonish him. Why build a city where it will be land-locked on three sides by water so it cannot grow? It was as if the fools had chosen the most impractical site out of a misguided attempt to create beauty.

The sun heated the back of his dark suit. But he had been born in heat; the heat was nothing. His trouble was closer.

His cell phone indicated incoming email.

He lifted 10 x 45 binoculars with an internal stabilization system. The red hull of the target's extravagant toy sliced the water. Two men stood on deck, as agreed.

He rotated until the field glasses faced the parking lot.

Pé's bruised face was visible in the back seat where she was handcuffed to her brother beside her. She stared straight ahead, expressionless, ignoring everyone around her. Especially him. Hating her own father. Such beauty and talent his number one daughter possessed. It saddened him that no matter how many times he tried to teach her the need to embrace the requirements of the family, she not only disobeyed, but outright rebelled. Family was the only security in a world of chaos—but it could only keep its members safe if each did his or her part.

This she had forgotten.

She had also forgotten they were at war. Not a war declared by old men sitting in chambers. A more fundamental war. A war of survival. A war that was as old as the human race. Fought between countries, races, religions and non-religions. There were many reasons to fight; man needed only one.

He shifted the glasses. His second son sat hunched forward in the front passenger seat. He worried about young Tuson's wounds. Dr. Fan had done his best, but to remain in a public hospital was too dangerous. The boy tried so hard, yet created such problems.

His glasses drifted back to his daughter's eyes. Dark eyes that had refused to meet his since this nonsense with the lawyer began. *She does not begin to understand the power of the secrets behind those eyes. She wants to go away. She will start to trust this fool. Whisper to him in the dark of night about the things she's done. A lawyer has connections. He will see an opportunity to profit from secrets. Following money—his only religion. The many years of work and sacrifice building hidden castles on three continents will dissolve like sugar in steaming tea.*

No. She can never be trusted. She must stay. If she refuses...

He lowered the binoculars and opened the email. He counted the packs visible in the picture. If Mr. Spooner had used real hundreds, the agreed upon amount was present. He answered the cryptic message with the digit 6: a number he knew to be favorable for his business.

The red boat moved to his left, deeper into the bay.

Another email arrived. *Sixth boat from the bay end. Galilee Park.*

So Spooner was coming to shore. Mr. Wu allowed himself a rare smile; the arrogant American was making this easy.

He strolled to his black SUV. He used the monstrous vehicle because Americans liked them so much that despite outrageous fuel prices and global warming, they were everywhere. He preferred black for the same reason.

He slipped behind the wheel and drove north on the highway

until he was well past Sausalito, then doubled back to avoid passing through downtown. In ten minutes he was parked near the Sea Trek Ocean Kayaking Center facing away from the bay, a stone's throw from the beach, and a few car lengths from tall windows under a wide blue awning with *The Book Passage* printed on it. The bookstore's windows provided sharp reflections that let him survey the entire parking lot. It was over half full. He counted four black SUVs, not including his.

He stared in the rearview and focused on releasing all thoughts to keep emotion in its place.

The red hull pulled alongside the outermost pier. A Caucasian male stepped from the yacht, carried the black pack shown in the email along the dock, boarded the sixth boat from the end, and ducked under the steering wheel. Whatever did Pé desire in such a gangly creature?

"Your Mr. Spooner has arrived, dear elder daughter. But there is still time to choose your future. Please give up this childish notion of romantic love that has filled your head. It is a foolish myth of the West. You are a leader in the orchestra. And the Geisha quartet. And the family itself. You have much skill, and a long, prosperous life ahead of you."

Pé said, "I don't care."

"I could send you back."

"I would run away."

"He will tire of you in a year. Then you will beg to return to us."

"I will slit my wrists and join Mother before coming back to serve you."

Wu found her eyes in the rearview mirror. She stared directly into him as he said:

"You do not serve me, dear daughter. We all serve our people. Like you, I must do my job."

Pé didn't avert her eyes. "I serve no one."

Wu blinked and faced forward. He wished for a moment he

could discover a third choice. One that he hadn't uncovered in the days and nights of deliberating on this conundrum of the disobedient daughter. It did not appear now. He said:

"Prepare her for the trade."

Prime stepped out of the truck and dragged Pé's left wrist behind him. They walked to the rear, lifted the hatch, and removed a leather suitcase with a sewn handle and two straps. He put it into her free hand, his eyes on the white cloth taped from her right temple to her chin. He reached back in to retrieve a violin case. She lowered the suitcase to the pavement and took the violin in both arms like it was a baby, his cuffed wrist following her movement.

Prime whispered: "Be patient."

Pé half-smiled and bowed. She clicked the latches and opened the case. The wood instrument glistened red-brown in the sunlight, then shadows from a tree branch moving in the wind darkened the wood. She stroked its slender body with the fingertips of her free hand.

Wu watched as Prime unlocked the cuffs from his own wrist, then from Pé's. She latched the case and put her hand through the soft leather handle. He intertwined his fingers over hers. He smiled at her. She bent to pick up the suitcase with her free hand. They walked together across the parking lot. At the entrance to the first dock, beside a small sign for the Kayak Center, they stopped.

She stared at him. Neither spoke.

Mr. Wu alternated his attention between his two children, and the white men in the red boat. They were now actors on the stage, and he had written the script.

Pé appeared like any other tourist in her blue jeans and light green blouse, jet black hair flowing down her back.

Prime left her standing alone and strolled out the weathered wooden dock toward the red yacht. He turned and boarded the sixth boat from the end. His head disappeared. Time seemed to suspend as Wu waited for him to count the money. Then Prime was on the dock walking back toward Pé wearing the pack on his back.

When he reached her, she hadn't moved, and was still holding her suitcase and violin.

He hugged her with both arms. If Prime was doing what he had been told, he would tell her: "Travel safe and far, little sister. Very far."

She looked up at him and smiled, but said nothing. Prime headed for the SUV. Her eyes followed him until he hopped into the back seat and closed the door.

"It's all there," Prime said.

Pé stood stock still, squinting directly at the SUV. Wu met her eyes in the wide outside rearview mirror. He could read her hatred even from a distance. Why hadn't he been able to train his own flesh and blood when the others obeyed? So many years invested—still she was not trustworthy. Her face provided the answer. Her mother. Her mother's blood pumped through her veins too.

Mr. Wu nodded and watched carefully.

She began walking slowly toward the red boat, favoring her left leg. She had traveled only a few meters when the squeal of tires caused her to turn, the fear clear on her face. Mr. Wu followed the sound. A small car had entered the parking lot from downtown, moving fast.

Pé hurried along the dock.

He lifted his binoculars and twisted in the seat to peer out the tinted rear window.

Pé grew closer to the red boat. Her friend Rudy Spooner smiled from the cabin. Pé's face told Wu that her heart was filled to bursting as her head danced with images of secluded beaches and a big house and the beautiful clothes the foolish American had promised her.

She struggled to walk quickly with the heavy suitcase, her

pain obvious to anyone watching. She reached the boat. Spooner extended his hand.

A thump, thump, thump like timpani echoed across the harbor.

Pé glanced over her shoulder.

Wu moved his glasses to the dock.

A white woman wearing sunglasses and pumping powerful arms was sprinting along the wooden planks toward the red boat at incredible speed—shouting Pé's name.

Wu moved the glasses back to the boat and lowered his window to hear better. Spooner's eyes showed fear as he grabbed the suitcase from Pé's hand—he didn't want this woman here, either. Pé turned to Spooner and put her sandal on the white deck.

The thumping continued.

The woman shouted, but she was farther away now and the only word that reached him was "Spooner."

Pé stepped to the floor of the boat and said something to Spooner that he couldn't hear. Spooner didn't answer. Instead he turned his back, leaving her alone between two frightening worlds, and being chased by this madwoman.

Spooner spoke to the other man.

The second man pushed the throttles forward and yelled. His face showed fear.

Who was this woman? A very good question; Wu wanted the answer. If there was a leak, he must find and fix it.

The bow of the fifty-four foot boat swung slowly into the bay as the props rotated the stern toward the dock.

The thumping ceased.

Pé twisted to stare at the woman flying through the air directly at her. She clutched her violin to her chest and dropped to the deck screaming.

Mr. Wu lowered the binoculars and retrieved a silver metal box the size of a cigarette case from the glove compartment in front of Tuson. He held it out to Prime in the back seat.

Prime didn't move. Instead he said, "I do not mean disrespect, but I prefer to face my enemies." He stared at the hovering box. "That is the coward's way."

"It is a mere tool," Wu said, pulling it away. He pushed a switch on the side upward; a tiny LED blinked red. He handed it to Tuson, who was leaning against the passenger door wheezing through his nose.

Tuson took it with his left hand without moving his head.

"I will tell you when," Wu said, keeping his eyes on the red boat in the mirror. He reached back into the glove compartment and removed a black weapon and a cylinder. He deftly screwed the silencer to the barrel not knowing what the next few minutes would bring, but knowing he must be prepared.

He had not anticipated police.

He considered driving away now, but Rutherford Spooner knew much—and may have guessed more. The man was also a lawyer schooled in the ways of American courts. With bad luck, the fool might attack the organization legally. Many questions would follow. Wu had much to hide; questions were unwelcome in his world.

He counseled himself to avoid lawyers in the future.

Prime twisted around in his seat. "I've seen that woman."

This surprised Wu. But this was the very reason he allowed Prime latitude, to bring in new information.

"Who is she?"

"She was with the men who came to the club to hire a rider."

"How can she know Pé?"

Prime shook his head. "I don't know. I've never seen them together."

Wu turned to the wheezing boy beside him. "You let Pé escape." He rolled the window down three more inches and placed both hands on the gun.

"Be ready."

CHAPTER 32

KANDY BRAKED THE MINI TO A SCREECHING halt at the far end of the parking lot pointing at the bay. She jumped out. Qigiq scanned the area from the passenger's seat. *Solicitor* sat at the end of the pier. A small beach to his right was unoccupied. Two sedans moved through the parking lot—either could have dropped Pé off. Three docks to his left a family of four were loading duffel bags onto a blue-hulled sailboat with faded teak trim. Two well-muscled young men pushed off from the far beach in yellow kayaks. Beyond them a bald man in a checkered shirt stood behind a cart selling hotdogs.

First priority: backup Kandy.

He slipped her spare pistol from the glove box and approached the point where the dock reached land, trying to see everything at once. He had closed half the distance to the red boat when its engines roared. Kandy was closer, sprinting out the plank dock.

The boat swung away from the marina, its stern banging the dock as it rotated. The gold letters of *Solicitor* were already ten feet away when Kandy leapt into the air.

Qigiq moved out the dock. Fast.

He watched Kandy land and collide with a fighting chair on a steel post bolted to the deck, sending it spinning. She moved with it until the skipper's spine stopped her forward motion, slamming him against the steering wheel. Her hand shot out and yanked both throttles down. The boat settled into the water, tossing everyone forward.

Voices carried across the water as he ran.

"Who the hell are you?" Spooner yelled as he struggled to recover his balance. "Dale, stop her."

Kandy sank her hand into Dale's curls and yanked his head toward her. His body bent backward and he screamed. She pushed his left arm up into a hammerlock and shouted:

"Police! Don't move."

The big diesels purred beneath the deck.

"Who the hell are you?" Spooner repeated, pulling Pé close to him near the entryway to the forward cabin.

"Are you deaf, Spooner? Police. You're under arrest for assault."

"Show me a badge and read me my rights, officer. Who have I allegedly assaulted?"

"And let me the hell go," Dale said. "You're breaking my arm."

Kandy dragged Dale away from the cockpit.

Spooner lunged to the wheel and pushed both throttles full up with his elbow.

Sixteen hundred horsepower lifted *Solicitor's* bow into the sky. The deck tilted like a teeter-totter gone mad, Dale lost his footing and the full six-foot-three two hundred and twenty pounds of him swept aft, dragging Kandy along. Her feet slammed into the stern. The force of Dale's body falling coupled with the forward motion of the boat folded her and Dale over the transom—and into the bay.

In seconds the boat was moving away at 40 knots. Dale splashed toward the dock, struggling to swim fully clothed.

Kandy wasn't visible.

Qigiq pulled off his boots as his eyes followed the boat's wake back to the point she had flipped over the stern. He gazed into the churned water and estimated where the wash from the props would push her body.

He dove.

The frigid saltwater swallowed him. Gray light streaked

from above like sunlight through a cloud after a rainstorm. He pushed with both arms and legs. Once. Twice. His mind flashed to blue-white images of diving under winter ice to save a young girl—he drove the past from his head. He pushed a third time; surfaced. He rotated his head, evaluating his position; a flash of flesh broke the water's surface. He swam with powerful, purposeful strokes, took a deep breath, and dipped under.

As he flipped Kandy's body a hundred cannons fired. *Solicitor's* cabin disappeared. The naked hull turned sharply. A fireball landed beside his left ear and hissed. He put a hand over Kandy's nose and mouth and pulled her below the surface.

He counted slowly to five while moving them away from the boat.

Qigiq kicked hard to get them back to the surface, then towed her carefully around smoldering debris to the empty beach beside the dock. As he dragged her up the sand, she coughed, rolled onto her right side, and wretched. Blood traced a tiny river behind her ear to her collar.

His eyes moved out over the water.

Solicitor's cabin roof was gone, the hollowed hull a cavern of fire. No bodies visible in the water. A crowd had formed at the end of the dock to gawk at the aftermath of the explosion. No familiar faces. The parking lot was already filling with cars trying to get a closer look.

The sound of a siren rose from the south.

A group of people formed a circle at the end of the dock.

Kandy coughed.

"You okay for a minute?" Qigiq asked.

She nodded between coughs.

He ran the length of the dock, pulled his badge, and gently ushered people aside until he reached the center of the circle. The man who had knocked Kandy off the boat was lying on his back with a red spot blossoming on his chest.

He wasn't breathing. And had no pulse.

_____

Kandy sat in the back of an ambulance as a technician checked her responses.

"So who's the gorilla?" she said.

Qigiq stood beside the open back door.

"According to his ID, *Solicitor's* new owner, the recently deceased Dale Walstein."

She moved her head slowly. "Headache is worse."

"I called Molly while you were resting. Your swimming buddy played hockey at Dartmouth with our friend Rudy. Owns a construction business now called Soonco, builds dream homes for the rich."

Kandy looked up. The tech waved a light in her eyes. "I've seen Soonco signs in the yards of McMansions. Their logo is a solid green rectangle, I figured it represented money." She touched the side of her head with two fingers. "That the only connection, hockey?"

"Spooner's firm has represented Soonco for the past three years."

The tech held up a finger, Kandy's eyes followed it. "A construction firm needs a lawyer?"

"The relationship started when a client sued Soonco for a building failure. People were hurt; two died. Soonco blamed a subcontractor's use of substandard materials. Spooner represented Walstein."

"Must have won."

"You sure you won't go to the hospital?" the tech asked. "Observation is a good thing with head injuries."

She shook her head slowly, "Dangerous places." She leaned her head against the side of the ambulance and closed her eyes.

The tech said, "Rest is a good idea."

"It's only Tuesday," Qigiq said. "Maybe you can take a couple of sick days to rest up, be ready for your vacation this weekend."

She smiled but kept her eyes closed.

"Look at the bright side," he said.

She opened her right eye to study his face.

"We have dead bodies now."

She blew out a long slow breath, and didn't smile.

————

Qigiq started Kandy's Mini and reversed carefully.

"You sure you can handle four wheels?" she asked.

"If I go slow enough."

She groaned.

He drove north for a few minutes and pulled up to a wide dock where a row of aging houseboats floated side by side. Shortly Kandy lay stretched out on Qigiq's gray couch and the smell of coffee filled the kitchen. She pulled her handgun from its thin holster in the middle of her back and placed it on the side table.

"Going to have to clean that soon. Salt water sucks."

He nodded and headed for his cleaning tools. "You sure you don't want to go to the hospital? Nice clean bed. People to watch over you."

"If I get dizzy, I'll consider it. Hey," she said, "you hungry?"

"I thought you were supposed to rest?"

"How can I rest if I'm starving?"

"What are you hungry for? I'll run out and get it."

She eyed him. "In my Mini?"

"Have to, my bike is still at the office."

"Maybe I'm not that hungry." They laughed. The phone rang an old-style metallic jangle.

"You get a new ringtone?"

"Yeah. I learned to sleep through the roaring motorcycle." He went to the bedroom to retrieve the one wireless handset in the entire floating house.

"Ah, you're home. I was worried when I couldn't reach you at the office."

"Hello, Ferdinand."

"Your presence is required at the Ton Up. There is something happening."

"Now? Kandy's hurt."

"Not badly, I hope. I'm here having lunch. I'll eat slowly. If possible, you have to see this for yourself."

Qigiq walked to the living room. "Ferdinand wants us at the Ton Up."

Kandy sat up slowly. "Perfect. I was dreaming of fish and chips."

"Kandy..."

"I'll clean it after lunch."

"I mean, the tech said..."

"I know. Rest. I can rest at the club. It's the drive over that worries me."

CHAPTER 33

QIGIQ PUSHED THE MINI AS FAST as he thought safe with his injured partner in the car.

"You always drive this slow?" Kandy asked.

"Only in a car."

"What did Ferd say?"

"The he'd take his time eating and wait for us."

"Cute. What's the big rush to get us to the club?" she said, eyeing traffic and frowning.

"He said, 'You have to see this.' But offered no details."

As Qigiq turned into the alley that led to the rear entrance of the Ton Up, a red bike flew past, raising dust from the gravel.

"Bags and windshield," he said. "Ready to travel."

They followed it toward the club. When the bike pulled over to park, Qigiq stopped the car.

Sitting along both sides of the alley was a rainbow of Triumphs, Nortons, small displacement Japanese bikes, and BSAs—maybe fifty on each side. They were loaded with side bags, or duffels strapped to the seat. Most were in the style of the café racers of the 1960s.

"Someone's going on a trip," Kandy said.

"Looks like they're evacuating the city."

The bikes occupied all available parking space so Qigiq backed the Mini out of the alley and found a spot on the street a block over. On the second try he maneuvered it almost parallel to the curb.

"The Eagle has landed," Kandy said as she flicked the latch to open the door and banged it into a high, tilted curb.

They walked along the alley like they were at a bike show. Qigiq stopped to examine one machine up close.

"Notice anything?"

"Lots of black," Kandy said. "And shiny stuff makes my eyes hurt."

"I thought these bikes all had custom frames. But this one that looks stock."

"So the bikes aren't identical." She stared up along the row. "They sure look it from a distance."

"The black ones are close. Some have expensive carbon parts. And half have knobbed tires. Where will they be riding dirt roads?"

Dozens of riders loitered in the alley behind the club, their age ranging from too-young-to-vote to retirement. One in five was female. Most wore the fitted jackets and tight black leather pants popular in the sixties. As Qigiq led the way toward the rear entrance bits of conversations reached him: "distance, sand, Mexico, heat, Nevada." A big ride. Made him want to mount up and join them.

They stepped through the door into near darkness. The place was bursting with bodies. A bubbling Wurlitzer jukebox stuffed against the left wall was blasting out a singer shouting, "Rev it up and go!"

Kandy pointed to the far corner where Ferdinand was seated with three dark-haired guys, all wearing worn leather. As she approached, the guys stood and offered their chairs.

"Ah, my colleagues, welcome," Ferdinand said. "We were just planning the spectacle."

Kandy lowered herself gingerly into a hardback wooden chair.

Ferdinand shot a quizzical glance at Qigiq, who said, "Bumped her head."

"I was wondering why you were moving slowly."

Kandy shrugged and waved her hand across the table.

"What's all this stuff?"

Ferdinand sat upright. "The plan. We are almost ready." A drawing with X's, a long spiral, measurements, and topology data covered the table.

"You're going to jump over barbed wire?"

Ferdinand shook his head. "We have a much more spectacular idea. However, since this is a reenactment of an actual event and not a computer graphics trick, I've decided to use the original height of the jump and the weight of the motorbike used in the film, which is heavy by today's standards. I'm also considering employing the terrain to act as the launch ramp."

Kandy said, "What's for lunch?"

A woman's voice from behind her said, "The fish and chips is good."

Kandy turned. The slender girl from their first visit smiled.

"Works for me," Kandy said. "Please hurry, Qigiq is trying to starve me."

"What about the rider?" Qigiq asked.

"The rider?" Ferdinand hesitated. "Our rider is lighter than Mr. McQueen or Mr. Ekins, but we plan to compensate while retaining the 60-foot distance."

The waitress returned with fish and chips for Kandy with shocking speed.

Kandy asked, "Could I have ice water, please?"

"Adding weight to the bike?" Qigiq said.

Ferdinand nodded. "Yes, to achieve balance. It will be spectacular. Let me show you." He rotated a sketch toward Qigiq. "Surely you're familiar with fuel in the frame as pioneered by Buell motorcycles. This was, of course, before Harley Davidson shut them down. We plan something similar."

"But more spectacular," Kandy said, chewing fish.

Ferdinand's cheeks widened into a big smile. "Precisely."

Fish arrived for both Qigiq and Ferdinand, though there

were already two empty plates on the table.

"There you go, Ferddy, pace yourself," the waitress said before disappearing.

Kandy choked. "Ferddy?"

"Yes, well...the young lady has been quite helpful."

Kandy pointed over her shoulder with a thumb. "She of the invisible panties?"

"Well, she doesn't always, um, apparently she finds them uncomfortable."

"What's her name?" Kandy asked.

"Petrushka. Born in California, though her parents are from the South Moravian Region of the Czech Republic, near Brno."

"Aren't you a walking Wikipedia," Kandy said.

Qigiq laughed. Ferdinand lowered an eyebrow toward Kandy, then began eating.

"What's with the crowd outside?" Kandy asked.

"They are preparing for the annual desert ride."

"Not much desert in San Francisco," she said. "How far can they ride old bikes?"

"Around the world if they can get parts," Qigiq said.

"That sound like cheating." She laughed, then touched her forehead with her fingertips.

"It's been done more than once," Qigiq said. "A guy named Fulton did it on a Douglas in the 1930s. Wrote a book called *One Man Caravan*. Where are they going?"

Ferd's jaw was working on fish so he waved a hand in a circle and managed to get out one word: "Teams."

Kandy sipped water. "More than one destination?"

Ferd swallowed. "More than one route."

"Everyone at once?" Qigiq asked.

Ferd nodded. "They've been gathering all day. Loading bikes, tuning engines. Petrushka says they leave before sunset and ride all night."

Qigiq examined the plans for Ferdinand's reenactment,

wondering which part was going to make it spectacular. He liked his tires planted on good old Mother Earth, though he recognized the courage required to launch hundreds of pounds of steel into the air and the skill to land it in one piece. He said:

"But we don't know the destination?"

"It's revealed at the last minute," Ferd said. "So no one can cheat."

A lanky six-footer walked up to the table. "Hey, you're the Guzzi man."

Qigiq recognized Murphy from the frame shop. "That's me."

"You never mentioned you knew Ferd. He thinks big. I like that."

Qigiq said, "Any luck?"

"I studied your pretzel. Couldn't locate engineering drawings, but found plenty of pics of Ambassadors. I can build a substitute. Better than the original: stiffer, lighter."

Qigiq smiled. "I'd sure like to have my bike back."

Murphy nodded. "The classics get inside you." His eyes moved to Kandy, but didn't say anything.

She gave a weak smile. "Fell off a boat."

Murphy laughed. "Salt water can be pretty hard."

"Ha."

He turned back to Ferd. "You have those dimensions for me?"

Ferdinand folded two of the drawings on the table. "These are my best estimates. They might need fine tuning once we begin testing."

"You going on this ride?" Kandy asked Murphy, gesturing toward the back door.

"Wouldn't miss it. This will be—"

Kandy lifted a hand to cut him off. "Let me guess...spectacular."

Murphy grinned. "You bet." He left with the drawings.

He was replaced by a tall guy with bronze arms. "Hey, good

to see you two again."

Kandy met his eyes. "Hi, Stolz. Do you live here?"

He chuckled. "Nah. But it's a good place to hang out. Especially this week with the ride happening."

"What's so special about it?" Kandy said.

Stolz shrugged. "Big. Lots of bikes. Great roads." He leaned forward. "More babes arriving every minute."

She raised an eyebrow and popped a chip into her mouth. "Bigger is better?"

"You said it." Stolz laughed. "It's an end of summer blowout we do every year over Labor Day." He held up a palm. "I know. This is California and we never stop riding. But the end of summer has an end-of-romance, back-to-work feel to it."

"Stolz, you surprise me. I never took you for the hopeless romantic type." She popped another chip.

He smiled. "You just haven't spent enough time with me. We could fix that."

"My head already hurts," she said.

"This ride open to anyone?" Qigiq asked.

Stolz shook his head. "Friends of the club. You want to come? I can swing you an invite. Got that old Moto Guzzi running yet?"

"Waiting for a new frame from Murphy."

Stolz bobbed his head. "It'll be good. But don't be in a hurry. Murphy isn't a hurry-up kind of guy."

"And Ferdinand got in line in front of me."

"Hey," Stolz said. "I heard about your jump. Have you figured out where you're going to do it?"

It was Ferd's turn to shake his head. "I am scouting locations. The original terrain was unusual, with a natural bowl to assist the ramp."

"Build it," Stolz said. "Get a golf course guy. They'll bulldoze the land into anything you want."

Ferd nodded while eating. "An excellent suggestion."

Stolz turned to Qigiq, "If you want to ride with us, let me know. I'll add you to my group."

"Not sure when I could leave," Qigiq said. "Work."

Stolz stood. "Gets in the way of living, doesn't it?" He headed for the bubbling jukebox.

"You thinking about going?" Kandy asked.

"Maybe." Qigiq leaned toward Ferdinand. "Do you really not know where this jump will happen?"

A smile emerged from inside the black beard. He said softly, "Of course I know, but then it wouldn't be a surprise." He reached into his jacket and extracted a folded sheet of paper. "Since we are together. Mrs. Chong's visitor had much to say. We must not let the excitement of the jump adversely affect the case it was designed to assist."

Kandy met Qigiq's gaze. He'd bet they were both thinking of *Solicitor* exploding.

Ferd placed the page flat on the table. It contained two columns of text: Chinese characters on the left, English phrases on the right. "The woman spoke softly, perhaps fearing microphones, making portions of the recording unintelligible. Such sections are indicated by Latin." He handed the sheet across to Qigiq. "This is what we have achieved."

His gut clenched as he read the words of a dead girl. Another innocent his cop world had failed to protect. Half of the first page was formal greeting, expression of concern for Mrs. Chong's physical condition, and repeated apology for being the cause. Then Pé said she was going away and would *make contact as soon as it is safe*. He turned the page over.

He treats us worse than the instruments.

I hate him. I hate all of them.

I will die before going back.

Time marks indicated a pause, as if Pé was wondering what else to say. Then:

I don't care about duty.

Fuck family.

Followed by a note that the speaker had stopped talking and begun to sob.

Qigiq blinked hard. He hadn't been able to save Pé. So far, he hadn't been able to do much. He slid the paper over to Kandy and stared out the back door of the club at the growing crowd milling in the alley.

CHAPTER 34

QIGIQ FOLLOWED KANDY UP THE STAIRWELL of their new, probably temporary, office building. As they turned at the top to head toward their corner, the Captain called out: "Dreeson, is that you?"

She cocked her head to catch Qigiq's eyes. He shrugged.

They entered an office freshly painted in light gray with a hint of tan. It held a pair of empty bookshelves, bare walls, and Captain Jasik's solid bulk seated behind a scratched mahogany desk. He studied them for thirty seconds, his dark eyes and dark skin revealing nothing of his thoughts. He finally asked:

"How's your head?"

"Hurts. Get dizzy if I move fast. But improving."

He nodded. "The investigation team sent a preliminary report. But you were at the scene."

"The SPOT system you hooked us into led directly to *Solicitor*. It was moored in Galilee Park when we arrived. I saw Pé, the girl from the cliff, walking alone down the dock." Kandy hesitated. "We attempted to prevent the boat and its occupants from going out to sea."

Jasik nodded. "Of course."

"Boarded the boat, identified myself, cleared the driver away from the controls. Spooner," she smiled slightly, "Rachel's lawyer husband, started yelling about badges and rights. Next I knew, the boat launches out from under me like a dragster on nitromethane."

She paused.

Jasik reached into his desk and came up with a bottle of

water. "Sorry it's not cold."

She drank before continuing.

"Spooner's friend Walstein, linebacker type, cleaned me off the stern as he fell."

"Two well-placed nine millimeter rounds," Jasik said. "He had just crawled out of the water. Hadn't made but a couple of steps onto the dock. No residue."

"From the parking lot?" Qigiq asked.

"Maybe," Jasik said. "But we haven't found a witness that saw or heard anything." He nodded for Kandy to continue.

"Hit my head on the swim platform. Blacked out briefly. This guy dragged me to the beach." She twisted a thumb at Qigiq.

Jasik turned to Qigiq, his face like carved onyx. He nodded almost imperceptibly. Then said: "Nice work."

"We were both in the water when *Solicitor* blew, or was hit by a grenade, or whatever happened," Qigiq said. "I never heard shots."

Jasik leaned back. His chair squawked. "Two shots while a fifty-foot yacht is exploding might not get noticed."

"Especially if they were well timed," Kandy said.

"Related?" Jasik asked.

"Have to be," Kandy said. "Whoever did the boat also did Walstein. They're not leaving loose ends. Besides. Walstein was supposed to be *on* the boat."

Jasik rubbed his chin, but remained silent.

"How's Mrs. Spooner?" Qigiq asked.

"Frantic," Jasik said. "She ran out of here spouting nonsense about wills and trusts and those damn kids are not taking my house."

"In mourning, huh?" Kandy said.

"Not yet."

Qigiq said, "I know it's early, but does the team have any thoughts on *Solicitor?*"

"Speculation," the captain said. "Patterson, the bomb guy, thinks homemade. No sign of technical explosives: C4, nothing like that."

"Dynamite?" Kandy said.

Jasik shook his head. "Believe it or not, he thinks it was gasoline. The GT54 caries 1250 gallons of fuel. All indications are it was full."

"Quite a bomb," Qigiq said.

"Ready for a long trip," Kandy added. "And made to look like an accident."

Silence.

"Bodies?" Qigiq said.

"Enough to know there was an Asian female and a Caucasian male on board. Not easy to get solid ID until we do DNA."

Kandy held her head and closed her eyes. When she opened them she said: "Of course."

Qigiq and Jasik gave her their full attention.

"Suitcase and a violin. Either is large enough."

"That explains how it got on," Qigiq said. "People on board were busy with Kandy. No one thought to check her luggage."

Kandy was quiet for a moment. "She didn't know did she?"

Qigiq tried to imagine Pé marching down that dock to a suicide on someone's orders. Reminded him of what the doctor had said.

"What about her feet?"

Jasik frowned and bent over for another bottle of water. He took a long swallow and recapped it. He said:

"I don't know if they found feet. But I didn't ask."

"Doctor Simmons over at General observed something while Pé was in the emergency room. The soles of her feet had been," he paused, searching for the word, "mutilated. Razor cut scars, burns." He stopped, struggling to even imagine such things.

Kandy added, "Some girls do it to themselves. The docs call

it DSH, Deliberate Self-Harm. But..."

Jasik sipped his water.

"Simmons mentioned two other things. One, he sometimes sees prostitutes in the ER that have injuries consistent with DSH, but that have, in fact, been inflicted by their pimps."

"Model citizens, those guys," Jasik said.

"Two, Pé's feet might have been bound as a child."

"Bound?" Jasik said. "As in wrapping the feet so they can't grow? I thought that was ancient history."

"Wasn't outlawed in China until the late nineteen forties," she said. "It was a strong tradition for a long, long time." She paused, then added: "Like slavery."

Jasik turned to her. Nodded. "Illegal since eighteen sixty-five. Yet people are bought and sold everyday: sex workers, fishermen, miners. I've heard estimates as high as thirty-million." His jaw clenched. He capped his water bottle and leaned back. The chair creaked again in complaint. He stared up at the ceiling like an angel was sending him a message. Then he leaned forward onto his elbows.

"What do we have? A stressed classical musician harming herself; not so uncommon with young people. She finds a rich boyfriend who wants to run away into a midlife fantasy. Someone decides blackmailing the rich guy is a smart idea. They run, get caught, shots are fired. She turns up on his boat moments before it explodes." He paused. Looked to each of them. "How does the DSH play into any of this?"

The office was quiet.

Traffic hissed from below. A car horn blared long and hard.

"Who's the blackmailer?" Qigiq asked.

"Someone with a motorbike and an SUV," Jasik said. "Which we only know about thanks to an anonymous individual with a telephoto lens who happened to be in the right place at the right time." He paused. "And is such a good citizen he sent his lovely pictures to the police as events unfolded like some kind of twisted reality show."

"Unlikely in the extreme," Kandy said.

Jasik nodded.

Qigiq studied the floor. The new carpet had woven swirls that reminded him of staring down at the windblown ice of a glacier, wondering what hid beneath the surface.

"How did they know?"

Kandy turned to him. "It started at the Chinese hospital with Mrs. Wong."

Qigiq shook his head without lifting it. "Before that. Who knew Pé and Spooner were together? Rich guy has a mistress from the second row of an orchestra. Who cares? Who would take the pictures we saw in Spooner's so-called contract?"

He sat motionless, eyes down. Time ticked by on his championship watch.

He jerked up.

"Did Pé know about them?"

CHAPTER 35

TENSION DRAINED FROM QIGIQ'S shoulders as he worked his bike toward the Golden Gate. He tried to convince himself they hadn't failed even as the roar of the explosion replayed in his head. Halfway across the bridge he checked his rearview mirror. A red Jeep rode close behind him, and a white box truck behind that. He was reminded of the two bikes that had led him to the Gallerie Electra.

And a dark BMW sedan.

He passed the gallery five minutes later and continued beyond Taste of Rome, then turned into the public parking lot for the docks. The police crews were gone and the hull of the *Solicitor* was missing: maybe sunk, or towed to a salvage yard. He dismounted, hung his helmet from the bars, leaned on the seat and stared out over the darkening waters trying to recall the faces of the two men who had stepped out of the BMW. When he had them in focus he walked back toward the Rome and took a table on the sidewalk. The air was cool near the water, and he was comfortable in his riding jacket. A waitress brought him a decaf in a to-go cup.

He studied the gallery across the street.

It was well lit. There was no movement inside. Halfway through his coffee, no one had gone in or out. At 6:11 pm he left cash on the table, took the paper cup, and strolled south along the water. Four blocks down he crossed Bridgeway and worked back toward the gallery. Once there he read a three-foot-high poster for an event called Burning Man: a rock-concert-sized gathering in the desert where people built extravagant art installations only to set them on fire. It seemed like a return to tribal times and sensibilities...and the unique dangers of humans in herds.

A gleaming black motorcycle frame sat on a white marble pedestal on the other side of the window. He recalled his Zen conversation with the biker. This object had no seams, making it appear carved from a block of black marble. A brass plate on the stand named the work *Naked*. It had to be coincidence, but seeing it made the dream feel like a premonition.

He moved a few yards down the sidewalk and examined paintings through the window. Many were seascapes, apparently chosen for tourists who wanted to take a bit of the ocean home with them. Wave after wave fused into a mash-up of a surfer's restless dream.

His gaze stopped moving.

Beyond the last wall, behind a glass counter that might be for checking out, though no cash register was visible, stood a six foot tall picture. It was leaning against the case so only the top third was visible. But in that top third he saw an eye, hair, and part of a nose of a girl holding a cigarette while standing beside a pillar.

The color was washed out it to nearly black and white. She appeared Asian. He pulled out his cell phone, took a photo, and emailed it to Kandy.

He continued around the building looking for indication of an alarm system, found it near the entrance facing the parking lot. He debated; checked the time. Not quite 6:30 pm. He held his gaze on the tiny tachometer etched in the face. The watch had been issued in honor of an American named Nicky Hayden winning the MotoGP Motorcycle World Championship.

It reminded him to pursue excellence.

He walked back around to the front and knocked on the glass. The sign on the door said the gallery had closed at 5:00. The interior hadn't switched to night lighting; possibly someone was still inside.

He knocked a second time. Sipped his now-cool coffee.

He was deciding whether to knock a third time when the lights inside dimmed—probably on a timer. A poster low in the corner caught his eye. He took three steps and crouched. Then he placed the coffee on the sidewalk and pulled out his phone to take its picture. A violist who had played a concert at the Nevada Museum of Art in Reno just yesterday was performing with a chamber orchestra at a nearby theater. The swoop of hair across the left side of her face was also present in the picture inside.

A dark BMW with no rear plate turned into the drive to his right. He stood and stepped out of sight. Before the car had stopped, the side door of the gallery opened and a silver-haired man exited. He'd bet Kandy five-to-one odds it was the man he had seen on his first visit.

Qigiq walked quickly toward the BMW. "Excuse me."

The man looked up. "I'm sorry, we're closed."

Qigiq nodded, but continued his approach.

"Sorry to trouble you. But could you please answer one quick question?"

The man had the passenger door open. "We open in the morning at eight."

"The girl in the picture smoking. Is she the one who played at the museum?"

The man's eyes narrowed. "Yes, that's Mylin, our violist. She plays very well."

"Thank you. How much are you asking for the picture?"

The man's eyes grew more interested. "That's a new arrival. It's not yet for sale."

Qigiq stopped, facing him. He wore a white shirt with a blue and silver tie beneath a suit coat. His face was creased, like a farmer who spent his days in the sun. He was calm, and not making telltale moves to adjust a gun in his jacket, or hide his hands.

"I have the perfect place for it."

The man waved a hand. "In a few weeks perhaps." He slipped into the car.

Qigiq stepped aside as the BMW backed out. He retrieved his coffee and strolled back toward the rental bike. His cell phone rumbled with the signature sound of the Guzzi he missed.

"How's your head?" he asked.

"Feeling better every hour. Got your email. Is that the girl from Mrs. Chong's place?"

"Her name is Mylin, plays the viola. Would you like to go to a concert tonight in Mill Valley?"

CHAPTER 36

THE BMW TURNED RIGHT onto Sausalito's main street. The two men rolled in silence as they passed the local police station. They followed the curving road to Highway One and headed south toward the Golden Gate Bridge.

"He was at the docks," Wu said, staring straight ahead.

They rolled onto the majestic bridge in the center lane. Wu scratched his nose, turned toward the driver. "With that woman you recognized."

Prime held the wheel steady with gloved hands. "He was at the club, too. With a third man. Rotund. Bearded."

"How?"

Prime had no intention of revealing his encounter on the sidewalk with this man and the wondrous woman called Kandy. He smiled inwardly at the name, and undressed her in his mind for a moment. That silly bitch Trina had told Kandy about the club. That's how this had started. But he wasn't planning to tell Father. Ever.

"How?" Wu repeated with emphasis.

"The third man. He is looking for a special kind of rider."

Wu straightened in the seat and turned back to the windshield. He reached in his pocket and slipped on dark sunglasses, even though it was dusk.

Prime glanced across at him. A golden view of the Pacific Ocean under a cloudless sky reflected from a lens.

"Those silly motorbikes you and Tuson ride," Wu said.

"They help us," Prime replied. "As you said about the radio-activated explosive in the violin...a tool."

Wu sighed. "Only a fool believes an American. But too much is at stake. She could no longer be trusted." He stared straight ahead. "Such waste."

Prime glanced at his father's drawn features as he drove. He hoped he never had to make such a decision.

Wu said, "Sad to sacrifice that instrument. But I knew Pé would need to look, and would have recognized a cheap substitute. Your sister lacked discipline. Had we refused, she would have become difficult in public, drawn attention, destroyed a delicate plan." They passed through the toll booth without speaking. "You said 'a rotund man.'"

Prime nodded. "Round, not so tall. Large hands, thick wrists. Talks like a university professor."

"And why does he want this special rider?"

"He is reenacting a famous motorcycle jump from an old movie."

Wu wagged his head. "Why would anyone bother with such nonsense?"

"As you taught me, America is about pleasure and instant self-gratification. Thrill is a kind of pleasure. He believes people will pay to see it."

"Pay to watch a motorcycle jump into the air?"

They turned east toward the marina. And Chinatown.

"Do we know who this man is?"

"Not yet. But Petrushka is near him."

Wu nodded slowly. "And the woman. She ran to the boat. Why?"

Prime shrugged. "Perhaps she was Spooner's whore. Did you see her leap from the dock?" Prime had seen it, and couldn't forget the raw power and beauty of it. "Or maybe she knew the other man."

"Who told her where to be? The location was fresh. And the coincidence: she is at your bike club, then at the dock." Wu fell silent. Spoke more softly. "Now this man who isn't a white devil appears at the gallery." Wu reached inside his jacket with his left hand and pulled out a dark red box. He removed a cigarette, lit it, and returned the box to his pocket.

"When are you going to stop that?" Prime asked.

Wu shook his head and waved at the smoke cloud in his lap.

"Never, I am too old. You give it up. You have many years to live."

The BMW eased its way into Chinatown. The architecture didn't change, but signs ceased to carry English, replacing it with characters unreadable by most Americans. The streets were narrower than in other parts of San Francisco, so progress was slow. Prime made a left turn, crawled up a hill, and stopped in front of a two-story building with a garage on the lower level. A red Prius was parked illegally in front of their driveway. Prime said:

"Doesn't anyone obey traffic laws?"

"Drive around the block," Wu said. He pulled out his cell phone, dialed, and spoke Chinese for a few seconds, then returned it to his pocket.

"When?" Wu asked.

Prime frowned. Glanced at Wu and back to the road.

"When is this jump?" Wu said.

"This week. The big American holiday called Labor Day. A special day set aside to celebrate workers."

Wu leaned back and drew on his dark cigarette. "In China, everyone works. We are all labor. Do they celebrate here in America the Chinese laborers who built their precious railroads one spike at a time?" He exhaled. "Lonely men, far from home, who cut tunnels a few inches each day with dynamite that often killed them as they placed it?"

Prime remained silent, knowing an answer wasn't expected, or welcome. He made another right turn.

"Where?"

"It's a secret," Prime said.

Wu's head whipped sideways. He stared at Prime.

Prime held up his right arm as if to deflect an attack. "I don't know. The big man won't tell anyone. And we haven't been able to find out who he's working with to set it up."

Wu settled back, reached his arm out until his cigarette hovered above the ashtray, and tapped the ashes off.

"He might tell Petr."

Prime nodded. "I've asked her to find out."

"Asked her?" Wu said. "*Tell* her to find out."

Prime shook his head. "It doesn't work that way. I'm trying to buy information. We don't own her like the others."

Wu blew two smoke rings toward the windshield. "Why does this man who wishes to make money from this jump keep secrets?"

The BMW turned the corner and eased up the hill. The red Prius was gone. Prime touched a button and a garage door opened on the opposite side of the sidewalk. He twisted the wheel to cross the walk, drove carefully because he had only inches of clearance on either side, pulled far in, and stopped.

He lowered the door and turned the car off.

"I'll push Petr for a location."

"Yes," Wu said. "However, it is more important that we understand this woman who knew Pé's name. If she gets too close..." his voice trailed off as he dragged on the last of his cigarette and put it out in the center ashtray. He made no move to get out. He said:

"How is Tuson?"

"Pale. Barely moves. And won't eat," Prime said. "Can't we get another doctor?"

"Western doctors don't know medicine."

"Chinatown then."

"He's been to the Chinese hospital," Wu replied. "Doctor Fan has done what he can."

"He needs a hospital with a breathing machine."

"Why? So the police can come and talk to him about what he was doing on the cliff, and why an American in an expensive car would want to shoot him?"

"Could we get him a nurse?"

Wu opened the car door and stepped out. He waited for Prime to do the same, then spoke over the roof.

"Tonight. Who will play in Pé's place?" Wu asked.

"Promote Yubi. She's diligent with practicing, and will be delighted to move to the first chair."

Wu brought his hand toward his face and realized he no longer had the cigarette. He covered his mouth with the hand and rubbed his cheek. "She plays well." He leaned his forearms against the roof rail. "Is she loyal?"

Prime had believed Pé was loyal. His own sister. "She has not been tested."

Wu stared at nothing in particular. "I contacted Gan. He has two suitable replacements. You will have to go, Tuson cannot travel."

"When?"

"There is no time for a cruise ship, so accommodations will be...basic. I instructed him to send both. Same channel. Ohio in nine days time." He stared into Prime. "If you fail to meet them, they will be sent back." He coughed. "At our expense."

CHAPTER 37

THE PLANE WAS IN THE AIR for three-quarters of an hour. Mylin napped until the jostling of a man struggling with his bag stuck in the overhead bin nudged her awake. She blinked to clear her vision. The concert started at eight. She was now at a gate of the enormous San Francisco International Airport. She glanced at the jostler's watch as he lowered a bag that she didn't think would pass the carry-on size test.

It was 5:30.

She retrieved her viola from the overhead compartment.

She was still wearing her green dress because there hadn't been time to go back to the shared rooms in Reno. She also had hundreds of dollars of Mr. Barth's money in her tiny purse. She was nervous she might lose it, or have it stolen. She trudged up the jetway and made her way to baggage claim.

There was no one waiting.

She had ridden with Joe all the way back to Reno and flown in because she thought they expected her to be on this flight. And now no one was here.

She knelt in a corner and opened her viola case. She looked around to see if anyone was watching, then removed the cash from her purse and slid all but a single hundred-dollar bill underneath the instrument. The hundred she slipped up under her skirt and over the waistband of her panties.

Feeling safer, she went out to stand at the curb. Cars pulled away carelessly, drawing horns from traffic in the outer lanes. What did they expect her to do? There had always been a car before. She bit her lower lip. Something had happened to make them forget. She wished Joe were here to drive her.

She could hire a driver.

She waved at a long black car. "How much to Mill Valley?" she asked the heavyset man with bushy eyebrows sitting behind the wheel.

"Flat rate is a hundred and five. How many people?"

"Just me."

The man smiled. "Well, little lady, for you I can discount the ride to ninety."

She nodded and jumped into the back seat, clutching her instrument.

The man struggled to twist around to face her. He finally gave up and looked at her in the rearview mirror.

"Where's your luggage, Miss?"

She shook her head. "No luggage. Just this." She held up the case. "Please hurry, I must play a concert."

He put the car in gear and executed a graceful curve into traffic. In a few minutes they were on a wide highway traveling north very fast.

Green hills became tightly packed buildings and many traffic lights. Buses came close to her window. The glorious Golden Gate Bridge lifted the car high up into the sky over treacherous water, followed by a road weaving among tall trees. Finally, a sign announced the village of Mill Valley, whose low buildings and wooden construction suggested a town trapped in the past. The entire way she asked herself: Who are you, Joe Roberts? Why did you take my picture in Michigan? What do you think of me, Mr. Roberts? Do you want me, Joe? You held me close at the rest stop. Thank you for helping me to see my grandmother. But Mr. Roberts, you cannot have me.

No one can have me.

The long vehicle stopped in front of a two-story hotel at 6:30 pm. She fumbled under her dress, then reached forward with the hundred-dollar bill.

"Thank you for the ride, sir."

"Where are you playing, Miss?"

She pointed past him across the street. His head swiveled to look.

"You're playing at the Throckmorton Theatre? That poster says there's an all-girl orchestra. Is that you?"

She nodded.

He got out of the car and walked around to open the door. He held out his hand.

She took it with one hand and kept her other arm wrapped around her viola.

"You have a nice concert, little lady." He tipped a black hat too small for his round head.

She was pleased that her hotel room was ready, and relieved that no one was there waiting to question her.

She took a shower. While washing carefully around her ankle bracelet she stroked its green stone three times for luck. She hand washed her under garments and hoped they would dry quickly. She toweled her hair dry and combed it out. Then she opened her case and practiced the demanding parts for tonight's concert while her hair and body dried. Fifteen minutes later she slipped on the tired green dress, her black heels, and took $200 from the case and put it into her purse.

A pleasant woman at the hotel desk directed her to a place called Ma Petite Folie, a store that specialized in imports from Italy and France. She walked the few blocks.

A woman in her forties wearing a long sweater of many subtle colors, black slacks, and heels approached. Mylin's head barely reached her chin.

"Hello, may I help you?"

"I need a blue dress," Mylin said. "Concert tonight."

"Oh, you're going to see the orchestra from Asia? That's wonderful. I've heard their playing is very precise." Mylin smiled. "Over here."

Only one was blue enough and small enough for Mylin. She loved the way the silky material glistened when she moved. It covered her knees, but hugged her hips. Mr. Barth would be happy.

"Bras?"

The woman shook her head. "Sorry."

Mylin looked down at her black heels, examining the scuff marks. "Shoes?"

"There are a few along the back. I'm not sure we have your size."

Mylin loved them instantly. Black, soft, with a tiny silver buckle. They sat alone at the far end of a shelf because they were too small for most Americans.

But they fit perfectly.

She paid cash and rushed back to the hotel to call room service. She didn't eat much before a performance, but she must eat something. And have milk. Chocolate if possible.

They delivered white milk with a salad and fresh bread, though she would have preferred rice. She ate wearing the green dress over nothing. The bedside clock showed 7:05 pm. She was due at the hall by 7:30. Was that clock correct? In America, she had found, clocks often lied.

Would an escort come by to fetch her? Or were they going to neglect that, too?

At 7:15 she opened the viola case and retrieved a bottle of Ferrari Red eyeliner with a calligraphy brush rubber banded to it. Father had insisted his daughters be skilled in the art of rendering Chinese characters. She used that skill now to place a tapering red line parallel to and below her right eyebrow, from the bridge of her nose to the tip near her temple where they almost touched. This line was her talisman for good luck, awakened her inner warrior, and gave her a place to hide ever since she was eight. The first time she walked on stage with the red stroke, having told no one she was going to do it, there was much whispering and pointing. After that brief performance in the home of a wealthy man named Jon Fong her father was trying to impress, he had said only: "Be brave in all things, little one. The future requires much of you."

He never once mentioned the red line.

She began to dress. Her undergarments were still wet so she skipped them. Her hair was damp, but presentable. She had been very lucky; the new dress was beautiful. She hoped Mr. Barth would be satisfied. Her mind drifted. Her secret desire was that Joe would adore her in it.

You sent him away. Stop.

What to do about the shoes? She was taking a chance because she must stand to perform the entire concerto and had no time to break them in. If her feet began to hurt, she would be forced to tolerate the pain.

She stared at the high heels of the dress shoes purchased with Mr. Barth's cash. Laolao had told her in loving whispers that part of being a strong woman was the ability to face pain: hours of practicing on steel strings, an abusive brother, loneliness. She asked the dragon gods to care for her grandmother, and vowed to return to her the moment Father would allow it.

At 7:23 on the lying clock no one had come. She tuned her viola, placed it carefully on top of the money, and clicked the case closed. She started walking to the theater, balancing carefully on the new heels.

Alone.

The feelings for her sister she had been keeping at bay rushed in and filled her chest. Her breathing quickened. A dizzying numbness invaded her brain.

Pé should be by her side right now, holding her hand. They would encourage each other. Chase away the pre-concert jitters by making jokes about all of the mistakes they could make and listeners would never know because most didn't pay attention.

Some even fell asleep. She and Pé had practiced together for so many hours, over so many years. And now...now she was alone. They had forgotten her. And Pé was...

She fought to keep her eyes dry.

She fought the hate rising up her throat.

She fought the desire to scream things she had wanted to say to men for so long.

Then she silently asked Pé why. Why, why, *why* did you cause trouble?

She touched the tip of her tongue to her lips. She needed just one cigarette. Like in Michigan when she had snuck out to avoid her father. But if she weakened, Father would smell it on her after the concert, and order Shen to punish her for disobedience.

When she arrived backstage the other musicians were there, but the brothers were not. Their absence made her wonder who had been riding that motorbike in the darkness, which made her mind replay Pé disappearing over the rocky edge. She hoped by some miracle Pé had escaped. And the rider, would he survive? She frowned as part of her hoped not, then she stopped herself.

Such thoughts were inappropriate.

She located the green room. As her fingers played warm-up exercises, her eyes wandered the empty space. A digital clock with red numerals hung above the door. She hoped it didn't lie. At 7:45 the sound of chairs scraping across a wood floor reached her. The orchestra was taking the stage. As the soloist, she would wait in the wings, and be introduced.

At 7:53 voices penetrated the door.

At 7:59 a knock interrupted her mini-rehearsal. She stopped in mid-stroke and opened the door. Her handsome brother Prime stood in the hallway in a tuxedo. He held out his arm to escort her to the stage. That meant Tuson had been on the bike. Joy freed her heart for the briefest instant, then she forced herself to feel nothing.

She walked onstage to modest applause. Pé wasn't with the

violins as she had secretly hoped. Mr. Bartholomew sat in the first row. He smiled broadly at her. She tried hard to give him a gracious smile back, then looked away.

She closed her eyes.

Concentrated.

The opening sounds of the orchestra filled her body. She lifted her bow and breathed. The long singing line of the Walton viola concerto melted from her instrument. It wasn't a complex piece, but contained great passion in the opening, and lovely dance rhythms as it evolved.

She paused at the end of the first movement and glanced up at the audience.

There, in the second from the last row. He wasn't holding a camera, but she could feel him capturing her.

———

An hour and twenty-six minutes later she was back in the green room still breathless from the fantastic Brandenburg Concerto for two violas. The arch of her left foot was cramping, and the shoes had started pinching her right pinky toe a half hour before. She wiped her viola and stooped to place it on top of the money. She paused, considering the future, then moved the cash to her purse. She latched the case carefully. She dabbed at her face with a tissue. The concert had gone well. The hall had a beautiful resonance. But the evening was not over.

She turned at the knock on the door.

The knob twisted and Prime stepped in. He closed the door and pressed his back to it.

"He is incredibly angry about Pé."

"I am not Pé."

"The two of you were close since you were kids. You must have known something."

She looked down at worn gray carpet where hundreds of great musicians had stood to warm up their hands before performing. He would expect her to lie—so she must not. She inhaled and said:

"Pé told me she was in love."

He laughed and moved to a curved plastic chair to sit.

"How is that relevant to anything?"

She met his eyes, then stood, clutching her case to her chest. "Where is she?"

"She's not coming back."

She took small steps backwards. Her shoulders touched the wall. She was holding her breath.

He shook his head. "What did you expect?"

She had expected her only sister to come to her senses and stop having foolish meetings with the fast-talking American. A lawyer with a sleek yacht that Pé had revealed in hushed tones would whisk them away to the ocean. A yacht with a luxurious bed and a kitchen and wine and no one to bother them for miles in any direction. Secret meetings Father had never approved.

"I." She wet her lips. "I thought it would all work out."

"It has. Pé isn't coming back. Yubi will be promoted to first chair." He paused. "And join the quartet."

She forced herself to remain stoic. Not ask why. Father had decided. There was nothing she could do to change that.

He said, "We'll fill Yubi's current chair later. You won't be affected."

She nodded slowly, but her eyes were focused on a faraway cliff. Her whole body twitched when a gun fired in her mind.

———

Mylin moved her mouth into a wide smile to show her teeth as she strolled into the reception on Prime's arm. The hundred or so attendees burst into applause.

Prime guided her across the room to the group containing Barth and Mr. Wu.

"I believe you two have met," Prime said.

Thomas Bartholomew's eyes studied the curves of her blue dress. He was smiling.

"I had business in San Francisco. Are you surprised to see me?"

"I had no idea we would meet again so soon. You must be a great patron of the arts."

"And artists in blue," he said. "You played beautifully tonight."

She doubted he could discern the difference between J.S. Bach and Amy Beach, but said:

"Thank you. Will you be staying long?"

His eyes flicked to Wu and back. "Uh, my team is still negotiating, so yes, I'll be staying the night at least."

She brightened her smile, knowing that would please Barth. And her father would expect no less.

A waiter approached carrying flutes of champagne. While he whispered to her father and gestured toward the side of the room, Mylin reached for a glass. She raised it to Barth and sipped. After the waiter left, Wu whispered to Prime. Then Prime came over and leaned close to her ear. He said:

"A man has requested to meet with you secretly. Find out what you can, then come see me and," he looked toward Wu and Barth chatting, "I will let you know about this one."

She nodded and excused herself. How would a "secret" meeting happen? She roamed the room, waiting to be approached. A six-foot high movie poster drew her eye to a cacophony of yellows and blues. She stopped in front of it.

A couple drifted up close on either side of her. He was middle-height and slightly dark-skinned. The woman was taller, with muscles that bulged like a weight-lifting supermodel. All three of them had their backs to the room.

"Hello," she said. They turned to face her. "My name is Mylin."

"I'm Qigiq, and this is my friend Kandy," Qigiq looked past her shoulder. "We must talk."

"Talk?"

"Yes," Kandy said softly. "About Pé."

Mylin's eyes grew wide; what did they know about her sister? She glanced over her shoulder. Father was in conversation with Barth, and wasn't watching her.

"Do you know—" she stopped herself, not wanting to be overheard.

"Let's get some fresh air," Kandy said.

Mylin deposited her glass on the bar on the way out. They stepped through the outer glass doors of the theater, passed its tiny stand-alone ticket booth near the sidewalk, and stopped beneath the tree in front holding Buddhist prayer flags in its scrawny outstretched arms. Mannequins in the dark windows of a clothing boutique across the street floated like dispirited souls awaiting sunrise.

They went left, three abreast, Mylin in the middle.

Antique green lampposts cast the shadows of trees over them; trees that lined both sides of the street and repeated every two car lengths as regular as a farmer's field. When they had traveled half a block toward town Qigiq reached into his jacket. He handed a picture to Mylin.

She stopped mid-stride. "How did you get this?"

Qigiq touched her elbow to start her walking again. He said:

"Found it in an apartment."

Mylin stopped again. Her eyes flashed from Qigiq to Kandy and back.

"Who are you?"

Kandy said, "Music lovers."

Qigiq added, "Is that you and Pé?"

Mylin stood stock-still on the sidewalk, trying to understand what was happening. Then an idea struck her.

"What did you tell the waiter?"

Qigiq said, "Please ask the elderly gentleman, would the soloist have a free moment for a discreet meeting."

Father usually made her meet a potential donor. Her eyes

moved from the picture to Qigiq's face to Kandy and back to the picture.

"Yes, her name is Pé."

"And is that you?" Kandy said.

Mylin hesitated, then rocked her head up and down. "We had just played a youth concert in China at the—" She bit her tongue. She had been taught never to reveal information. "We were celebrating."

They walked. In another block, a pair of pine trees in a traffic island split the road in two. They reached a circular bench in front of a bank. Someone had chalked "Cookies" and an arrow on the bricks. The faded wooden bench enclosed a lonely tree with buds, but no leaves. Scraggly grass encircled its trunk. They sat.

On the far side of the street a white Honda hybrid backed toward an empty parking space. The next spot was occupied by a red motorcycle whose helmeted rider was fumbling with a saddlebag. She hoped the rider noticed that car.

"Can anyone hear us?" Qigiq said.

Mylin frowned. "We are alone."

"But can they hear us?" Kandy said. She reached for Mylin's purse.

Mylin held it. Mr. Barth's money was inside. She shook her head no.

Kandy didn't let go.

Mylin opened the purse with her other hand and removed the hundred dollar bills. She squeezed them in her hand as if they could keep her safe.

Kandy slipped the purse from Mylin's shoulder and hid it in the grass near the tree. Then they walked away.

"They will wonder why they cannot hear me," Mylin said.

"Tell them you forgot your purse," Qigiq said.

She shook her head. "They will punish me for carelessness. We must return quickly."

A noisy sports car approached. Qigiq glanced at Kandy, who shrugged. He said softly:

"Mylin, we're police detectives."

Mylin curled the toes of her aching feet tightly. She didn't speak. Or blink. Father had taught *no police* since she was old enough to speak. She had never even been this close to one.

"Tell them a detective is interested in getting to know you. They may see an opportunity, or sense a trap. Let them choose."

The sports car's exhaust rumble faded.

She turned toward Qigiq. Men said "know you" when they meant something else. She said:

"You desire sex with Mylin?"

He shook his head. "No, Mylin." He hesitated. "Pé is dead. She and Rudy Spooner were killed when his boat exploded a few hours ago." They turned a forty-five-degree corner in silence. "We want to find the people responsible. Please help us."

Mylin stopped walking. She stared at Qigiq. Her mouth opened, but she didn't speak. She wrapped her arms around her torso as if she were standing in a freezing wind.

"My sister…"

She hugged harder.

"My sister…he said she wasn't coming back."

Kandy touched her shoulder.

Mylin jerked away.

"My sister is dead?"

———

Inside the reception hall champagne glasses floated on waiters' trays and a five-foot-tall ice sculpture of a grand piano began dispensing martinis from its pedals. A chocolate fountain and mountain of shrimp appeared while the girls from the orchestra mingled with the crowd of concertgoers. Mylin flew directly to her father and brother, and pulled them toward a corner.

"The man says he is a detective. He would like to get to

know me better."

Wu interlaced his fingers in front of his chest and rubbed his palms together. "A detective who wants to know Mylin. Today of all days. Yet. Such an obvious approach. No one is so stupid."

Prime remained silent, but his dark eyes shifted to his father's face and held there.

Wu said: "You have a date with Mr. Bartholomew tonight. Keep it. But tomorrow night, you will meet our new detective friend. Obtain a phone number where you can call him. Insist. And give him your cell number."

"My personal cell?"

"Yes. I want him to be able to reach you at any time. Let us see how anxious he is."

Mylin turned to go find Barth; if she kept him waiting too long, she would be punished. Behind her, she heard Prime speak softly to her father: "Keeping your enemies close?"

She hesitated, wanting to hear Father's response, stood on tiptoe and craned her neck to scan the crowd. Barth was at the far side of the room near the ice piano. She was glad she had been ordered to exchange phone numbers; Mr. Qigiq's card was already in her shoe, and she had memorized his number.

Her father said: "Not close. The great Sun Tzu taught, 'Know your enemy and know yourself, and you will win a hundred battles.' We must study this enemy. Observe with clear eyes, my son."

Mylin shuffled across the room to drift up beside Bartholomew, who was drinking with one hand, eating with the other, and talking with both to two men wearing gray ill-fitting suits. She didn't know them, but smiled and waited for him to stop talking about what a great sport fisherman he was but he never had the time; and how living in Reno was just too far from the ocean and too much hassle to fly even though he had his private jet land directly in Half Moon Bay. Eventually he turned toward her and placed his drinking arm gently around her shoulders.

"And this, gentlemen, is the finest violist on the west coast."

He squeezed her body against his briefly and released her.

She smiled and bowed slightly to each of them.

The men returned her smile and nodded. One mumbled, "Pleasure."

Barth raised his glass, the others followed suit. "To Mylin, who makes such beautiful music."

Three glasses tipped up.

Mylin tugged on the sleeve of Barth's jacket; he leaned his ear close to her lips.

"I am ready to go. Do you have the Bentley? It is such a beautiful night."

His face collapsed. He spoke loud enough for all to hear. "I flew in today and have a crappy rental car."

She gazed at him. "Oh, I was hoping for a topless drive."

The three men grew more attentive.

She motioned with her hand. "Top down is so nice in evening air."

They laughed.

"Sorry, Mylin. The rental is just a plain old sedan."

The man on the left curled a finger at Barth and drew him aside. The remaining man, whose eyes were both shifty and half-closed, glanced at Mylin and looked away. He stood in silence, sipping red wine. She didn't really care about the convertible so much; they wouldn't be in it long anyway. She just knew older men loved to talk about their fancy cars that they thought made them virile and attractive.

When the men returned, Barth was smiling.

"Mylin, John here has offered to let me borrow his Volvo so you can have your topless ride. We have a meeting tomorrow and can trade back. Isn't he great?"

She beamed and stepped forward. "Thank you, John. That's very sweet of you." She stood tall on her aching toes and gave him a quick kiss on his left cheek.

He blushed and broke into a huge smile. "You're welcome. I loved your music."

"Thank you." She backed away until her arm touched Barth.

"I guess we should be going," Barth said. "Appreciate the loaner, John."

Barth shook hands with both men, took Mylin by the arm, and made his way to the main door. She stopped short.

"My viola!"

CHAPTER 38

MYLIN CARRIED HER VIOLA in her left hand, purse over her shoulder, and held Barth's arm with the right as they walked along the tree-lined street, nearly retracing the steps she had taken with the detectives. A bleep and a flash of amber lights on a shiny black Volvo with sparkles in the paint identified the borrowed car. The expanse of black between the snowy white sedan parked behind and a white van in front carried her thoughts to the *Silent Pool* by the amazing artist Cai Guo-Qiang. She had played melodies from the Brahms Requiem in a Shanghai museum as a teenager while standing beside a lake of black ink surrounded by construction debris. As she played, the events of her life—from her mother's death to sacrificing her virginity to the most recent man who had tied her ankles to the bed and almost broken her precious ankle bracelet—emerged from the shattered concrete, twisted rebar, and bottomless black of hopelessness right there in the room before her.

The car's metal top began folding in half, pulling her mind back to the lonely street—and her job.

"Will it be warm where we're going?" she asked.

Barth grinned, but didn't answer.

She placed her viola in the trunk and wiggled into the bucket passenger seat. She hadn't lied; she really did like convertibles. So much sensation all at once: motion, howling wind, breeze on her cheeks, slow rising song of a powerful motor like a glissando from eight cellos—it filled her body with so much qi energy her skin tingled.

Barth backed the car out, and headed away from the town.

She tilted her seat back, closed her eyes and stretched.

When the car began weaving from side to side a few minutes later, she opened them. Two-lane blacktop painted stark gray by moonlight flowed through grassy hills. The freshness of the Pacific Ocean in northern California filled the air. Above her the sky was a mesmerizing pattern of stars, the fog having stayed behind in San Francisco.

She lifted her arms up high behind the headrest and arched her back, pulling to increase the intensity of the stretch. She sighed. California was filled with so much beauty it almost made her cry.

The car slowed.

Mr. Barth's hand grazed her shoulder, then traveled down her side and across her hip, outlining her body. He said:

"It's warmer here."

He was speaking the truth. The farther they traveled from San Francisco, the more the air caressed her with its warmth. She let him touch, and did nothing but listen to the night. Wind swirled, the turbine-powered thrum carried them forward. From far away, the high-pitched whine of a distressed gull reached her.

Barth's hand moved to her left thigh, and squeezed.

She rolled her face toward him and forced a close-lipped smile.

Driving with his left hand, he became more bold with his right, inching the blue dress up with his fingers until her kneecap was exposed, then her thigh. He stroked her leg above the knee and shifted his hand to the inside—and up. It was time to focus on her job. Not only must she give him what he wanted now, but also make him want more...much more. She said:

"Should we go topless?"

His eyes jumped to her face and back to the road. He smiled and put both hands on the wheel.

"Sure."

She leaned forward and swept the blue dress up over her

head. Lingerie drying in her room left her naked on the supple leather, except for her shoes. She had yet to meet a man who didn't like high heels, so she left them on.

He squeezed the wheel and twisted his neck back and forth between eyes-on-the-road and eyes-on-her-breasts.

"Well, well."

She reached out with both hands and placed them over his right hand. Then she eased his hand away from the wheel and brought it to her left breast. She was small but firm, and most men enjoyed the hardness of her nipple against their palm.

Barth drove and grinned.

Mylin moved his hand gently against her, feeling the mushy palm of a businessman who avoided physical labor more difficult than swinging a golf club. And the wind. She so loved wind...swirling, swirling around her entire body like eddies in a stream, cleansing her with its touch.

She guided his hand across her flat belly. Closing her eyes, she mentally replayed her concerto as she pushed his hand lower, reaching her jade gate, pressing, rocking her hips gently forward...back...forward. Men obsessed over carrying her to the zenith; it made them feel strapping and powerful like the heroes they imagined themselves to be. Even the clumsy ones could be successful if they accepted direction.

If not, she was a skilled faker.

She sighed out a long breath. To increase positive energy for the upcoming night she gave thanks that Father hadn't given her a worse job, which he could do at his whim if she failed to perform: Fenfang picking rice under the hot sun in a muddy field, not considered pretty enough to entertain men; or Huidai serving two dozen customers a day in a dirty brothel like the others who had failed to learn their musical instrument; or Kwong sweating over a sewing machine in a factory where the bosses raped the women, even while they were pregnant.

An angry buzzing filled her ears.

"What the...?" Barth said, pulling his hand away and grabbing the wheel.

The car jerked right. She popped her eyes open. Two wheels hit gravel. A thunderous hiss was followed by pings of ringing steel. The car bounced wildly on the rough shoulder.

A blur of red motorcycle flew past on the left, the rider tucked in tight behind a tiny windscreen. An instant later it had become a tiny spec of taillight.

Barth fought the wheel and twisted the Volvo back onto pavement with a shudder and chirp from the tires.

Mylin hugged her arms over her breasts. Her eyes followed the red light as it shrank like a fading ember in the fireplace at music school when she was little. It wailed a tortured cry very different than the motorcycle on the cliff. Her imagination filled her eyes with the Volvo careening over the edge into the Pacific Ocean, plunging Barth and her to their deaths.

She screamed.

Barth's hand squeezed her left forearm. His voice shouted over the wind: "It's all right, Mylin, we're safe. Relax. We're safe. It's all right..."

She stared at a gentle curve of black road; the soft crash of surf replaced the screaming machine.

"Damn biker could have killed us."

She stared straight ahead. Silent.

"Sure ruins the mood, huh?"

Her nakedness in the breeze abruptly interrupted her fear, reminding her why this American was beside her, what she was there to do—and who she was. She leaned toward Barth and placed her head on his shoulder. Reaching forward with her right hand, she touched him between his legs. Lifting her lips close to his ear so he would feel her breath, she whispered:

"We know where the mood lives. We will find it again."

―――

The Volvo turned onto a narrow strip of cracked, whitened blacktop and stopped beside a steel pole. At the top of the pole, a sign lit from inside its plastic sheets by a flickering tube read: Sea and Sky Bed and Breakfast. Below that, a separate white-on-red sign glowed: VACANCY. The top motored up. No other buildings were visible as far as she could see along the road in either direction. Two cars were parked on the opposite side of the pole lit by moonlight and the sign. Both looked older and cheaper than the borrowed Volvo. Neither compared to Mr. Barth's Bentley.

She wiggled back into the blue dress while Barth's eyes roamed over her in silence. When she had it situated, he said:

"This isn't a fancy place like in Reno, but I wanted to be near the ocean—the two of us, close to nature. I reserved their best ocean-view room." He pointed up. "Number four, second floor on this side. I'll get the key and meet you." He stepped from the car and leaned into the opening. "Casino crowds, making small talk after a concert, all okay. Out here we stick out, people jump to the wrong conclusions." He half-smiled. "Better if we're not seen together." He closed the driver's door and strode across the small lot.

She stared into the night with soft eyes. Another man who wanted things he wasn't proud of. The waves kept her company. She silently asked the universe to care for Pé's spirit.

She twisted her head around to look through the back window. The white building had freshly painted blue trim, but was merely a large wooden house separated from the ocean by a tiny parking area and a wide beach that appeared gray in the moonlight. The surf repeated a gentle, relaxing adagio as if in no hurry to get anywhere. She reached down, found her purse, and got out. Paused. She would be busy in the hotel room; her instrument would be safer staying in the trunk.

Since he didn't want to be seen with her, she needed a way to room 4 that didn't pass through the lobby. There were no stairs on this side, so she walked the length of the parking lot and followed a gravel pathway to the back of the building away from the ocean. The surf was quieter here. Blue stairs led upward from a small garden area with single weathered bench. She took the stairs carefully, her new heels wobbling on the uneven wood.

At the top she followed a walkway around the perimeter of the house. She reached a door with a 2 hanging upside down from a single nail; no lights shone through its curtained window. A few more steps took her to a door with the number 4 screwed to it. She gazed out over the ink-dark water, again remembering *Silent Pool*. She searched for the moon; found it low in the sky, nowhere near full. As the water swelled and receded, she pictured Pé's body rocking beneath the waves at the bottom of the sea.

Why did this have to happen?

She knew. Pé had caused trouble. Become untrustworthy. A liability. Father taught that if you could not be trusted, you became the enemy. She and all the others...including Mylin...were expendable. Pé had forgotten.

Footsteps approached behind her.

As Barth came near, she turned her mind to the gentle ocean waters and fabricated a wide smile. The corners of his lips twitched upward, but she couldn't tell if he was returning her smile, or was nervous that they were standing at the door to a hotel room where they might be seen.

He unlocked the door and led her into a musty room with a high bed piled with half a dozen colorful pillows. She caught a glimpse of them side-by-side in a narrow mirror on the back wall, a scene from ten thousand rooms in a hundred countries—an anxious rich man longing to use the body of his submissive little whore.

She looked away, admonished herself for wishing for a different life, and hopped onto the bed. She tossed off her shoes and dress, then bounced gently on her knees. Her breasts swelled and dropped. She reminded herself that her job was much more than letting him have his way with her for one night. She must enter deeply into his thoughts, and stimulate him so intensely and in so many ways that he could never forget her—no matter how hard he tried.

His eyes followed her. He flicked off the light and began to remove his jacket, but stopped. He said: "Wait."

In the darkness he retrieved the blue dress he had requested and draped it carefully over the back of an upholstered chair with wings. He removed bills from his wallet, and placed them under the dress.

"How about black next time?"

"Black is very dramatic."

"And a bra and thong to match, just to spice things up?"

"Yes, Mr. Barth. And new shoes. Those hurt my feet."

He had his shirt off and was working on his belt. "All the shoes you want, Mylin."

A sliver of moonlight leaked through brown threadbare curtains. She hopped from the bed and located her purse on the floor. She placed it on the nightstand, retrieved the condom she knew she would need soon, and reached into a front pocket covered with clear plastic to touch her cell phone with her pinky finger. It came alive instantly, no code, no security, just a barely perceptible red dot in the center of the screen to indicate the special recording app was running. Father wanted her to be fast at times like this, but the app must be running if no one else was available. Record. Always. She turned and dashed across the room into Barth's arms, almost tripping him as he struggled to step out of his pants.

He held her close for a long kiss, then lifted her to the bed and caressed her entire body while he stood admiring her. His hands moved around the ankle bracelet she always wore, its green stone Father said had once belonged to her mother capturing the moonlight, to massage her feet—the one thing she welcomed after her foolishness of wearing new shoes.

Neither spoke; they simply breathed each other's energy.

She reached her right hand out to improve his mood. He reacted quickly. The sound of the surf mixed with his accelerating breathing...and something else: a cat-at-the-door scratching. The scratching became a lost memory as he crawled onto the bed, his body dwarfing hers, its spongy softness touching her everywhere. With experienced hands she unrolled the condom into place. With ever shorter breaths he positioned himself above her. Touched her jade gate. Thrust. The moment of entry shot through her body like an unwelcome surprise.

The room filled with light.

Had he lit a lamp to see her naked? No, Barth's eyes were wide with shock. Their heads twisted, seeking an explanation.

Her throat clenched.

A figure stood in the doorway wearing head-to-toe black riding leathers and a helmet with a mirrored face shield. Its right arm stretched straight at them holding a handgun with a fat barrel.

A scream crawled up her throat; she stifled it to a whispered, "No."

The room was still except for the surf.

Barth began to move; the helmet shook left to right.

The gun motioned. Barth shifted his body away. She squirmed out from under him.

She walked slowly toward the barrel, her heart thumping fast above a tumbling stomach. She was doing everything they asked, why was this man here? His face was hidden, but she knew it was a man. And not one of them—he was too tall. Which meant someone else. Someone they had hired was in her hotel room with a gun and a backpack.

She crossed her arms over her breasts.

Gloved fingers proffered a piece of paper.

She unfolded the note. The first thing it said was *Read this aloud*. So she did. And kept reading. *Mr. Bartholomew, Mylin is leaving with me. Remain in this room for thirty minutes, then drive back to San Francisco. Say nothing to anyone. Do anything else, and you will be sent to meet Pé.*

"Who's Pé?" Barth said.

Silence.

Mylin swallowed hard, choked. Then said softly: "Pé was in the orchestra with me. She's dead."

Barth's face sagged and whitened. He nodded slowly, holding up both hands palms forward.

The gun waved; Mylin stepped toward her dress.

The gun wagged; she froze.

His left hand beckoned her. She moved barefoot toward the door, her eyes riveted to the dark eye of the barrel.

His free hand wrapped tightly around her wrist and dragged her out of the room.

She ran naked behind him along the wood walk, rough beneath her bare feet, and down a flight of stairs. At the bottom he stopped and pointed the gun at her face as he dropped his backpack at her feet.

She looked from the gun to the mirrored face shield down to the pack and back to the gun, too frightened to move and unable to stop worrying about what she had done wrong. Then, staring in the mirrored shield, with crystalline awareness her heart stopped—they had decided to send her to meet Pé.

She twisted away, searching for a place to run.

The gloved hand grasped her hair and pulled her to her knees. She covered her face with her hands for protection from the blow she knew was coming.

Nothing happened.

She peeked between her fingers; he was pointing at the bag. She pulled two long zippers apart. A helmet rolled out. She turned to him and back to the bag, the gravel of the walkway digging into her bare knees. She pulled out boots, gloves, a one-piece black suit like his.

He wasn't going to kill her here.

She dressed quickly while he pointed the gun at her chest. The helmet went on last. He grabbed her arm and dragged her across the back of the building. At the edge of the garden a red motorcycle sat quietly ticking.

He stuffed the empty pack into a case on the side of the bike, shoved the gun into his jacket, and zipped it closed.

She must run. Not back to Barth; he was the kind of man who would move mountains to protect himself—but didn't even want to be seen with her. He would do nothing. But she could steal the keys to the convertible and race away. That red flash had flown by so fast while Barth fondled her; she'd never get away from it. She could run to the ocean; the bike wouldn't be able to chase her across sand.

But the gun could.

He was sitting on the bike, its motor now growling, motioning for her to mount behind him.

Her mind raced: her precious viola, Mr. Barth's money, the new dress—but only for an instant. She put a foot on a silver peg and stepped up and over as if mounting a pony. She wrapped her arms around his body. Maybe she could reach inside his jacket—and get the gun.

The engine shouted.

The bike shot forward. In an eye-blink they were racing away from the moon on the black highway beside the midnight ocean, the wailing engine matching the howls trapped in her chest as she anticipated her own death.

His helmet blocked her view, so she turned her head toward the water and tried to think of a way to save herself. Her purse, clothes, money, cell phone were back in the hotel room. She had nothing of her own except the bracelet around her ankle.

A green sign read: *Stinson Beach 20 miles*. She inched forward to peek at the speedometer. When they reached Stinson,

Barth's time would be almost up. Would Barth come to save her? No, he would find a replacement. He even had the money hidden under her new blue dress to hire her.

They raced the roaring wind; no cars passed from behind.

She was shivering inside the leather suit when the bike suddenly slowed and leaned left.

The parking lot was empty.

He leaned the bike onto its stand, stepped off, then held out a gloved hand to help her dismount. Her eyes roved the beach, begging both the dragon gods and the Buddha her grandmother loved to send help. If she ran, he would shoot her in the back. She would collapse to the sand, and bleed to death.

She waited motionless.

He removed his right glove. Caucasian. More danger; why would they hire a white devil?

He knelt. A wide red sheet screeched as he peeled it away from the machine; the side magically became black. He transformed the entire bike in seconds, rolled the red sections into cylinders, and stuffed them through the metal flap of a garbage can.

He motioned her toward him.

She moved slowly, watching his hands for the glint of a knife, though all men didn't need a weapon to kill. No matter what—she would fight.

He prodded and pulled at her helmet, and then his own, changing them from black to white. He went to the bike. Exhaust rose from its tail into the cool night air. He removed a small bag. She listened for a sign from the Buddha.

Only the surf spoke.

He dragged her to the curb and pulled off her left boot. He unzipped her riding leathers to expose her leg, then removed a tiny pair of pointy pliers from the pack.

He was going to torture her. But why? She had no secrets to tell.

He put a finger under the wrapped strands of metal that held the polished jade stone to her ankle.

She pulled her foot away, shaking her head. "It was my mother's. I wear it in her memory. Please don't. Please don't steal it."

The eyeless helmet stared at her.

"I...I...my father will be very angry if I lose it."

He grabbed her leg and yanked it toward him. He pointed a finger directly at her to remain still. She started to cry but felt like a fool. He was going to kill her, and she was worried about a stupid heirloom from a mother she had never known.

He unwound the braided band until it was separate strands. From his case he extracted clips like tiny alligator jaws. Wires connected one to the other in pairs. He attached the clips to the exposed strands, then cut the strands and moved the bracelet slowly over her heel and off her foot. He dragged her one boot and one bare foot across the deserted beach to the lifeguard station on slender stilts. He pushed her down on her knees under the station and motioned for her to dig.

She dug with both hands, tears dripping down both cheeks inside the helmet, imagining her life ending beneath this rotting hut, her body buried in a grave she had to dig herself with gloved hands.

He pulled her away, carefully placed the bracelet in the hole she had dug, then made her kick loose sand over it until the surface matched the rest of the beach.

In a fleeting moment they were again on the bike, racing the moon.

The bracelet had been a part of her for so long that its absence made her feel more naked than riding in Barth's convertible. Tiny spiders seemed to crawl in circles around her ankle. Stop. Then crawl in the opposite direction.

He tapped her thigh and pointed to a bulge on the side of his helmet. With one finger he pressed it. A red light glowed. He pointed at her.

She lifted her left hand toward her helmet; wind tugged at her arm. She leaned closer to his body and tried again. Her finger found the bulge, but she had to guess where the button was located. She pressed three times before finding it.

A soft sizzling filled her ears. The bike leaned to the left and she squeezed him tighter until it was around the corner and back upright. The sizzling continued.

A hollow voice she couldn't recognize said from inside her helmet: "Relax. We'll be riding for hours."

CHAPTER 39

THE VOICE HADN'T LIED. Mylin's rear was numb, her neck stiff from holding the helmet against the wind, and her back was cramping from hours crouched on a tiny pad. She had been cold, then hot, then cold again as they swept through hills. She guessed they were far away from the ocean; she hadn't seen or smelled it since burying her gemstone. The continuous rush of shadowed pine trees racing past like a crazed video game combined with the whine of the engine to create a cocoon of stimulation that left her feeling like she was traveling across a dream planet on a space mission. The smells—first of wildflowers, then pine, open pasture...and a skunk—hit her nose with a brilliant clarity so intense it seemed fake.

Time roared past. Then stood still, suspended in the black night as stars disappeared behind invisible clouds. Then roared again.

Her overstimulated mind despaired the future—would he kill her? Take her back to Asia? Torture her to reveal something she didn't even know? Spiders inched around her ankle—a constant reminder this was no joyride, or another client, but that something had gone very wrong in her world.

She had played well, then gone off with Mr. Bartholomew like any other assignment. She had even tried harder with him because she didn't want to slack off as she grieved for Pé inside her heart. They would be watching.

What had changed?

The detectives.

But she had only done what they ordered: exchange phone

numbers. She was still trying to find a reason for being on this
buzzing machine when it slowed and turned into a deserted rest
area isolated amid slender pines. It had parking spaces for only
six cars. One small lightbulb encircled by flying insects glowed
over the door to a single restroom. It wasn't deserted; there was
one other vehicle: a dusty orange pickup truck with a high
camper on the back that made it look like a giant sea turtle. They
stopped three parking spots from the truck. The dense trees
blocked the view of the road, trapping her in a private chamber.

The engine stopped.

The rider beckoned her off.

She swung her leg up and over and stepped off into the
darkness of that lonely bulb so far away. The spiders started a
chill that ran up to her fingertips. Suddenly she had the urge to
pee.

He knelt. Worked under the rear fender. Put a license plate
into a side bag. Began to unstrap the bags.

She would run away while he wasn't looking. First into the
woods where the riding suit would protect her skin from sharp
branches and undergrowth. Its blackness would make her
invisible among the trees. Or no, maybe she should run to the
truck and beg for help. *He had a gun.* Why would strangers help
a girl who had ridden with a man carrying a gun? She selected a
spot in the dark forest to aim for, tensed her entire body, and
sprang behind the bike.

A vise clamped down on her wrist. She spun and pulled hard
to get away. He squeezed harder and dragged her behind him
like a toy on a string.

Toward the truck.

When they reached the back of the camper he opened the
door, shoved her through, stepped in, and locked the door behind
them. She stood in a narrow space surrounded by a sink, stove,
bed at the front, table against the wall, and a narrow door that
could be to a closet. A dozen boxes were scattered about. She

turned around and stared into his face shield.

He slapped the door three times with the flat of his hand.

The truck's engine came to life; the vehicle backed up. She swayed at the motion and grabbed the edge of the sink. He sat down at the table and motioned for her to sit across from him.

The truck gained speed. He removed both gloves. She had been right: Caucasian. Then he unbuckled his helmet and looked down to peel it off.

When he lifted his head, Joe Roberts said: "Hello, Mylin."

———

She stared in shock from inside her helmet, blinking to be sure she was seeing clearly. In all those hours of imagining who had abducted her, she hadn't considered her photographer for an instant. She wanted to know what madness was inside his head. She wanted to know why he hadn't stayed away—she had told him clearly. She wanted to tell her father this wasn't her fault. But she said:

"I didn't know you rode motorcycles."

He burst out laughing. "Learned a bit from a friend in college; I'm nowhere near an expert. That bike is borrowed. Someone will pick it up later." He paused. "After they determine it's safe."

She sat icy still. Not wondering what to do, not feeling anger, just numb with the realization that the mysterious helmeted man was not an assassin. Then she remembered the gun with the fat barrel and confusion flowed up her spine like rising floodwaters. It occurred to her for the very first time that maybe their meeting at the art show on the beach, the pictures in Michigan, maybe none of it had been accidental.

He reached across the table and undid her buckle. She lifted the helmet off the way he had and placed it on the table facing her like a disembodied head. She shook her hair and covered her left eye. Fearing the answer, she said:

"Now what?"

The truck lurched sideways. She held the table for support.

"Now," he said. "I get to see you again."

She slumped against the wall behind her. He watched her, but didn't speak.

"My viola is in the trunk of the convertible."

"I'll find a way to get it."

"They'll come after me."

"They won't find you." He paused. "That green stone we buried can be tracked. That's why we left it."

She ran gloved fingers through her hair. Tears formed. "Father told me it belonged to my mother many years ago. He wished for me to wear it always." She paused. Blinked tears away. "But they found Pé."

"The girl who jumped?"

She nodded. "My sister." She wiped her right eye with the back of the stiff glove. "My silly old sister who just had to disobey." She glanced down at the dark spot of moisture on the black leather. It looked like a bloodstain. "My only sister."

The truck lurched. Springs squeaked as the seat pounded her sore bottom through the leather pants.

"Who's driving?"

"Not someone you've met." His head shook slowly. "Better you don't know. In case..." His voice drifted away. It came back with: "Do you want to go back?"

She had been ordered to be with Mr. Bartholomew. He would be gone. And he had her viola. No one expected her back until morning.

"Not yet." She paused. "Where are you taking me?"

"Black Rock City."

She knew nothing of such a place. "Why?"

"To become lost."

She looked around the inside of the turtle's back and said:

"Can we stop at a restroom? I really need to pee."

CHAPTER 40

QIGIQ WOKE ON HIS GRAY COUCH and stared at the ceiling. A soft thud came from the stern. Was that the first, or had a previous one roused him? Another, from the direction of the kitchen. He pushed the olive green afghan he had brought with him from Alaska onto the back of the couch and rolled his feet to the floor.

Clunk.

He pulled on black pants and yesterday's T-shirt and walked to the kitchen. He said:

"You been up long?"

Kandy absentmindedly rocked her chair back on two legs. It tapped the wall softly. She was wearing midnight blue jeans and an aqua T-shirt with *Bang!* over the left breast in white. The parts for her new Kimber Micro 38 were spread across the table, including 14 rounds of ammunition and two magazines.

"Half hour. Slept like a baby." She pointed to the bandage on her head the EMTs had applied. "No problems with the head. Thanks for being the observer so I could stay out of the hospital. Those places make me nervous."

He headed for the brewing coffee. "You always rock non-rocking chairs?"

"Sorry, nervous habit, I'm used to living alone. It's already seven-fifteen Wednesday morning and we have a message from the fearless Ferd. He has forensics on *Solicitor*." She pointed at his cup. "Be careful, I can't spell decaf."

Qigiq stared at the dark fluid wishing caffeine were visible. Sipped.

"I thought you were a revolver girl?"

"I am, Sig Sauer. But this is thin, light and accurate. So I'm experimenting. Plus, it's easy on my back. Kind of a mini-1911."

"Did Ferd give us anything?"

She nodded while polishing the barrel. "Two words: *No money.*"

He slipped the second chair out from under the table with a bare foot and sat down.

"How could Spooner and Pé run with no cash?"

She placed the part on the table. "They can't. So either they weren't running, or he had a stash he was running to."

Qigiq waited for the coffee to cool. "That would mean nothing on the boat to be found by an inspection. Just three people out for a joyride." He paused. "Maybe anticipating a customs inspection."

She stood to get more coffee. "Want to go see Ferd, learn what else he has?"

"Sure." He paused. "I'd like to call Mylin first."

"Business or pleasure?" Kandy laughed.

He shook his head. "She's beautiful, talented, and intense. Better stick to business. Think it's too early to call?"

"Depends on your hypothesis. If they sleep in, it's way too early. But if they need to get back to San Francisco today, they'll want to beat traffic. In that case, now would be good."

Qigiq went to the living area, adjusted the afghan on the back of the couch, and found his cell phone on the bookshelf in front of a book titled *The Perfect Vehicle*. He dialed.

"I hope she recognizes my number."

Kandy nodded from the kitchen without looking up from pushing a bullet into a magazine.

Qigiq waited, hung up, and slipped the phone into his pocket.

"Five rings, then voice mail."

"Was it Mylin's voice?"

"Phone company robot." He walked back to the coffee dripper. "Oatmeal and toast, or we go out?"

"Cuisine a la Qigiq, please. I'm still recovering from your driving."

———

Kandy drove herself to the office. Qigiq followed and parked his bike near the trash bin in the spot that no one wanted. They walked in together and wandered past Jasik's office. The captain was out. Up another floor they found Ferdinand staring at the computer with three monitors.

Kandy said, "Knock, knock," as they entered.

Ferdinand tipped bleary eyes toward them. "Hello, detectives. I have results for you."

"Ferd, you look exhausted. We working you too hard?"

He shook his head slowly. "Not at all. My special project is keeping me up late. I must ensure there are no mistakes."

"You mean like Knievel trying to jump the Snake River canyon and making it only half way?"

"Yes, I mean no." He wagged his head. "Such a result would be far below my standards."

"Not spectacular," she teased.

"You will see," Ferdinand said with a tired grin.

"You say when and where. I'll be there. Unless by some miracle we wrap up this case and I get to go on vacation."

Qigiq studied the images on monitors that in combination showed a wide-angle view of a long spiral, crisscrossed fence posts, and a truck.

Ferdinand said, "Where will you be going, Detective Kandy?"

"Camping trip into the desert for an art festival. I go every year."

His eyebrows lifted. "How bizarre. A festival in the desert?"

"Well, it's not really a festival so much as a sort of tribal gathering of fifty thousand or so like-minded nature lovers."

"Is there a race?" Qigiq said. "We draw big crowds for the Iditarod Trail sled dog race every year."

Kandy shook her head. "No race. The playa has speed limits."

Ferdinand noticed Qigiq studying the truck. "I've designed this event to be portable with that single vehicle, including the motorcycle. We can pull into an area, set up in thirty-eight minutes, perform the event, pick up, and be gone in another thirty."

"Impressive speed, Ferd," Kandy said. "Why the big hurry?"

Ferdinand stroked his beard. "There are several issues; the ideal terrain is number one. Without it I must include a ramp, which reduces the authenticity of using a dip in the terrain as implied by the movie."

Kandy pointed at the spiral on the screen. "Is this what your rider is going over?"

"Correct. It is the precise dimension of the spool of barbed wire jumped in the original. But it isn't barbed wire."

"I'll bet it's more spectacular," she said.

"The other problems?" Qigiq asked.

Ferdinand was quiet for a full fifteen seconds. "Let us just say that acquiring permits for this kind of event is a complicated matter."

Kandy laughed. "You're going to cut and run, so you have to be mobile. A man after my own heart."

Ferd said, "I did not say *cut and run*."

She continued laughing. "Okay, and I didn't hear it. Anything new on *Solicitor?*"

Ferdinand rolled his chair two desks over. "I mentioned that we found no cash. We also found no explosive that can be traced."

"Keep going Ferd, you're helping me a lot."

"We did find spruce and ebony wood splinters embedded in the inside of the hull. These are not woods that would be used to adorn a modern yacht."

"Inside the violin?" Qigiq asked.

"Precisely." Ferdinand played a movie on the computer in front of him. "Here's my reconstruction of the explosion. The violin case was near the stern. As are the fuel tanks. Eight ounces of gasoline inside the violin body, properly ignited, would provide the explosive power of two sticks of TNT. Miraculously, one of the yacht's fuel tanks remained intact. The top of the second ruptured and assisted with the fire."

"Residue?" Kandy asked.

"Splattered Radio Shack parts. Untraceable."

They were silent while the looping movie showed the expanding shockwave ripping through the roof and fly bridge of *Solicitor*.

"What bothers you the most, Ferd?" Kandy asked.

"The money."

She frowned. "You said there was no money."

"Precisely."

Kandy paced back and forth in front of the exploding yacht. "There was money at the cliff. Now there isn't. So the money disappears and the girl shows up."

"A trade?" Qigiq said.

"That's the most obvious explanation," Ferdinand said. "Cash for the girl."

"Then kill everyone," Kandy added. "Spooner, Pé, even Walstein, the curly-haired guy driving the boat. No witnesses."

The room fell quiet.

Qigiq slipped out his cell phone and walked to the window. He redialed Mylin's number. It was answered on the third ring.

"Hello?" A male voice answered.

"Is Mylin available?"

"I don't know a Mylin. Who is this?"

"Detective Qigiq with the San Francisco Police Department. You are holding Mylin's phone."

"Is that who owns this? The maid found it in room four this morning. Wasn't even slept in. The guy who rented it took off last night."

"Does the guy have a name?"

"Jack Phlash, with a P. H. We have a phone number he doesn't answer, and an address that's probably on Mars. He paid cash in advance."

"Was there anything else in the room?"

"High heels and a blue dress. Might put them on eBay, since I can't reach him."

"Please hold everything for us. We're in the midst of a homicide investigation. Your hotel is a crime scene. What's your address?"

He hung up and crossed back to Ferdinand's desk. "Strange happenings at the Sea and Sky B&B north of Marin."

Kandy looked away from the explosion. "How strange?"

"Clerk has Mylin's dress, shoes, and cell phone, but no one has seen her. A man arrived last night in a black Volvo; rented a room for one night. It hasn't been slept in."

"I bet it's the guy she left the party with," Kandy said. "I asked around, he's a businessman from Nevada. CEO of Tomba Mines. Name is Thomas Bartholomew."

Ferdinand typed on the computer that was looping the explosion simulation.

"There is no Tom or Thomas Bartholomew in Nevada or California who has registration for a Volvo."

"You're fast, Ferd."

"A rental?" Qigiq asked.

"That will take longer to determine," Ferdinand said.

Qigiq turned to Kandy. "Feel like a drive up the coast to retrieve Mylin's phone?"

"Nice day for a bike ride," she said. "I'll stay here, take it easy like the medical people keep telling me, and dig into the *Solicitor* data with Ferd."

Qigiq walked down three flights to the front door, stopping once to flex his recovering ankle, and hopped on the rented 850 he wished had a clutch. The ride north took him within a mile of his houseboat so he decided to stop. By the time he reached the dock he had almost convinced himself that Mylin was just a girl with a load of musical talent who had simply left a boring party with a rich guy. He wanted to know when, how, and by whom the incriminating pictures in Spooner's contract had been taken. That made him think of Pé. Which made him wonder if, why, and by whom her feet had been bound as a child. And could possibly have something to do with the web of blackmail they were trying to unravel.

He added a fleece layer under his jacket for the ride to the ocean, then headed west through the hills on CA-1. Flowing through mile after mile of curves reduced the tension that had been building since Kandy called about a traffic accident. In less than an hour he arrived at the Sea and Sky, dismounted, studied the lot, and tried to guess where the Volvo had parked. He entered through the front door into a small lobby adorned with a vase of artificial white orchids that needed dusting. A white male about thirty-five who hadn't shaven in a few days sat behind an open counter.

"Hi, I'm Detective Qigiq. I talked to—"

"Yeah. Here's your stuff." The man put a smartphone, black high heels and a blue dress on the counter. "You going to give me a receipt?"

"Sure. Can I borrow a page of your letterhead?"

The man pushed a single sheet of paper onto the counter and slapped a plastic pen on top of it, then went back to staring at his computer.

As Qigiq wrote the receipt he looked over the items. Had Mylin been wearing anything else? If so, why wasn't it here? Why discard a dress and shoes? Unless Bartholomew had bought her a new outfit, making this one obsolete.

"Who was on duty last night?"

The man looked up. "Me. I close the desk here around 9:30, sleep in back, then open again at 7:00."

"So you saw Mr...uh...Phlash?"

"Yeah. Tall guy, needs to work out. Maybe fifty but looks closer to sixty. Those city types that come up here are all the same: way too much stress."

"Think you'd recognize him?"

The man contemplated for half a minute. "Only maybe. I didn't pay much attention and he wasn't here long. I never saw her," he pointed at the dress. "She wasn't hanging on his arm saying, 'Oh honey, I love this place' like most of the wives."

Qigiq nodded. "May I look at the room?"

The man shook his head. "Not now, I put a couple from SoCal in there. Honeymooners. Probably won't come out until dinner."

"Anyone else around that was here last night?"

"Just me. Midweek the guests move on. Travel up the coast, or head for the city."

"Sorry for the cop-show question, but did you see anything unusual last night?"

"You mean other than a guy coming in alone? Happens from time to time. Business guy traveling through wants a little slice of nature to calm his nerves. He listens to the waves, gets all teary-eyed about his surfer past, that kind of thing."

Qigiq remained quiet, hoping the guy would fill the space.

"Yeah. One thing. Two, actually. The couple in 1-A out back. She yapped at me this morning about how can we let people with motorcycles stay here and ruin the quiet for nice people like her. I told her no one with a bike was registered. She swears one," his voice went up an octave and became a pinched nasal sound, "'Made an awful racket right outside my window while I was trying to go to sleep. My husband's snoring is bad enough, now I have to listen to those death machines.'" Back to normal he said, "I didn't hear anything here in the office, so it couldn't have been that loud."

Qigiq took notes on the page he carried in his pocket. "Any guess at the time?"

"She had watched the eight o'clock horror flick, because she complained about her TV not being big like in *real* hotels. So I'd guess around ten, plus or minus thirty."

"You said there were two things."

"Oh yeah. You said unusual. When a guy comes in alone, he sleeps all night, even if he makes an early start the next day. Sure, some guys bring a girl in and frolic for awhile, but those guys stay all night too. No one drives all the way to the ocean to use us as a by-the-hour no-tell motel. So I'm at my desk at seven this morning, and the Volvo is already gone. Maid claims the bed wasn't slept in. I can't figure it."

Qigiq couldn't figure it either, but he wrote it down. He thanked the clerk and took Mylin's property to his bike. He put the shoes in a plastic evidence bag and strapped them across the seat, then folded the silky blue material of the dress into another bag, and stuffed it into his jacket. He bagged the phone and put it in a pocket. He would dust it for prints, but didn't hold out much hope.

He started the bike and crossed the parking lot. At the highway he looked north and south, trying to sense which way they had turned. He went north, away from the city.

More privacy.

The rented Mana hummed below him. Salt air teased his nose. How far would they drive before stopping? What would cause that first stop?

He had been riding for fifteen minutes when his cell phone rang inside his helmet.

Kandy said: "I'm here with a friend."

"Where's here?" His voice rang hollow inside the shell of the helmet.

"Bartholomew's San Francisco office. Instead of tracking down the rental, I decided to ask Tom directly. He's behind his desk ten feet from me, making me wait while he reads a contract."

Qigiq wanted to know who, then, was with Mylin? But he said: "Does he have a rental?" while forcing himself to concentrate on the road.

"Yes he does, but it's a Chevy. Says he drove it to the concert in Mill Valley last night. Then went straight back to San Francisco. Doesn't know anything about a Volvo."

"I've got a night man at the desk that thinks yes, maybe, sort of, he can ID the guy who rented the room."

She spoke so softly her words were barely intelligible over the wind noise. He slowed.

"Tom seems white-knuckle nervous here."

"Afraid his wife will find out?"

"More like he's...wait a second, he's getting a call."

Qigiq flipped on his signal and took the exit for Stinson Beach. He found a parking place between a hand-painted VW bus and a brown Subaru with a surfboard strapped to it. He shut the bike off and stared out at the ocean over the round lid of a trash can.

A scratching sound came through the phone, then Kandy said softly, "He put the caller on speakerphone, apparently wants me to listen in."

The next voice sounded like a talk-show host through a cheap radio.

"Once more, Mr. Bartholomew. When was the last time you saw Mylin?"

The talk-show host had had a long day.

"At the concert last night," Bartholomew answered. "No, after the concert at the reception. We had a little wine. Then I split."

The host laughed. "Yes, you did. I have in my possession a

picture of a black Volvo convertible with you and a beautiful female musician, Mr. Bartholomew."

Bartholomew's voice became more strained. "We had a fight. I left her at the bed and breakfast."

"But she is not there. So where is she?"

"I don't know."

"Start remembering. You were with her last."

The caller's line became a dial tone. Then Qigiq's own line went dead.

He waited. Low waves washed the beach. His phone rang.

"Bartholomew asked me to leave, so I'm on the sidewalk in front of his building," Kandy said. "Nice digs. Apparently he has a bigger main office in Reno. You should have seen him talking to our mystery caller. Ghostlike. Verge of panic."

Qigiq sat down on a parking curb near his bike. "Any idea who it was?"

"Someone who knows how not to be traced. He got off the line before I could even begin to put a finger on him."

"So Bartholomew really was driving a black Volvo?"

"According to the caller. He also thinks Bartholomew knows Mylin's whereabouts. My guess from looking in Tom's eyes? He knows plenty that he's not saying."

"I thought they would be together. A repeat of the Pé-Spooner scenario."

"I'll put guys on Tom, see if he leads us to her. He claims he met her for the first time Monday night at a charity auction at the Nevada Museum of Art in Reno."

Qigiq stared at the ocean, surf in one ear, poor cell connection in the other.

"Did you look at her phone?" Kandy asked.

"I was going to have Ferd do it," Qigiq said.

"Good plan. But you might glance at the recent pictures."

"I'll call you back."

Qigiq fished Mylin's cell phone from his pocket.

The surf crashed loud from a rogue wave.

He poked at the phone. It came alive without even asking for a security code.

CHAPTER 41

FERDINAND RAN THE EXPLOSION simulation for the fifty-third time. The eruption near the stern filled the cabin and blew out the windshield, probably killing Pé and Spooner instantly. The secondary explosion from the tank was powerful enough to remove the roof and fly bridge. He was impressed that *Solicitor* hadn't sunk immediately. The conclusion appeared straightforward. The girl carried the violin case onto the boat. It had been rigged with a simple radio detonator. Not much range, but it wouldn't need much range in a straight line over water. Boom. Nothing unusual for him to discover.

He switched the movie off.

Working half the night on his spectacular event was affecting his ability to think, which could affect his job. He had to get more sleep—and have less fun.

He turned to the recordings sent to the police by the unidentified photographer. He had established the range and location of the sighting vehicle, but his detective friends had found little useful evidence. Image analysis had merely confirmed Spooner driving and Pé leaping. The motorcycle rider's face was covered by a helmet his technology couldn't penetrate as it had with the first rider. The men who stepped out of the SUV had wisely faced the ocean. The one left to clean up had prepared to ride, so he also wore a helmet. Likely the same helmet after the rider was placed into the SUV.

He played it again.

A knock on the lab door coincided with the handgun flash from the driver's window of the Mercedes, making him jump from the unexpected audio. He glanced at the computer's clock: precisely noon. He wasn't expecting anyone.

The door flung open. The tattoo of high heels on tile preceded the aroma of corned beef.

"Hi, Ferddy."

He smiled at the abominable distortion of his name.

"Hello, Petrushka." His eyes passed over short black boots with four-inch heels, bare legs, a tiny skirt, and an oversize forest green sweatshirt that matched half her hair, the other half being almost black. "Whatever are you doing at my office?"

"I knew you would be hungry. You've been, uh..." she half-smiled, "working too hard."

She placed a brown bag on his desk and leaned in to give him a tiny kiss on his bearded cheek.

"This is a secure area. You know my profession is not to be shared. We agreed."

"I haven't shared a thing. But men are trivial creatures. I told the guys downstairs I had a delivery of sensitive material for a person named Ferdinand. After they finished staring at me, they directed me to this room."

He shook his head as he stood. "Now that you're here, will you be staying for lunch?"

She pulled up a wheeled desk chair, plunked into it, and crossed her legs. "Since you asked. I was hoping we would review Pumpkin Eater." She grinned with lips the color of bing cherries.

Ferdinand fumbled the bag open and placed the drinks and sandwiches across the desk near the triple monitors. "Your timing is excellent. I was being frustrated with night footage from a crime scene."

She opened a round sandwich wrapped in white paper and took a huge bite. With her mouth mostly full she said:

"May I see?"

He studied the slender face of this woman he had only

known for days, yet it seemed much longer. She was completely serious.

"That would violate proper protocol, Petrushka."

"You're so silly, Ferddy. Hire me as a consulting crime-scene investigator and I'll give you my expert opinion when we're done. In writing if you like. Then it's all legal and proper for you."

Ferdinand pulled a tab on the top of a blue Pepsi can; it hissed away pressure.

"Yes, I have contracted with experts before. What are your credentials in this matter?" He smiled.

"I do a lot of work at night."

He choked on the soda. She leaned over and patted him on the back until he was breathing normally. "I see," he managed.

"Meaning, I have good night vision. And I've been living in San Francisco for years. Maybe I'll see something helpful."

He took a bite of his sandwich. "You do work at the Ton Up. Perhaps you will be able to identify…" He opened a drawer, pulled out a form, and slid it across the table to her. "Let's interview you as a witness, see what you recognize."

"You mean whom?"

"Possibly." She signed the form. He pointed to the left monitor. "I will humor you for the moment, then we will review Pumpkin Eater." He started the video and found a bag of chips to open.

She watched carefully without breaking stride in her chewing. The video stopped after the cleanup guy removed evidence with the spinning rear wheel of a motorcycle. The overlook area was now empty, the air filled with dust.

Petrushka continued to stare at the screen, moving nothing but her jaw. She reached across the desk and stole a handful of chips from Ferdinand and shoved them into her mouth. She washed them down with her own Pepsi.

"OK. Ask me a question," she said.

"What happened? Sorry, I mean, why did it happen?"

She held her eyes on the monitor, even though the movie was frozen on the last frame, which showed only an empty road and shoulder.

"The rich guy in the Mercedes was trying to run away with that Asian girl. The other three guys were told to stop them. Maybe hired to stop them."

"You don't think the men were told to eliminate them?" He examined her eyes, the curve of her nose, the high cheekbones.

She blinked slowly as if meditating. "No. Stop them. Things got out of hand only because the Mercedes driver fired a gun."

Ferdinand considered this. "Who are the three men?"

"Gang. Mafia. Family. Something like that. The girl looks Asian. I'd guess a Chinese gang."

"Hmm," he said. "Who is the man on the motorcycle?"

"That bike is one of our special Brits. See the curve of the frame cradling the engine? Means it's either someone from the Ton Up, or someone who has a connection to someone from the club. No one else would have that bike."

"The rider walked across the dirt before being shot. Did you recognize who it was?"

"No, but we can find out."

Ferdinand's eyes widened in surprise. He glanced at the bag of cookies.

"And how would you go about doing that?"

Petrushka turned toward him, her face a sea of calm. "Everyone and his brother's friend's sexy little sister is out for the big ride. Get the club roster, find out who's missing. If we assume the rider is a club member, the roster will lead you to a name. If he's a friend...well, that'll be harder."

Ferdinand felt foolish that a waitress had to explain strategy to him. "Of course, process of elimination. The list of club members is a fixed set. Most of the set can be identified. Intersect that list with all Chinese riders known to be associated with the club. Petrushka, you're a genius."

"So I've been told." She smiled. "Though not usually while sitting upright." She laughed.

Ferdinand started coughing. When he recovered, he said, "But isn't that list private?"

"I'll provide it with my expert's report." She popped up from her chair and kissed his cheek lightly. "Got to get back to work. I wish my job were as easy as yours."

His eyes landed on her green hair while forcing himself not to consider the presence or absence of undergarments. "Tell me, Petrushka. Why is a woman with your talent waiting tables in a biker bar?"

"Art, my dear Ferddy. You know I'm studying for my painting degree at San Francisco State. Artists must live near an edge to remain fully awake. Since my childhood included a bit of dirt riding with my 'wish-you-had-been-a-boy' bike-obsessed father, the club was a natural fit. Hanging with the Ton Up retro-boys and their irrational dedication to iron objects provides stimulation I wouldn't find elsewhere. Plus," she moved her blue eyes from his black wingtips up slowly until they met his tired face, "you meet interesting people who inspire your work."

"Ahem. Yes, well…"

"And Ferddy. Those guys in the video aren't the ones you really want."

He stopped chewing.

"They're part of a clan. Find the dragon head. No way he, or she, was on that road in the middle of the night."

CHAPTER 42

KANDY PACED ON THE BRICK SIDEWALK outside Bartholomew's San Francisco office situated in a glass and concrete structure 20-stories high. She had been waiting 48 minutes, hoping he would make a run for somewhere, while the shadow from the nearby Transamerica Pyramid inched its way toward her. But Bartholomew hadn't emerged, and she was out of patience. She jogged back to the Mini feeling about 80% her usual self and headed for the Ton Up. On the way over Ferd called. She mulled over his *process of elimination* approach all the way to the turn into the alley.

She didn't pass a single bike until reaching the rear of the club where two black clones bookended the door. She got out. The only thing that looked different from what she remembered was that these machines were new-from-the-factory clean. She snapped close-ups of the bikes, and was slipping her phone into her pocket when a voice behind her said:

"If it isn't the detective's girlfriend. You're supposed to ask before taking pictures of a man's bike."

She turned around. Prime and Michael in blue jeans and T-shirts, the first two Ton Up boys she had ever met, were framed in the doorway.

"I'm no one's girlfriend."

"Maybe we should change that," Prime said, grinning.

"I prefer guys who are tougher than me," she said, taking a step toward the door. They didn't move. "You going to let me get lunch?"

"Not here," Michael said. "We don't like cops."

She faced them, sizing up who would move first. Reminded herself she wasn't in top form after the dive off *Solicitor*. "I have cop friends, I have robber friends." She shrugged. "So what?"

Michael shifted his weight to his opposite foot. "So, maybe you should go somewhere else for lunch. We're closed for the holiday."

Kandy pointed over her shoulder with a thumb. "Why are your bikes so clean?"

Their eyes shifted. Concern.

"Just back from Murphy's," Michael said.

Prime's eyes shot sideways. Kandy read them as wishing Michael would shut up.

The three stood in early afternoon sun shining through cool air, typical of a San Francisco summer.

She waited. They didn't move. She waited.

Prime ended the standoff with, "Get out of here, we're busy."

She said, "I enjoyed the concert. When is Mylin performing again?"

Prime's eyes narrowed as he stretched to his full five-nine height.

Kandy smiled, spun one-eighty, went back to the bikes, pulled out her phone and started taking pictures.

They both moved forward.

Michael said, "We told you not to take pictures."

She rotated the phone to landscape mode and squatted next to an engine.

"No, you didn't. You said I should ask permission."

They got close and stood over her.

Prime raised his voice: "Stop, bitch. Stop now."

She lowered the camera, looked up at Prime. Rose slowly, said:

"Pretty bikes. I figured I should take pictures before they get dusty."

Prime stepped back, trying to act nonchalant. "What makes you think we'd let them get dusty?"

A hundred bikes with knobbed tires and the trips Stolz had mentioned gave her a fifty-fifty shot.

"Because it's dusty in Mexico."

Prime's face stiffened before he got control of it and laughed. "Who would ride a vintage bike so far?"

Bingo. Now if she only knew why. "Bye, boys."

She jogged to her car and was driving down the alley before either moved. She glanced at the rearview. They were staring at the back of the Mini as her dust settled on their shiny toys.

She turned right at the street, drove three blocks, turned right again and pulled to the side of the road in the shade of a gnarled black walnut tree. She switched off the Mini, checked the mirrors, waited; then dialed Qigiq, who answered on the first ring.

"Two very clean vintage bikes at the club."

"Long video on Mylin's phone of her post-concert tryst with Bartholomew."

She stared at the rearview. Empty. She said:

"Prime and Michael chased me away when I tried to take pictures. I'll email them to you."

"The video shows a helmeted rider, fully suited, raising a silenced handgun at the couple on the bed. He dragged Mylin out of the room naked."

Kandy frowned. "Dragged her out?"

"Just the way she was on the bed. Not even shoes."

"In a hurry?" she asked.

"Maybe. But first he made her read a note to Bartholomew that told him to wait thirty minutes and threatened him with Pé's fate."

"No voice, no face, no prints."

"Correct. About six foot, comparing him to Mylin. No hint of race, jacket collar was too high."

Kandy stared out the windshield. A new crime, too few clues. "I'm going to stake out the club."

"I'll take Mylin's video to Ferdinand. See you in the lab."

She ended the call, studied her pictures, found nothing special about the bikes, then emailed the pics to Qigiq and Ferdinand. She stepped out, locked the car, touched her hand to the lump on her head—winced. She flexed her neck left and right. No dizziness. She touched the weapon at her back beneath her jacket, then ran.

Two blocks forward and three back brought her near the west side of the club. She ducked between two buildings and kept a gray cement-block warehouse with a rusted roof to her left; between her and the Ton Up. She stopped at the far corner. An iron fire escape hung from the back of the building. A cable wrapped around a cement counterbalance held the stairs she wanted to climb horizontal—and out of reach.

The bikes behind the club were now on the far side of a six-foot high chain-link fence entangled with scrub no one had bothered to clear. While calculating how much noise that fire escape would make if she lowered the stairs, Michael's girlfriend Trina came out the back door of the club and leaned against the building. She lit a cigarette.

Kandy glued her eyes to the young girl.

Trina gazed up the alley. She turned and studied the fence between the club and the warehouse that was hiding Kandy. She looked to the far side of the alley where graffiti had converted the back wall of a garage into a Jackson Pollock. When the cigarette was half gone Trina casually dropped it in the gravel and ground it under the toe of a pointy black boot that rose over her calf.

The moment she did, two people stepped out of the club wearing black riding leathers. The first one out checked the alley as Trina had done. Then the other did the same. Though helmets prevented identification, Prime and Michael was an easy guess.

They each carried two lumpy duffle bags, one in either hand, that looked to be filled with marbles, or rocks, or ball bearings.

Kandy pulled her head back and inched her phone past the corner until its camera could see the club.

Trina scanned the alley again.

Kandy shot video of the two men flopping open the side cases and placing a bag of marbles on each side. They tightened leather straps over the top, then mounted. Helmets swung like beacons. One nodded. Trina disappeared into the club.

Kandy mumbled under her breath, frustrated they were getting away.

Trina reappeared in a jacket and helmet and mounted the near bike.

Kandy let the video record as the machines rumbled down the alley trailing streams of gray dust. She considered having them stopped and searched, but if they were clean, that would be it for the pooch.

She stopped recording and leaned her back against the building, the blocks cool through her jacket. She played the video on her phone and studied the sacks carefully. Drawstrings held the tops tightly closed—no way to peek inside.

She slipped the phone away and jogged back to the street, down a block, around, and up the alley she had driven through minutes ago. Staying in shadows on the side, she crept along until she could peer into the dark room. Chairs were stacked on tables like someone was about to mop the floor. A figure moved behind the bar. Her phone showed 1:18 pm. No lunch crowd; the place really was closed.

She crouched at the corner of the club. In three minutes the door to the alley closed from the inside. Locks clicked. She worked her way between the club and the fence until she reached the front corner of the building. She pressed her back against the wall to wait.

The front door creaked. A male crossed the sidewalk

carrying a green canvas bag over his right shoulder. He crossed the street and the lights flashed on a plain white pickup truck towing a box trailer. His back faced her as he stepped into the driver's seat.

She slowed her breathing and remained still.

The truck started. The driver's window rolled down. The driver stuck his head out and looked back down the street to check for oncoming traffic.

Murphy.

CHAPTER 43

AFTER DELIVERING MYLIN'S belongings to Ferdinand's lab, Qigiq sat in the corner office with a crumpled page of notes flattened on the desk in front of him, trying to reconstruct the events at the Sea and Sky. An unknown person points a gun at Mylin. The same person uses a written note to threaten Bartholomew—but the threat is nothing like the one in the Spooner contract. A woman hears a motorcycle.

He rubbed his temples with the thumb and middle finger of one hand. Multiple pieces. How many different people wanted Mylin? That voice on the phone suspected Bartholomew stashed her, so that person hadn't seen the video from her phone. Maybe the man with the gun was working for Bartholomew, creating a twisted plausible deniability for the lawyer.

The door to the office flung open and Kandy marched in, dust covering the left side of her dark pants, white flecks in her hair.

Qigiq said: "What's the other guy look like?"

She smiled. "I went on a treasure hunt."

She reached out her hand and placed five colored balls on the table.

Qigiq leaned forward to examine them. "You hunt gumballs?"

She dropped into a chair and brushed fingers through her hair. White grit crackled to the floor like concrete snowflakes.

"I watched Prime, Michael and Trina load bags onto two bikes. They rode out. Then Murphy left via the front door after locking the club up awfully tight for lunch hour."

"And you happened to be there with a warrant."

"Exactly," she laughed, "and my toolbox. They really should put newer locks on that clubhouse; someone might break in. The bags looked like they were filled with ball bearings. I found these stashed in the clubhouse basement inside empty beer cases. There are hundreds, maybe thousands, sorted by color."

Qigiq picked one up. It was like rice paper filled with air, but stronger. He shook it.

"Plastic?"

She shrugged. "No idea. Could be made from corn for all I know. I figured Ferd would need a good look."

"So you borrowed a few."

"Easier than explaining."

The door rattled with a double knock, then immediately twice again.

Ferdinand entered carrying photographs. He spread them across Kandy's desk, gently moving the gumballs to one side.

"It is fortunate the video camera recorded high definition."

Four prints of Mylin on her back on the bed, Bartholomew over her. He scanned the background, trying to find what had his colleague excited.

Ferdinand pointed with the capped end of a red ballpoint pen to the first picture.

"She placed the camera beside the lamp; we were quite fortunate with angles. Notice the full-length mirror hanging on the back wall in this first picture."

They nodded.

"In that mirror we see the door to the room."

"It's not very big," Kandy said.

"That is why I am pleased with the resolution. It allows me to zoom. In the third picture, the door to room four is ajar. Whoever is opening it remains out of sight."

Qigiq checked. Ferd was right, it looked like a ghost had eased it open.

"But as the opener pushes the door further into the room, and turns toward the bed, we see this picture." Ferd pointed to a blow up of a small section of the mirror that contained an open door, shoulders, and a helmet. "There," Ferd announced proudly.

Qigiq and Kandy stared at a reflection in the curved face shield that had reflected from the mirror and into the camera. Qigiq leaned forward. Squinted. Moved closer still. He said:

"Red Honda VFR parked in the garden behind the hotel. Not the big model, the 800. That woman in one-A really did hear a motorcycle start up."

Ferdinand grinned.

Kandy leaned back, put her feet on her desk. "Qigiq told me the mystery man dragged Mylin out of the room naked."

"That is what the video shows," Ferdinand said.

Qigig turned to the window, then back to the reflected image of the bike.

"It has bags. Might contain clothing."

"Premeditated," Kandy said. "How many of those bikes are on the road?"

"It was replaced by a 1200 cc version years ago. But then Honda came out with an updated 800."

"Think we can find one in a haystack?" she asked.

Ferdinand pushed his photos into a pile. "It is worth a try. I wouldn't expect there were many of this model riding last night at ten PM in the vicinity of the Sea and Sky. We can localize the search area nicely. But this man will not be in charge; we must find the dragon's head."

"Your language is getting more colorful, Ferd." Kandy stood. "But you're right. Whoever is pulling the strings is likely invisible. I'll start with the traffic folks. Maybe we'll get lucky and he ran a red light. Might even get a picture."

She left and pulled the office door closed behind her. The frosted glass rattled.

Ferdinand pulled out two large phones from deep within his

lab jacket pockets and placed them on the desk.

"I suggest we keep in close touch regarding this case over the holiday weekend. I'll be leaving this afternoon to set up Pumpk....uh, my project, but I will be available by satellite phone at all times. I've asked the forensics team to contact me if they uncover anything new regarding the explosion. And of course, I will update you regarding Mylin's belongings."

"Thanks, Ferdinand. Would you have time to look at these?"

Qigiq rolled the gumball spheres with the side of his pencil into a row across the far edge of his desk: red, blue, yellow, blue, green.

Ferdinand lowered himself into Kandy's chair, which squeaked as he studied the balls through thick glasses. He reached forward with his pen and rolled the green one around on the desk, then did the same to the other four.

"Hmm. Is this all we have?"

"For now. Kandy can get more if necessary."

"I would like to cut one open. But I am reluctant to perform destructive testing with so few samples."

Kandy kicked the door open. "Sorry to interrupt your brain, Ferd, but we got a hit."

"The probability of such an event is impossibly low," Ferdinand said, without taking his eyes off the balls.

"So says you, Mr. Mathematics. But I have a response here from a Grass Valley patrol officer. She found a Honda VFR last night, apparently abandoned, at a remote rest stop along Route 20. There's only one problem."

"Ms. Kandy, never in my life has talking to you created only one problem," Ferdinand said.

"That's why you love me, Ferd: I keep life interesting." She paused. "It's black."

Ferdinand sat up. "Black?"

Qigiq's eyes turned toward Kandy.

"I know, I know. It's red in your picture. How long does it

take to change the color of a motorcycle?"

Qigiq envisioned Murphy's shop. "Would depend on how careful you had to be."

Kandy placed three prints on the desk. "This is what they had handy. Taken with a cell phone."

Qigiq reached for one of the right side of the bike.

Ferdinand took the left and removed a jeweler's loupe from his pocket. He placed it over the picture and began scanning the bodywork.

"Do you have a whole lab in your coat?" Kandy asked.

"Just the necessities."

Qigiq looked the bike over carefully. There was no sign of overspray on a wheel or the silver parts of the bike that a hurried paint job might cause.

"Did Honda make this model in black?" Ferdinand asked.

"For at least two years," Qigiq said.

"And red?"

"Their most popular color."

"Hmm..." Ferdinand said softly. "Ms. Kandy, did the registration tell us anything?"

"The bike has a hideaway holder under the rear fender. But no plate."

"Have they traced the vehicle identification number?"

"Totaled two years ago. No salvage title ever issued."

Qigiq placed the picture back on the desk. "Whoever used it knew we wouldn't be able to locate the owner."

"Here," Ferdinand said. "Very clever!" He moved aside and handed the loupe to Kandy. "Red tape peeling off along the very bottom of the fairing."

Qigiq came around the desk to look.

"I hypothesize," Ferdinand said, "that this bike was covered in cheap peel-off plastic, similar to the material used to protect new cars in transit. The rider drove away on a red bike, pulled over, peeled off the plastic, and continued on a black bike in an effort to confound anyone following him."

"But that tiny strip tore along the bottom," Kandy said. "I'll confirm that's what we have with Grass Valley. But let's say this is our getaway machine. Now what?"

"Now," Ferdinand said, "I must take my leave. But you have the satellite phone. If I think of anything at all, I will call you immediately." He rolled the five balls into a small evidence bag he withdrew from his pocket, and departed.

Qigiq looked from the reflection in the face shield, to the thin red strip along the bottom of the black bike's fairing.

Kandy sat directly across from him chewing gum and staring out the window. She said:

"Doesn't feel right."

"Mylin was dragged out of the room naked, but he had riding gear for her. Too careful?"

She nodded. "Yeah. The guys who pushed Spooner were more brute force."

"Maybe this dragon head Ferdinand mentioned brought in a professional."

She dropped her feet to the floor. "At the after concert party when we talked to her. Did you get the feeling she was trying to run?"

"No. When we met after the concert, she seemed like the star employee striving to please everyone. I was even supposed to call to confirm a date for tonight."

Kandy laughed. "Looks like you're going to be stood up."

"So where do you think that bike was headed? And why didn't it get there?"

Kandy typed on the laptop on her desk, twisting her mouth around the gum. "Looking at where he's been, he's heading northeast. Maybe Reno, maybe somewhere north of Reno..." her voice drifted off.

"Or he dropped the bike and backtracked to the coast so we'd go looking all over Nevada."

"That's hours of effort on his part just to misdirect us." She lifted her eyes. "And he won't be thinking about us. No way Bartholomew would call the cops; too much risk to his fat-cat profile. It was a fluke you already had Mylin's cell phone number, or we'd know nothing about last night."

Qigiq put both elbows on the desk. Wished for a coffee. "You think he's running from someone else?"

"Or covering his trail so when the body is found it can't be linked to him."

Qigiq put his face in his hands; the image of Mylin on a slab in the morgue gnawed at his insides. Mrs. Chong's motorbike accident had become a very strange business.

"So we have to find Mylin fast."

Kandy nodded. "That's our best shot at the bad guys."

Shuffling in the hall preceded a firm knock.

Kandy whispered, "Now what?" Then louder, "Come in."

Captain Jasik swung the door open for a man in a dark suit with a barely visible pinstripe. Qigiq recognized him instantly from the concert the night before. And from the parking lot of an art gallery.

"Detective Qigiq, Mr. Wu came by this morning and mentioned he knew you. So although this isn't strictly a homicide issue," Jasik's mouth curved into a half-smile that didn't reveal what he was thinking, "I figured you two would be anxious to lend a hand." Jasik ducked out the door leaving Wu standing in the middle of the office. They were all still for a moment, then Kandy and Qigiq stood.

Mr. Wu bowed slightly. "My daughter Mylin is missing. Would you please help?"

CHAPTER 44

KANDY AND QIGIQ STOOD ON THE STREET corner outside their office waiting for a walk signal.

"Burgers or Mexican?" Kandy asked.

"Burgers," Qigiq replied.

They walked east toward J-Burger on Lassiter, so named because the owner's name was Jong. In ten minutes they were seated with a coffee and a chocolate shake, waiting for sandwiches. Kandy tapped her index fingers together aimlessly. She said:

"Wu didn't seem to be aware of the video we found on Mylin's phone."

A waitress called out, "Mary," and pushed an order across a silver counter at the far end of the room.

"He seemed surprised she's missing," Qigiq said. "Shocked that such a thing was even possible."

"Claims it's never happened before, that she always lets him know where she is."

"Why Mylin? And why now?"

"Cue-gee," the waitress called. He stood and weaved between tables to make his way to the long counter. Just as he reached it, Kandy's name was called. He carried two burgers with sweet potato fries back to the table.

"Your second question: why now?" Kandy said. "A girl tries to run, ends up dead. Wu says, 'I understand there was a terrible boating accident.' The *very next day* another girl from the same orchestra goes missing."

Qigiq took a bite of his burger before saying: "Competition?

Someone trying to put Wu out of whatever business he's in. Pé is killed. Mylin kidnapped." He paused. "I don't see the connection from Mylin's disappearance to Spooner."

"Turf battle?" she said, shoving a fry into her mouth.

"Between?"

She shrugged.

Qigiq sucked the cool sweetness of the shake through a fat straw, but craved coffee. "Last known location is a rest stop in Grass Valley, assuming she was on the bike when it stopped. There are exactly two detectives assigned to this case," he pointed at Kandy, then turned the finger on himself. "Do you have a secret tracking device like that SPOT we can use to find Mylin?"

Kandy held up a finger and manipulated her phone with the other hand. She frowned. Tapped at it with both hands. She shook her head and lifted her mug of coffee. "Nothing on the major social networks. Bet there aren't many 20-something musicians *not* on social networks. That's weird all by itself."

"Maybe she's read Stallman's essay: *Reasons not to use Facebook*."

She locked eyes with him over the top of her mug. "Mr. Vintage Motorcycle reads Richard Stallman?"

"Only once. Stalking case in my department up in Fairbanks. Guy posing as Icy the Snow Clown tracking teenage girls. Wasn't my case though."

"Snow Clown?"

"All white outfit, including the nose where he hid the blow. No kidding. People joked about it for months. The captain sent Stallman's article to everyone, trying to educate us."

Kandy sipped. "And I thought San Francisco was the freak capital of the world. So, how would you track Mylin in Alaska?"

"Follow her footprints." He laughed. "Really. Far less densely populated. Following a person is sometimes possible just by talking to bystanders along the way. Won't work here."

He paused. "We could get a bunch of volunteers to stomp through the bush to scare her out."

Kandy frowned. "Or find the body."

Qigiq leaned back and took a deep breath. "Your natural optimism inspires me."

"Sorry, frustrated. This show lacks action. Find me someone to punch." She blew across the top, then sipped her coffee. "What do you think the gumballs do?"

Qigiq ate fries one at a time. "They were feather light...like they were empty."

"Filled with a gas?"

He stopped chewing. "You mean explosive gas?"

Kandy lowered her coffee to the table and tapped the handle with her middle finger. Dialed her cell phone. Conversed for a minute. Shook her head. "Ferd says the gumball he destructively tested had air in it. And there was nothing special about the air."

"Can we track the bikes you saw at the club?"

"We can try. I have pictures of the license plates. Maybe we get lucky at a toll booth or one of our highway cams. I'll touch base with Molly when we get back. She's good friends with Samantha over in Traffic."

"Doesn't help with Mylin."

She nodded agreement.

He worked on his basket of fries in silence. As he finished the last of the milkshake, his cell rumbled. He glanced at it.

"Dispatch operator," he told Kandy. "I'll take it outside." He moved to the front door and found a place to stand ten feet upwind of a young couple smoking cigarettes.

"Qigiq here."

"I'm so glad I found you. I have a hysterical woman who called your office number. Says she has a date with you tonight. You know I shouldn't put personal calls through the switchboard. But she sounds *frantic*. What have you done to this poor girl?"

"Thanks, Shannon, you made the right decision. She was kidnapped last night. Please put her through."

"Kidnap...she was...what?...uh, sure, right away."

The phone clicked and he begged it to stay to connected.

A whisper. "Hello, hello? Are you there?"

"Hello, Mylin, this is Qigiq."

"Oh, Qigiq. They're coming after me and I didn't run away, really I didn't. Please help me. They will hurt—"

"Where are you?"

"On winding road. Orange truck with little house on back. I want to come home, but I'm afraid—"

The line fell silent. It didn't come back.

He dialed Shannon to request a trace, hoping Mylin had been on a cell and the towers would provide a location. But the call had been so short; he didn't hold out much hope.

He went inside and repeated the conversation to Kandy, word for word, including his request to Shannon.

She drank the last of her coffee. "California is a maze of winding roads."

"When did they find that black bike?" he asked.

"After midnight. If they've been driving since then," she glanced at a wall clock, "they have a fourteen-hour head start. At least five hundred miles, even in the hills. Unless they're on gravel."

Qigiq looked into his shake: there was nothing left. "What if they put up for the night, maybe started out this morning?"

A shrug. "Still four or five hours. A couple hundred miles from that rest stop on Route 20."

He dug around the paper container and found two burnt fries. "Why would you drive an orange truck?"

"I wouldn't." She smirked. "But if I did, it'd be because I wanted to be noticed. Not a lot of orange on the road."

"You kidnap a naked girl, disguise your motorcycle, then drive an orange truck?"

She wrapped both hands around her coffee mug like she was trying to prevent it from being stolen. "Doesn't add up. Not if we're right about this guy being careful."

Qigiq gazed at traffic through an outside window hand-labeled with the day's tuna melt special, including a drawing of the sandwich. A green cab rolled by, and a white utility truck.

"I see green and white on the street. No orange."

A long pause. Then: "He sure is clever." She crumpled the paper that had wrapped her burger and tossed it cleanly into a trash can eight feet away. "He's driving orange because Caltrans, our friendly California Department of Transportation, drives orange. People treat those trucks like they don't exist. No one will remember seeing it."

Qigiq gave up on his shake and tossed the cup toward the can, trying to recall the last time he had seen a Caltrans truck. He couldn't. The cup missed. He walked over to retrieve it.

Kandy was shaking her head when he got back. "It gets better, Qu, much better. I know where he's going."

"With an orange utility truck?"

Kandy stood and brushed salt off her lap. "Look at his path. Starts at the ocean, heads northeast. Toward what? The Sierra Nevada mountains? Utah? Canada? But wait, Mylin said the truck has a house on the back. That means camper. I think he's going where things are so crazy, and there are so many people, we'll have a hard time finding him even knowing he's there in a bright orange truck."

"Vegas?"

"Better. The biggest event around and my vacation paradise: The Burning Man Festival."

———

On the walk back to the office Kandy expounded on the 1960's style be-in, art show, city, party, performance extravaganza that was created each year in the Nevada desert by 50,000 attendees. Qigiq imagined it as a tribal fertility rite writ large.

Kandy said: "It's a perfect plan. Grab Mylin, change the color of the bike, use a maintenance truck no one will notice, take winding back roads, camp along the way like the other Burners. He blends into a moving circus of vehicles that are ever more strange, so he goes unnoticed. Unfortunately for us, once he gets to Burning Man, the size of the crowd alone will make her invisible, not to mention costumes and art cars and stationary exhibits five stories high surrounded by thousands of people."

"Better than a 200-mile radius," he said.

"Agreed. But it's just a hunch."

"Best hunch we have. Way better than beating the bushes with sticks."

Kandy looked at the empty wall. "I have to get my clock put up. I miss it."

"How about we get a new one?"

She shook her head. "Can't replace my lucky Dunlop tire." She glanced at her phone. "Twenty after two. It's a three- or four-hour drive." She frowned. "I'll need to double the supplies: tent, food, water—there's absolutely nothing up there, just open desert. Going to take a bit of time to pull it together."

"How can I help?"

"Your leg good to ride?" she asked.

"Two hundred miles? Sure."

She leaned toward her laptop. The chair squawked. She stroked keys and talked at the same time:

"You said Mylin sounded frantic. How about you hightail it up there? Who knows how much time we have before she disappears to another country. Keep Ferd's satphone handy. I'll call after I get the Mini inside with our luxury accommodations."

CHAPTER 45

WU ATE THICK NISSIN NOODLES from a Styrofoam bowl in the driver's seat of his black Cadillac SUV. He avoided driving, especially in the suffocatingly narrow streets of San Francisco. Driving interfered with thinking. But Tuson was still weak, though less pale. Through the windshield he kept a careful watch on the motorbike parked near a green garbage bin, wondering if perhaps he had been wrong and the detective didn't know how to find his daughter.

He swallowed a noodle.

It angered him that Mylin was gone. How could she, too, defy him? She must have removed her bracelet as Pé had; it had been stationary for hours near the ocean. A precious stone from her mother—enhanced by his own clever electronics designed with the aid of the Internet—and she probably tossed it into the waves, thinking she could escape her eternal duty to her ancestors.

He sighed.

Pé forced him to use extreme measures. But Mylin was not Pé; she was younger, and wiser. He glanced in the rearview mirror. Tuson was stretched across the back seat asleep. He turned his eyes back to the motorbike.

Finally.

The detective descended the steps from the rear entrance two at a time.

Wu set the noodles aside and waited without moving. Motion triggered the hunting instinct in predatory animals.

The detective mounted the bike, buckled his helmet, and

rode down the alley.

Wu pulled into traffic and turned right at the first corner. He leaned forward to activate the navigation system, then switched to aerial view. Two dots pulsated on a map, blue for the location of his Cadillac, bright red for the motorcycle. He relaxed as the bike moved smoothly toward the Bay Bridge about half a mile ahead of his location. His instincts had been correct; the detective wasn't going to let him down.

Two hours later, Tuson shifted and sat up slowly in the back seat. He blinked himself awake.

Wu said, "We have passed through Sacramento, heading east." He waved his right hand at the navigation screen. "Your GPS tracker is working perfectly. How are you feeling?"

"Hungry," Tuson said.

"There are cold noodles in the bag." Wu changed lanes to the left and accelerated. "He stopped for petrol just before Sacramento. I suspect he'll stop again in an hour or so; bikes don't have much range. If you want to wait, we can pick up something hot. You need your strength."

"I'll eat them cold."

A pair of motorcycles covered with chalky white dust flew past in the inside lane.

Tuson leaned forward to study them from the back seat, but said nothing.

Buses and vans, cars and trucks, were all heading east. Some had symbols painted on the back or smudged onto dirty windows. The most common was the letter X with a circle above it, reminding him of a man standing with arms extended. Others resembled a drunkard with a mop swirling garish colors, the result far worse than even the horrible abstracts he placed in the gallery for the tourists from the East Coast. He would never understand human desire.

He smiled for the first time since Mylin had turned up missing.

He had no need to understand—so long as he had the opportunity and means to exploit it.

CHAPTER 46

QIGIQ'S HEADLIGHT WAS VISIBLE on the road ahead by the time he reached the exit for Pyramid Lake. As Kandy's directions indicated, he refilled his gas tank at Gerlach, Nevada along with a steady stream of other travelers, then rode a few miles on potholed blacktop to reach a fork. He turned right. The bouncing high beam of his Mana brushed strokes of blue-whiteness across desert sand churned into crud. His street tires slipped and twisted. He stood on the foot pegs and slowed. Shortly, a sign with a thin arrow indicated:

The Burning Man Project.

He reached a gate held up by guy wires between billboards welcoming him. *Temporary.* He waited in line as car after car in front presented admission tickets. When he reached the gate he was greeted by a young woman wearing a sleeveless dress made of horizontal black strips that covered very little of her athletic body. Her face was painted green, and she wore a huge smile beneath pink hair that glowed iridescent in the fading light of the setting sun.

"Ticket please?"

He pushed his goggles up on to his helmet. "I'm sorry, I don't have one. I'm a police officer tracking a missing person."

Her eyes opened wide and round, azure against green skin.

"Missing?"

"A woman's been kidnapped. We have reason to believe she's been brought here."

"To Burning Man?"

He nodded. His bike burbled beneath him.

She turned slightly, shifted to her other foot and stepped closer. The black stripes turned with her, but didn't cover much from the side either. She spoke as if she didn't have quite enough air to activate her vocal cords.

"Amazing. Is kidnapping a kind of performance art?"

Maybe it was, but he didn't understand how that would matter. Unless his answer got him inside.

"Not a good kind."

She nodded, agreeing with something.

Her green forehead creased. "You don't have a ticket?"

"I'm sorry, no. We just found out she was here. I rode up from San Francisco right away."

Her eyes grew wider and rounder. "You rode a motorcycle from San Francisco? I'm from there too." She moved closer and touched his riding jacket, which had been too hot crossing the valley, but was near perfect for the cooling desert. "I love motorcycles. Especially Italian ones. They're so sexy."

"This is Italian. Hand made in Noale."

She stepped back and squatted, causing the black stripes to shift. Her hand reached out and he feared she'd burn herself. But she carefully ran her fingertips along the frame tubes as if they were speaking to her. Without warning she popped straight up and hopped onto the back of the bike, almost toppling them onto the sand in the process.

"I'll get you in." She stretched her arm and index finger past his right shoulder. "Over there." She was pointing at an RV parked sideways. A yellow plastic banner strung across it read: *Volunteer Burners.*

He rode to the RV, she jumped off and ran inside, the stripes twisting with each stride. In a minute she was back with a lanyard and badge. She worked it over his head, barely fitting over the helmet, and let it dangle outside his jacket. Then she peeled the back from an official looking decal and slapped it over the tachometer.

"The bike needs a ticket?" Qigiq asked.

She nodded vigorously, the pink hair trying to follow. "You can't drive on the playa without an art-car pass."

He assumed this made sense to someone, so he didn't press. He looked ahead to a wide open desert with movie sets of alien cities randomly dropped onto it.

"Thanks for your help." He had no idea who she was. "My name's Qigiq, what's yours?"

"Here, I'm KD."

The letters stirred a memory. "Like K.D. Lang, the musician?"

She shook her pink hair and smiled a green-cheek smile. "No, like the detective in San Francisco. I saw her kick butt on the TV news."

Who would that—? "You don't mean Kandy Dreeson, do you?"

"Yeah, that's her. She's so together. All style and skill." KD made karate flashing motions with her flat palms.

Qigiq tried not to laugh, wondering if Kandy knew she had a fan way out here in the desert.

"You're not going to believe this KD, but Detective Dreeson is coming here tonight."

KD stiffened as if her nervous system had gridlocked. "Really?" Her eyes blinked four times to an unseen metronome. "I'll get to meet her?"

"If you like. Would you be able to arrange a pass for her? She'll be arriving in a black Mini in a few hours."

"For Kandy? You bet."

KD disappeared into the volunteer hut for another minute and returned at a full run wearing a bright green bicycle helmet with pink hair sticking through the openings. "Done. Boxy will watch for her, give her the pass, and tell her where to find us."

Since Qigiq had no idea where he was going, how would Boxy know?

KD jumped on the bike declaring her intention of going with him.

"Let's go," she said. "Toward the man."

Qigiq rode through the gate, then past cars and bicycles and pedestrians toward a ten-story structure in the distance with the a huge stick man standing on top. The Mana tires regularly reminded him they preferred asphalt.

"A couple more minutes and we turn left," KD said. "Five O'clock and Istanbul."

Being in the desert surrounded by randomness was disorienting, so he was happy to have KD on board, even though much of what she said sounded like transmissions from a far-off galaxy. He idled along in a straight line, marveling at the diversity of the populace; as yet, no one appeared normal, even by San Francisco standards. Closer to the man structure the crowd became denser; some frowned at his bike. Two guys wearing nothing but orange jockstraps spit in his direction.

He turned his head to speak over his left shoulder. "The natives aren't friendly."

"You're supposed to have an art car out here. Turn left by the pink bunny."

There was indeed a 20-foot-tall pink bunny sitting in the desert. Though it had three wheels, it wasn't moving. He turned left.

"How do I get an art car?"

"Your bike." Her left arm came around his shoulder and pointed at the tach he could no longer read. "That's why I got a sticker for you." Her long fingernails alternated between green and pink.

She led him to a campsite with a squarish RV in the middle of a city of campsites. Its sides had been painted the green of her face, and the top sprouted colored tubes as much as a foot in diameter, hanging in huge arcs, nearly touching the ground on all sides. Two men and two women, wearing nothing against the coming desert cold except the bottoms of brightly colored bathing suits—blue, black, pink, red—and green body paint on their arms and faces, were running from one tube to the other, pounding them with mallets. The resulting jumble of thumps conjured images of the war drums of a species preparing to attack Earth. Inside the windshield of the motorhome, a hand lettered sign declared: *The Porcupine Band.*

He guided the bike between the arm-like structures, paddling with his feet, finally parking beside the motorhome in the fading shadows of the waving tubes. She hopped off. The drumming ceased. Five green people huddled ten yards away. The exhaust from the bike began collecting beneath the tube umbrella, so he switched it off.

Drums in the distance pounded out a tribal rhythm that made him want to dance the way he had as a child. He hadn't felt that free for ages.

The group rushed over and surrounded him. KD pointed and said, "Qigiq, this is Blue, Black, Pink and Red." They each nodded as their color was spoken.

"Nice to meet you," he said.

Everyone disappeared into the RV except for KD. She examined the bike closely, then motioned him off. He found solid footing for the stand and stepped away. She crawled in the sand, circling the bike, touching parts to test if they were hot, and polishing spots with her fingers.

Since she was busy, he checked his cell phone. No signal. No messages.

KD popped upright: a jumping jack released from her box. "I've got it."

She also disappeared into the band bus.

Qigiq retrieved the satellite phone and was re-buckling the side bag when the five green folks came out of the RV single file. Red carried a bucket of water and a mitten sponge with which she set to cleaning his bike. He warned her about the hot parts. She nodded, smiled and continued cleaning, oblivious to his efforts not to stare at her.

Pink wiped the bike dry with a white cloth.

Blue followed Pink with a noisy hair dryer running, dragging a power cable that disappeared under the motorhome.

KD placed a shiny can beside the bike and stirred gooey brown liquid.

Black sorted an armful of colored tubes an inch in diameter and several feet long: miniatures of those on the motorhome. When he had them arranged, he bent each tube and shook it until it began to glow.

Qigiq was about to ask what they were planning just as the image of a glowing porcupine bike leapt into his head. He dialed Kandy's cell number on the satphone and was tossed into voice mail. He left the message that he was at Burning Man near Five O'clock and Istanbul, then called Ferdinand.

"Sorry, Ferdinand, I'm not going to be able to make it to your spectacular show. Kandy thinks Mylin has been taken to a place called Burning Man. I rode up here to see if I can find her."

"You're at Burning Man?" Ferdinand said, his voice slightly delayed over the satellite connection.

KD brushed liquid over his gas tank, fork, swing arm, fenders. He hoped it wouldn't damage the finish, or void his rental agreement.

"Arrived ten minutes ago. Unusual place."

"Yes, at least that. Since you are here, you must come to the event. We jump at ten PM sharp. The vector along Six O'clock and Vine."

Clocks and streets, time and space, were a bit disorienting. His phone showed 6:38 pm. Would Kandy arrive by ten? Then Ferdinand's words fully registered.

"You're jumping at Burning Man?"

"Where else would we find an instant appreciative audience

of thousands, no regulations, and plenty of space? It's a natural fit for this kind of statement, though a bit dusty."

Qigiq hesitated to dampen Ferdinand's enthusiasm, but said: "I've got to find Mylin."

"Ah, yes, the string player. Have you found her instrument? It may lead you to her."

"Bartholomew admitted to being at the Sea and Sky with her. I suspect he has it." Five green faces glued on colorful tubes. The bike looked more like a glowing rainbow blowfish than a porcupine, but he genuinely appreciated their efforts. Coming from the calm spaciousness of Alaska, San Francisco was complex but manageable; here, he struggled to remember he wasn't dreaming.

"How will you find her, my friend?" Ferd asked. "There are over fifty thousand people here in the desert."

"Find an orange truck."

"If it's still orange." A sigh told him Ferdinand was out of ideas too.

"I'll call after I talk to Kandy. Good luck with the jump."

"Thank you. I hope it will be all I've imagined. There is always risk of unforeseen complications."

Qigiq ended the call and smiled at the transformation of his bike, wishing he was doing more of something.

Five green heads stood as one.

"What do you think?" KD asked.

The seat was barely visible. Every available surface, including the headlight, taillight, both fenders, and gas tank had the end of a long glowing tube protruding from it. The free ends of the tubes waved in the wind. A sudden urge to ride it overtook him.

"Wait, I'll be right back," KD said. She spun and dashed into the motorhome.

Qigiq approached the bike. Four people stared as he flicked the end of a yellow tube with a finger. It bobbed as if agreeing to a silent suggestion.

"Beautiful work. How can I repay you?"

They all smiled, shook their heads, and spoke as one. "It's a gift."

The girl with the pink bikini bottom swept her hand across the desert landscape. "All of this is a gift. No one expects payment."

He wanted to ask why he needed a ticket if this was all a gift, but kept quiet.

KD returned holding his helmet festooned with short tubes that looked like they had grown from a white skull. They glowed shades of green. She had also donned the bicycle helmet she had worn earlier, only now it emitted purple tubes.

"Let's go find her."

Qigiq appreciated her enthusiasm, but he shook his head. "Too many people. Worse than a needle in a haystack."

Pink stepped forward. Qigiq looked up to meet her eyes.

"The problem is easy: X-ray, metal detector, or magnetism can find a needle. You just need the right technology."

Digital technology had undermined his last case in Alaska. He had taken a sabbatical in an effort to better understand technology so he could solve more problems. And here a topless girl with a green face stood telling him the very same thing.

Blue said: "What are we looking for?"

Qigiq took out his cell phone and found the video from Mylin's phone that Ferdinand had copied for him. He paused it at a frame where her face was clearly visible.

"Her." They jostled each other to get close to the screen. "She was kidnapped at gunpoint near the ocean north of San Francisco. Between ten PM and midnight last night."

They stared at the phone.

"Why do you want to find her?" Red asked. "Is she your girlfriend?"

Qigiq decided not to mention his pending date. "Her father

came to us this morning. Reported her missing."

"She looks over eighteen," Red said. "Can do what she wants."

Qigiq nodded but asked, "Does it look like she left of her own free will?"

They all frowned into one wide green tightly furled forehead.

"She has ink. Hip," Pink said.

"That's good," Black said. He didn't elaborate.

KD whispered in his ear, "Tell them about Detective Dreeson."

"What about her?"

"That you know her. That she's coming."

"Why?"

"They'll want to impress her."

This mystifying environment made Qigiq feel like he had traveled a lot more than three and a half hours from San Francisco. But the group had been helpful and cooperative, so he said:

"KD thought you might like to know that my partner is coming to join the search. She's also a detective with the San Francisco Police Department. Her name is Dreeson. Kandy Dreeson."

Four mouths opened.

Pink found her voice first. "Kandy is coming *here?*"

Red. "She's your *partner?*"

Black and Blue together: "OMG! OMG!" They high-fived each other.

The four huddled again.

KD grabbed his arm and pulled him toward the RV.

"You have to change clothes to ride our art bike."

CHAPTER 47

KANDY POUNDED HER FOREHEAD against the steering wheel. Two hours to round up desert supplies, several more to make the drive. Now creeping along—clutch in, clutch out—toward the entrance to Burning Man.

She moved two car lengths.

The gate was visible ahead, but she had at least a quarter mile to go at about a half mile per hour. She gritted her teeth and squeezed, released, squeezed, released the hand exerciser in her right hand, the spring groaning with each compression. The rumble of engines drew her attention to the right side mirror. Two single headlights were ignoring the line and raising clouds of powdery dust as they moved toward the front. She debated stopping them, but it would slow her down.

The dust-covered riders appeared like a black and white movie in the dance of car headlights. But one thing registered: size. One large, one small.

Her satellite phone blipped on the seat beside her. A red light in the antenna flashed. She picked it up while inching the Mini forward. "Dreeson here."

"Hello, Detective Dreeson. This is Samantha Roster over in Traffic. Molly asked me to run motorcycle plates for you this morning. I left the search active so I would be notified if they were stopped for speeding or other violation."

The bikes shot past, their taillights dimmed by dust. Those bastards were almost to the front of the line in seconds.

"Hello, Samantha, thanks for calling. You get a hit?"

"Maybe. According to my computer, both bikes were on a

plane to Tucsan this morning. Then they showed up crossing into Mexico at Nogales."

Kandy focused. "A plane?"

"But get this. Then they were ridden back into the U.S. through Sonoyta."

"Who's riding them?"

"Richard Bachman and David Axton. Same two that rode them into Mexico."

Kandy rolled the Mini forward. The names weren't familiar. But she'd bet on Prime and his buddy Michael—two guys with fake passports and clean bikes that had just come back from Murphy's.

"Samantha, why do you think two guys would ride to Mexico for a couple of hours?"

"The few bikers I know? Typical boy stuff: Tequila, girls, drugs. Then they race back to work. Bikers like the freedom of riding fast down there too—apparently the cops are a bit more, uh, lenient."

A baby-faced kid in a yellow top hat gestured to the riders at the gate. The Ton Up Club. Named for riding at 100 mph— illegal on any road in the United States.

"They come back clean?"

"As a whistle. A quick in-and-out like that, our customs guys are thorough. Only found saddlebags full of tequila."

What, she wondered, happened to those bags of air-filled colored balls?

"Thanks, Samantha, you sure do good work. Let me know if anything else pops up on your screen."

Kandy thumbed the phone. The taller rider reached into his left bag without dismounting, extracted an object, and handed it to the guy with the yellow hat. The bikes were waved through.

The yellow hat gazed down the line of cars, motionless, as if counting. He dropped to one knee, placed the object beside a gatepost, and started jogging along the line of waiting vehicles.

The bikes rode out of sight, so Kandy followed the cloud of dust being lifted by them with her eyes. It turned right.

The guy with the hat was still running her way. When he reached the Mini he stopped and tapped on the driver's window. She rolled it down. He bent slightly forward, breathing hard. "Are you Kandy Dreeson?"

She studied his soft face and blond curls, but couldn't generate a memory. Maybe the yellow top hat was throwing her off.

"Yes. Who might be asking?"

"Hi, I'm Boxy." He reached his hand in to shake.

His body was skinny and frail, not boxy. She'd bet there was a story there.

He took a few breaths like a fugitive on the run. Then said:

"KD asked me to get a pass for you." He pushed a lanyard through the window. "She's at Five O'clock and Istanbul. Here's a map." He handed a folded sheet of paper through the open window. "Pull to your right and head up front. I'll let you through on the far side. It's for official vehicles, VIPs, that sort of stuff."

Right where the bikes had gone.

"You want a ride back?"

He smiled and ran around the car. She moved her satphone out of the way as he slid inside.

"Hey, Boxy. Can I ask you a question?"

"Sure. KD's going to flip out when she meets you. Do you really punch people?"

Wondering who KD was, she said, "Only if they need it. So, Boxy, what did the biker boy give you?"

"Tequila, I think. But I don't drink alcohol. Do you want it?"

She wasn't even through the gate and someone named KD had given her a pass, and Boxy wanted to share his tequila—the wonders of Burning Man continued to amaze.

"I appreciate the offer, but you keep it. You know, lots of

girls like tequila."

He grinned. "Good idea. Thanks."

She pulled right, following Boxy's finger.

"Boxy is an unusual name."

"It's just a reminder."

He didn't elaborate. She tried to convert balls of air and bottles of tequila into a question for her new friend before she dropped him off. Came up blank. So she said:

"Reminder?"

"Yeah. That we all live in a box of our own making dictated by our mindset, history, philosophy, acquired habits, and received knowledge that is mostly bullshit. It reminds me to constantly think outside the box if I want to improve my experience of the world."

"You're in a good place for that."

He grinned again as he hopped out to raise the VIP gate, and waved his bottle of tequila as she drove through. She didn't recognize the label, but maybe that bottle contained something important. Then again, Prime wouldn't give anything important to a kid at the gate in a yellow top hat.

On the other side of the gate, the Mini bumped over rutted sand until she reached the spot where the dust cloud had turned right. She stopped to orient herself to the tall structures that had been raised above the desert by artists who love the freedom of Burning Man. A temple. A hollow tower. The man himself. Pieces built only to be set afire later in the week—a kind of cleansing antidote to hoarding consumerism. Each year the loosely structured chaos reminded her to keep moving—her last move having been to adopt the sabbatical guy from Alaska.

So far, so good, though they were only on their second case.

She hugged the outer edge of pedestrian activity, following those two bikes. She switched to parking lights only because headlights blinded people in the darkness of the open desert. The art vehicles were lit more to be seen than see, and rolling snail slow. Like the guy and girl riding a steel tricycle with a front wheel ten feet in diameter sporting an umbrella shooting flames out its top.

She traveled in a wide arc, studying campsites to her left decorated to Las Vegas levels: giant shark, cabana with palm trees and pink flamingoes, laser-lit disco, motorhome with tubes protruding from the roof like a melted pipe organ. She searched for something that would lead her to the tequila bikes, not really expecting to find it.

But she did.

Sitting between a rainbow VW Vanagon and a bright blue school bus with a galvanized metal chimney sat a plain white pickup truck hooked to a box trailer, both covered in chalky dust. Behind the trailer five motorcycles were parked tightly in a neat row like sardines in a can. From a distance they looked suspiciously similar to each other. Behind that row of five bikes stretched dozens of partiers of both genders, many wearing black leather against the coming coolness of the night. She didn't recognize anyone, but could make out past their heads a makeshift nightclub with a dance floor and a motorcycle where the jukebox should be pumping out rockabilly. A sign had been hung above the entrance: *Ton Uppers Paradise*.

She braked. She had driven the Mini to the club. They would recognize it instantly.

She slipped the car into reverse and eased the clutch out. With the artistic contraptions driving around the desert, no one would notice one car that happened to be moving toward its taillights. She retrieved her satphone and dialed while scrunching across the playa at a walking pace.

"Qigiq here."

"Arrived at Burning Man a couple minutes ago. I think Prime and Michael are here. Weird story about those bikes I saw this morning."

She stopped the car and stepped out onto gritty sand. A

purple man with flat computer screens hanging front and back over his shoulders like a sandwich board sign walked past wearing combat boots and dark ski goggles. She barely noticed him. What stopped her eyes was images of Mylin on the front screen above the words *HAVE YOU SEEN ME?* in English, Spanish, Japanese, and a few she didn't recognize. But she knew the pictures—they were from the video taken by Mylin's camera at the Sea and Sky. They focused mostly on her face. Mostly.

"Forget the bikes for a second, Qu. I'm looking at an electronic sign with Mylin's face and body on it. Someone is looking for her."

"The signs are out already? These people are fast, Kandy."

She paused. "This wouldn't be someone named KD would it?"

"Exactly. She's dying to meet you. Her friends had the idea for walking billboards. Given the way people dress out here, they suggested including more than face shots."

"This KD person, what's her name?"

"Don't know. She's going by your initials at Burning Man. Says she saw you kick butt on television."

"I avoid cameras. They make my butt look fat." She leaned against the idling Mini, trying to remember the last time she was on TV against her will. Too many reporters were misinformed, stupid, trying to pick a fight, or all three. She preferred lying low—tough to do in a sea of smartphones. The purple man strolled away. A blurry close-up of Mylin's hip filled the departing monitor. She said:

"Got it. Guy in Noe valley. Couple months ago. He ran for it. I convinced him it was a bad idea without drawing blood. Heard later that a bystander sold video to KRON News 4, but I've never seen it."

"KD didn't elaborate. She wants to hear about it from you."

"Have to wait. If Prime and Michael are here, they're going to see that sign."

The line was quiet for a few seconds. Then Qigiq said, "Will they lead us to her?"

"Might." She paused. "Or vice versa." She looked past the placard man to the pickup. Three guys were pushing a bike, that might be black under the dust, up a ramp into the trailer.

"I'm leaving the Mini here." She looked around for a landmark then remembered, removed the satphone from her ear, and read the GPS coordinates to Qigiq. She clipped the phone to her belt and checked her weapon. She gazed out over the playa. People everywhere; no safe place to discharge a firearm. She flicked the Mini off, left the emergency flashers on, locked it, and pocketed the key. With luck, it would be mistaken for an artistic statement about the value of smallness in a bigger-is-better world and not be bothered.

She stood beside the car. The sand was warm underfoot, the air cool. What mattered at the moment was the growing crowd that wore silver space costumes, welding masks, lingerie, less than lingerie, Sargent Pepper jackets— essentially anything but street clothes. Street clothes would draw attention just when she needed to be invisible. She pressed the key to unlock the Mini's rear doors and ducked around the back. She swung the doors open and positioned one to block the view from the trailer, then dug her Leatherman multi-tool out of a black plastic toolbox.

She tossed her jacket to the floor behind the front seat and peeled off her black shirt, boots and jeans; leaving her standing in a black bra, panties, and a lightweight holster designed by the Israeli military. She tied the shirt and cut eye holes, making a cap that reached the tip of her nose. She held up her jeans, sighed, cut the legs off and stepped into short shorts, then back into her boots. She slipped the T-shirt cap on, stuffed her auburn hair up underneath so it wouldn't attract attention, and considered using the jacket to hide her gun.

"Hey."

She turned around. Four people, guys based on their size,

stood a few yards away staring her way. They all wore rust-brown monk robes tied with gold rope. Their hoods were flipped up and hanging forward, hiding their faces.

"Hey," she said, with a wave.

They approached slowly, as if shy. The shortest one spoke.

"We were watching you, uh, tailor your clothing."

"Show's free."

He cleared his throat. "Uh, yes, well, sure. Lot of girls don't wear much out here."

She studied at him through her shirt-mask, one hand on her hip, the other behind her back hiding her weapon from view.

"You registering a complaint?"

"No way," the guy on the left said. "We were just wondering."

While meeting his gaze, waiting to find out what he was wondering, she planned. The jacket would be too obvious, but she didn't have another shirt. That meant working in a bra and shorts. Possible, but sand wasn't the friendliest of surfaces, and the temperature was dropping.

"Uh, yeah, we were wondering if you might like a buckyball?"

She searched her memory. That term registered as something to do with the physics of carbon atoms. And a game. Yes, she was sure it was a game.

"Maybe."

The four approached as one unit, like a brown wave about to slosh on the shore. The little guy held out his hand. A red sphere rested in his palm.

She frowned without meaning to.

"You don't like buckies?"

"It's not that." She stepped closer.

"We want to give you a gift, the way you gave us the gift of your incredible body."

Burning Man. She was no longer in the city that saw the

Summer of Love. Even its liberal rules didn't apply in this desert basin. She wasn't sure if any rules applied.

"Why, thank you."

She picked up the ball between her thumb and index finger. Her eyes flicked to the trailer a hundred yards away, then back to the ball. It was the same size and texture as the ones she had lifted from the Ton Up. She was sure of it.

The four guys stared at her. A tall monk said: "Have you ever done one?"

She shook her head. "Never even seen one."

"It's amazing. You control it by how many holes you poke in it, and how hard you suck on it. Take your time and it'll last for hours, or you can open it and take it all at once." He shook his head inside the hood like a sorcerer bringing bad news. "But please don't do that if you've never had one."

She slipped the ball into the pocket of her new jean shorts. "So, you guys are monks?"

To her surprise they all nodded yes.

"Real monks, live in the mountains, celibate, that kind of stuff?"

Their eyes moved one to the other.

"Well..."

"Not..."

"Exactly...."

Three of them managed to assemble.

The fourth lifted his hand palm upward.

"We are instruments of the power of chant." He stepped up beside Kandy, faced his three colleagues, lifted both arms, and began conducting.

She was instantly enveloped in weird choral swooshing sounds. The oddity of standing in her bra under an evening desert sky listening to ancient music woke her up. She needed to get back to work. She held up both hands to stop them.

"Guys, you sound great, fantastic. Come over here." She

beckoned them into a huddle.

All four glanced down at her breasts as they leaned in.

————

Four robed monks followed a diminutive figure in a drooping black leather jacket whose face was covered with a black hood. The hooded figure walked backwards, conducting. The group moved with the rhythm of their chanting: step pause, step pause. As they passed the Vanagon they sang more loudly and shifted direction. When they reached the trailer behind the pickup truck, the five grouped into a tight circle and raised their hands together into a human pillar.

They held this position for a full ten seconds, stretching the syllables of the chant to a climax, before lowering their hands. The hooded figure took two steps backwards to lead the group across the playa. Three monks followed.

Kandy scooted across the sand on her back and elbows while the pillar of monks hid her from sight, the underside of the trailer inches from her nose. With the sound of chanting still in the air, she moved quietly to the center of the trailer and twisted her head to place an ear against the floor above her. Boots scuffled. A whirring. The screech of a saw blade biting into something hard. The softening of the sound as the cut completed.

Silence.

A hiss of air, like a tire deflating. A series of light thumps: Halloween candy being dropped into a child's paper bag. She counted 20, 30, and the thumping continued. She wanted a peek inside the trailer; considered the red ball in her pocket. She worked her hand inside the borrowed robe and came back with the satphone. She muted the sound and carefully prepared a text message.

Gumballs are drug dispensers. Targets in trailer. Ask for buckyballs. The "monks" sent you.

She added her GPS location.

The cutting and thumping continued above her; still no

conversation.

She rested her head gently on the ground and wished some tech genius in Silicon Valley would invent X-ray glasses to see through the floor of a trailer. Her imagination told her Prime and Michael (and maybe Murphy) were inside that trailer selling those buckyball drugs that the monks were sharing. Dealing that involved motorcycles making a fast run up from Mexico. That was international drug trafficking, even in the desert gift culture of Burning Man.

The desert.

She had a satphone. Call in Reno people? They were a hundred miles away. That wouldn't be fast unless they sent a chopper. A lot to ask for half-a-hunch.

A motorcycle coasted silently across the sand and stopped beside the trailer's wheel.

Qigiq was right, KD and her friends did move fast.

A green legging inside a black leather boot planted itself six feet from her head. A pair of feminine legs dropped onto the sand behind it wearing leopard-skin flip-flops. Kandy reached around to her back, brought the pistol to her chest, and prepared to roll. This should be simple, but many times she had thought things would be simple. Life was full of surprises.

The girl knocked on the back of the trailer.

The thumping ceased. All quiet inside. Not even a shoe scratched across the trailer deck.

Another knock.

Someone inside yelled, "Yeah?"

KD began singing a decent imitation of the monks' chanting.

The floor-to-ceiling locking rod of the trailer's back door groaned as it released.

"Hi guys. Monks say buckyball show way to happiness."

No voices, just the sound of paper money being flipped like playing cards.

"Thanks," the girl's voice said. "You bring much joy. I will honor you in song." She sang in a language foreign to Kandy as the leopard flip-flops danced back to the bike and lifted out of sight. Clumps of white sand dropped from slowly turning tires as the machine pulled away at a quiet idle.

Kandy listened intently. They had sold buckyballs. That was good enough for her. Time to confiscate the evidence. She tried to connect the balls to Pé or Mylin, but a male voice from inside interrupted.

"Those monks are a human billboard."

A different voice. "Maybe we should pay them."

"In a gift giving culture?"

Quiet laughter.

At least two men inside.

The thumping began anew.

She rotated until her head pointed toward the rear of the trailer, then used elbows and heels to inch silently across the sand until the doors were directly above her face. As she had hoped, the handle that rotated rods to hold them closed was drilled to accept a padlock.

But she didn't have a padlock.

Or wire. Or even a coat hanger. And her zip-tie handcuffs were in the jacket she wasn't wearing.

She crabbed back along the sand toward her feet until she was back under the trailer.

The thumping ceased.

She ejected the magazine and extracted a 38 mm bullet, studied the diameter of the shell casing, placed the weapon on her chest, and felt along her side to locate the gold belt. Carefully she removed the braided cloth from the robe, then yanked it taut between her hands.

She worked her way out from under the trailer, stood, silently slipped the bullet through the padlock hole, and wrapped the belt around the handle to prevent the bullet from moving. She stepped right to put the trailer between her and the foot traffic that was now as dense as a crowd leaving a rock concert. With her left foot she pushed a black block gently away from a trailer tire. She checked the hitch, then ducked to heel-toe around the front bumper to the driver's side. She tested the door. Unlocked. Slipped inside. With a shared campsite in a place with no cell phones, the obvious thing to do...she flipped over the floor mats, felt under the driver's seat, checked the center console, and finally found a single key wedged under a cup holder built into the rear seats.

Kandy pulled the monk's hood around her face, turned the key, double-checked for pedestrians, and eased the truck into gear. The boys probably had an escape plan involving those parked motorcycles; she needed it to fail. She yanked the wheel left and pulled away fast enough to disorient anyone in the trailer. She rolled across the playa as fast as safety allowed, which meant not much faster than hundreds of people wandering aimlessly in a starlit desert could get out of the way. Pounding emerged from the trailer; unintelligible voices shouted. She swung right, gunned the diesel, and approached a sign marking Three O'clock and Istanbul.

An island floated from the Three O'clock street across her path.

She slammed on the brakes.

The rolling mound inched along covered with brown sand, iridescent blue waves painted around its edges, palm trees and, at the very top, a cabana beside a hot tub containing four girls waving Jolly Roger flags at the night sky.

The driver was hidden inside.

The island moved slowly. The trailer rocked on its springs, letting her know the boys inside were up to something. Could three of them force that door open? Then she remembered a motorcycle being pushed up a ramp.

As if reading her mind, the roar of a bike erupted from the trailer.

She put the truck in reverse and gunned it for ten yards, slapped it back into drive, and made a hard left. The mud tires of the pickup dug into the sand and shot her and the trailer around the front of the island. The four pirate girls screamed obscenities down at her. She cut back to continue down the street, blasting her horn. This was very poor Burning Man etiquette, but she was confident a 500-pound motorcycle could rip through the trailer door.

She couldn't let that happen.

Five O'clock scrawled on cardboard flashed in her headlights. Huge curved tubes emerged from the darkness. An overgrown neon houseplant with two wheels sat amongst them. She pulled into the camp with all six tires raising dust and swung the driver's door open before the truck fully stopped. She dropped her boots to the ground and pulled her weapon as she made for the rear of the trailer while shouting:

"Move away from the door."

A shirtless person wearing tights and a helmet with green tubes shooting out the top exited the porcupine RV. He was painted green.

"Kandy."

She recognized not the man, but the voice, untied the monk's belt, pulled the bullet from the handle, and leapt away.

The trailer was still.

She moved farther back, aware they were likely armed.

"The door is unlocked," she shouted, her gun steady, though firing with so many people around was the last thing she wanted to do.

The handle rotated; the right barn door opened six inches. Michael's face emerged near the floor of the trailer. He struggled to breathe as he crawled to the dirt, swinging the half door out of his way. Between gasps he managed:

"She's got a gun."

Qigiq dropped to a squat. Michael fell onto the sand and

crawled toward the RV. Murphy stuck his head out, gripping the edge of the closed door with two hands. He took long deep breaths of the fresh desert air.

CHAPTER 48

MY FINGERS WERE ROUGH all the way to their tips from the high-desert air as I worked the tiny buttons on the back of the camera reviewing pictures. I switched it off, slipped it into my jeans, found water under the miniature kitchen sink, and drank half a bottle.

Mylin had been gone a long time.

I stepped out into a cold wind, locked the tall rear door to the camper, and circumnavigated the orange truck Bear had suggested we use. The drifting sand was a bit deeper; the orange truck whiter. Not much had changed in the past few hours.

I strolled across the playa marveling at the sights and sounds created by thousands of people with no responsibility other than to survive. I pulled out my camera and clicked a flash shot of a dozen stuffed animals in rainbow colors dangling from an address post. In the distance a purple face strolled across the playa carrying a computer, reminding me of Martians and sci-fi stories from the twentieth century.

I squinted.

I lifted my camera; pushed it to full zoom.

Mylin's face glowed on his chest.

I spun open the cap on my water bottle and drank while fighting panic. It was from the hotel where I grabbed her. That building was an old converted house. I had verified it didn't even have security cameras.

So who took that picture?

I turned on my heel and trotted towards where I had left Mylin playing a borrowed fiddle like a busker on the New York subway. When I got there, she was gone.

I tried harder not to panic while turning in a full circle. Hundreds of people moved in every direction; a discotheque shot colored lasers into the desert sky; fires in fifty gallon drums burned in a dozen locations. I lifted my camera and did the same 360 turn with the zoom. Slower. Checking faces.

She was three drums down still wearing the fur coat Bear had hung in the truck.

I ran, constructing in my head the conversation we needed to have.

Flames roared six feet high from the steel drum; sparks disappeared into the night as if being vacuumed up by an alien force. She had formed a band with a busty girl on clarinet, and a brown-skinned man with dark hair to his waist kneeling in the sand beating rhythms on auto hubcaps with the metal tips of unlit flares. A crowd had gathered to listen to music that reminded me of the cantina scene from a Star Wars movie— otherworldly, yet somehow inspiring one to dance.

I glanced over my shoulder; the purple man continued his approach. I shot a picture in his direction, then elbowed through the crowd, not making friends along the way, and dropped to my knees beside Mylin. I shouted:

"Drum solo!"

The members of the band looked at me, so I yelled again.

"Drum solo!"

The brown man smiled, the two girls finished their phrase, and the hubcap tapping grew more intense.

Mylin said: "What are you doing?"

Smiling toward the percussionist and nodding my head in rhythm, I held the camera up. "There's a man approaching with your picture from the hotel room on a computer screen. I don't know who he is or how he got it, but we have to get you out of here."

She lifted her instrument and started playing staccato bursts of double stops to counterpoint the hubcaps. Then she began working her way through the crowd—toward the purple guy.

"What are you doing?"

She continued playing. "I'm going to ask him how he got my picture."

"But—" I wanted her to run away. From what? To where? I followed close behind the brown fur as it swayed with her playing. In moments we reached the purple man; seconds later he recognized her.

"Are you Mylin?"

She continued playing while studying her picture. "Who wishes to know?"

The photos flipped on the display: a nude Mylin, a blurred face, me in riding leathers. The angle of the shot told me where the camera had been located in the hotel room.

The purple man said: "Our green friends send a message: 'Qigiq is looking for you.'"

She smiled. "Where?" He recited a time and city. "Don't tell anyone," she told him. "I'll find him when I'm ready."

The purple man nodded as if completely understanding a dark mystery they shared, then continued his walk across the playa with two tablet computers showing pictures of the girl he had just found.

She had told me about the detective who attended her concert. But she had also said *no police* a dozen times. I said:

"What do you want to do?"

She pursed her lips and finally stopped playing. A long moment of silence was followed by:

"I want to kill him."

I swallowed and choked. She gazed straight up into the sky where desert stars gleamed like a thousand droplets of molten silver. I waited, feeling tiny, isolated, and overwhelmed by the vastness of the desert surrounding us in the black night. Eventually she whispered:

"Where are you now my dear sister?"

I touched her shoulder gently; held on until she looked at me, then wrapped my fingers around her biceps. "Let's get out of sight."

My heels dug into the desert floor as I ran; she didn't resist. In minutes we were back to the dusty orange truck. I closed the door behind us. And locked it. Twice.

She placed the borrowed fiddle into a cardboard box. "I must return this."

I wanted her to focus, so I said: "Qigiq?"

She sat down at the folding dinette table. Through the side window her eyes tracked something far out in the desert.

"He said he would help me."

I felt a pang of jealousy before admitting there wasn't much more I could do. I had yanked her out of an environment that was threatening to collapse on us.

"We both can help you."

Her eyes focused on my face. She smiled. "Yes. Let's go together to see Qigiq." She stood.

I held up a finger. "Wait. With those monitors walking around, you'll be recognized."

I shuffled to the front of the camper, found our riding gear, handed out her boots, unzipped the jacket, and gave her the leather pants. I blinked, remembering the energy that had zapped through me when she stood naked behind the hotel before stepping into the leathers. Later she had been afraid, then slowly took on a strength, finally she wanted to *escape*. I still didn't know if she meant physical or emotional.

"No jacket," she said. "Obvious."

I turned around and she was standing in boots and pants with nothing above it.

"We should cover you."

She smiled. "You no like?"

I stared at her breasts. "Yes...but." I shook my head.

"Obvious, obvious."

That made her giggle; both of us trying to ignore the stress surrounding us like a dust storm.

I dug in the tiny closet beside the bathroom and came up with a blue and white plastic box. Inside, as I had hoped, was a tan Ace elastic bandage in a tight roll.

"Lift your arms." I pressed one end against her ribs and unrolled the stretchy materiel around her torso, covering from her breasts to a few inches above her navel. She looked at herself in the long mirror on the bathroom door, turned sideways, turned her back to the mirror. Smiled.

"Helmet?" I asked.

She took the white full-face helmet, held it in both hands and stroked the surface. She pointed her finger and wiggled it.

I opened drawers. Ballpoint pen, two pencils, red marker. She tried the marker; it wouldn't write on the smooth helmet. That sticky plastic I had used on the bike would work, but it was back at Bear's shop. I found a toolbox. More pencils. Blue chalk line. Black grease pencil. A permanent marker in orange.

I tossed the marker to her.

She placed the helmet on the table and sat down. She started tracing a line very slowly from the front chin bar upward.

"Shouldn't we—"

She held her palm out. "Shh."

I waited in jeans and a spotted dress shirt I wore when mounting pictures, sipping water against dehydration, feeling useless. I decided to wear my leather jacket; it would match her pants. I disabled the flash on the telephoto camera and placed it in a left pocket.

Mylin remained engaged in drawing curlicues and musical notes and the occasional flower on her helmet.

I enabled the flash for the close-up camera; debated about taking the gun used for the kidnapping. One of Bear's collection. I could hit a standing target at 50 feet since I turned sixteen.

Even beat my dad half the time. But I'd never used a gun for anything else. Still, better to have it and not need it. I put it in the inside jacket pocket, creating a bulge. But so did the armor under the shoulders and elbows. One more bulge didn't matter much.

Her marker tip reached the back of the helmet: up and down, back and forth.

She stopped, having lifted the orange tip but once.

"There." She looked up. A big smile. "I like your jacket."

I snapped her picture holding the uncapped marker above the helmet. She blinked after the flash, lifted the helmet, and slipped it on. The shield turned to face me as she rose. Her mummified space warrior in a designer helmet would be right at home the moment we stepped outside. I said:

"Ready?"

The squiggles nodded.

"If we get separated, come back here." I hesitated. "If I can't get back, lay low for three days, Bear will be here Saturday to help you."

She bowed slightly.

I pushed open the door of the camper and checked all directions like a spy in enemy territory. To my right, fires had been started in a long row of oil drums as if a plane were about to do an emergency landing. People milled about. No one seemed to pay us the slightest attention. I stepped down the metal stair that hooked under the rear bumper and helped an unrecognizable Mylin down after me. We retraced the steps of the purple man. Campfires flickered near nylon tents creating a geodesic rainbow village moonscape. I took her hand. A question that had been haunting me slipped out.

"Who?"

Her upturned face questioned me. She kept walking.

I said, "Who do you want to kill?"

"Him. Them. All of them."

I was on shaky ground with the cops after kidnapping her.

But I said:

"Will this detective help?"

The helmet shook side to side. A muffled voice came out. "He is police. He will only protect me." A pause while we crunched forward a few steps. "Us."

So she was willing to go to the police for protection. From them. Him. The people who had chased Pé off a cliff. We turned right at Istanbul. I stopped at the Three O'clock cross street and asked:

"Are you sure?"

The helmet tipped. "I know he will find me eventually."

"And when he does, Qigiq will protect you?"

Her eyes were hidden. She didn't speak. I reached out and hugged her, the elastic material of the bandage rough against my palms. The glass-smooth surface of the helmet's visor bumped my chin. I twisted my neck and placed my cheek against the top of the helmet. It was as cold as the desert air.

"Perhaps," she whispered.

I tried to think of a better option. Failed. "OK. Let's go do this, Mylin. Whatever you're involved in, I want to help you *escape*, like you said before."

The helmet moved up and down against my cheek, though not very fast.

I took her hand and headed for Five O'clock. We approached a motorhome with tubes jutting from its roof where a monk was pointing a gun at two men: one flat on the ground, the other hanging out of a covered trailer with half the door open. A few yards to the right a green man in black boots squatted low. A truck engine idled. Everyone seemed to be waiting like a cat ready to pounce.

I pulled out my telephoto camera. "Who are they?"

She didn't reply right away. Finally, "They are dressed strangely."

We blazed a trail through a hanging tube forest until

reaching tubes we could hide behind.

"Please go inside," I whispered, pointing to a door halfway down the left side of the motorhome. If guns were going to be fired, I didn't want Mylin out here. I didn't want to be here either, even though forty or fifty people had gathered to watch — but I did want pictures.

She leaned her helmet close and returned my whisper. "They are very dangerous." Then she disappeared into the tube forest in the direction of the entrance.

I lifted my camera and snapped a couple shots of the guy holding onto the door, then repositioned myself lower and to the left for a better view inside the trailer. The tube in front of me swayed in the wind so I wrapped an arm around it and hugged it to my side. I switched to ten frames per second burst mode, feeling in my gut that whatever was about to happen, would happen very fast.

The grinding of a starter emerged from inside the trailer. I put my eye to the viewfinder. The guy leaning against the door pushed it open fast with both hands, and hung on as his body swung around to the far side of the trailer, like a kid playing in the park.

The grinding sound became thunder.

From inside the cavelike darkness of the trailer a brilliant light blinded me.

I pushed the shutter.

A motorcycle leapt out, its helmeted rider pressed low against the fuel tank. When it hit the ground the spinning rear wheel shot a wall of sand at the robed figure.

The monk ducked.

The bike fishtailed.

The green man sprang forward from his crouch like a poked frog. A silver blade glinted and slashed at the rider's left arm.

Handlebars twisted.

The bike crashed on its left side, spinning in place, the rear

wheel throwing grit that ricocheted off the tube in front of me. I
hopped around to point my camera at the rider whose hand still
held the throttle as he fought the machine. The image of a silvery
creature flashed on the side of the helmet. The rear wheel
struggled for grip. He leaned into the bike, the wheel dug in, and
he hopped on side saddle.

Pointed straight at the crowd.

People scrambled to make room as the headlight illuminated
frightened faces. A woman wearing a Native American
headdress, feathers trailing down over her bare breasts, froze in
the beam like a startled deer—and screamed.

I turned the camera toward the trailer, engulfed by dust
swirling in the night air from the departed bike. Exhaust fumes
filled my nostrils. The man who had pushed the door open was
gone. The second man lay on the ground, not moving. The green
man with the knife stood over him. The robed figure was on one
knee holding a gun in an outstretched arm. I framed the shooter
and pressed the shutter.

The gun came down. The monk ducked and peeled the robe
off in a single motion to reveal an athletic woman in short jeans,
boots, and a black bra.

I rotated the camera to follow as she sprinted through the
motorbike's dust cloud directly at the crowd. The bike was out
of sight; a roaring engine told me it had found open space.

Mylin!

I spun fast only to see her standing beside the RV with five
green people shadowed by light glowing from the plastic tubes.
Two males and two females were color-coded in Black, Blue,
Pink and Red bikini bottoms. The fifth was wearing black stripes
over her green body and pink hair spiked into a Mohawk above
huge sunglasses. Mylin was now green from her waist to the Ace
elastic band, and her neck all the way up to the helmet.

I instinctively photographed them.

The color-coded four each spoke a single word as if their

brains were wired together into a single cosmic circuit: "We." "Saw." "What." "Happened."

The man with the knife handcuffed the guy on the ground, then turned his gaze to follow the running woman. Even green, I recognized his face from the concert—the detective. He took three steps and jumped onto a two-wheeled machine that looked like fireworks in mid-explosion.

The man in Blue trunks reached up, touched his arm and said: "We will slow him down."

The rider nodded; the bike revved.

A tablet computer showing a map appeared in the hands of the woman in pink. She spoke to it. "Walkers. Black motorcycle moving fast across playa. Please log sightings. Be prudent, it is evil."

The green people stared at the screen. The fireworks motorcycle made a U-turn and started rolling. I stepped clear of the tubes and held up my hand. He stopped.

"Detective, I brought Mylin." I pointed to the orange-squiggled helmet. "She said you would protect her."

The rider's head twisted toward the group and back to me. Wheels crunched gravel behind me.

A full-size SUV, its tires chalk white from playa sand, pulled across the path of the detective's bike. A young Asian man in the passenger seat stared at us with wet glassy eyes. A man with white hair wearing a dark suit made black by the night jogged around the front of the vehicle.

The four color-coded people whispered excitedly, and ran off.

The suited man stopped beside the rider and ran his eyes over the strange machine.

I shuffled soundlessly backward and ducked behind a tube.

"Thank you, detective, for finding my daughter. I had every confidence in you." He turned towards the two women standing beside the motorhome. "Come, Mylin. This nonsense must stop."

No one moved.

"Daughter, do not make this more difficult for yourself. You have made enough trouble."

The tight black leather pants floated forward with small steps. I shot a picture of her framed by the back of the man's head. She stopped six feet from him and wagged the squiggled helmet.

"She doesn't want to go with you," the detective said.

His name popped into my head.

"Her desire is of no importance. My daughter is in America on a visa through my company. If she stops working, she will be deported."

"She could stay with her mother," Qigiq said.

The man faced the rider. Seconds ticked by in slow motion.

"Detective, her mother has been dead since the day Mylin was born. Karma for the disobedient wife who insisted on having another girl baby."

The rider moved a hand down his left leg and scratched his knee. He said:

"She could seek asylum. Become a witness. No fake visa required."

The man's laugh shook his narrow shoulders. "What fool country would believe a whore?" He shot forward and grabbed the wrist of the mummy girl. "Come, Mylin."

She followed him for two steps, then soundlessly spun on her heels and tried to run.

He held her.

The rider stood and pushed the jumble of tubes that was the motorcycle over, striking the older man's leg. The man called out and reached for his knee with both hands as he fell.

The girl raced into the darkness.

The man lay sprawled on the ground half-under the fallen bike, his suit covered by desert sand.

I turned toward the whir of an electric motor. The passenger window of the SUV was gliding past glassy eyes. The muzzle of a gun rose into sight. A deafening rumble filled the air. The tube hiding me vibrated hard against my cheek as if it had come alive.

I stuffed a hand into my pocket, ran to the rear of the SUV, and pressed my chest to it. The window stopped rolling with four inches to go. I sidestepped past the rear doors. A fat barrel came over the glass. I reached my arm into the open window—and pressed the shutter.

In the desert darkness, the flash fired inches from the man's retinas.

He screamed but didn't shoot.

I brought my forearm down hard against the barrel. The armor of my riding jacket absorbed the impact as the metal barrel slammed against the top edge of the glass, spiraling the gun into the air. It landed a foot from the white-haired man who had been hit by Qigiq's falling motorbike. He grabbed it, struggled to his feet, and set off with a limping run after the girl.

Qigiq picked up the fireworks motorcycle. The starter ground for a few seconds but nothing happened. He tried four times before the bike came to life.

I leapt away as the SUV started moving, taking pictures fast. It was out of sight in seconds. When I turned around, the motorcycle rider was gone, too.

The door to the motorhome slammed closed behind the girl in the striped dress.

The thundering noise continued unabated from the green people on top of the RV drumming incessantly on tubes like fallen angels trying to awaken the underworld.

I scanned for a picture.

The handcuffed man face down in the dirt was alone.

Without thinking, I followed the limping man chasing Mylin, reminding myself that he had a gun.

CHAPTER 49

KANDY RAN FLAT OUT ACROSS SAND softened by the feet of hundreds of burners, the cooling desert air chilling the sweat on her body. Prime's motorcycle wailed in the darkness ahead. If he bolted for the highway, she would need the Mini. Getting to it would consume precious minutes. But she figured him for circling back to help his buddies to avoid the nasty possibility of their testifying against him.

So she kept chasing the sound of the engine, hoping the desert floor would be slow going for a street bike.

Deep resonating rhythms emanating from behind followed her across the playa. A woman in a gold gown sitting beneath a gramophone the size of an oak tree pointed to her left. Kandy turned. The woman nodded vigorously, then applauded as if Kandy were part of a stage play.

Moonlight revealed the tropical island rising from the black sand like a mirage to a dying traveler. A throng had gathered around it. A stopped motorcycle pointed at the palm trees.

Prime stood over it screaming.

Locking her focus on his silver and black helmet, she increased her pace. Prime spun the bike, circled back about thirty yards, made another fast U-turn—and headed straight for the unmoving island. At the precise moment he lofted the front wheel, the bike slithered up the side of the island, narrowly missed four girls in a hot tub, and disappeared over the top.

The crowd roared.

The island float began to move.

Kandy waved to the topless girls in the hot tub as she ran

past.

She was now within a hundred yards as the bike struggled to part the crowd. People jogged, slowed, or turned haphazardly into Prime's path as if guided by an unseen hand. She ran faster, barely warmed up, still plenty of gas in the tank.

A campsite on her left displayed a glowing yellow sign for *Pee Funnels*, and one on her right read: *Free Titty Wash*. Not far ahead Prime made a sweeping turn.

Toward open desert.

She angled onto the hypotenuse to shorten her distance to him, but lost perspective as the bike approached people three sizes too tall leapfrogging across the playa.

Stilts.

Further out, house-sized multi-colored fish sprang alive when touched by the bike's bouncing headlight. She ran into the heart of the darkness, hoping the desert wouldn't offer up a leg injury; she hated losing her prey.

———

Standing on the foot pegs, Qigiq coaxed tires designed for asphalt through the slippery sand between rows of RVs. He knew Wu was chasing the helmeted Mylin, but had lost both of them in the maze of psychedelic costumes, colossal structures, and campers. So he was reduced to guessing which way she would run as his bike's tubes glowed and burners shifted out of his way.

A few applauded. Two booed.

He rode past a bug statue and a mirrored disco. The crowd became thinner. Staring into the darkness hoping to catch a glimpse of the limping Mr. Wu, he was startled by an orange flash that spread across the desert like a bursting star.

He aimed his bike at the afterimage.

A tube broke off and caught under his arm. He grabbed it with his left hand and stuffed it between the tank and the frame. In the distance a spiral of fire ignited from one end, looping around and around until it filled the horizon like a monster slinky toy stretched across the earth illuminating the faces of thousands of people standing in the desert. He reached over the handlebars and yanked a tube off his headlight.

The rough grayness of desert sand grew brighter.

He twisted his wrist.

———

Kandy had been following the pinpoint of red from Prime's taillight when it blinked out near the edge of a crowd assembled in the open blackness of the desert. She pounded across the sand—steady, even—sweat dripping from her entire body despite the cool air. She lifted her eyes to an imperceptible horizon where the empty desert met dark sky, seeking anything that would attract so much attention.

Brilliant light exploded against her retinas so hard it hurt.

Blowtorch blue tongues burned outward from a fat snaking spiral twenty feet in diameter.

She tried to pick up her pace, but her legs resisted.

She focused on where the taillight had been, and estimated how far he could have ridden.

The drumming that had been in the air since she began running ceased, leaving only the sound of air rushing past her ears. The crowd ahead parted like the waters of the Red Sea, and she was staring at hundreds of lights in two long rows. A motorcycle raced into the void. She ran straight toward it, then into the opening between the pinpoints of white. She ran and ran until reaching a dusty yellow bulldozer parked on the sand like an abandoned moon car.

She stopped, chest heaving, wiping her eyes with the back of a hand.

On the other side of the dozer, a ravine had been cut deep into the desert floor. On the far side of the ravine, crossed timbers formed a fence a yard high. Beyond that, the burning coil of wire glowed in the black sky. She stopped at the edge.

Prime was in the ravine, his bike rolling down and up the sides like a skateboarder preparing a trick.

Vapor rose from her body. Her chest heaved.

He started up the near side of the ravine.

She leapt in.

She stripped him off the bike with one arm, landed on his chest, and pressed a forearm across his throat beneath the chin bar of the helmet. To her great surprise, he didn't resist. The bike slid to a stop below them; still running.

From somewhere in the darkness another engine wailed a hellish redline scream.

———

Qigiq caught sight of a business suit for a split second before Wu disappeared into a throng of bodies. To the far left, light rose from within the crowd, as if thousands of people had turned on flashlights at the same time. He rode through the throng until forward progress became impossible, then abandoned the bike. He elbowed past people while asking which way the man with the gun had gone until a murmur of voices preceded him and the crowd began to part even before he arrived.

He reached a barricade constructed of DO NOT CROSS tape that was holding back the crowd. Ghostly dancing light thrown by the spiral's flames silhouetted two moving bodies: a helmeted girl in black pants, and a man chasing her with his right hand held low.

A motorcycle engine screamed in the distance.

Without conscious effort his mind conjured: Triumph twin.

———

Kandy held Prime's throat. His left arm flipped up the face shield, then lifted to point up into the darkness, the jacket sleeve soaked with red-brown liquid.

"Please," he choked out. "I saw them. He'll kill her. Save my sister. Arrest me later."

She followed his finger, but they were too deep in the ravine to see beyond the fiery spiral.

The screaming engine grew louder.

She gazed down into his eyes, looking for truth.

A thundering blur swept through the ravine. A rider, helmet painted with orange flames, astride a black motorcycle used the deep curve of the ravine as a ramp and flew into the air. As the bike floated above the spiral of fire, Ferd's spectacular version of barbed wire, the rider's coat burst into flame.

The crowd roared like the winning Super-Bowl touchdown had just been scored.

Kandy switched priorities and released Prime's throat, letting him slide downhill toward his still-idling bike. She ran hard across the ravine and clawed her way up the other side with her bare hands. When she reached the burning spiral she became keenly aware of her exposed skin, twisted sideways to scissor-step through the blazing heat, then paused to regain her bearings. The girl was on the ground, the man moving toward her. Someone beyond him jumped the security fence.

She squinted into the flickering darkness.

Qigiq.

Her hand automatically reached for her weapon as her eyes searched for a safe line of fire that wasn't there.

CHAPTER 50

WU'S LEGS WERE HEAVY WITH FATIGUE, his fine Italian loafers filled with coarse sand. He panted through his mouth, bending forward at the waist from the ache in his lungs. His knee throbbed where the fool detective's motorcycle had banged it. He craved a cigarette.

Mylin would soon pay for his pain.

The motorcycle flying overhead had startled her into sprawling on the ground. But he had remained calm, closing the distance. He knew she would tire first; a mere woman, even a young one, was no match for him.

She was within firing range. He kept running.

She rose to one knee. A motorcycle stopped to his right. The rider's burning jacket tossed shadows onto her shiny black pants. The frenzied crowd cheered. He could shoot her here; the silenced sound would be lost.

His lungs burned like they were being branded.

If he shot her, he would have to move quickly to escape the detective. He was old now, and unsure he would be able to escape the younger man. He must recognize his own weakness, as well as his strength.

Wu glanced over his shoulder. The green man had crossed the barrier. As he turned back toward Mylin the half-naked female detective appeared in the distance. In the blink of an eye he weighed options:

leave now, deal with Mylin later
one shot, disappear into the night
grab her, fade into the crowd.

It was no crime to help his daughter. He slipped the weapon inside his jacket.

She started to run. He swept his front foot in an arc; she tripped and fell to the dirt. He dropped and rolled her onto to her back, pinning her arms above her head.

"Mylin, stop. It is over. Come quickly. We must avoid the police."

She said nothing; her eyes hid behind the shield of the gaudy helmet.

He squeezed until she cried out in pain. A motorcycle engine revved above the crowd's cheers. She struggled to throw him off.

She was strong.

He frowned and yanked her right arm up, then rubbed her wrist with the sleeve of his jacket to remove the green body paint.

She punched him, but the blow glanced off his shoulder.

He released her arms; flicked up the face shield. A green face held blue eyes.

The noise of the revving engine grew louder.

Her right hand swung wide and fast in a smooth motion, catching him on the side of the face and twisting his neck with such force he struggled to retain his balance.

The crowd cheered on.

The hand pulled back and punched up into his Adam's apple. He reached for his throat with both hands, his breath frozen in his chest.

She began to slither away, then went rigid—her blue eyes turned upward at the night sky.

He gasped, fighting to understand what was happening so he could regain control.

She screamed.

He followed her gaze to the left...and up.

A motorcycle.

Black. Smoking. Roaring.

Descending from the sky like the claw of the dragon god.

CHAPTER 51

QIGIQ WAS TWENTY YARDS BEHIND WU when the flames shooting from the spiral went out, washing the crowd and desert in the ghostly blackness only seen far from the light pollution of cities. Within that darkness, the second motorcycle dropped from the sky. The spinning rear wheel struck Wu's forehead and crushed his skull.

The bike pivoted in midair.

The front wheel hit sand and bounced. The rider flew forward over the bars, contacted the desert floor, rolled. The last wavering light from the burning spiral coated his body and reflected from a silver design on his helmet.

The helmeted girl lay flat on her back. Kandy was heading toward her from the opposite direction shouting words that the crowd noise blanketed.

A motorbike pulled up beside Qigiq. The rider flipped up the face shield on a helmet painted with orange flames. A woman's voice said:

"What did you think of that?"

Qigiq listened to her, but kept his eyes glued to the two motionless bodies. He doubted she had seen the second bike arrive. He said:

"You made an amazing jump."

The helmet came off and she shook out her hair. "Ain't Ferddy great? He told me I could do it with practice. He was right!"

He turned. The slender waitress at the Ton Up in the short black skirt gazed at him in the darkness. He didn't hide his surprise. "You made that jump?" A man in a blue EMT uniform appeared beside Wu. Of course Ferdinand would have medical personnel standing by. But from where he stood, Wu was dead. He wasn't sure about the second rider.

She smiled from ear to ear and spoke fast, as if the adrenaline from the jump were powering her mouth. "Didn't you love the retro-rocket jacket? He has so much cool tech. And he worked so hard to be sure this jump was perfect for me." She took a quick breath, her heart rate no doubt well above normal. "Even though I know it all started just so you guys could hang around the Ton Up to gather intel."

Ferdinand was full of surprises. Maybe that voice in the background in the middle of the night.... Over the rider's leather-clad shoulder he saw Kandy reach the prone girl. Two more EMTs were attending to the downed rider. The crowd noise subsided as everyone realized that without lights, this show was over.

An irrelevant question came to mind. "What do you wear under a burning outfit like that?"

Petrushka smiled, but didn't answer.

———

Kandy reached the orange-squiggled helmet as a motorcycle pulled up beside Qigiq a few yards away. She hadn't known Ferd had planned two jumps, though she wouldn't argue that two was a spectacular idea. She knelt and checked for a pulse.

The girl's eyes popped opened. Then grew large, like she was at a horror movie. A helmet-muffled voice said:

"Are you Kandy Dreeson?"

Not the first words Kandy expected, but she nodded.

"Awesome! I so wanted to meet you."

Kandy stared at the green face inside the helmet.

"We met after your concert, Mylin."

The girl wriggled the helmet off her head, revealing blond and pink hair, and blue eyes.

"I swapped clothes with Mylin back at Porcupine camp. She's wearing my dress." A shy grin. "I call myself KD here, but my name is Jill."

Kandy sat cross-legged in the sand and shook hands with the young girl.

"That was a dangerous thing to do."

"It was just trying to hide her. I didn't know there would guns. Everyone expected her to be wearing the scribbled helmet and Band-Aid," she pointed to her chest. "So they didn't bother much with the green girl in the black stripes."

Kandy smiled.

Jill said: "This will be so amazing for my senior project."

CHAPTER 52

QIGIQ MADE A RIGHT TURN AND PULLED into a parking spot fifty feet beyond the entrance to the Chinese Hospital. As he turned the bars to full lock, he noticed gray dust deep down in the triple clamp of the steering. He sighed. He had washed the rented Aprilia three times, and was still finding bits of the Nevada desert on it.

He swung his leg over, leaned against the seat, and glanced at the bike's dash: not yet 8:00 AM Friday morning. A light fog hung in the air, but early rays of sunshine beaming through promised a clear day by lunch. The floating moisture felt like cold soup on his skin after the romp in the dry high desert. Part of him had wanted to hang out with KD and the green percussionists to experience that Burning Man tower going up in flames.

But loose ends, and Captain Jasik, were calling loudly.

He crossed his arms. The sticky remains of green grease in his pores made him want to take another shower. Alaska had impressive sled dog races, but nothing like the Burning Man Festival. He recalled the sight of a rider on fire flying through the air on a street bike—a rider that turned out to be a painter who waited tables for a living. Maybe no one had anything like Burning Man.

A car shifted gears near redline. Kandy's black Mini appeared at the corner. Drum rhythms pumped into the street. The music stopped. The car rocked to a standstill.

He walked three parking spots as its passenger window rolled down, then leaned in to speak through the window.

"New music?"

"Recommendation from the Porcupine Band. They really know drumming."

"Impressive the way they communicated across open desert."

She grinned. "Didn't you beat drums to send messages across the tundras of Alaska when you were a little tyke?"

"Telephones and snowmobiles. Oh, and I had a walkie-talkie once."

She laughed.

He glanced into the back of the Mini. The rear seats were folded down. A black tube structure occupied most of the available space.

"Is that the sculpture from the gallery?"

"Nope."

"A Ton Up bike?"

"I left those with Ferd. He's confident they were using air pressure to pack the buckyballs inside the frames of the bikes. Dogs apparently can't detect drugs sealed inside carbon fiber very well. And what inspector would pull a fully sealed bike frame apart without good reason?"

"Air pressure?"

"To move the balls through the tubing. That's the thumping I heard from under the trailer: balls shooting out of the frame and into a bag. The boys then sell for top dollar."

"Top dollar. In a gift culture?"

"Gifts have to come from somewhere. People run out of drugs. Want to try something totally unique. Have to find the perfect gift for that special someone. Apparently, every year they sell all they can carry in."

He reached a hand in and stroked a frame tube with his fingertips. The carbon fiber was glass smooth. It would look great painted. He said:

"You finally going to decorate your apartment?"

Kandy popped a mint into her mouth, shook her head.

Qigiq studied the shape. Walked around the back of the Mini and looked it over through the rear window.

"You're kidding. Murphy got it done?"

"Yep. He drove the pickup right back to his shop after Prime rode out of the trailer and got to work. Not sure what he's thinking, maybe that we don't have much on him personally."

He wrapped a hand around a tube and shook it. Solid, and clearly lighter than steel.

"Not a bribe, is it?"

Kandy reached into the glove box and handed him an invoice. "Not at these prices. I figure when we're done here at the hospital we run it over to Grojini. Maybe you'll get your Guzzi back sooner rather than later."

He grinned, imagining sweeping through a turn to the song of his old Guzzi twin.

"Speaking of sooner than later," she said. "Rachel Spooner left a voice mail for us with Molly. You really should be sitting down, so hold on. She called to thank us for our help in trying to free her Rudy from the evil people that were after him."

"How much does she know?"

"From her message she knows his buddy went with him. Heck of a shock. She sounded almost contrite. Like suddenly nothing was his fault and she wants him back. However—" Kandy stopped to pop a mint into her mouth. "However, she also knows that she gets everything: the house, cars, bank accounts, maybe the insurance policy on the boat given the timing of the transfer of ownership, and, of course, the life insurance policy carried by the law firm."

"If I didn't know you better, I'd say that sounded cynical."

Kandy rolled the mint around on her tongue like she was thinking of a comeback. But only smiled.

They strolled through the hospital's main entrance and asked for Mr. Wu's room. When they arrived, Prime was in a cast from his waist down to his left ankle. His left arm was heavily bandaged.

Kandy stood in the doorway. Qigiq sat opposite the foot of the bed in a white wooden chair.

Prime was awake. He gestured toward his arm with his head. "Thirty-seven stitches. Slowed me down or Ms. Kandy wouldn't have caught me."

Qigiq said, "Didn't stop you from making that jump."

Prime was quiet for a moment. "Lot of history with a famous jump like that. Your bearded friend gave me a rare opportunity to see if I measure up."

Kandy shifted to her other foot. "You still want to testify?"

"Yes. My father is gone, now is the time to end it. I've hated life since turning thirteen, when he sent me miles away to rural villages to buy girls no one wanted. Some could learn to play. We kept those, sold the others to the highest bidder."

"What about your brother Tuson?" she asked.

Prime shifted on the bed, pain reached his jaw, then his eyes.

"Ah yes, younger brother Shen, the number two son. Father never let him forget his place in the family hierarchy. If he doesn't die from the bullet wound, please arrest him for the hit-and-run of my grandmother: a foolish move using her as bait to force Pé to return." He paused for a breath. "Though it worked. He supported my father...always." Prime hesitated, staring out the lone window. "And raped the girls. Sometimes after what he called *punishing* them. He preferred they fear rather than respect him."

Qigiq recalled the doctor's comments about pimps and feet.

Prime turned slowly toward Kandy. "Yes, including our sisters." He paused, his jaw working in silence. "Shen desperately wants the business, and despises me for being the favored son and *not* wanting the business."

"You have proof of the blackmail?" Kandy asked.

"Father trusted no one outside the family. As eldest, I was

treasurer, and have access to all records. The first date. The gifts the mark bestowed upon the girl. We didn't charge for sex, you know; that's illegal in most states." He laughed softly, coughed, moaned, shifted his weight to his right side. "I have expense records for music lessons, instruments, travel. And of course the contracts, payment methods, offshore accounts."

No one spoke. The HVAC fan stirred the antiseptic air all hospitals seemed to use. Prime reached out slowly for a round wooden tube on the nightstand, held it to his right eye, and stared toward the window as he rotated it between his fingers.

Qigiq imagined the colors inside the kaleidoscope a kind nurse had probably given him to pass the time. Prime would need something bright about now. He said:

"Why?"

Prime understood immediately. "I wanted out. Had a secret scheme to vanish one day." He inhaled a long breath through his nose and shook his head. "Slave girls in the twenty-first century. Hard to believe." He paused to return the tube to the table. "Did you know there are more slaves today than at any time in the past? Fishermen. Miners. But most of all, sex workers. How's that for human progress?" He took time to fill his lungs slowly. "My father was ruthless. No one who crossed him lived to tell about it." His gaze shifted back to the window. "So I stayed and tried to protect the girls." His eyes tracked something. "A private source of income gave me options." He rolled his head toward Kandy. "It was Michael and me. The club had nothing to do with it. The guys have been making that high-speed run down to Mexico then up to Burning Man for years. It's really just an excuse for a great ride, but they pick up tequila to share with burner girls in their desert clubhouse. I saw a way to make good money, at low risk."

"Murphy?" Kandy said.

Prime nodded his head slowly, as if being careful not to disturb it. "Hired him to build frames and procure the edible balls. He never touched the end product. Michael and I moved it, and shared the proceeds." He cleared his throat. Kandy picked up a water bottle from the table beside the bed, removed the cap, handed it to him. He drank, passed it back with a nod.

"We hired him to prepare the frames before we left for Mexico, so we could seal them with no visible marks. If you've seen his sculptures, then you know his level of skill. Then he'd open the carbon tubes and pressure the balls out up at Burning Man. I never told him exactly what we were running."

The HVAC had stopped. The room was quiet save for Prime's breathing from the effort of speaking.

"The frames," Qigiq said. "Why so many of the same style?"

Prime's face slowly filled with a wide smile. "Norton featherbed. Best chassis ever devised for a Triumph-powered café racer. People combine the names, call them Tritons. The ones we use are Murphy-engineered carbon. You want to be fast at the Ton Up, you get that frame, and tune up a Triumph motor."

Qigiq shook his head, knowing that's exactly what he would have done as a young rider.

"And," Prime said. "Cops get confused when the bikes look the same in a street race...especially in Mexico after Ben Franklins change hands."

———

They stopped in the hallway after leaving Prime's room. Mrs. Chong's voice floated Chinese along the hallway. Kandy unwrapped two sticks of Juicy Fruit and folded them into her mouth.

"What have we got?"

Qigiq pulled a crumpled sheet of paper from his pants pocket.

"Dismantle the blackmail operation. Arrest Shen, aka Tuson, for the double murder of Pé and Spooner, assuming Prime testifies. After we find Shen, of course. If he's still alive." He paused. "And Prime's cooperation gets him a plea-bargain on the drug charges."

She chewed noisily for several seconds. "Something's bothering you."

"What happens to forty lovely musicians who are here illegally? No management. No friends. No visas. Not even a port of entry. They get sent back to be sold all over again?"

She drummed her fingers against the wall behind her. Then said:

"Anything else?"

"That second jump. Ferdinand didn't plan a second jump. Or second rider. The first jump was 60 feet, and Petr's bike could have been a stand-in for the Triumph Trophy used in the movie. Even the ravine Ferd dug was as close as he could calculate from measurements on the film. He added fire only because she jumped at night; he wanted the audience to be able to see the action."

Her fingers accelerated. "How about we ask Prime why he did it?"

"Would his answer help? He might have jumped to prove he could do it, like he says; or to get close to Mylin faster to protect her; or to chase his father away. Best we'd get is an involuntary manslaughter charge. Probably not even that because an elderly man crossed a clearly marked barrier and was hit during a show in the middle of the desert."

"You think Prime saw an opportunity?"

Qigiq's dark eyes turned down the hallway toward Mrs. Chong's room.

He didn't answer.

CHAPTER 53

MYLIN CROUCHED IN A BACK CORNER of Bear Naked Leathers, full of smiles, tuning the viola that had just arrived via Fed-X. A homeless woman, carrying a long white box in her arms, had walked into the San Francisco police station asking for Kandy Dreeson. She claimed the box contained flowers from a secret admirer who offered her $200 to make the delivery. The viola had been hidden beneath two dozen pink roses. I was happy Kandy had shipped it quickly.

I clicked the shutter to capture Mylin. I wasn't happy about much else.

Bear worked a silver wrench inside the red Harley sitting at eye level on the backmost lift. He said:

"You going to send the detective dude those pictures?"

I was on the opposite side of the bench staring through the bike frame. My camera held hundreds of pictures taken in multi-shot mode the night Mylin and I had gone to find Qigiq at Burning Man, including some of him in green paint and tights. I hadn't shown them to anyone. In the Internet age a picture could take on a life of its own and cause trouble where there hadn't been any before. I didn't want to cause trouble—for me, or anyone else. Especially not for Mylin.

"Haven't decided. There are a lot of unusual shots."

Bear shrugged and placed his wrench on the lift. He found an orange spot on a rag that was mostly black with oil. Wiped his hands.

"So what? Maybe they dig into it, find something to help put those guys away. Like the one you hit with the flash."

Maybe I didn't want to admit that Mylin had been standing a few yards in front of me, scantily clad in black stripes (albeit with pink hair, painted green, and wearing sunglasses), and I hadn't recognized her. It was more obvious in the pictures. But at the time, my eyes had followed the helmet. Mylin had arrived wearing the helmet. Even her own father went with it.

"You're right, Bear. I'll talk to the detectives. But they were both witnesses; maybe they don't need my pictures." Or maybe I would put them on a thumb drive and store it in a safety deposit box until all of this blew over.

Mylin began playing a slow melody. When she caught us listening, she stopped.

"Sorry to disturb you."

I hadn't yet known her a week, and was trying to digest the extent of craziness she had lived through in her young life. I had gone half crazy myself just to be near her. I walked to the corner and sat beside her.

"What happens to the orchestra now?"

"Number one brother will inherit everything. He will decide our future. He is the firstborn male child."

That didn't seem entirely fair to me. "Prime is going to jail. Any money will be confiscated."

She frowned and pulled in her lower lip.

I knew I was on shaky ground, because if I were honest, I'd bet she had no idea what to do next. Or even what her options might be. I said:

"What would you like to do?"

"I like to play music."

I took a chance. "Where do you want to live?"

She didn't answer right away. Then said, "Not many places have been good to me. Somewhere new. Here in America. Or maybe Taiwan."

I hoped photographers in Taiwan were paid well.

Bear's bike roared to life.

We both jumped, then laughed. I went over and lifted the long garage door at the end of the store to let the fumes out and fresh air in. I leaned against the doorframe and gazed at the Biggest Little City in the World—Reno, Nevada, where gambling among silver miners was all the rage long before Las Vegas was even founded. The neon and glass of the casinos looked dusty reflecting morning sunlight, like a car that hadn't been washed in a long, long time.

I sighed.

Bear's bike stalled.

Mylin appeared and leaned against me the way I was leaning against the doorframe, like two dominoes unable to fall, though they wanted to.

"Well aren't you two just making this place cheery?" Bear said. "What's the trouble? Maybe Doctor Bear can help."

Mylin didn't move. Neither did I.

"My problem is I long for a chance to get to know this lovely lady here."

Mylin lowered her eyes.

"Her problem is that she's presently an illegal alien with no money, no job, and no place to stay—unless she wants to bunk in a truck with a poor photographer who travels from town to town selling pictures."

Bear popped the top off a beer bottle with an opener on his key chain and chugged half of it. He belched.

"Not bad so far."

"The larger problem is that she has forty girlfriends who are in exactly the same predicament. Minus the photographer."

Bear turned the bottle up again, wiped his mouth on a clean spot of the orange rag.

"They play like Mylin here?"

"Yes," she said without hesitation. "Stringed instruments." She made a bowing motion with her right arm.

Bear's eyes scanned the street, then shifted to me, and back to the street.

"So a promoter could assemble string quartets for weddings and corporate yahoos, an orchestra for big concerts, duos, trios for recording studios, stuff like that?"

Mylin asked, "Like the solo recital I gave at the art museum?"

"Yeah, like that," Bear replied.

"I've heard the orchestra," I added. "They got a good review from the *San Francisco Chronicle*."

"Is that where they are?" he asked.

"Sau-sa-lito," Mylin said, pronouncing the name carefully. "We stay in a big house near Father's art gallery." Her entire face tightened, as if she were straining to play difficult music. "What will happen to our house now?" she said softly, as if reading a fairy tale. "Where will we go?"

A red pickup truck that needed a new muffler roared down the street.

She looked more lost than that night at Burning Man while talking to the purple billboard man.

"You travel a lot," I said. "The house is probably rented month-to-month."

Bear finished his beer.

"OK," he said without preamble, and headed back into the shop.

Our gaze followed him. He picked up the handset of the office phone. She leaned against me a bit harder. Sunlight fought the grime of the city, struggling to make it beautiful. I said:

"I bet Taiwan has many beautiful places to take pictures."

She was quiet for a moment, but she didn't pull away.

"No home in Taiwan. We have nothing, anywhere. All of us are lost children."

Two motorcycles rumbled down the street. They parked at the curb ten feet from where we stood. Two six foot guys, slender like runners, stayed with their bikes. I didn't recognize them.

Mylin slipped her hand under my arm.

"Qigiq said he would look into agencies that help illegal immigrants," I said. "We'll find someone."

A group of four bikes arrived from the south. These riders wore vests and loose clothing, maybe college age. They parked beside the first two.

I looked behind me. Bear was punching at his phone's keypad with a greasy thumb.

A lone rider on a chopped Sportster rode in, the deep orange metal flake of the tank shimmering in the sunlight. Three guys wearing colorful leathers arrived on silver sport bikes. From the little I knew, sport riders and Harley guys didn't ride together often. I glanced at Bear; he was busy with the phone.

Mylin's shoulder pressed against mine as the street filled with motorcyclists from the greasy to the greased. Leather, jeans, little helmets, big helmets, black, white, silver, yellow, orange. The street in front of Bear Naked Leather morphed into a curbside bike show. A couple dozen guys and four women milled about drinking coffee from Peet's café around the corner.

Bear arrived astride his Harley, paddling it along with his feet, three open beer bottles in one hand. He gave one to Mylin, the other to me.

"My friends, we are forming BNO, the Bear Naked Orchestra. A toast to our success." He clinked his bottle against ours and drank. I looked at Mylin, touched my bottle to hers, and drank along with Bear, having no idea what he was talking about. She sipped and choked, dribbling beer onto the sidewalk.

"American beer?" she asked.

"An acquired taste," Bear said. He brought his Harley to life, filling Bear Naked Leathers with smoke and noise. He glanced at the two of us and shouted over the racket:

"Let's go fetch our orchestra."

I looked from the grinning bearded biker to Mylin. Sunlight

on her face penetrated strands of purple and black hair to reveal a hint of her left eye.

Hope glowed there.

If you would like to hear about what's next from Joe Klingler, please sign-up at: www.joeklingler.com

If you enjoyed *Tune Up*, please write a review on Amazon.com to help spread the word about Joe Klingler's books. Thank you.

Also By JOE KLINGLER

RATS

Summer greets the land of the midnight sun as a lone rider races across the last American wilderness. He has many names, but the world only knows a shadow—the Demon. Army sniper Claire Ferreti sips sake in Washington D.C. with her lover, a young, ambitious General whose specialty is classified. When a boy finds an unusual machine, Claire and the Demon embark on a collision course that leads to tests of skill, a clash of ideologies, and Claire's unconscious body lying in a typhoon-ravaged jungle. She becomes the hunted, and the Demon's tool for survival.

MASH UP

Too slow to solve a high-tech crime that leaves a key suspect dead, Qigiq (Inuit for hawk) points his motorcycle from Alaska to San Francisco and his new partner, the hyper-intense Kandy Dreeson. When a violinist named Robina arrives holding an Amazon box with a thumb inside, they confront a torrent of cyberclues: YouTube videos documenting torture, thousands of disappearing music files, a virus spreading on the Web. A twisted mind threatens their lives as they strive to untangle a string of 'accidents' before the killer plays a trump card—to be delivered anonymously, digitally, and within the hour.

MISSING MONA

As Tommy turns 29, his smartphone convinces him it's time for a change. So he embarks on the path of the beatniks—hits the road—and meets a damsel in hitchhiking distress. She leads them to the bright lights and dark clubs of Chicago. On a summer Saturday they settle into a fancy hotel overlooking Lake Michigan. On Sunday...she disappears. But she leaves behind more than a sweet memory that involves Tommy in a brand new cash-flow problem. While trying to stay on the right side of the law, he meets a criminologist who helps him, a DJ who doesn't, and a librarian who teaches him the art of the makeover. Now he is desperate to help Mona...if he can find her.

71222574R00282

Made in the USA
Columbia, SC
23 May 2017